P9-DNT-328

Praise for Valerie Hansen

"*Her Brother's Keeper* is a fascinating look at long-buried secrets."

—*RT Book Reviews*

"Valerie Hansen's story offers a heartwarming romance with enough suspense to keep the pages turning."

—*RT Book Reviews* on *Out of the Depths*

"Kudos to Valerie Hansen for writing an exceptional story with a puzzle that's nearly impossible to solve."

—*RT Book Reviews* on *Hidden in the Wall*

"[I]nteresting characters and plenty of action and suspense."

—*RT Book Reviews* on *Nightwatch*

Praise for Hannah Alexander

"With its suspense, danger, characters and other strong elements, Hannah Alexander's *Hidden Motive* (4.5 stars) is an excellent story that's sure to keep you up late."

—*RT Book Reviews*, Top Pick

"The rapport of Alexander's characters is both realistic and engaging in this tautly thrilling tale."

—*RT Book Reviews* on *Eye of the Storm*, 4.5 stars

"Alexander's skill at meshing spiritual truths with fascinating suspense is captivating."

—*RT Book Reviews* on *Safe Haven*

Valerie Hansen
and
Hannah Alexander

Frontier Courtship
&
Hideaway Home

H **HARLEQUIN**® LOVE INSPIRED®CLASSICS

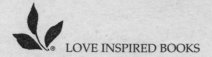 LOVE INSPIRED BOOKS

ISBN-13: 978-1-335-89585-1

Frontier Courtship & Hideaway Home

Copyright © 2018 by Harlequin Books S.A.

The publisher acknowledges the copyright holders of the individual works as follows:

Frontier Courtship
Copyright © 2008 by Valerie Whisenand

Hideaway Home
Copyright © 2008 by Hannah Alexander

www.Harlequin.com

Printed in U.S.A.

CONTENTS

Valerie Hansen was thirty when she awoke to the presence of the Lord in her life and turned to Jesus. Married to her high school sweetheart since age seventeen, she now lives in an old farmhouse she and her husband renovated with their own hands. She loves to hike the wooded hills behind the house and reflect on the marvelous turn her life has taken. Not only is she privileged to reside among the loving, accepting folks in the breathtakingly beautiful Ozark mountains of Arkansas, she also gets to share her personal faith by telling the stories of her heart for all the Love Inspired lines.

Books by Valerie Hansen

Love Inspired Historical

Wilderness Courtship
High Plains Bride
The Doctor's Newfound Family
Rescuing the Heiress

Love Inspired

The Perfect Couple
Second Chances
Love One Another
Blessings of the Heart

Love Inspired Suspense

Her Brother's Keeper
Out of the Depths
Deadly Payoff

Visit the Author Profile page
at Harlequin.com for more titles.

FRONTIER COURTSHIP

Valerie Hansen

Be merciful unto me, O God, be merciful
unto me: for my soul trusteth in thee: yea,
in the shadow of thy wings will I make my refuge,
until these calamities be overpast.
—*Psalms* 57:1

To Joe Roe for helping me understand mules
the way he does. And to my husband, Joe,
for talking me out of buying one
and breaking my fool neck trying to ride it!

Prologue

Ohio, 1850

Clouds boiled black. Threatening. Lightning shot across the sky in endless jagged bursts of fire. A blustery gale swept the hilltop as if bent on clearing it down to the last blade of grass.

Alone, Faith Ann Beal stood her ground in spite of the scattered drops of rain that were beginning to pelt her. She leaned into the wind for balance, determined to withstand the rigors of the early spring storm long enough to place flowers atop her mother's resting place. After the horrible tempest they'd all weathered mere days ago, it was going to take more than a little wind and water to deter her.

Faith kissed her fingertips, bent to touch them to the damp earth, then paused for an unspoken prayer before she said, "I'll keep my vow to you, Mama, no matter where that duty takes me. I promise."

Shivering, yet loath to leave, she straightened and took a shaky breath. Everyone's life had changed in literally seconds when the tornado had mowed a swath through Trumbull County. It was still hard to believe her own mama was gone to Glory, along with so many of their closest family friends.

There was little left of the farm where nineteen-year-old Faith and her younger sister, Charity, had grown up. The lower part of the chimney still stood behind the iron cookstove, but the rest of the house had been reduced to a pile of useless kindling. The roof had blown clean off the barn Papa had built, too. Most of the livestock that had survived the storm had been rounded up and quickly sold for traveling money.

A hooded bonnet partially sheltered Faith's cold-stung, flushed cheeks and she clasped her black wool cloak tightly to her. Despite that protection, her body still trembled from marrow-deep chill. The sweet, peaceful life she had taken for granted was gone. Over. She felt as if her soul had been trapped and frozen within the numbness that now filled her whole body.

Looking down to where her mother lay beneath the freshly turned earth, she gained comfort by imagining her dear one asleep in the arms of Jesus, instead.

"Oh, Mama, why did you have to leave us?" she lamented. "And why did you make me promise to take Charity and look for Papa? What if I can't find him? What if he's lost forever, like so many of the other men who went to seek their fortunes?"

Bittersweet memories of her father's initial departure, his last hugs and words of encouragement to his family, rushed to soothe Faith's wounded spirit. Would she have reneged on her deathbed promise to her mother if she'd still had a comfortable home in which to wait for her father's return? Perhaps. Perhaps not. It was a pointless question. No choice remained.

"Oh, dear God." Her prayer was as plaintive, as wistful, as the wind that carried it. "Please, please show me what to do. Spare me this obligation."

No reprieve came. She hadn't truly expected divine intervention to lift her burden. Instead, she found herself remembering how she'd clasped her mother's hand and listened intently as the injured woman had spoken and wept, then had breathed her last with a blissful smile softening her features as she passed on.

"Lord willing, I will come back," Faith vowed, making peace with the past as best she could. In her deepest heart she feared she would never again climb that desolate hill to look down on those verdant valleys and farms of Ohio.

Bending over, the edges of her black cloak flapping wildly in a sudden gust of frigid air, she laid a bouquet of dried forget-me-nots on her mother's grave, turned and walked resolutely away.

Behind her, the storm tore the fragile flowers from their satin ribbon and strewed tattered fragments across the bare ground, destroying their beauty for the moment in order to plant the seeds of future blooms.

Chapter One

Fort Laramie, early summer, 1850

"Look out!" Faith yanked her sixteen-year-old sister to safety, barely in time. Massive wheels of an empty freight wagon ground across the footprints they'd just left in the powdery dust.

True to her nature, Charity gave a shriek. She cowered against the blunt end of a water trough while she worried the strings of her bonnet with fluttering fingers.

Faith caught her breath and waited for her heart to stop galloping. Fort Laramie was not at all what she'd expected. It was more a primitive frontier trading post than a real army garrison. No one seemed to care a fig about proper deportment, either. The rapidly rolling freight wagon that had just cut them off would most likely have run them down without a thought if they hadn't dodged in time!

As it was, she and Charity were both engulfed in a gritty brown cloud of powdered earth, undefined filth and bothersome, ever-present buffalo gnats. The tiny insects had been driving their mules crazy since before they'd reached the lower Platte. Not to mention getting into everything. Even her biscuit dough. She grimaced at the thought.

Waiting for the worst of the blowing dust to clear, Faith spied an opportunity, took hold of her sister's hand and dragged her back out into the fray. "Come on. We can't stand here all day."

"Ouch! You're hurting me." Charity's voice was a childish whine, far less womanly than her budding body suggested it should be.

At that moment, Faith's singular intent was surviving long enough to reach the opposite side of the roadway, whether Charity liked the idea or not. She refused to slow her pace. "Oh, hush. Stop complaining. You'd think I was killing you the way you carry on."

Charity's blue eyes widened. "You might be!" Planting her heels, she brought them to a staggering halt in front of the log-and-adobe-walled trading post. "I don't like it here. It's so…so barbaric. And it stinks."

Faith couldn't argue with that. Between the passage of hundreds of draft animals, plus careless, slovenly local inhabitants and travelers, the place smelled wretched. Though the high adobe walls surrounding the fort were obviously necessary for protection, she couldn't help thinking they'd all be better off if the tightly packed settlement was more open to the cleansing wind and rain of the plains.

Intent on finding the best in their situation, she nodded toward a group of blanketed Indians sitting silently against the front of the trading post. "Look, dear. Isn't all this interesting?"

Charity pressed a lace-edged handkerchief over her mouth and nose. "Not to me, Faith Ann. I think it's awful." She lowered her shrill voice to a whisper, her sidelong gaze darting to the stony-faced Indians. "Do you suppose they understand what we're saying?"

Faith boldly assessed the native women. They were short, like herself, but twice as wide and far more rounded, and seemed to be cautiously avoiding meeting her eyes. Even the smallest children were careful not to look up at the sisters.

"I suspect they may," Faith said, a bit ashamed. "Else why would they act so shy?" Lifting her skirts, she urged Charity up the high step onto the boarded walkway. "We probably hurt their feelings."

The blue eyes grew even wider. "Do you think so? Oh, dear." The fair-haired girl blushed as a tall, manly, cavalry officer in a uniform of blue and gold doffed his hat, bowing graciously as he passed.

Faith's quick mind pounced on the occasion to raise her sister's spirits. "There," she said quietly. "See? Aren't you glad you washed up and put on your best bonnet?"

"Captain Tucker already said I looked lovely, today," Charity countered, blushing demurely and twirling the tails of the bow tied beneath her chin. "I think he's wonderful."

Her sister was appalled. "Handsome is as handsome does, as Grandma Reeder used to say." Faith likened the horrid wagon boss to an unruly billy goat, bad to the bone and just as dangerous a creature to turn your back on. She knew better than to criticize him openly, of course, because he literally held their future in his hands. But that didn't mean she had to pretend to admire him. He was a necessity. Nothing more.

Leading the way into the trading post, Faith took one whiff of hot, stale air and wished she could hold her breath indefinitely. The cloying smells were no improvement over the pungent aromas of the street, they were simply more varied. Spices, coffee beans, vinegar, molasses and salted fish added their own tang to the almost palpable atmosphere.

Judging by the overwhelming odor of sweat and smoke liberally laced with dried buffalo dung, most of the customers had long ago abandoned any notion of bathing, too. Not that Faith blamed them. Now that she and Charity had spent two long months traveling from Independence, Missouri to Fort Laramie in the Territories, they, too, realized how few of their old customs and manners fit the wearying trek.

Glancing around the crowded room for the proprietor, she spied an older woman with a topknot of gray hair. Faith watched her deftly wrap and tie a package, hand it to a matron in a dark wool dress, accept payment, then turn to help the next of the noisy, milling customers.

"Come on." Taking her sister's hand, Faith began to lead her between the piles of flour sacks, kegs of tar and barrels of pickles to wait their turn to order supplies.

They were quite near their goal by the time Faith paid full attention to the tall, broad-shouldered man at the counter ahead of them. He was as rustic as anyone present, yet different. Intriguing. For one thing, he didn't smell as if he never bathed! While his back was turned, she took the opportunity to study him.

Long, sandy-colored hair hung beyond the spread of his shoulders. Worn buckskin covered him from head to toe. When he moved even slightly, he reminded Faith of the sleek, sinewy cougar she'd seen stalking a herd of antelope through the waving prairie grasses along the lower Platte.

Embarrassed to have been so bold, she lowered her focus. The man was speaking and his voice sent unexpected shivers up her spine. Her cheeks flamed as if touched by the summer sun. Surprised by the uncalled-for reaction, Faith nevertheless set aside her ideas of proper etiquette once again and peered up at him, listening shamelessly.

The storekeeper was looking at something cradled in the man's outstretched palm. "Sorry, son. It's been too long. I can't say for certain. Maybe. Maybe not."

Sighing, the man turned to go. With the Beal sisters directly in his path there was little room for polite maneuvering.

For a heart-stopping instant his troubled gaze met Faith's. Held it. His eyes were the color of smoke, of a fog-shrouded mountain meadow at dawn. And his beard, almost the same hue as his buckskins, continued to remind her of a stalking mountain lion. Faith caught her breath.

The man nodded politely, pushing past them toward the door. Charity gave a little squeak of protest and fell back as he passed. Faith stood her ground. She had never felt so tiny in her entire life. Yet she experienced no fear, even though the plainsman was rough-hewn and dusty from the trail.

The gray-haired woman noted Faith's watchful interest. "Feel kinda sorry for him, I do."

Faith frowned. "I beg your pardon?"

"That big fella. He's lookin' for his betrothed. Might as well be lookin' for a will-o'-the-wisp. Got about as much chance a findin' one."

"Oh, dear. I'm so sorry."

Faith saw him pause to show something small to several groups of people, then square his hat on his head and leave the trading post. Thinking of her own home and family, her heart broke for the poor man. She knew all too well what it was like to lose a loved one. As she absently laid her hand over the heart-shaped onyx pendant containing a lock of her mother's hair, she vowed to add the stranger's quest to her nightly prayers.

The shopkeeper shrugged. "Happens a lot out here. Folks windin' up lost, I mean. Now, what can I do for you ladies?"

Focusing on the reason for their visit, Faith took a scrap of paper from her reticule and handed it over. "We'll need these supplies. Do you have them all?"

"Coffee'll cost you dear," the woman said, licking the point of a pencil and beginning to check off items on the list. "The flour's no problem, though. And the bacon. You'll have to go across to the mercantile if you want a paper of pins."

"All right." Faith couldn't help glancing toward the doorway where she'd last glimpsed the intriguing man. Sadly, he'd gone.

"Indians steal pins if I keep 'em here," the shop-keeper went on. "Candy, too. Regular thieves, they are."

Charity grasped her sister's arm in alarm. "You see? I told you we shouldn't have come."

"Oh, nonsense. Surely you don't think there were no thieves at home in Ohio." Faith shook her off.

"You in a hurry?" the proprietress asked. "Other-wise we'll have this packed up and ready to go in an hour or so. Have to send Will out to the smokehouse for another side of bacon. You put aside enough bran to pack it in a barrel real good like?"

"Yes. And there's no hurry," Faith assured her, ig-noring Charity's scowl. "Our friend Mr. Ledbetter is at the blacksmith's getting a wagon wheel fixed. No telling when we'll be ready to go back to the train."

"I got lots o' pretty Indian trinkets," the woman urged. "Or you could do what most of the ladies do and go wonder at the dry goods in the mercantile. They got twenty…thirty new bolts o' calico since winter. Been meanin' to go have a look-see myself. Never seem to find time." She wiped her hands on her apron. "Tell 'em Anna Morse sent you."

Faith thanked her for her advice. "We'll be back in a bit, Mrs. Morse. We're the Beal sisters. This is Charity and I'm Faith. We're with the Tucker train."

"Yes," Charity added proudly. "Captain Ramsey Tucker is kindly looking after us."

Faith noticed an immediate change in the woman's countenance. Her gray eyebrows knit, her wrinkles becoming more pronounced as her eyes narrowed in a wary expression. It was somewhat of a relief for Faith to see that she, herself, was not the only one disturbed by references to the captain.

That realization gave her pause. What might Mrs. Morse know about their wagon train? And would she reveal the truth, if asked?

Faith glanced nervously at her sister. Any candid conversation must not take place in front of Charity. The silly girl was too smitten with Tucker to be trusted to hold her tongue, especially if the news was disturbing.

Pondering alternatives, Faith recalled their schedule. They were to lay over in camp the rest of today and tomorrow before pushing on to California. In that length of time she was bound to be able to sneak back into the fort and make some discreet inquiries of Anna Morse. She only hoped she could live with whatever secrets were revealed.

The sun had crested and started toward the west as Faith waited on the plank walkway in front of the trading post. A small bundle from the mercantile, wrapped in brown paper and tied with string, lay at her feet where it had been for the past three hours. The rest of their purchases remained inside.

Shielding her eyes from the afternoon glare, she seemed oblivious to the people pushing past. She fanned her burning cheeks with an embroidered handkerchief while looking left and right in anticipation of the arrival of the Ledbetters' wagon. Repairs to the wheel must be taking a very long time.

Charity tugged at her sister's sleeve. "It's fearful hot

and dusty out here. I'm going back into the store." She pulled harder. "Come with me."

"Just a moment more." Faith pushed her slat bonnet off the back of her head, letting it hang down her back by its strings while she dabbed away the drops of perspiration on her forehead.

"No. I'm frightened," Charity insisted. "I told you, Ramsey... Captain Tucker...warned us not to come into town at all. He said he'd take care of buying our supplies for us. He was right. We should have listened to him."

Faith could hardly tell her gullible sister that the nefarious captain was not going to get his hands on any more of their money if she could help it. Not even to run simple errands. She'd paid dearly for their spot with the train because she hadn't known any better. Now, she knew they'd been cheated. She wouldn't play the fool twice.

Instead of arguing she merely said, "We'll be fine."

Cupping one pale hand around her mouth, Charity made a pouting face and leaned closer to whisper. "The Indians get more terrible looking all the time. See them scratching? I hate to think why. Makes me want to dip the hem of my skirt in kerosene to ward off the fleas!"

"You're being a silly goose." Faith took her sister's shoulders, physically turned the girl to face the door to the trading post, shoved the paper-wrapped bundle into her hands and gave her a push. "All right. Go on. Suffer in the stench of those stacks of awful buffalo hides if you want. I'm perfectly happy out here."

Charity turned back. "The captain told us to stay together."

"Captain Tucker is merely our guide," Faith said flatly. "I will not pretend we aren't beholden to him, but neither will I cede to his every command."

"I can't believe you're being so mean. He's a brave and wonderful man."

"That remains to be seen." Faith took a deep breath and made a decision. "Look, I can't abide standing here wasting my time any longer. I have wash to do and food to prepare back in camp. Fixing one loose wagon wheel shouldn't take this long. I'm going to walk to the blacksmith's and see what's delayed Mr. Ledbetter."

Charity gasped. "You can't do that! Not here. Not alone."

"Then you'll come with me?"

The pale girl stepped back quickly, clutching the package to her breast. "I can't. It's not fair to ask me."

That reaction was what Faith had counted on. Two months as her sister's constant companion and chaperone had been an insufferable trial. If the Lord hadn't granted her an extra dose of patience, she'd surely have throttled the girl by now, especially when Charity had claimed she'd accidentally lost both their black dresses while washing them in a flooded river and they'd been forced to cease wearing mourning for their mother far too soon. For Faith, a few minutes respite from her familial duty would be like a breath of cool breeze in the midst of oppressive heat.

She composed herself, then said, "All right, Charity, dear. Then why don't you go inside and check the rest of our order to be certain everything is exactly as it should be?"

"I could do that." The younger woman began to blink

and smile sweetly. "The captain would be proud of my efficiency, wouldn't he?"

"Undoubtedly. I'm certain Mr. Ledbetter will tell him you are the picture of virtue. And you needn't worry about me. It's obvious the army has plenty of men here to keep the peace."

"Oh. Well, if you're sure you'll be all right..."

Wheeling quickly, Charity gathered her skirts and darted through the door.

Faith breathed a relieved sigh as she turned away to look down the street. She'd often thought it must be a sin to wish for self-serving favors from heaven, yet there were times she couldn't help hoping some suitable young swain would soon rescue her from her sister's trying foolishness.

Tiny flies continued to buzz around Faith's head. Beads of perspiration gathered on her temples while sweaty rivulets trickled down her back between her shoulder blades. Ignoring the discomfort, she squashed her bonnet back on her head, whipped the ties into a loose bow and started off.

Wide cracks between the rough-sawed boards of the walkway captured the narrow heels of her best shoes, forcing her to either descend into the street or chance taking a bad fall. Since Charity had never learned to handle the mule team, Faith certainly couldn't afford to be incapacitated. Not unless she wanted to be compelled to put up with whatever form of retaliation or retribution the unctuous Captain Tucker decided to arrange.

Since their last set-to over his brutality toward one of her mules that very morning, she'd suspected that the captain would shortly come up with some lame excuse why relief drivers, Ab or Stuart, could no longer be spared to handle her wagon. Well, fine. It would be her pleasure to show Ramsey Tucker that at least one Beal sister was capable of something besides giggling helplessness. If he wouldn't provide the assistance he'd promised when she'd joined the train, Faith would handle the lines herself, just as she had at home in Ohio.

She set her jaw. Tucker had underestimated her for the last time. She'd stood up to him before and she'd do it again. And, oh, was he going to be scalded!

Faith shuddered at the memory of his dark, penetrating eyes, the way he'd stared at her, spitting that disgusting tobacco juice at her feet. He was not a person to be taken lightly. But then, neither was she.

Clouds of choking dust billowed from beneath passing rigs as Faith hurried down the street. Grasping the brim of her bonnet, she pressed it closer to her cheeks. The din around her was so loud, so packed with shouts, curses, strange tongues and the sound of rolling wagons and clanking harness traces that Faith didn't see the danger or hear anyone call out a warning until a melee erupted directly in her path.

A door flew open. Glass shattered. Shutters banged. Three uniformed cavalrymen careened off the walkway and down into the street, tumbling, pushing, swinging and cursing as they went.

Faith jumped aside. One of the men, a thin, filthy fellow who reminded her of a rickety calf, was bleeding from his nose. He wiped the blood on his dirty sleeve, then flung it aside, dotting her skirt with ugly red splotches.

Disgusted, Faith was wiping at the stains in the green calico when a fourth man lurched off the porch. He hit her a jarring blow with his full weight. Breathless, stunned, she went sprawling in the dust.

For an instant she lost track of where she was or what had happened. All too soon, it came back to her. Raising up on her forearms she tasted the gritty substance of the well-traveled street and found her mind forming thoughts quite inappropriate for a lady. Her only clean dress was a grimy mess, her bonnet was askew and, worst of all, no one in the crowd seemed to even notice.

Pausing on her knees, she assessed her pain. Something was very wrong. If she hadn't been in such unexpected misery she would very likely have lectured the careless men on the impropriety of brawling in the streets. As it was, she knew she'd be doing well to merely maneuver out of harm's way.

One of the soldiers had collapsed, gasping and retching, in a drunken haze beneath the hitching rail. The larger of the two remaining was beating the rickety-calf man to a pulp.

Gathering her soiled skirts, Faith lifted them above her shoe tops with one hand, lurched to her feet and stumbled around a corner. Finding a bare wall, she leaned against it and closed her eyes.

It hurt to move. To breathe. She pressed both palms hard against her aching side. Dear God! As much as she hated to admit it, Charity was right. The streets of Fort Laramie were no place for a stroll.

At the passage of a shadow across her flushed face, Faith's eyes snapped open. The muscled shoulder of an enormous reddish-colored horse was a scant three feet from the tip of her nose. She heard saddle leather creak as its rider leaned forward.

"You should have better sense," he grumbled.

Her blurry vision focused. That beard. That hair. The buckskins. It was him. The man from the trading post who was searching for his lost bride-to-be. She drew a short breath and winced as pain shot from her side to her innards. "Sarcasm is quite uncalled-for, sir."

"Where's your man?"

"I hardly think that is a proper question," Faith shot back, grimacing in spite of herself.

He dismounted beside her, his tone a little more gentle. "You're right. My apologies. Guess I've been alone on the trail too long. Are you badly hurt?"

Suddenly not certain, Faith sagged back against the wall. "I… I don't think so." Taking a deeper breath, she assessed the searing pain that increased every time she moved or dared inhale. "Oh, dear."

"Can you walk?"

"Of course." What a silly question. Why, she'd never had a sick day in her life, not even when she'd been left to try to cope after Mama had died. Faith bit her lower lip. Today's problems were sufficient for today, as the Good Book said.

The plainsman stood by, waiting, his mere presence lending her added fortitude. She would straighten up, stand tall and prove to him she was fine. The moment she tried, however, agony knifed through her body, bending her double. She bit back a cry.

"Have you got a penny?" he asked, sounding disgusted.

The slim cords of Faith's reticule were still looped

around her wrist. Had she been in better command of her faculties, she might have questioned his request. Instead, she raised the drawstring bag to him without speaking.

"Good, because I don't. I'd hate to waste a whole dollar on this."

Although pain was coursing through her like the racing water of a rain-swollen stream, she was still capable of a modicum of indignation. "I beg your pardon?" Her mouth dropped open. What audacity! The man had invaded her reticule to withdraw the asked-for penny.

"This will do." Flipping the oversize copper coin into the air and catching it several times, he whistled at a young boy who was passing. "Son! Over here."

The boy's face lit up when he spied the coin. "Yessir?"

Connell bent low, holding out the penny as inducement. "I want you to fetch that Mrs. Morse from the trading post. You know her?"

"Yes, sir!"

"Tell her a lady is hurt and needs her. Then bring her here and I'll pay you for your trouble."

Young eyes darted from the coin to the pale, disheveled woman leaning against the wall. "Did you hurt her, mister?"

Faith managed to smile. One hand remained pressed tightly to her ribs, but she put out the other and laid it on the buckskin-clad arm of her Good Samaritan. "No," she said. "There was an accident and this gentleman came to my rescue. Now, hurry. Please."

"Yes, ma'am!" The boy was off like a shot.

Breathing shallowly to minimize her pain, Faith

peered at the man on whose sturdy arm she was leaning. Soon, she would release her hold on him. Just a few seconds more and she'd feel strong enough to stand alone.

"I do thank you for looking after me," Faith managed. "No one else seemed to even notice."

"They noticed." How delicate she seemed, Connell McClain thought. Her skin was soft, like the doeskin of his scabbard, only warm and alive. And her eyes. No wonder they had reminded him of a deer's the first time he'd looked into them. They were the most beautiful, rich brown he'd ever seen.

He scowled. Better to keep the woman talking and draw her thoughts away from her injuries. She didn't look well. If she passed out on him before Mrs. Morse arrived, he didn't know what he'd do with her.

"The Indians wouldn't help you because they don't dare touch a white woman," he explained. "And if the soldiers got involved, they'd have to admit they were the cause of your troubles. That could mean the stockade."

"Oh." The woman glanced at the street and seemed to realize passersby were eyeing her with curiosity. "I'll bet I look a fright."

"You have looked better," he said, remembering the strong response he'd had when he'd almost bowled her over in the trading post. Some of the pins had come loose from her hair and it was tumbling down over her shoulders. He hadn't imagined that the coffee-colored tresses under her bonnet would be nearly as comely as they actually were.

Nodding, she folded her arms more tightly around

her body in an apparent effort to cope. Between the sweltering heat and the pain she was evidently experiencing, it was little wonder she was struggling so.

"I expect they think I'm your kin, so they're leaving us alone," he offered.

"I'm truly sorry to have inconvenienced you, sir. If I had money to spare, I'd gladly repay you for your kindness. My sister and I are on our way to California. After arranging our passage I'm afraid we have very little left."

A sister? Connell vaguely recalled that there had been another woman with her in the trading post, but for the life of him, he couldn't picture what she'd looked like.

An unexpected twinge caught her unaware and she gasped before she again gained control of herself. Tears gathered in her eyes. He hesitantly cupped her elbow with as light a touch as he could manage and still support her.

"I'm sorry for being such a ninny," she said, with a faint smile. "I'm usually quite brave. Really, I am."

"I'm sure you are, ma'am."

"I can't be seriously injured, you know." She looked east toward the wagon camp. "I may have to drive the team when we leave here." Her voice trailed off. She could tell from the way the man was looking at her that he had already decided she was, indeed, badly hurt. Coming on top of so much throbbing pain, the thought of not being able to function on her own was too much for her.

Darkness pushed at the edges of her vision. Flashes of colored light twinkled like a hundred candles on a festive Christmas tree. Nausea came in waves. She fought to keep her balance, but it was no use. Closing her eyes, she began a slow-motion slide toward the ground.

Connell saw her going out. The doe's eyes glassed over, then rolled back in her head. He cast around for help. Where had that fool boy gotten to?

The plainsman instinctively grabbed Faith's arms, then made the split-second decision to catch her up in spite of his misgivings. Next thing you knew, he'd probably be shot by the woman's jealous husband or brother for trying to help her. They'd bury him on the prairie in an unmarked grave and forget he'd ever lived. Then, who'd be left to find out what had happened to poor Irene?

Connell lifted the unconscious Faith in his arms, trying not to jostle her ribs as he swung her across his chest. She was so tiny. Barely there. He couldn't just walk away and ignore her plight. He wasn't going to leave her until he'd seen to it she was safe and well cared for.

He could only hope that someone, somewhere, was doing the same for his intended bride.

Chapter Two

Connell met the breathless boy halfway to the trading post.

"She die, mister?"

"No. Fainted. Where's Mrs. Morse?"

"She ain't comin'. I told her what you said but she didn't believe me." He trotted alongside, struggling to keep up with Connell's long, purposeful strides. "Kin I have my penny, anyhows?"

Connell muttered under his breath. No telling what had happened to the coin. Chances were he'd dropped it when he'd had to catch the girl.

He glanced down at the eager child. "Look in the dirt, where we were before. If it's not there, follow along and I'll get you another. And bring my horse. His name is Rojo. That's Mexican for red. Call him by name and he won't give you any grief. He's a full-blooded canelo I picked up in California and I'd hate to lose him. I'd never find another one like him out here."

"Aw, shucks. You said…"

Connell was in no mood for argument. "Go, before

somebody else finds your money." The boy seemed to see the logic in that suggestion, because he took off like a long-eared jackrabbit running from a pack of coyotes.

Crossing to the trading post, Connell and his frail burden solicited few inquisitive glances. He looked down at the sweet face of the girl. Her cheeks were smudged and her hair nearly undone. The bonnet hung loosely by its ribbons. Her doe eyes were closed, but he could still picture them clearly.

She stirred. Long, dark lashes fluttered against her fair skin like feathers on the breeze. She was so lovely, so innocent looking, lying there, the sight of her made his heart thump worse than the time he'd fought with Fremont against the Mexicans in San Jose in '45.

The quick lurch of his gut took him totally by surprise. He stared down at the girl. She was all-fired young. Much younger than Irene. Couldn't be more than eighteen or nineteen if she was a day. That made her ten or so years younger than he was; about the same distance apart in age as his mother and father had been.

Clenching his jaw, he tried unsuccessfully to set aside the bitter memories of his childhood, the mental image of his mother's funeral and the cruel way his father had behaved afterward. If it hadn't been for Irene and her family taking him in and showing him what a loving home was supposed to be like, no telling what would have become of him back then.

Connell took a deep breath and started across the street, his purpose redefined, his goal once again in focus. It didn't matter how attracted he might be to this woman. Or to any other. It was Irene he had to think about, Irene he had sworn to find. To marry. If he had to spend the rest of his life looking for the truest friend he had ever had, then he would. Without ceasing.

The unconscious girl moaned as Connell mounted the walkway in front of the trading post. Several Indians edged out of his path.

As he made his way into the store, all conversation ceased. He headed straight for the proprietress.

Anna Morse clapped a hand to her chest. "Land sakes! The boy was tellin' the truth."

"Obviously." The plainsman reached her in six quick strides, his tall cavalry boots thumping hollowly on the floor. "Where can I put her?"

"Let's take her upstairs," Anna said. "Her sister's right over…" Pointing, she snorted derisively. Charity had fainted dead away. The girl lay draped across a stack of flour sacks while two other women and a child patted her hands and fanned her cheeks. "Never mind. We'll see to her, later. Bring Miss Faith this way."

Faith. Connell turned that name over in his mind. He'd have guessed she might be called after a flower or some famous woman from the Bible, like Sarah or Esther. Hearing that she was, instead, Faith, gave him pause. Yet it fit. A strong trait, a gift necessary for survival especially when crossing the plains, Faith was appropriate. How was it the scripture went? Something about…"if you have faith as a grain of mustard seed, you can say to a mountain, move, and the mountain will move." This tiny woman was going to need that kind of unwavering faith if she was to survive the many rigors that would face her on the trail.

The upstairs room Anna led him to was small but clean. An absence of personal items led Connell to believe Mrs. Morse probably rented it out whenever she could. Careful not to jostle his limp burden, he lowered Faith gently onto the bed.

As he straightened and slipped his arm from beneath her shoulders, he reached up to gently smooth the damp wisps of hair from her forehead. The act was totally instinctive. Until the older woman cautioned him, he didn't think about how improper his actions must look.

"That'll do, mister. We're beholden to you for totin' her here." Anna wedged between him and the prone figure, which was beginning to stir. "I'll take good care of her."

Connell nodded and touched the brim of his hat. "Yes, ma'am. It doesn't appear the sister'll be much help, that's a fact." Keeping his voice low, he added, "This one got herself knocked down by a bunch of drunken horse soldiers."

"Figures. I swan, this old world has got to be nearin' judgment day."

"Don't know about that, ma'am, but there's four boys in blue who will be when I get ahold of them."

"You ain't plannin' on startin' trouble, are you?"

"No, ma'am." Connell took a few backward steps toward the open bedroom door. "Finishing it."

Anna made a noise of disgust. "Bah! All men are fools. Every bloomin' one of 'em."

At that, the plainsman managed a half smile. "You're probably right." Peering past her, he tried to get another glimpse of Faith. "You think she'll be all right? I reckon her ribs are broke."

"Soon as she comes to, I'll be able to tell for sure."

Turning toward the door, Connell paused. "I'll be back to pay you for whatever the girl needs."

The older woman shook her head. "You ain't her kin. You done enough."

He scowled, his helpful attitude hardening into determination. "I told you why I was here. Whatever I do for Miss Faith, it'll be like I'm doing it for my Irene, too. Understand?"

Anna nodded solemnly. She wiped her hands on her apron. "That, I do. Long as you remember your money buys you no rights to the Beal sisters."

The growing smile lifted Connell's mustache. "Oh, it won't be my money," he said. "I aim to collect damages due from the sons o'—'scuse me, I mean the *soldiers* who did the hurting."

That seemed to satisfy Anna's sense of decency. "Good for you. Think they'll pay up?"

For Connell, the question was already answered. His decision was firm. It wouldn't take but a few minutes of his time to enforce justice on Faith Beal's behalf. To see to it that she was recompensed. He was certain that was what Irene would want him to do.

"Yes, ma'am, I do," he said flatly. "Those four boys'll be real tickled to help out. You'll see."

Anna shook her head. "I don't want to see any of it. You do what your conscience tells you to do, son, but leave me out of it. You hear?"

Tipping his hat, Connell nodded in affirmation and left her. By the time he'd reached the bottom of the staircase, his anger in respect to Faith's plight was white-hot. How dare those drunken fools abuse a refined, gentle soul like her and then ignore what they'd done without so much as a backward glance or a word of apology?

He left the trading post, jumped down to the street and started off toward the saloon. Very little time had passed since the incident. He had no doubt he'd easily be able to locate the perpetrators.

The door to Maguire's Saloon swung back with a bang as he straight-armed it and headed for the bar. The place wasn't fancy red velvet and sparkling chandeliers like the plush parlors of San Francisco. Nor was it any cleaner than the rest of the fort. At each end of the bar stood gaboons, wooden boxes filled with sawdust, that served as poor men's spittoons. By the look of the floor, no one there took very good aim.

Connell scanned the crowd. Nearly a dozen men were dressed in the blue of the cavalry but only a few were as filthy and bruised as the guilty parties he was looking for had to be. Bellying up to the bar, the largest of the four was lifting a glass and laughing as another member of the disgusting quartet gave his impression of Faith's shocked facial expression after her fall.

Silent, Connell approached, his jaw set, his fists clenched. The loudmouth had reddish hair and a swollen eye as purple as a ripe plum. When Connell tapped him on the shoulder, he turned, still chuckling, with a sarcastic what-do-you-want? look on his face.

Connell reached up and whipped off the man's hat, turning it over to serve as a collection basket.

"Hey! What the…?"

"For the lady you boys hurt," Connell said. The low, menacing timbre of his voice was as threatening as his words. "Ante up."

The man cursed. "Now wait a…"

Connell had grasped the redhead by the shirtfront and hoisted him high in the air before anyone could interfere. As formidable as the soldier was, he was no match for such ferocious rage and brute strength. The others began to edge away.

"All of you," Connell shouted. "Freeze where you are and fill the kitty." His head cocked toward the hat, which had landed on the bar when he'd grabbed the loudmouth. "Now."

He waited till three soldiers had complied before releasing the fourth. "Your turn."

"I ain't got no money to waste on no stupid settler."

Connell's fist connected hard with the man's jaw, sending his body sliding along the front of the bar where it finally came to rest in a heap near the gaboon. He gestured to the man's friends. "Pick him up."

The smallest of the three shook his head violently and backed away, his hands in the air. Thin and much shorter than the others, he'd obviously gotten the worst of the brawl. "No way. He wakes up, he'll kill me."

"Judging from what's left of your sorry face, it looks like he nearly did, already." Connell glanced at the remaining two. "You think your friend would be interested in making his fair share of the contribution?" He held out the hat. The few coins it contained chinked together.

"Sure, sure. Ol' Bob, he's a regular fella. He just gets nasty when he's keepin' company with John Barleycorn, is all." The closest one reached into his companion's pockets and came up with a fistful of coins. "This do ya?"

When the soldier dropped the money into the hat, Connell gathered it in his hand, briefly calculated how much there was, then threw the empty hat across the face of its unconscious owner. "He wakes up, you tell him for me that the lady is much obliged."

"Yes, sir. Sure will."

Turning away, Connell stalked out. He was certain neither Miss Faith Beal nor Mrs. Morse would approve of his methods, yet they'd have had to admit they were effective. There was no need to go into detail when he delivered the "donations" to the women. It was enough to know that he'd righted a wrong. An innocent young woman wouldn't have to suffer more hardship because of the yahoos who'd harmed her.

Thinking about Faith's vulnerability, he took a deep breath and exhaled noisily as he reentered the trading post. Near the door, the pale girl with corn-silk hair still sat atop the filled sacks. White flour dusted the back and shoulders of her blue dress, a clear reminder of her fainting spell. An older man and several women were fussing over her. Unsure of whether or not to approach, Connell paused to listen to what they were saying.

"No! I can't stay here. I just can't," the girl whimpered. "Please, take me back to camp with you."

"Now, Miss Charity," the man was cajoling, "you'll be perfectly safe with Mrs. Morse. Your sister might need you."

"No! No, no, no." She stamped her small foot. "It wasn't my idea to come here in the first place and I'll not stay. I demand you deliver me back to Captain Tucker."

One of the matrons patted Charity's hand. "There,

there, dear. Of course we'll see that you get to the captain. I'm sure your sister is in good hands."

Shaking his head in disgust, Connell watched them leave before he started for the staircase.

Anna Morse met him halfway up and solidly blocked his path. "Well?"

"The sister left," he said, scowling.

"Figures. What about the fellas what done the hurting? Did you clean their plows for 'em?"

"Enough to get their attention. I never did intend to start another set-to." He transferred the money he'd collected to the proprietress. "If you want more..."

"No need. This'll be plenty. I bandaged her myself. You was right. She's got a few sore ribs."

"You bound her tight?"

"'Course. I did fine and so did she. She's a spunky one, that Faith."

Connell nodded. "That she is."

"Too bad about her ma."

They made their way to the base of the stairs, Connell in the lead. "Her ma?"

"Got kilt by the same twister that wiped out their house and most of their belongings," Anna told him. "That's why she and that worthless sister of hers are on their way to Californy to look for their pa."

"Alone?" Connell couldn't believe how many women tried to cross the plains without proper help or preparation. He didn't fault them for their courage, only for their lack of common sense.

"That's right. Ramsey Tucker's supposed to be lookin' after them. To my thinkin', they'd be better off all by themselves than trustin' him." Heading toward the busy young man who was trying to wait on three families at once, she slipped the coins Connell had collected into her apron pocket. "I'm comin', Will."

Connell followed and asked, "When does the Tucker train pull out?"

"Tomorrow." Anna smiled with understanding. "Don't fret. Our girl'll be able to travel just fine. Now, scoot. I got work to do."

It wasn't till Connell was outside that he remembered what Faith had said about having to drive her own team. Well and whole, she might be able to do it. Hurt the way she was, the pain would be dreadful. Besides, she might make her condition worse. Maybe even puncture a lung.

Muttering and gritting his teeth, Connell argued that Faith wasn't his concern. Irene was. He found his horse where the boy had left it, rechecked the cinch on his saddle, then mounted. It was time to head for Maguire's or some such place. The drink and eats he'd promised himself a whole lot earlier were way overdue.

Standing in the upstairs room in her chemise and drawers, Faith listened at the slightly open door, then quietly eased it closed. Thanks to the tight bindings around her midriff, she'd managed to get out of bed without too much discomfort. She hated corsets. Always had. But she had to admit wearing one might have spared her poor bones.

Placing her forehead and palms against the wood of the door, she closed her eyes for a moment, hoping that somehow, when she opened them again, her current predicament would prove to be no more than a bad dream.

Such was not the case. Breathing shallowly when she really wanted to sigh deeply, she straightened and took a long look at the room. The bed sagged in the middle where the ropes had stretched, but at least it was clean. Mrs. Morse had hung her soiled dress on a peg next to the pine washstand. On the floor in front of it was a small rag rug, just like the ones Grandma Reeder used to make, and laid across the foot of the bed was a plain lawn wrapper.

Barefoot, Faith crossed to the bed and slowly threaded her arms into the wrapper, folding it closed. The process was painful, though not nearly as bad as she suspected trying to put on her dress would be. Pensive, she tied the sash and padded across the cool wooden floor, in search of a breeze from the open window.

The wide, busy street lay below, it's clattering traffic an ongoing performance. Wagons of all shapes and uses were passing, as well as riders and enough foot traffic to more than fill the fondly remembered old streets of Burg Hill. In the midst of all the hubbub sat a man in buckskin astride a giant horse the color of a rusty rose.

With a trembling hand, Faith drew aside the lacy curtains and studied the traveler who had so recently borne her to safety in his arms. It was a kindness she hadn't expected here in this wild country. She fingered her pendant and thought of home. Of family. Oh, how she wished her mother were there to be a companion in her travails, to understand her the way Charity never could.

Well, at least her Good Samaritan had the hope of someday finding his missing betrothed, Faith mused, looking down at him and stifling a tiny twinge of jealousy. She would never again see her dearest ones or the home place she'd loved, no matter how hard she wished or prayed or toiled.

Suddenly realizing she had taken her deliverance for granted, Faith was penitent. Not only had she been spared the fate her poor mother had suffered, she'd been rescued a second time since then. Given the unsympathetic reactions of the other travelers she'd encountered at the fort, it was a wonderment she was not still lying in a heap in the street.

In retrospect, Faith realized she'd drifted in and out of consciousness while being carried to the trading post. She'd felt the rumble of the man's voice beneath his buckskin shirt as he'd told the boy she'd fainted. There was also a vague recollection of a gentle hand on her face as someone touched her to brush back a lock of hair. Could that have been him?

Stepping in front of half of the curtain, she toyed with the loose curls that hung down over her shoulders. Decent, grown women didn't let anyone but their husbands see them with their hair thus, Faith reminded herself. And they certainly didn't stand in a window clad in nothing more than their chemise and a wrapper. Yet she didn't move away, even when the man's head tipped back and he gazed boldly in her direction.

Did he know who he was watching? He must. If not, why stare like that? There was plenty to see in the street below without bothering to peer into a tiny window fifteen feet above the entrance to the trading post.

Faith knew she should step back into the shadows. Displaying herself was indecent. Wanton. Still, there was the remembered touch of a hand on her cheek, the pounding of a strong heart beneath her ear as he bore her away in his arms, and the concern she'd glimpsed in his eyes as mental darkness had overcome her.

One more look, one more thought of intense gratitude wouldn't hurt. She knew she'd never see the man again. He had a quest of his own—the search for his bride—while she must complete her own journey. That their divergent paths had crossed at all was amazing. She only wished she'd had an opportunity to thank him in person.

Wanting to memorize the image of her rescuer so she could later pay proper homage to his compassion, Faith swayed closer to the thick, white-painted casement. Beneath his beard and mustache, she thought she saw a smile, though it was impossible to be certain at such a great distance. Hopeful, she raised her hand as if bestowing a blessing.

In reply, the man tipped his hat, then squared it on his head, reined his horse hard and rode off.

Faith's heart pounded as she watched him go. Clearly, he'd entered her life to profoundly influence it. No matter how far she traveled or how many more years she lived, she'd never forget him.

Sudden awareness made her breath catch. Of course! The man on the red horse had been the answer to her fervent prayers for deliverance. Accepting that notion tempered her perspective of the ordeal in which she was currently embroiled. Without his amazing intervention she might actually have died, alone and ignored.

And gone to be with Jesus, she countered, certain her lonely soul would approve of the idea, just as it had ever since her mother's fatal accident. This time, however, Faith found she was no longer looking forward to joining Mama in heaven. Yes, she wanted to see all her loved ones again someday, but her earthly tasks weren't complete. Not yet.

By proving she wasn't truly alone in her current trials, a heaven-sent stranger had inadvertently opened her eyes—and her heart—to the possibility of a bright, worthwhile future.

And she didn't even know his name.

Chapter Three

Near evening, the sun turned the adobe walls of Fort Laramie a pale crimson. Myriad cooking fires were burning in the distant wagon camps. Anna brought Faith a bowl of warm gruel with pork trimmings and a cup of broth made with boiled, dried vegetables.

"I'd a fetched you more if I'd figured you could hold it," she said, setting the small pewter tray down on the top of the washstand.

"Whatever you've made is fine." Faith managed a smile and arose with care, her bare feet silent on the wooden floor. Thoughtful, she paused. "I don't know when I'll be able to repay you for all your kindness. If I were going to be here longer I'd offer to work off my bill."

"Ain't necessary. It's been paid."

"But...how? Surely my sister didn't..."

"Not her. Forgive me for sayin' so, but she's about as worthless as a pocket on a pouch."

Blushing, Faith stifled a chuckle. The analogy was funny and most apropos. "Then, how was it paid?"

Tempted by the aroma of the hot broth, she raised the cup to sip while Anna spoke.

"Them fellas what busted you up took up a fine collection—with a little prodding."

Faith paused as the liquid trickled down her throat, warming her against the cool of the evening. "Prodding? I don't understand." But in her heart, she did. Unless she missed her guess, her buckskin-clad benefactor had once again come to her rescue. A faint smile began to lift the corners of her mouth.

Anna snickered. "From the look in your eye, I'd say you've got the right idea. Didn't see it happen, myself, but talk is, your Mr. McClain dusted the floor of Maguire's with them boys in blue."

"Oh, dear." Faith pressed her free hand to the base of her throat, over the mourning pendant. It was strange to hear the big man referred to as her Mr. McClain. So, *that* was his name.

"Quite a sight, they say, and I can sure see why. That boy's a big one, all right. Strong as Finnegan's ox."

"He's hardly a boy," Faith observed, sipping more broth to cover her urge to smile at the ridiculous comparison. "Did he say what his given name was?"

Anna raised an eyebrow. "Can't say as he did. Why?"

"I just wondered."

"It's good you've got a friend like him, considering the mess you're in."

Lowering the cup of broth, Faith set it aside before taking advantage of the comment to ask, "When you say mess, are you referring to my injury, or to our business dealings with Ramsey Tucker?"

"Both. Mostly Tucker, I reckon."

Faith reached for the older woman's callused hands, clasping them tightly. "Please. I must know everything you've heard."

"You won't like it."

"Ramsey Tucker has made more than one inappropriate suggestion regarding my lack of a husband or father to care for me and my sister during the crossing. I'd hardly be shocked at anything you'd tell me about his character. He's detestable."

Nodding, Anna led Faith over to the edge of the rope bed and they perched together on the wooden frame. "You're right about him. He's passed through here seven or eight times. I liked him less every time I laid eyes on him."

"But why? I've seen that he's cruel. He's even whipped my poor, innocent mules for no reason except pure meanness. But there must be more. I feel it."

"Maybe so. Not that I have any sworn word on it, mind you, but I hear your captain's been made a new widower on just about every trip." She paused, patting Faith's hands for comfort. "They say he picks out a woman of property, sidles up to her, and before she knows it they're married. Trouble is, his brides don't reach Californy."

Faith's eyes widened. "And he inherits?"

"Every penny. And all his dead wife's possessions, to boot. Makes himself a pretty piece of change, what with sellin' off their rigs and all."

"Oh, dear Lord!" Faith's hands fluttered to her throat again. "He started making up to my sister after I rebuffed him."

"That ain't good. Not good at all."

"I know. But what can I do? We have to get to my father somehow."

"Stay here then. Wait for the next train to come through and join up with them."

"We can't." Ringing her hands, Faith began to pace, oblivious to the pain in her side. "Tucker has most of the money I was able to raise by selling what was left of the farm. We can't afford to pay again. And we might not be able to talk another party into accepting us, even if we could. Not two women alone."

Shrugging, Anna got to her feet. "You're probably right about that." She reached into her apron pocket, came up with a fistful of coins, and placed them in Faith's hands. "Here. Take this. It's not much but it'll help."

"Oh, I couldn't."

"Have to, as I see it," the shopkeeper countered. "It ain't my money. It come from the soldiers I told you about. Way too much for what little your stay here cost."

"Well…"

"Good girl. Take whatever the Good Lord supplies and don't ask questions. That's the way to get by out here."

"Thank you." Faith smiled with gratitude. "Now, what advice can you give me about handling Ramsey Tucker?"

Snorting in derision, Anna shook her head. "That's another kettle of burnt beans, ain't it? As I see it, all you've got to do is keep your little sister locked up tight for the next couple o' thousand miles. Anything so's

she don't go gettin' all het up about marryin' that son
of perdition—excuse my plain speakin'."

"No pardon necessary. I've thought to call him worse
than that myself, once or twice."

"I'll bet many a sensible woman has. It's the foolish
ones what get taken in and pay so dearly. I'll be prayin'
for you, Faith. I truly will."

"Thank you. Please do. I suspect I'll need all the help
I can get before I ever set eyes on the American River."

Dozing in the soft, slightly sagging bed, Faith was
nudged into wakefulness just before dawn by the low
timbre of a man's voice. Before she was fully aware of
what she was doing, she'd donned the wrapper again
and tiptoed across the floor to her door, opening it a
crack so she could listen.

The voice was unmistakable, both in its inflections
and its concern. She knew if she looked out her window to the street below, she'd no doubt see a big red
horse waiting at the hitching rail.

The trouble was, she couldn't make out what her
self-appointed defender was saying. Nor could she hear
Anna's quiet responses. At home in Ohio she never
would have ventured out onto the upper landing dressed
as she was, but this wasn't Burg Hill. This was the frontier. Her need to know was greater than any false mod-
esty. Nervous, she crept to the railing and looked down.

The plainsman had slicked back his sandy-colored
hair and, hat in hand, was speaking with Mrs. Morse
at the base of the stairs. One booted foot rested on the
bottom step.

"You're sure she'll be all right?"

"Fine," Anna said. "She's a strong one. Stubborn."

"Her ribs?"

"Prob'ly cracked, like we figured. No fever, though. I checked on her twice during the night."

He took a deep breath, releasing it noisily. "Thanks."

Anna merely nodded. "Soon's I get the store ready for today's business I'll take her up some breakfast. The train fixin' to pull out soon?"

"Looks like it. Think she'll be able to travel?"

"Oh, it'll hurt, that's for certain. But she'll do."

Connell muttered an unintelligible curse. "What are idiotic women thinking when they try to make a journey like this practically alone?"

Still poised one floor above him, Faith closed her hands tightly over the banister. She'd heard it all before. Too often. Who had made the rule that women ought to live their lives according to the rigid rules men set down for them, anyway? It didn't have to be that way.

Her father had left his family to pursue gold. Wealth. Supposed happiness. Waiting behind, her mother had adjusted beautifully to life without a husband to sanction her daily decisions, and Faith had every intention of following that good example. Nobody, least of all a drifter, was going to tell her what she should or shouldn't do. The fact that he'd helped her once didn't give him any right to criticize her personal choices.

The hackles on the back of Connell's neck began to prickle. He'd spent the past eleven years making his way through varying degrees of wilderness. The ongoing experience had honed his natural senses to a keen edge. Either an Indian was about to chuck an arrow his way, a hungry rattlesnake had a bead on his ankle, or Faith Beal had overheard his last comment. For the sake of his hide, he hoped it was the latter.

Raising his eyes, he looked up the stairs, intending only a quick glance. What he saw changed his mind in a blink.

The rising sun was coming through a window behind her, giving her a golden, glowing aura. The plain white wrapper was belted at her waist, its long sleeves gathered at her wrists, the skirt reaching to the floor. And her hair! Soft brown curls framed her face and cascaded in a tousled sheet of silken beauty over her shoulders. Most of the women he'd known, including Irene, had plaited their long hair at night. The wild, untamed look of Faith's tresses took his breath away.

Nodding, he acknowledged her. "Ma'am."

In spite of Anna's sputtered protest, Faith did not withdraw.

"I apologize if I offended you," Connell said, seeing undisguised ire on her face as he spoke.

"Not at all," Faith said. "I'm quite used to men assuming that because I'm a woman I'm about as dumb as an old muley cow."

Connell stifled a chuckle. "Some of those ol' mossey-backs are pretty smart critters. It might be a compliment, ma'am."

"I doubt it. At any rate, my sister and I do thank you for your care and concern, even if it is uncalled-for."

"A pleasure. Can I take a message to your sister for you? I'm headed out that way."

It was a reasonable enough offer, considering. And she did need a way to either get word to Charity or find her own ride to the wagon camp. "Yes, please. Ask for the Beal wagon and have my sister send Mr. Ledbetter back for me, if you please."

With that, Faith stepped away from the railing and disappeared into her room, shutting the door firmly. She was suddenly weak, dizzy. Not that she intended to admit it to anyone but herself.

Pouring fresh water from the ewer into the shallow basin, she splashed her face and breathed as deeply as her ribs would allow until her head cleared some.

Anna had managed to rinse most of the previous day's grime out of her green calico and had returned it to the peg beside the washstand. Though Faith would have preferred to sponge off her whole body before getting dressed, she logically decided against removing the tight bindings and chancing further injury.

Back home, she'd seen Gunther Muller die from a rib that poked into his lungs. It wasn't a pretty sight. He'd lingered for hours while neighbors gathered to pray and offer their support. In the end, he'd died gasping for air. When he'd breathed his last, Hilda had gone out to the corral and put a bullet into the prize bull that had stomped her husband to death.

Faith shivered at the memory. Before she left Fort Laramie she'd be sure to pick up some extra muslin for bandages so Charity could replace her bindings when it became necessary.

Thoughts of the days and weeks ahead before she was fully healed made Faith's heart lodge in her throat. So far, their trip had been fairly easy compared to some of the stories of hardship and loss she'd heard. From now on, however, it was going to be dreadful. Pure and simple.

* * *

Not sure she'd have time to eat before the Ledbetters came for her, Faith concentrated first on buying the muslin. Accepting a parcel of fresh biscuits from Anna in lieu of a morning meal, she then waited inside the store, scanning the busy street.

Will had been going in and out, loading goods for a teamster headed up the Platte toward the Black Hills and Deer Creek. He stuck his head back in the door to holler, "Wagon's here for you, Miss Beal."

She rose stiffly from her perch on some sacks of beans and said politely, "Thank you." Approaching Anna, she held out her hand in parting and found herself swiftly swept into a gentle but encompassing hug.

"You take care, you hear?" the older woman warned, her eyes suspiciously moist, her wrinkled forehead creasing even more as she spoke. "Watch your back."

"I will. The Ledbetters are good people. They'll stand by me, I'm sure."

"Still…"

"I know. I'll be careful," Faith vowed. "I promise. If you're ever out Sacramento way…"

Anna stood back. "Doubt I will be, but thank ya."

It was hard to make herself break away and leave the haven of Anna's presence. "Well…"

"Have a safe trip."

"Lord willing."

Turning away, Faith stood tall and walked out the door into the bright morning sun, shading her eyes with her right hand. Her bonnet ribbons, reticule and the string around the small bundle of muslin were looped over her opposite wrist.

Ledbetter's spring wagon was waiting, all right, but Ramsey Tucker was in the driver's seat! The sardonic grin on his face set Faith's teeth on edge.

"What are you doing here? Where's Mr. Ledbetter?"

"He had chores in camp."

"Chores you assigned him?"

Tucker spit tobacco juice over the off side of the wagon. "Maybe. So what? Get in."

She started to place her hands on her hips, realized the motion made her left side hurt worse and lowered her arms. "I'd rather walk, thank you."

"You do and you'll be walkin' from here to Fort Bridger, missy. I'll see to it."

"Don't you dare threaten me."

Tucker cursed. "Come on. Get in. I'm tired o' foolin' with ya." He reached down and grabbed her arm, giving it a mighty tug that lifted Faith's feet off the ground.

She stumbled and swung against the front wheel of the wagon. Searing pain shot through her. Set knives to her spine. Made her cry out.

So far, the package of unbleached muslin had padded her side. It slipped slightly off center when she banged against the wheel rim a second time. If only Tucker would let go of her she'd gladly board! *Anything* to get him to stop jerking on her arm.

Gathering what breath she could muster, Faith struggled to get her feet back under her. She glared up at him. "Stop! That hurts!"

He just laughed. Tucker's meaty hand dwarfed her wrist and her fingers were already turning white from his tight grip. Surely, Charity had told him about her injuries! Therefore, he must be inflicting this horrible pain on purpose.

Suddenly, a buckskin-clad arm shot past her shoulder. A stalwart hand closed like a vise on Tucker's thick wrist, forcing the man to his knees in the wagon bed. The captain let go. His adversary did not.

Faith, clinging to the wheel for needed support, knew instantly who had come to her rescue. The glimmer of fear in Ramsey Tucker's eyes was a truly blessed sight to behold!

The plainsman's voice rumbled. "Are you hurt?"

Rubbing her wrist, she backed away from the wagon. Pure truth could do irreparable damage. Like it or not, without the captain's guidance, she and Charity would never make it all the way to California.

Faith made the necessary choice. "No," she gasped. "I'm fine. There's no problem here. Captain Tucker and I just had a little misunderstanding."

The plainsman regarded Faith, his doubt evident. "You're sure everything is all right?"

"Positive." She labored to make her voice sound stronger, more convincing. "Now, if you'll excuse me, I was just about to get into this wagon and start back to the train. We're pulling out soon."

"Whatever you say."

He released Tucker's wrist, nodded to them both and started away without further debate. Faith could tell he didn't believe her assertion. Not for one minute. And no wonder. The statement, though partially true, had burned on her lips it was such a blatant lie.

She squared her shoulders. With her left arm held tightly against her waist and side, she faced Tucker.

She knew there was loathing in her expression. "Back off and I'll get in."

"You meant what you told him? Well, well." Chuckling with satisfaction, he offered his hand.

Faith gritted her teeth, gathered her skirts, put one foot on the step and managed to boost herself aboard without his help.

"I need a ride and you've come to fetch me. That's all," she said icily, wrapping her skirts around her legs so they wouldn't touch even a smidgen of Tucker's person. "Nothing else has changed between us."

He slapped his knee, guffawing rudely. "Feisty little thing, aren't you? Aw right. If it's a wagon ride you fancy, a wagon ride you'll get." Lowering his voice, he added, "Other kinds of things, you and me'll discuss after you've healed up."

Faith's face flared in anger and embarrassment. Of all the insulting, vulgar... She held her temper, saying nothing. Tucker had the upper hand, for now. Someday, though, she'd best him.

She swore it on her mother's grave.

Chapter Four

Connell stomped down the street, pulling his hat lower over his eyes to shade them from the morning sun. It was going to be another scorcher. Pretty normal for this time of year hereabouts.

A green spring wagon clattered past, stirring up a cloud of dust. Ramsey Tucker rode the driver's seat. Beside him, her back ramrod straight, her bonnet strings blowing behind her, sat Faith Beal. The bad blood between her and the captain was as thick as flies on a dead buffalo, so why had she insisted on letting him have his way?

Connell cursed under his breath. Why should he care? He had enough trouble already. He had to find Irene.

Pushing on the door to the saloon, he paused a moment to let his eyes adjust to the dim light. The place was sure busy. Him, he'd rather have a steak than a slug of whiskey for breakfast. But here was where the drovers from the Tucker train had congregated, so here he'd stay. At least as long as they did.

What few chairs and crude benches the place had to offer were already taken. Connell leaned against the far, canvas-covered wall with some other latecomers and studied the crowd.

A short, slight man with a wary look in his eyes and a Colt revolver stuck through his belt sidled up to him and spoke. "You're not with the Tucker train, are you?"

Connell shook his head. "No. Why?"

"Just wondered. It's a big outfit, but I didn't think I'd seen you before."

"I rode in alone. You?"

"Lookin' for a party going back to Missouri," the thin man said. When he smiled, Connell saw he was missing his front teeth. It didn't look like they'd been gone very long either, judging by his swollen lips and gums.

Noting the focus of Connell's glance, the man closed his mouth as tightly as his injuries would allow. "Saw you face up to the cap'n this mornin'. Wished it'd been more of a fight. He needs to be taken down a peg."

"You know him?"

"Too well." The man rubbed his jaw. "Too blamed well."

Nodding, Connell reached into his pocket for the miniature of Irene and held it out in his palm. "Ever see her before? Last trip, maybe?"

"Your woman?"

"Irene Wellman. My intended."

"Nope. Sorry. You might ask them two by the door. If she was ever with Tucker, they'd know. They been his drovers for years."

"Which ones?"

"Tall, fat fella with the beady eyes in the black vest and beat-up gray hat is Stuart. The shorter, weasely one next to him is Ab. He walks, you'll see he limps a might. Understand he got hurt around St. Jo last trip."

The hair on the back of Connell's neck was bristling. "What makes you think my Irene might have been with Tucker?"

"It figures. You been payin' a lot of attention to the captain's affairs. If it was me and I was lookin' for my intended, I'd start backtracking. Her trail lead you here, did it?"

Connell took a chance that the man really did have a grudge against the wagon boss. "In a manner of speaking."

"Thought so. Word is, Tucker has a bad reputation with women. No offense, but was your lady the kind to change her mind about waitin' for you and marry up with a fella like him, instead?"

"Marry *him?*" Remembering his recent meeting with the wagon boss, he didn't see how any woman would consider agreeing to such a marriage bond.

"No. Irene isn't like that," Connell said. "We've known each other since we were children. If she'd changed her mind, she'd tell me straight out."

"Well, like I said, if it was me, I'd talk to Ab and Stuart. You never can tell." Pulling his battered brown felt hat lower, he used the floppy brim to partially hide his face. "Just don't let on I sent you, all right?"

Palming the miniature, Connell agreed. He began at the closest end of the bar for his informant's sake, asking after Irene as he worked his way along. By the time he reached the door, the fat man named Stuart was already gone. Ab, the weasel, seemed ready to bolt as well.

Connell touched the brim of his hat. "Morning."

"Mornin'." The shifty-eyed little man glanced toward the open door and shuffled his feet.

"I wonder if you could tell me…?" As Connell lifted the portrait, the man looked the other way, muttered something about being late and darted out the door.

Tucking Irene's image away in an inside pocket with her last letter, Connell followed. He was in time to see the two drovers mount up and ride. For fellows who were just honest, hardworking hands, they were acting awfully suspicious. If they didn't know anything about Irene, why refuse to look at her picture?

He swung easily aboard Rojo and trailed them at a distance. They made a dash straight for the Tucker train, then split up. The shorter man stopped at one of the wagons to help a lone woman harness a mule team. The same woman Connell had rescued twice.

Pondering all he'd learned, he squared himself in the saddle to watch and think. It was starting to look like the key to locating Irene might lie in that wagon train. Her last letter to him had been written while she was at Fort Laramie and she had mentioned a Captain T., without actually spelling out the man's name.

Beyond that clue, Connell had no other leads. Perhaps a kind Providence was trying to tell him something. He had planned to follow the same trail the wagons did, anyway. Why not do it as an actual member of Tucker's train?

Once the wagons were lined out and rolling, Connell figured he'd simply ride along by the Beal rig and offer his services. He already knew the women needed a driver. If he kept his eyes and ears open, someone might inadvertently give him a clue to Irene's whereabouts. And in the meantime, he'd be able to keep a close eye on Miss Faith and her addle-brained sister.

It never occurred to him she might turn down such a sensible offer.

Riding drag for the first hour, Connell figured he'd picked up enough trail dust in his beard to grow potatoes. Shaking it off as he cantered forward, he drew up beside Faith's wagon. There was no sign of her sister.

He tipped his hat. "Morning."

"Good morning." Her glance was cursory. "If you came to judge whether or not I was capable of handling my team, you can plainly see that I am."

"Oxen would be better for a hard crossing like this," Connell said, trying to steer their conversation in another direction. "You could pull a much bigger wagon."

"I grew up with two of these mules, the lead jack, Ben, and one of the jennies. The other two came cheap. A good ox cost more than I could afford. So did a Conestoga." She eyed him curiously. "Now that we've discussed my livestock, why are you really here?"

"Just passing by."

"In the middle of the plains? Really, Mr. McClain."

"Hush. I'd appreciate it if you wouldn't use my name."

"Why not?"

Connell shot a glance at the empty portion of the seat beside her. "Your sister isn't with you?"

"Not at present. You haven't answered my question."

"May I come aboard?"

"No! I told you, I'm perfectly able." She heard him mutter a string of epithets that reminded her of her father's mood just prior to his leaving for the gold fields. Before she could protest further, Connell had urged his horse closer and stepped off onto the wagon seat as easily as if he did it every day.

His presence crowded more than her body. Her senses were full of him: his earthiness, the scent of the soap he'd obviously applied so liberally while at the fort. And his strength! Oh, my! He exuded the power, the controlled force of someone who knew his extraordinary capabilities and took care to harness them as long as he deemed necessary.

To her relief and surprise, he didn't try to wrest the lines from her. Still, she ordered, "Get out of my wagon."

"No."

"It's not fitting for you to be here or to talk to me that way."

He lowered his voice. "If I'd come to court you, Miss Beal, you'd be right. But I have no such intentions. I'm here to speak to you man-to-man…as much as possible. So please keep your voice down and try to look relaxed."

Staring ahead, he propped one booted foot up near the brake and laced his fingers together around his knee. "You're going to hire me."

"I'm *what?*" Faith's voice squeaked. She was still struggling to digest his odd suggestion that they speak man-to-man.

Connell laid a finger across his lips. "Shush. Some of Tucker's people might hear you."

"What if they do? I have no intention of hiring anyone. I already made that quite clear."

"I know, I know. You're a regular mule skinner. Fine. Say that's true. Who's going to spell you along the way? Your sister?"

Faith pulled a face. "You know better."

"Ab or Stuart, then?"

She scowled over at him. "How do you know them?"

"I get around."

"They used to help me out. The last time Tucker beat poor Ben, I stood up to him and caused him to lose face, so now he doesn't want either of them to come near me. This morning, Ab helped me harness up and the captain flogged him across the shoulders for his trouble."

"Nice fella."

Faith couldn't help agreeing with the sarcastic observation. "I wish my sister didn't really believe that."

Taking off his hat, Connell ran his fingers through his thick hair to comb it back. "That's the only part that's got me buffaloed."

"What does?" She was so caught up in their strange conversation she was almost able to forget the shooting pain in her side every time the wagon hit a rut or bounced over a depression.

"Mrs. Morse tells me Tucker's been acting interested in your sister. I can't figure out why. Not that she isn't a pretty little thing."

Faith kept her familiar twinge of sibling rivalry to herself. For as long as she could remember, people had remarked how lovely her younger sister was.

"Charity is comely," she said.

"So's a butterfly, but men don't go around courting them. No. There's got to be something else." He pondered a bit, then shook his head and replaced his hat. "Blamed if I know. From what I've heard about Tucker, he only goes after women of considerable means."

Faith gasped, nearly dropping the reins. "Oh, no! Why didn't I think of that?"

Connell reached over and relieved her of the lines without incurring any protest. "Think of what?"

"The mining claim."

"What claim?"

Faith shifted her body sideways. She wanted to watch her companion's expression while revealing the family secret. "Papa's been gold prospecting. Last we heard, he'd been quite successful. I'll bet Charity told Tucker. She's just foolish enough to have spoken out of turn."

Connell's eyebrows raised. "So that's why you're headed west by way of Sacramento City."

Since they hadn't yet come to the place where either of the trails to California branched off from the Oregon trail, she was surprised he knew. "Yes, but how…?"

"I've been asking around and keeping my ears open. Same as anybody could do. Chances are, Ramsey Tucker's not the only one who's heard about your papa's good fortune by now, either."

"Oh, dear."

She grasped the wagon seat and held on tight while they jostled across an unusually rough area. The wagon creaked with the stress. Late spring rains and the passage of earlier wagons had left deep, uneven ruts. Now that drier weather had come, the roughness bound the wheel rims and put a twist on the wagon's undercarriage that made it squeal in protest.

"I'll work for *found*," Connell offered, expounding on his original offer. "You won't be the first traveler to need extra help on the trail. Just feed me and give me a place under the wagon to sleep and we'll call it even."

"I couldn't do that," Faith said flatly. "It wouldn't be fair to you. It's been over a year since my father's last letter home. We may not even be able to locate him when we reach California. I couldn't guarantee any pay, even then."

"I never asked for it," he countered gruffly.

Reaching into his pocket, he withdrew the miniature of Irene and held it up. "See this woman? Her name is Irene Wellman. We've been friends since we were children. She disappeared on her way to marry me. I figure, if she was traveling with Tucker on his last trip, she probably mentioned my name plenty. That's why I didn't want you to use McClain. I don't want anybody to get suspicious and shut up before they can spill useful information."

Gently, reverently, Faith took the picture. The woman was young, in her early twenties from the look of it, and pretty in a plain sort of way.

"After my mother died," Connell said, "I lived with Irene's family for a few years and we grew close. She gave me that picture when we parted and we pledged to marry someday. I was sixteen and headed for the mountains to make my fortune trapping. By the time I finally sent for her, she'd decided her bounden duty was to help her father care for her invalid mother, instead."

"What does all this have to do with me?" Faith asked.

"Irene and I kept in touch as best we could. After her parents both died she had no family left, so she finally wrote and agreed to come to California to join me. That was a year ago. Far as I can tell, she never reached Salt Lake. Nobody will admit to knowing what happened to her."

"And you think Tucker may be responsible? Why?"

"Because he's the most likely prospect I've come across, for starters. The only connections I've been able to come up with are the first initial of his last name and the funny way his drovers started acting when I was asking about Irene. I know it isn't much to go on, but it's all I have. I need this job so I'll be in a position to learn more."

Faith gave back the miniature, sighed and turned to face the west where heaven-knows-what awaited her. How awful not to know for sure what had happened to a loved one. Was wondering worse than knowing the worst? She thought it might be.

Her mind made up, Faith held out her hand. "All right. Shake on it," she said. "You're hired."

As soon as there was an easy opportunity to do so, Connell pulled the Beal wagon out of line. Halting the team, he called to Rojo. The gelding responded by obediently trotting up.

"You'll ride him for a while," Connell said, climbing down and holding out his hand for Faith to follow.

"There's no need."

He gritted his teeth. Why did she have to be so

proud? "It's not a favor, it's common sense," he argued. "You don't weigh as much as a good-size calf, the horse is making the trip anyway, and your ribs will heal faster if you don't go bouncing around all day on that hard wagon seat." He started to make a token effort to get back into the wagon. "But, if you don't want to…"

"I see your point," she said begrudgingly. When he started to reach up to grasp her by the waist then stopped himself, she reassured him with, "I can manage. My side hurts less when I move without assistance."

Standing by the side of the horse, Connell laced his fingers together to give her a boost up, wincing as he watched the signs of pain flash across her face. You could see from her eyes that she was hurting a lot more than she'd let on. To his surprise, she swung a leg over to ride astride. Her skirt hitched up to her boot tops, showing a bit of white stocking.

Seeing his quizzical expression, Faith adjusted the fabric of her dress and gave him a half smile as she took up the reins. "I was raised riding mules like old Ben without the benefit of a saddle. A body tended to wind up in the brambles if she didn't sit her mount sensibly."

Without comment, Connell climbed back aboard the wagon and called to the team to move out. Nothing Faith Beal did or said should surprise him, yet it kept happening. She was an enigma: a frail-looking beauty with the strength and stubbornness of a mule and more than a few useful skills many men didn't possess.

Connell smiled to himself. Looking at her, he'd never have guessed just how capable she was; nor did he think it wise to tell her what he thought for the present. Something inside him kept suggesting that Faith was the key to finding Irene and he tended to trust his gut feelings. Besides, she made an interesting traveling companion.

He looked over at her astride his horse and sighed. It had taken him months to acclimate himself to life among the Arapaho but he'd eventually adjusted, thanks to the love of Little Rabbit Woman. A Pawnee raid had ended her short life. He hadn't let himself care for a woman that way since. Nor had he wanted to.

Connell cast another sidelong glance at his new boss. No God-fearing Christian woman would submit herself the way Little Rabbit Woman had when they'd been married in the Indian tradition. That was as it should be. So why was he suddenly feeling let down?

Ab and another outrider were the first to notice Faith astride a horse while someone else managed her team. She saw Ab's shocked, nervous expression as the two men wheeled their mounts and rode rapidly away.

Pulling abreast of Connell, she called out, "I think we're about to have trouble."

"I saw. Ab, I recognize. Who's the other man?"

"Calls himself Indiana. That's all I know."

Connell nodded. "When Tucker gets here, let me do the talking."

"In a pig's eye. That's my rig. You work for me, remember?"

With a grin, Connell cocked one eyebrow and pulled his hat lower over his eyes. "Yes, ma'am."

"And you needn't pretend to be subservient, either.

We both know you don't feel that way, so stop taunting me."

His resultant laugh was deep and mellow. "You're a hard one to please, Miss Beal. Do you want me to be your equal or your slave? Make up your mind."

Faith had only a few moments in which to send Connell a warning glance before Ramsey Tucker reined his lathered horse up beside the wagon. It made no difference whether or not her new driver had permission to speak for her. As far as Tucker was concerned, she may as well have been invisible.

He glared at Connell. "Who the blazes are you?"

Deferring, Connell nodded toward Faith. "Miss Beal has engaged me as her driver. Seems all her usual assistance is unavailable."

Tucker snorted and spit. "You talk pretty fancy for a drover. Where you from?"

"Around."

"Oh, yeah? Well, you're not welcome here. Get on your horse and scat."

"Nope."

"What'd you say?" Shouting, Tucker was reaching for the coiled bullwhip tied to his saddle by a leather thong.

Connell's eyes met Faith's, their message clear. While Tucker was distracted, she let the canelo fall back a bit, quietly slid the plainsman's heavy Hawken rifle out of its scabbard and held it ready in both hands. At Connell's nod, she tossed it to him.

His left hand closed around the barrel. He swung the long gun around in one fluid motion, laying it across his knees with the business end pointed toward Ramsey Tucker.

"No," Connell repeated. "I'm staying."

Faith saw terrible anger in Tucker's face, vitriol in his eyes. She also sensed raw fear. He'd met his match in the rough-edged stranger and he knew it.

The captain's nervous mount danced beneath him and he jerked hard on its bridle. "What'd you say your name was?"

"Folks call me Hawk," Connell offered. "I rode night hawk for Fremont out in California. The moniker stuck."

"We could use a good hand with the stock." Tucker's voice was filled with false bravado. "You take your turn as a wrangler with the other single men and you can stay."

"Mighty neighborly of you." Connell smiled over at him, his steady regard a warning he'd not be deterred. It wasn't until Tucker had ridden off that the smile became truly genuine.

Faith was grinning broadly. "You'll do."

"I thank you, ma'am."

"And quit with that false politeness, will you? If I'm going to call you Hawk, you'd just as well call me Faith."

"The other respectable ladies would have my hide if I did that, and you know it. Think of all the loose talk that kind of familiarity would cause."

"Let them talk. It's gotten so I don't give a fig what they say." Faith was warming to her subject. "Every one of them has stood by while Ramsey Tucker abused my animals and ordered me around like some worthless chattel. The way I see it, you've earned the right to call me anything you like." She giggled. "Did you see the look on his despicable face when I tossed you that rifle?"

"That, I did." Connell sobered. "I should have thought to strap on my forty-four again once I left town. Did it hurt you to lift the Hawken?"

"Honestly? A bit. But it was worth every twinge to see Tucker running off like a mangy cur with his tail twixt his legs."

"Do you have a pistol of your own?"

"Papa's Colt Walker. Why?"

"Because I intend to drive, eat and sleep with my revolver. I want you to begin wearing yours, too, right out where everybody can see it." With a grin he added, "I assume you have extra cap, ball and powder and know how to shoot."

"Of course I do. What's so funny? Did you figure I couldn't handle a gun?"

"Not at all. I was just marveling at the fact I knew you'd say you could. I assume you're a good shot, too."

"You'd better believe it!"

She nudged her heels against the horse's side to keep him in line with the front of the wagon. Whether Hawk McClain was teasing her or was dead serious, at least he'd quit assuming she was totally helpless. For a man like him, that was pretty good progress, considering they barely knew each other.

"I never shoot animals for sport," she warned. "Only when we need food."

There was genuine admiration in his tone when he

said, "You'd make a good Indian. Little Rabbit Woman would have liked you a lot."

"Who?"

"Little Rabbit Woman. She was my Arapaho wife," Connell said quietly. "In another life. She died a long time ago."

Empathy flooded Faith's heart. "I'm so sorry."

"I believe you actually mean that."

"Of course I do. Why wouldn't I?"

"Because she was an Indian and I'm not. Lots of folks would hold that against me."

"Do you think Irene will?"

Connell shook his head, a look of benevolence and calm on his face. "No. Not Irene. We haven't seen each other in years, but I wrote and told her all about my past with the Arapaho before she made the final decision to travel to California to finally marry me."

"I'm glad," Faith said. "That speaks well of her."

"Yes," he said with a lopsided smile that made his eyes sparkle. "It speaks well of you, too, Faith Beal."

Chapter Five

The tight bindings around Faith's midsection were chafing in the heat something fierce by the time the wagons stopped for nooning. Normally, she and Charity shared a cooking fire with the Ledbetters and the Johnsons, but this afternoon the reception she received from the others when she approached was decidedly unfriendly.

In pain and more than a little put out, she returned to the solitude of her wagon.

Connell had finished putting the mules with the other stock being herded out to graze and was about to remove his horse's saddle. The dejected look on Faith's face made him stop what he was doing and go to her.

Gently, he touched her shoulder, then quickly stepped away and apologized for the undue familiarity.

"No need to worry," Faith said with a shrug. "Thanks to the captain's lies, everybody thinks I'm a soiled dove already."

"A sporting woman?" Connell laughed aloud. "You?"

"You think I'm not pretty enough? I don't blame you."

"Hey. Hold your horses. I never meant anything of the kind. It's simply obvious to me that you're one of the most honest, upright women I've ever met. I can't imagine how anyone would believe such idiotic rumors."

Faith held herself proud in spite of the lingering soreness around her middle. "Thank you."

"You're welcome. Now that we have that settled, what's for dinner? I'm starved."

She sighed and made a disgusted face. "We'll have to kindle our own fire. I'm afraid I'm no longer welcome at the others' camps."

"Their loss," Connell said. He glanced at the calfhide "possum belly" strung under the wagon to make sure it contained enough kindling and dry buffalo chips for Faith to start a fire without having to go out gathering. "So, what do you fancy? Rabbit, antelope or sage grouse?"

Raising an eyebrow, she began to smile. "You're going hunting? Now?"

"Unless you've figured out a way to get the critters to jump into the pot on their own."

"Very funny. Just bring back whatever you see and I'll cook it, no questions asked."

"That could be dangerous."

She laughed. "Not with you eating out of the same kettle. Now, skedaddle. I'm hungry, too."

Watching him mount up and ride away, she sent a silent prayer of thanks heavenward, adding a postscript plea for his missing bride's safety. If Tucker was truly involved in the woman's disappearance, no telling what had become of her. Faith hoped, for Hawk's sake, that he was wrong about that possibility. Perhaps Irene had simply found herself a husband among the emigrants on her train and gone off to wherever that man was bound.

But what if Tucker had been her choice? Faith thought the idea quite discomfiting. And what of Charity? If there was even the slightest chance that the captain was guilty of purposeful harm, how was she going to protect someone as innocent and gullible—and stubborn—as her sister?

Faith glanced at the communal fire where Charity was assisting in the preparation of the large noon meal. It was no great surprise to see Ramsey Tucker's horse tied to a nearby wagon.

Angry that she'd been rendered powerless by circumstances beyond her control, Faith began to lay a separate cooking fire. Her mind was whirling and darting like the eddies in a fast-moving mountain stream. Too bad she couldn't really tie Charity up till they reached their destination, the way Anna had jokingly suggested.

Other than doing exactly that, she had no idea how she was going to save her from herself. None at all.

While her new boon companion was away, Faith managed to bake corn bread in the Dutch oven and also boil a pot of beans using side-pork for flavoring. When Connell returned, they added a spit and roasted the hare he'd bagged. All in all, the meal was as tasty as any she'd eaten in a long time, due in part, she was sure, to the good company.

Hoisting the nearly full bean pot by its wire handle,

Connell stored it in a box packed with straw in the rear of the Beal wagon. Thus secured, it would ride safely and continue to cook from its own internal heat for some time, making it easy to fix supper after the long day of travel still ahead of them.

When he saw Faith grimace as she bent to clean their dishes, he went to her and crouched down by her side. "Let me do that."

Wide-eyed, she looked at him as if he'd handed her a poke full of gold nuggets. "You? Why?"

"Because it pains you."

"It's woman's work," she said.

"A man learns to do lots of things when he's on his own in the wilderness. Let's make a bargain. You go hunting next time and I'll help with your chores now."

"Don't be silly." She scrubbed harder, her hands flying over the gray surface of the tinware.

"I'm not. You claim you can shoot straight."

"I can, but…"

"But, what?" Taking the dish from her hand, he looked it over carefully. "If you rub this any cleaner, it's liable to end up so shiny it'll start a prairie fire."

Faith wasn't about to admit how much his close presence had dithered her. "Cleanliness is next to godliness."

He drew a hand slowly over his beard, bringing his fingers together at his chin. "While we're speaking of such things, do you happen to have shears and a looking glass I can borrow?"

"In my trunk in the wagon," she said. "I'll get them for you presently." Hawk had fallen into the rhythm of her work and was relieving her of each piece as she finished with it. Since there had been just the two of them for dinner, there wasn't much left to clean up. "I can trim your hair for you, if you like," she offered. "I used to cut Papa's."

He eyed her mischievously. "I trust he had hair to cut?"

"Of course, he did!" Straightening stiffly, she batted him with the corner of her apron, then used it to wipe her hands.

With one eyebrow raised, he warned, "Just a trim, mind you. It's been ten years since I had a city haircut. The back of my neck is real used to the shade." Seeing her heading for the wagon, he followed, reaching out to stop her. "Let me get the shears for you so you don't strain."

Faith halted and wheeled to face him, her hands planted firmly on her hips. "Look, mister. I don't mean to sound ungrateful, but you're being so solicitous you're driving me crazy. I've been hurt before. I've healed. And I'll do it again, with or without you."

He tried to look chagrined when, in truth, her fortitude pleased him greatly. "Yes, ma'am."

Catching the wry humor in his reply, she hoisted herself into the wagon and looked down at him with a smirk. "You'd best not tease me, sir. Not when you're about to turn your barbering over to me."

"Is that a threat, Miss Beal?"

"Take it as you like," she offered, slipping the scissors, a wide-toothed comb and a small hand mirror into her apron pocket.

Once again, Connell tentatively held out his arms to her. Situated above him as she was, allowing his help in descending was the sensible thing to do. This time, Faith acquiesced.

"Okay. Easy," she said, placing one hand on each of his shoulders and leaning forward.

His hands circled her slim waist, almost fully spanning it, and he lifted gently, slowly and with great care, bringing her closer, then lowering her till he felt her feet brush the toes of his boots.

Breathless at his nearness, Faith was loath to let go. She was remembering how marvelous it was to be cradled against this man's broad chest, to be held the way a loving husband might hold his wife.

Only she and the plainsman weren't husband and wife, nor would they ever be, she reminded herself. Not only was he betrothed to someone else, he was little more than a stranger to her!

Shocked by the wild thoughts racing through her head, Faith decided they must be sinful. She'd always been taught that no good Christian woman desired a man's arms around her, so why did this moment seem so right, so meant to be, as if her whole life had been nothing but preparation for her extraordinary encounter with the plainsman?

Connell knew he should let go of her, yet kept granting himself one more breath of the natural fragrance of her hair, another second to plumb the wondrous depths of her dark, expressive eyes. If they had been alone, he knew he might very well have leaned down and kissed her. Then there'd be a fracas for sure, wouldn't there?

"Did I hurt you?" he finally asked as he released her.

Faith cleared her throat. "Um, no. Not at all."

"Good. Where do you want me?"

For some reason, her brain seemed as befuddled as it had been immediately following her accident at Fort Laramie. "Want you?"

"To sit. For my haircut."

"Oh." She took as deep a breath as her ribs would allow, then gestured toward one of the packing boxes they had used for chairs while they ate. "Over there. Take off your hat."

Connell seated himself, hat in hand.

"You'd better take your shirt off, too," she warned. "Papa always complained I got bits of hair down his neck."

"I'll be fine the way I am."

Faith knew she should let him have his way, especially since his reply had sounded so gruff, yet a perverse part of her nature insisted otherwise. "You act as if I've never seen the top of a man's union suit before," she taunted. "I guess if you're afraid to remove your shirt in my presence we'll just have to make do as is. I won't be responsible, though, if you itch something fierce afterwards."

Casting her a sidelong glance that was more an irate glare than an expression of admiration for her boldness, he reached down, crossed his arms and drew the soft buckskin hunting shirt off over his head. There'd been times when he'd stripped to breechcloth and leggings while stalking buffalo or antelope, but when among those he considered the polite society of his upbringing, he'd always remained fully clothed. Till now.

"Okay. Remember this was your idea," he said.

Hearing muffled gasps from somewhere behind her, Faith clenched her teeth. When Connell tried to swivel his torso to see who was making the fuss, she stopped him with a firm hand on his bare shoulder, a reflexive action that did not go unnoticed by anyone, she was sure.

She bent closer. "You could have mentioned that you weren't wearing a union suit under your buckskins."

"You didn't ask," he grumbled. "I suppose the fat's in the fire now."

"Let it be," she said, rancor in her tone. "All my years I've tried to live a pure, untainted life, just like the Good Book teaches. Soon after Charity and I started this pilgrimage, I realized I'd have to make many concessions in order to survive. The more time that passes, the more certain I am that I'm right."

Taking up the scissors, she handed him the small mirror so he could watch as she began to cut. Instead, he angled it so he could observe her reflection. He thought new maturity had come to Faith in the past few days—maturity and awareness. He saw her glancing openly at the muscles of his bare back and wondered what female notions might be going through her head.

There were certainly plenty of ideas passing through his. In lots of ways, she reminded him of his late Arapaho wife, while in others, her daring spirit far surpassed even his most unrestrained fancy. Knowing she was innocent of any wrongdoing, Faith was willing to stand up to everyone in the entire traveling party to affirm it. Women usually set great store by what their peers thought. Surely, Faith Beal was no exception. She, however, had the backbone to assert her innocence by both word and deed. Such courage was its own reward.

Connell closed his eyes to better enjoy the pleasant sensations of the comb passing through his hair, the slight tug of the shears, the whisper of Faith's apron against his lower back. When she stopped, took up a corner of the apron and began to brush his shoulders off with it, he stood and stepped away, rather than let her see how much her tender ministrations had affected him.

"Thanks, I can do the rest," he said, finishing the job with quick swipes of his hands.

"All right."

She held out shears and comb to him, then watched while he propped the mirror on the side of the wagon and went to work on his beard. It was just as well he'd taken over, she mused. The way her hands had begun to shake, no telling how the rest of his haircut would have turned out if she'd continued.

Suddenly exhausted, she sank onto the packing box Hawk had vacated and tried to regain control of her heightened senses. What was wrong with her? Was it her own unseemly thoughts and actions that were at fault, or was an outside force trying to undermine the purity of her motives and thereby destroy all the good she was attempting to do?

And another thing, her conscience was quick to interject, *look how you're dressed.* Custom dictated that she and her sister should still be in mourning for Mama. Yet, truth to tell, she'd felt a surge of relief when Charity had returned from a trip to the river to do the wash and had reported that their black dresses had been swept away by the current. With so little extra money at their disposal, replacing the somber clothing was out of the question, especially while traveling.

Should she have dyed another of her frocks dingy black no matter what? Faith wondered. She didn't think so. Surely, the Good Lord understood her present predicament. After all, hadn't He sent her a guardian to watch over her?

A brief glance toward the wagon showed just how rough around the edges that so-called guardian was, in spite of his recent tonsorial efforts.

Faith smiled and turned away. Even with an imagination as creative as hers, there was no way she could convince herself the plainsman was actually an emissary from God.

Her smile faded. On the other hand, it wasn't at all hard to envision Ramsey Tucker being a faithful minion of Lucifer, himself, was it?

The afternoon sun was high, the prairie affording no shade except what little could be found under the wagons. Prairie vastness that had once been lush and green was spoiled now. Swaths of bare land miles wide on each side of the emigrant track meant the travelers had to drive their livestock off to find fresh pasture, let them graze, then bring them back so the journey could continue.

Faith knew that. Her heart, however, coveted the presence of her only remaining ally. When Hawk made ready to take his turn as a drover so other men could come into camp and eat, she found herself wishing mightily she could go with him. It wouldn't do to ask, of course, for what good was a protestation of gentility if a body then followed up with such an unacceptable suggestion? Therefore, she'd wait as the other women did and ready the wagon for travel while Charity stayed with the Ledbetters and Hawk rode off to do men's work.

"Take care," she called as he mounted.

Whirling Rojo in a tight circle, he paused and leaned closer. "Watch your back, Faith. Get out the Colt and strap it on like I told you."

"I will."

Connell straightened. "Do it now."

She snapped off a mock salute. "Yes, General."

It was clear from his lack of levity that her jest hadn't pleased him. Well, too bad. As long as she followed orders, why should he care how it was accomplished? Being around him made her feel silly and giddy and altogether unhinged, with an excitement coursing through her that she hadn't even dreamed of before. Daily life was supposed to be mundane. The feelings the plainsman was awakening within her were anything but.

Climbing stiffly into her wagon, Faith let down the flap for privacy before she loosened the bodice of her dress and slipped it off. The muslin bindings had bunched beneath her breasts, their roughness coupling with trail dust to cause an irritation in spite of her soft cotton camisole.

Padding the bandages along the edges with tufts of lamb's wool, she hoped to find enough relief to carry her through till evening when she'd ask Charity to apply clean dressings. At this point, it was hard to decide which hurt worse, her cracked ribs or the cure. Cautiously, she threaded her arms back into the dress sleeves.

Papa's Colt lay beneath the clothing in her trunk. Probing under the piles of folded garments, Faith lifted the holster and heavy pistol. The belt was much too big, as she knew it would be. Preparing to make the necessary adjustments, she seated herself on the ticking she and Charity used for their bed.

The straw-filled softness beckoned, making her admit how much the trying day had already taken out of her. She'd rest for just a few moments, she thought, lying down on her uninjured side, the Colt beside her, her eyelids so heavy she could barely keep them open.

Camp noises from outside the wagon became a muffled din as sleep overtook her. Drifting in and out of awareness, she only vaguely heard a man say, "I'll kill him before I let him ruin my plans to marry Charity Beal," but that was enough to snap her to wakefulness. She held her breath and listened.

A different voice asked, "Aren't you afraid of him?"

"Naw. I don't care who he really is or who he fought with in California. He'll bleed to death easy as any man."

Faith's eyes were wide, her lethargy gone. There was little doubt who the men were discussing, especially since she recognized the bloodthirsty speaker as Ramsey Tucker and the other as his cohort, Stuart.

"I imagine he'll be shot by renegade Indians real soon," Tucker said, laughing.

"What about Miss Faith?"

Tucker shushed his companion. "Watch your mouth, you lamebrain. She may be about."

Stuart protested that he'd already checked the camp, then began to whisper. Faith could only catch a word here and there. "…trail…problems…accident…"

She yearned to move and press her ear to the canvas but the straw in the ticking would surely rustle if she tried. Once her presence was discovered, there was no telling what might happen next.

Slowly, cautiously, she reached for the Colt. Her fingers closed around the grip and drew it closer till it rested on her stomach. The firearm was heavy, weighing at least four pounds. She held it tightly with both hands, her eyes on the loose flap of canvas covering the rear of the wagon, her thumbs ready to pull back the hammer to cock and fire, if necessary.

It wasn't. Hearing the men walk off, she let out the breath she'd been holding and slowly sat up. Rapid-fire pounding of her heart accentuated her worst fears. Tucker was planning to do serious harm to Hawk McClain, with the help of Stuart and probably others of his henchmen.

And it was all her fault. It wasn't McClain they had started out to best—it was her. By allowing the plainsman to come to work for her, she'd unknowingly placed him in mortal danger!

Maybe it wasn't too late to save him by sending him away, Faith reasoned. Certainly she'd be no worse off than before, and since she now had indisputable proof of Tucker's nefarious character, she'd be doubly on her guard. As long as she carried the Colt and stayed close to the other wagons, she was certain Tucker wouldn't dare harm her, not if he really wanted to win Charity's heart.

The idea of her poor sister in the wagon boss's bed turned Faith's stomach. It didn't matter how much he slicked himself up and minded his manners for courting, the evil shone through. Given time, Charity would see that. She must. Their future depended upon it.

Chapter Six

When the men returned with the sated animals, Faith helped her hired hand harness the mules. They were fastening the trace chains to the hames when she quietly told him, "As of tomorrow, you're fired."

He scowled over at her. "I'm *what?*"

"Fired. It's for your own good."

"What about Irene?"

"Nobody will talk to you anyway, thanks to Tucker. After you've gone and things have settled down, I'll ask around and keep my ears open. If we rendezvous later on at some place like Independence Rock or Fort Bridger, I'll tell you whatever I've learned. I simply can't have you traveling with Charity and me anymore."

Connell ducked under the heads of the lead mules and came closer, his countenance dark. "What's happened?"

"I don't know what you're talking about." Faith turned her face away, afraid the imperative lie would be too plain to miss.

Two strong fingers lifted her chin. "Yes, you do.

Something made you change your mind about me while I was gone. What was it?"

She jerked away. "I just decided it would be better for my reputation—and for my sister's—if I didn't encourage any more spurious rumors. That's all."

"And you really want me to go?" His hand had come to rest lightly on her forearm, the contact as necessary for him as was breathing. If she truly did mean to part company, he wanted this brief moment to become seared into his memory the way his idyllic days with Little Rabbit Woman had been.

Connell's heart leaped to his throat at the comparison. *No,* his mind shouted. *No! Not like that. Never again like that.*

To care too much was to invite loss. He should know. He hadn't been able to prevent his mother's death or his father's drunken tirades. And he'd been away hunting when the Pawnees had raided the Arapaho camp and killed his bride. Now, not only was Irene missing, he was beginning to have strong feelings for Faith Beal, as well.

Connell muttered and turned away. Faith was right. The best thing he could do was comply with her wishes. He'd been fooling himself into believing she needed him a lot more than she really did. Without him around to sully her reputation, she'd be free to implore some of the other men for help—men who were more civilized and more to her liking. Besides, nothing said he couldn't keep out of sight and dog the train from a discreet distance without her knowledge.

"All right," he said, rechecking the mule's harnesses while he spoke. "The Sweetwater River passes by Independence Rock. You won't get there by Independence Day, like Fremont did when he named it, but you should arrive sometime in mid-July. I carved my name at the base of the western face in '43. Since you're the only one around here who knows it's McClain, you can watch for me near that mark without causing suspicion."

Faith nodded. "What's your Christian name?"

"Connell," he said quietly, feeling a prickle at the back of his neck as she echoed it ever so softly.

"I like it. It suits you," Faith told him, thinking sadly of their proposed parting. She'd prepare a special meal tonight, something he could also take along on his journey to remember her by.

"How's the pain?" he asked.

"Nearly gone." She hated to lie to him again, but she knew if she told the absolute truth, he'd never leave. And if he stayed, Tucker's men would kill him for sure.

"Good." Scooping her up, he lifted her easily yet gently, set her in the wagon and handed her the lines. "Think you can handle the team from here on out?"

"Yes, but…" She watched him mount Rojo. "Where are you going?"

"No sense waiting till tomorrow to part company," he said flatly. "The longer I stay, the more gossip it'll cause." He gallantly touched the brim of his hat, nodded and said, *"Vaya con Dios."*

Faith had heard that phrase before among the Mexican wranglers. It was a parting benediction.

In her heart she knew she'd done the right thing for Connell McClain. Sending him away was her wordless blessing on his quest.

She only wished there was some way of letting him

know the underlying reasons for what she'd done and how much she truly cared about his welfare.

Following parallel, the sun at his back, Connell managed to easily keep the Tucker train in sight. If anyone noticed him, he figured they'd probably think he was just one of the extra drovers, rounding up loose stock, or maybe a lone Indian on a scouting mission. There were sure plenty of those around since the emigrant trains had cut such a wide swath through the plains.

Two days out, he came upon a Cheyenne and Arapaho hunting party in search of buffalo. Seeing members of the two tribes together had become a common sight, especially after the summer council of 1840 had drawn them, plus the Kiowa and the Comanche, to the Arkansas River to make peace amongst themselves.

Ascertaining that he and the hunting party were moving in the same general direction as the Tucker train, Connell spent the next three days riding with the Indians and communicating by means of rudimentary language and sign. To his relief, the hunters treated him like a long-lost relative.

The young men in the party were upset about the presence of so many wagons crossing their hunting grounds, and rightly so, Connell thought. Westward migration of Eastern settlers as well as the influx of Mexicans from the south was unstoppable, and the tribes were only now beginning to realize what all that meant to them.

In the course of the evening meal on the third day, he'd shown them Irene's picture. To his great surprise, Lone Buffalo had nodded solemnly.

"You've seen her?" Connell asked.

Another nod.

"Where?" He had trouble feigning calm in the face of such news, but he knew if he demonstrated much excitement, his cautious companions might choose to tell him no more.

Lone Buffalo pointed north. "Black Kettle camp."

"In the Big Horn Mountains?"

The young Indian recoiled at the use of the settlers' name for such a sacred place, but he nevertheless nodded affirmatively.

None of the others in the hunting party could confirm the sighting. Still, the lead provided the first glimmer of hope Connell had had in months. Could the woman with Black Kettle really be his Irene? Maybe. And if not, he still had the God-given responsibility to visit the camp and try to rescue whoever was being held captive there. He might not be a Bible-quoting zealot or a churchgoing man, but he was a believer just the same.

Although he'd prayed fervently and long that he'd find Irene in a white man's settlement, he knew she could have done worse than to wind up with the Cheyenne. Of all the Plains tribes, they were the least likely to force her into a quick marriage, since their normal courting rituals took from one year to as long as five. Then again, if she was considered a slave instead of having been adopted into the tribe, those customs wouldn't apply to her.

Connell's jaw clenched. He forced himself to consider various options. If, by tribal custom, she now belonged to one of the Cheyenne families, that relationship could pose a worse problem. It was far easier to purchase a slave than it was to convince a bride's father, adoptive or not, that he'd make a worthy husband.

It would be better to make a formal appeal than to simply grab her and make a run for it, he reasoned. Black Kettle would definitely not take kindly to having one of his band spirited away, no matter what the reason.

What he needed, Connell decided, were twenty good, fast horses as a show of his wealth and importance. Trouble was, he had so little money that, unless he intended to adopt the age-old Indian custom of stealing them, that particular option was out of the question. It was times like these that he wished he hadn't been raised with Christian values. To the Indian, stealing wasn't a sin, it was merely a contest of skill and daring, a besting of one's enemies. Instead of feeling guilt after a raid the way he would have, they celebrated victory.

Bedding down by the communal fire, Connell worked out his next moves in his mind. First, he'd return to Faith, explain what he'd learned, and tell her not to look for him at Independence Rock. Then he'd head for Black Kettle's camp and try to convince the chief that, as Irene's betrothed, he had the right to claim her no matter what her current status. Even if the woman captive turned out to be a stranger, he'd liberate her and see her safely to the nearest fort before he resumed his original search. The plan was simple. All he needed were trade goods, courage and a colossal marvel.

Early the following day, Connell packed the fresh buffalo meat he'd been given for his participation in the hunt, bid his traveling companions goodbye and headed out to intercept the emigrant trail. It was nearly sunset when he finally spied the smoke from the cooking fires of the Tucker train.

Reining in his horse, he paused on a slight rise to watch the activity in the camp and see where Faith's modest rig had wound up when they'd stopped for the night.

As was the routine, each wagon was backed up over the tongue of the one behind, forming a large circle and leaving only a narrow passage from the outside into the enclosure. Stretched across that passage, wheel to wheel, was a heavy chain that formed a gate and kept the loose livestock secure for the night.

Connell spotted the Beal wagon just to the right of the makeshift gate. Inside the circle, oxen milled around with horses, mules and an occasional goat brought along for milk when no freshened cow was available. Attached to the side of several of the wagons were slatted coops containing laying hens, although he imagined they'd wind up in the stew pot before long rather than have precious food and water wasted on them.

Dismounting, he led Rojo behind a hill where they could hunker down against the rising north wind and dropping temperature. No chance to keep a fire going tonight, not with the weather worsening.

He shivered, looking up at the gathering clouds and smelling the moisture in the air. Chances were, he and everything he owned were going to get good and soaked before morning.

"Over my dead body," Ab grumbled as he climbed into the supply wagon.

Stuart snorted in derision. "That can be arranged. I don't make the rules, old man."

"But criminy, Stu, we're gonna freeze out there and get soaked to boot. Why couldn't he pick a dry night?"

"How do I know? Probably figures most folks'll be inside, keepin' out of the storm, so's we won't be so likely to be seen. You ought to thank him." He reached into a burlap sack and pulled out a beaded band of bedraggled feathers and three sorry-looking arrows.

"Don't suppose any of these green settlers will notice that's a Blackfoot headdress and Sioux arrows, do ya?" Ab remarked, stripping off his shirt and sitting down to remove his run-down cavalry boots.

"Naw. Not a chance. To them, an Indian's an Indian. Besides, we'll be in and gone with the girl before most of 'em even wake up."

Ab sighed. "One of these days we're gonna get shot playin' Injun for Tucker."

"Just as long as we don't get separated like last time. You're lucky you were able to handle the Wellman woman alone."

"Yeah." Ab busied himself lacing up the tall tops of his moccasins.

"Tonight, we sneak in together, grab this one and ride. No fancy stuff, you hear? The cap'n said."

"Okay, okay." Ab stood, shivering in the icy dampness that had invaded the supply wagon. "Get the blasted war paint and let's get this over with before I freeze to death."

Stuart soon finished decorating himself and his unwilling companion, picked up the arrows, selected one and put the others back. "We'll have to barter for more of these man-stickers pretty soon if Tucker wants a sign left every time we pull a raid."

Peering first into the darkness to make sure they wouldn't be seen, he led the way out of the wagon and faded into the night. As soon as the rain began in earnest, they'd work their way back to the camp, shove the arrow into the canvas cover over the Beal wagon and make off with Faith, just as the captain had instructed.

That was the easy part. What came next was going to be harder to stomach. He'd kind of taken a liking to the girl. Slitting her throat, scalping her and burying her body in the wild was going to be a lot rougher than most of the other folks he'd killed. He almost hated to do it this time.

Frightened by the lightning and nearly continuous rumble of far-off thunder, the draft animals enclosed by the circle of wagons milled restlessly. A lone dog barked in reply to the distant howls of coyotes.

By the time rain began to pelt the canvas above her pallet, Faith was already up and dressed, preparing to go outside and reassure her mules.

Charity, having made a temporary peace with her sister, was huddled beneath their quilts instead of sleeping in the Ledbetter wagon as she had been of late.

"I don't see why you have to go out there," the younger girl whined, peeking over the top of the calico fabric, her fair hair in total disarray. "Come back to bed before you hurt yourself again. Captain Tucker will see to our stock for us."

"He won't touch those mules while I still have breath in my body," Faith said flatly. "Go back to sleep."

"How can I when you're running all over the camp

like some hoyden? Look what it got you back at the fort."

Faith made a face at her. "You didn't think of that all by yourself. Who's been calling me names?"

"Nobody. Not exactly. Mrs. Ledbetter just says you should remember you're a lady, the way I do."

"Oh, she does, does she? Well, don't waste your time worrying about me. I'll do what I have to do."

Charity's response was to hunker down in the bed and pull the covers up higher.

Faith belted the heavy Colt over her hips beneath an old, oversize India-rubber slicker that had belonged to their father, stuffed her feet into an old pair of shoes she'd walked holes in before they'd reached the valley of the Platte, and tied her slat bonnet on her head. The cotton fabric wouldn't afford much protection against the driving rain, but she needed to wear something familiar so Ben and the other mules would recognize her. Otherwise, she'd have little luck approaching them, especially when they were already so spooked.

Calling to Ben, she threw back the canvas flap and climbed down out of the wagon. Water borne on the unseasonable gale stung her cheeks like freezing sleet, its force whipping at her skirts and making her stagger. Bumping against the sideboards, she was thankful Charity had rewrapped her bruised ribs so tightly.

From where Faith stood, it appeared that few others had left their warm beds to check on their livestock personally. She wasn't surprised, since the makeshift corral did offer considerable protection and there were regular guards posted at the four points of the compass.

Ben quickly responded to her call. His long ears

were up and alert and he seemed truly glad to see her as he trotted over and tried to tuck his velvety, graying nose into the front of her slicker.

Stepping behind him for shelter from the wind, Faith hugged his neck and chuckled. "You're spoiled rotten, you know that? Trust me. If I had an apple I'd give it to you. Honest, I would."

She'd been treating the old mule with fresh apples for as long as she could remember, often sneaking into her mother's root cellar to help herself to them after picking season was long past. Undoubtedly, Ben was the reason they'd had fewer winter apple pies than most families she knew.

"Where's Lucy and Lucky?" she asked Ben. "You see them lately? And how about Puck?"

Ben tossed his head and laid his ears back. The rain-slicked hide of his neck and shoulders twitched, his concentration focused beyond the perimeter of wagons.

"What is it, boy? What's wrong?"

Faith turned to scan the darkness in the direction Ben was looking. She soothed him with one hand on his withers while she wiped the cold rain out of her eyes.

"Settle down, Ben. There's nothing out there."

But the mule wouldn't be placated. A clap of thunder set him to dancing and nervously stamping his forefeet.

If she hadn't been so close to their wagon, Faith might have thought Charity needed help and the mule was sensing it. However, she could see the rippling canvas plainly every time the sky flashed bright and all seemed as peaceful as could be expected during such a violent storm.

Stroking the mule's nose, she repeated soothing words of comfort. "Easy, old boy. Easy."

Suddenly, the atmosphere reverberated with a piercing scream. Ben jumped in unison with Faith.

A bolt of lightning split the sky, illuminating the shocking scene before her. Two war-painted figures were exiting her wagon bearing Grandmother Reeder's favorite quilt between them! And the rolled bundle of bedding was writhing and emitting strangled cries.

Faith's heart leaped. Charity! Good Lord in heaven, wild Indians were making off with Charity!

Giving no thought to her own safety, Faith gathered her skirts and dashed forward, her small feet flying across the slippery ground.

Launching herself into the air behind the nearest kidnapper, she grabbed him around the neck and hung on, oblivious to her earlier injury.

He muttered an oath as he spun around. His beefy elbow shot back, clipping her hard in the ribs. With a cry, she doubled up and fell to the muddy ground in a haze of pain.

"Look!" one of the Indians muttered. "We got the wrong one."

Suddenly, Faith felt herself being lifted, dragged, then thrown over the wagon tongue and out onto the soggy prairie. Resting on hands and knees, she shook her head to clear it. Something was dreadfully wrong here! The few Indians she'd heard speaking at Fort Laramie hadn't sounded like they came from some place back east, yet this one certainly did.

As she struggled to regain her footing, she remembered the pistol trapped beneath her slicker. She had to reach it!

Hands dripping with mud and water, she clawed frantically at the copious length of rubberized cloth, finally managing to raise the hem enough to expose the butt of the Colt. Her slick fingers slid off the grip!

Before she could try again to grab onto the revolver, someone pinned her arms from behind. The man she'd attacked at the outset faced her and drew back his arm. Surely he wasn't going to *hit* her!

Camp lanterns that had been quenched began to flicker to light. Charity was thrashing around in the mud with Grandma's quilt all askew beneath her.

The younger girl screamed for help as she pointed to an arrow sticking out of the canvas of their wagon.

Then, Faith felt a jarring blow to her jaw and everything went black.

Chapter Seven

This storm had Rojo spooked more than usual, Connell thought, watching his fidgeting horse with interest. The strange thing was, he seemed to be feeling the same unexplained nervousness the animal was.

There was bad medicine in the air, as his Arapaho friends would say. He'd already moved down into a draw to avoid being an easy target for lightning. Not that it couldn't strike where it pleased, as many a plainsman had seen. It even took out a buffalo, now and then. He'd never personally witnessed such an event but the stories were numerous. It wasn't a pretty sight. No matter how hungry Indians were, they refused to eat the charred flesh, considering it tainted by evil spirits.

Shivering, Connell arose from his crouched position. He'd donned the oilskin coat he carried and hunkered down beneath the piece of buffalo hide he'd had his meat wrapped in, but it had afforded little shelter. Nothing helped much in the midst of a prairie storm as bad as this one. Soon, the draw he was in would fill with racing water and he'd have to climb to higher ground. If he wasn't already soaked by that time, he soon would be.

He stamped his feet to work the kinks out of his legs and warm himself. This wasn't the first time he'd been caught miles from any decent place to take cover. He'd live. A traveler on horseback couldn't carry his shelter along the way the emigrants did.

Pausing, he listened. The noise of the storm blotted out everything, as far as he could tell, but the canelo seemed to be growing more agitated. He hoped there wasn't a twister brewing!

Connell approached and took up the loose reins. Rojo, ears pricked, was staring toward the distant wagon camp.

"What is it, boy?"

The horse snorted and tossed his head, then went right back to staring into the distance.

Connell peered along the same line of sight to no avail. The rain was falling too hard and fast for him to see much. Yet something had caused the hackles on the back of his neck to prickle. Maybe his nervous horse was spooking him, he argued rationally. And maybe not.

The urge to mount up and ride closer to check the situation was getting too strong to ignore. He'd intended to wait till morning to approach the camp. That way, there'd be lots of activity to cover his arrival and he'd be less likely to be shot by an overeager sentry or one of Tucker's henchmen when he tried to speak to Faith.

Now, however, his instincts insisted on immediate action.

"You're crazy and so am I," Connell told his horse

as he lifted the left stirrup to reach under and tighten the cinch before mounting.

Rojo snorted and stamped.

"Yeah. I don't know why, but I think she needs us, too," Connell said, his voice barely audible. He swung into the saddle and nudged the horse into action. "Let's go."

Closing on the wagon camp, Connell heard a ruckus. Folks were milling about, shouting to each other. A flash of lightning outlined two bent figures sneaking away. His first instinct was to follow them.

Thoughts of Faith gave him pause. Once he'd seen her and talked to her—made sure she was all right—he could go after the suspicious men. Trouble was, in this storm and at night to boot, there wasn't a chance in a thousand of successfully trailing them once they got a head start.

He peered in at the camp. Looked like no one had started to saddle a horse for pursuit. By the time they did, the marauders would be long gone.

A continuing barrage of lightning gave Connell further glimpses of the fleeing men. The taller one was carrying a large, dark object draped over his shoulder while the other walked sideways and backward, apparently watching to see that they weren't being followed. Judging by their headdresses, they'd be Blackfoot, except he'd never seen braves from that tribe so far west or south before.

Connell urged Rojo forward so he could keep his quarry in sight. A pair of horses waited several hundred yards from where he'd first spotted the men. They hoisted their burden, threw it across one saddle, and the smaller man swung up behind it. As soon as his partner had mounted, they whipped their mounts and began to put distance between themselves and the wagon train.

Connell knew now what he must do. Indians sometimes rode saddles of their own making, but he'd never seen a brave yet who could abide a high Spanish cantle.

He spurred the canelo into a gallop, oblivious to the dangers of traveling so fast over prairie-dog-ridden ground. The question was no longer *who* he was tracking but *what*.

One thing was certain. They weren't real Indians.

"I think she's comin' to," Ab warned, reining up beside Stuart. "And I'm half-froze to death. I don't know why we couldn't wear buffalo robes or at least hunting shirts the way the real Indians do in foul weather."

The heavier man grunted his disapproval. "Shut up, old man. He let us keep our long pants, didn't he? Stop your complaining or I'll shoot you on the spot and leave your sorry carcass for the buzzards when I dump the woman."

"I don't think we should keep doin' this for Tucker," Ab whined. "Trouble comes, you know he ain't goin' to fess up. We'll be stuck payin' for his crimes."

"Not me. I got enough on Tucker to see he rots in some stinkin' prison like the one I seen once in Yuma. Man, it was hot there."

"Don't talk about hot." Ab's teeth were chattering. "It reminds me of Hell, where you and I are probably goin' fer doin' this. How far do we have to ride, anyways?"

"Couple a more miles." He glanced at the slicker-covered bundle across Ab's saddle. "You said she was comin' to. She ain't moving much."

"Quit about as soon as she started. Probably fainted. You know women."

Stuart chortled. "Yeah. If we wasn't on a job here, I'd sure like to see if that one's as good as she looks."

Horrified and dismayed, Faith held her breath, biting her lip to keep from crying out every time Ab's horse took a step. The saddle horn was pressing into her stomach, thank goodness, but her sore ribs got a painful jolt at every stride just the same.

They were going to kill her. That was evident. She'd been a fool to think she was safe simply because she was in the emigrant company. Clearly, a nefarious man like Ramsey Tucker was not above kidnapping her to implement his scheme to get to Charity.

Cautiously, she tried to wiggle her fingers. Ropes held her wrists fast. The same with her ankles. When they'd secured her, they'd apparently looped the rope under the horse's belly because when she tugged the bindings on her wrists, the pressure on her legs increased.

Her mind whirling, Faith tried to reason through the panic that was eating away her ability to think logically. The voices of her captors were all too familiar, yet perhaps that could work to her advantage. From what little she'd heard, it sounded like Ab was the least committed to her demise. Perhaps, if she prayed hard enough, God would make Ab speak up and give her a chance to plead for her life before it was too late.

She held her breath. *Dear Lord!* They were stopping! Tied facedown she couldn't see much, but it was evident the men were dismounting. In seconds she was loosened, pulled from the saddle and released to fall painfully onto the soggy ground. That was the last straw. Unable to keep quiet any longer, she cried out in agony.

"She's awake!" Stuart shouted. "Get your gun on her."

"What gun?" Ab started to laugh like he was crazy in the head. "In case you ain't noticed, there's no room for a holster or a pistol in these danged costumes."

"Then hit her over the head with a rock."

"You hit her," Ab argued. "You're the one who likes that kind of thing."

"I never said that."

"Then why wouldn't you help me save Miss Irene?"

"'Cause Tucker'd a killed me if she'd a got away, that's why."

Ab continued to cackle as if he'd taken leave of his senses. "Then you'd best get ready to meet your maker 'cause that little gal is alive and well."

Stuart shouted a string of curses.

Lying in the mud at his feet, Faith began to give thanks for what she'd just learned. Now, if she could only escape, she could take word to her friend Hawk that his future bride was all right.

It was also a relief to hear that the men were unarmed, since the Colt was still snug in its military holster beneath her black slicker. The trick would be reaching it and using it to defend herself before her kidnappers figured out she had a gun.

She snaked her right arm inside the oilcloth while

she tried hard to keep the rest of her body from moving. The dark, rainy night helped mask her cautious movements.

Arguing loudly, her attackers moved off a bit, thereby giving Faith the opportunity she needed. Her cold fingers touched the leather flap over the top of the holster and lifted it out of the way. Under the cover of the slicker she eased the heavy pistol from its sheath and raised it to point toward the two men in case they noticed she was fully awake and getting to her feet.

She need not have worried. Neither man was the least bit interested in her at the moment. Stuart was pushing at his smaller companion's shoulders over and over. Ab was fighting back with angry words.

"I don't care what you say. I done the right thing and I'm not sorry."

"You will be when the cap'n hears."

"Go ahead. Tell him. I ain't goin' back there, anyhows."

"Oh, yes you are."

"No, I'm not."

Ruing the added weight of her wet, muddy skirt and petticoat, Faith edged herself partially behind the weary horse she'd been tied to, then pulled the black slicker off the pistol barrel. Having the gun would do no good unless she took careful aim before ordering the drovers to surrender.

Gathering her courage, she shouted, "All right. Hands up, both of you!" How weak and puny her voice sounded in the vastness of the open prairie!

Ab lifted his hands over his head with a wild laugh. "Ha-ha. I see *somebody* remembered to bring a gun!"

"Shut up, old man," Stuart ordered. He began edging away from his companion, making a split in Faith's target.

Not sure which man to continue to point the gun at, she wavered, her eyes blinking fast against the falling rain.

Lightning flashed. For a moment she was blinded. Something told her Stuart was lunging for her, but not wanting to shoot without being certain, she held her fire.

He hit her low, like a cowhand bringing down a steer from the back of a running horse. The blow made her squeeze off one wild shot.

In an instant he'd wrestled her to the ground and torn the pistol from her grasp. The next lightning flash showed him standing over her, the menacing-looking Colt pointed right at her head.

"Nice of you to bring your own gun, Miss Faith. It makes my job much easier."

"I was always good to you." She hugged herself to ease the pain in her side. "Why are you doing this to me?"

Stuart cocked the hammer of the pistol to bring another loaded cylinder into play. "Don't want to," he said. "It's just the way things worked out. No hard feelin's."

His uncaring attitude made Faith boiling mad. He might actually kill her, but she wasn't going to Glory without giving him a piece of her mind no matter how much it hurt to breathe and talk.

"No hard feelings?" she spit out. "You bet there are, mister. I'm going to be mad as a hornet at you if you pull that trigger. Maybe I'll even come back to haunt you. Do you believe in ghosts?"

Ab appeared at Stuart's elbow. "You'd better listen to her. There's talk on the train she's got special powers. Just might be able to do as she says."

"I didn't hear no such talk."

"Well, there was." The thin man raised his trembling right hand. "I swear."

"Bah. Get away from me, you old fool. I got work to do." With that, he raised the pistol higher and took aim.

Connell hadn't been more than a quarter of a mile behind the riders when they and their burden had stopped. He thanked the Good Lord over and over when he recognized Faith's discarded bonnet and realized exactly who he'd been following and what was apparently going on.

He'd dismounted to approach on foot when he heard her shout "Hands up!"

A single gunshot cracked amid the thunder.

Faith cried out.

The sound tied Connell's gut in knots.

It was clear that at least one of the men had doubted she'd really shoot to kill, because Connell had seen a dark, crouching figure run at her and knock her to the ground.

When the man scrambled to his feet, Connell glimpsed the reflection of a shiny object in his hand. Faith's pistol! His heart sank. He'd left Rojo behind in a ravine so he could sneak up on the abductors more easily and his Hawken was still in its scabbard. That left only his .44, a much less accurate weapon than the rifle, even under the best of conditions. Which these were not.

It was dark except for the scattered clusters of lightning flashes. Rain was falling in bursts, as if someone were emptying buckets on him from above.

Connell knew if he chanced a shot and missed, the man with the gun would fire, likely hitting Faith. Yet if he waited until he was within better range, it might be too late. Unless…

Using a trick he'd learned from Little Rabbit Woman's people, he pulled his hunting knife and began to slice off thick bunches of grama grass. The idea was to make his swiftly moving shadow resemble a large, dangerous animal like a mad buffalo.

It would have been much better to use a real animal's hide but he'd left that behind, as well, so a substitute would have to do. The ploy didn't have to fool anyone for long. It was meant only as a delaying tactic and a way to get closer to Faith and the men.

Growling, snorting and making as much animal noise as he could, Connell started off at a dead run toward the three people. He was counting on surprise to keep them from firing at him. He was wrong.

Wheeling, Stuart squeezed off a shot. The bullet whizzed through the grama grass bundles. Connell dropped them, hit the ground, rolled away in the darkness and sprang to his feet with the speed and agility of a pronghorn antelope.

Plunging headlong into the danger ahead, he raced over the wet ground as if he knew every inch of it and with no thought of personal risk. This was the way the Native People felt about the land, about nature, he realized. It had been literally years since he'd sensed such a oneness with a Greater Power and it made him feel almost invincible.

There was no time to pause and draw his .44. Stuart was turning back to Faith and bringing the gun to bear.

With a soul-deep roar of rage, Connell lived up to his nickname and launched himself into the air with a mighty leap, his arms reaching like a hawk's talons for its prey.

Stuart's scream was cut off by the attack almost before it began. He fell beneath Connell. The Colt flew from his hand to disappear in the mire.

A soggy, muddy mess in spite of the heavy slicker, Faith scrambled to her feet and pushed her limp hair out of her eyes with her hands. The furor died down in mere moments. "I can't believe you found me out here in the middle of nowhere. How did you do it?" she asked, sounding amazed.

Connell shook his head. "It was just a feeling I had. I guess you could say the Good Lord sent me."

"I don't doubt that. I've been asking Jesus to send help ever since these two grabbed me."

"Well, I guess He heard you because here I am." Connell got to his feet and gazed down at the muddy, disheveled woman. "Are you all right?"

"I think so." She managed a smile. "Stuart, I see. What happened to Ab?"

"I'm right here," the weasely man squeaked. His hands were raised high over his head and he was trembling visibly as he edged closer. "D-don't shoot."

It was a natural reflex for Connell to reach for his pistol anyway. Faith stayed his hand. "No. Don't. He tried to help me. Even made up a story that he'd heard I had supernatural powers." She brightened. "And he says he helped your Irene, too."

"What?"

Grabbing him by the upper arms, Connell lifted Ab overhead, gave him a mighty shake and held him there while rain cascaded off him like the headwaters of the Mississippi.

"I did. I helped her," the little man sputtered.

Connell wasn't convinced. "Prove it."

"She's...she's with the Arapaho. I took her there myself, I swear."

"When?"

"Last year, when the wagons came through these here parts. Tucker married up with her, like usual, then told me and Stuart to get rid of her." Ab's thin voice broke. "Only I couldn't do it. She reminded me of my ma."

It wasn't exactly the same story Connell had heard from the Indian hunters, but it was close enough to re-affirm the good news that Irene had survived Tucker's planned destruction.

Angry, Connell thrust Ab aside. "I doubt you had a mother! How could you be a party to such cruelty?"

"It was me or them!"

"All right, all right. Shut up. I believe you," Connell replied. "At first light, you'll take me to Irene. Understand?"

"I... I can try. The camps move around, ya know. Follow the buffalo. Might not be there no more."

"Then we'll keep looking till we locate the right band."

Shivering now that all the excitement was over, Faith tugged at Connell's wet buckskin sleeve. "What about me? And what are we going to do with Stuart? We can't just ride away and leave him here."

"He can rot where he lies for all I care," Connell said. Nevertheless, he gestured at Ab. "Help him up and let's try to get out of this rain before we all take sick."

The thin little man reached for his companion's arm. "I can't lift him."

With a grunt of displeasure, Connell yanked Stuart's limp body to its feet, then hesitated, feeling for a pulse in the man's throat and finding none before releasing him to fall back onto the sodden prairie.

"The Good Lord is wiser than we are," he said flatly. "This man is dead. I think his neck is broken."

"We should bury him." Faith's tone lacked conviction.

"Not if it means we're overtaken by a search party from the wagon train while we dig the grave. Surely they must be out looking for you by now. Tucker has to put on a good show of concern for the benefit of the other folks."

"There's…there's a hole already dug," Ab stammered, pointing. "Over that ridge, I think."

Faith gasped. "It was meant for me, wasn't it?"

Ab said, "Yes," and Faith staggered as if she was going to faint for the second time in her life.

Chapter Eight

The night seemed to drag on forever. Huddled under a rock outcropping with the buffalo hide pulled over them, Faith, Connell and Ab waited impatiently for dawn. Head down, his rear to the wind, Rojo stood quietly nearby.

"I wish you'd let me share this slicker with you two," she said. "It's way too big for me and we could make a fair shelter out of it."

Connell was quick to say, "No," even though Ab was shivering like a quaking aspen in a gale.

Sleep was impossible, given their cramped positions and the continuing noise of the storm. Thankfully, the lightning had moved off to the northeast so at least the danger of being roasted alive had passed.

"We have to go back and get Charity," Faith said.

Both men turned their heads to stare at her. Connell said, "Out of the question."

She wasn't surprised at his attitude. However, she didn't intend to change her mind. "Then I'll go alone."

"You'll do nothing of the kind."

"You have no right to tell me what to do."

"Well, somebody better," he replied. "You aren't thinking smart anymore."

"I can't leave her there!" Faith's voice broke as she fought a strong urge to weep.

Ab interrupted their conversation by saying, "It ain't good for the cap'n to know you're alive, missy. Might rile him up and make him change his plans."

"But…"

Nodding, Connell agreed. "You know what he has in mind, then?"

"I do." The thin man cleared his throat. "He's after the Beal gold mine. Figures it'll set him up for life. Only this time he's got to work it out different. If something happened to Miss Charity before the train reached Californy, her pa wouldn't take kindly to it. That's why I know fer certain he won't hurt her."

"I have to see her again. To reason with her," Faith insisted.

"Well, you sure can't go back to the wagons." Connell sounded gruff. "What do you want me to do, kidnap her and bring her to you?"

"Oh, would you?"

"Absolutely not. What makes you think your sister would listen to you even if you had the chance to speak your mind? You've been arguing with her about Tucker for as long as I've known you and she hasn't learned a thing."

"But this time I can tell her what he tried to do to me," Faith said. "That should open her eyes."

"What if she doesn't believe you?"

"She will. She has to."

Ab cleared his throat. "'Scuse me, missy. I think you're wrong about that. It's my guess she'll be married to the cap'n 'fore the train moves again."

"No! It can't be! What makes you say that?"

"'Cause it's his plan," Ab explained. "Me and Stuart was to pretend to be Indians and do away with you. Then Tucker would move in on Miss Charity and tell her she couldn't travel all alone on his train because she wasn't a married lady. Unless you know of some other young fella she might marry up with, it's my guess it'll be Ramsey Tucker. He's the law out here. He can do anything he wants, even perform his own weddin' if he can't find a rightful preacher."

Faith was glad the darkness beneath the buffalo robe hid her tears as they slid silently down her muddy cheeks. If Charity chose to wed, there was nothing she could do about it. The sanctity of marriage had to be respected.

Given a choice, she would have mounted Stuart's horse and galloped back to the train right then. Trouble was, she had no idea how to find her way back to the wagons without some kind of trail to go by. She had no doubt Connell would not aid her. He was too dead set against her going.

Thinking about asking Ab for help, she decided that wasn't safe, either. Under the present circumstances he seemed innocent enough, but put him back where Tucker's influence could corrupt him again and there was no telling how he would act.

Turning to Connell, she laid her hand gently on his sleeve. "Please, Mr. McClain. I know how badly you want to find your bride. Try to put yourself in my place.

What if it were Irene about to marry Captain Tucker and you found out about it in time to stop it. Wouldn't you try?"

He turned away as he mumbled something she couldn't quite decipher. From his tone of voice and attitude, though, Faith decided it was probably just as well she hadn't been able to make out the words. They were most likely not at all genteel.

Rising suddenly, Connell flung off the buffalo robe. "All right. You win. But we do this my way, is that clear?"

"Yes, sir."

Grinning broadly, Faith ducked her head so he couldn't tell how happy she was and therefore change his mind simply because of stubborn pride. She'd learned long ago, by watching her father and mother argue, that men were happiest when they didn't think women had anything to do with their decisions —especially the important ones.

Ab, too, arose. He stood there shivering, pulling the wet, heavy fur robe around his scrawny shoulders. "What about me?"

"You stay," Connell said.

"I'll freeze to death out here!"

"Not before morning. It's my guess this place'll be plenty hot once the sun rises. Usually is."

"At least leave me a horse."

"So you can warn Tucker or ride off to alert the Indians that I'm on my way? Not on your life."

"I won't. I swear!"

Mounting Rojo, Connell rode to where the other

horses were hobbled and loosed them to lead. "Stay put. We'll come back for you," he promised Ab.

"What if you get kilt?"

Sobering at the suggestion, Faith stood on a raised, flat rock to climb more easily onto Stuart's mare. "I guess you'd better pray hard that we don't," she said. "I imagine the Lord will even listen to the pleas of a skunk like you, providing you truly repent. I'd give it a try if I were you."

She took up the reins of the extra horse as well as her own and looked to Connell. "I'm ready. Let's go."

Activity started in the wagon camp before dawn. There were animals to harness, food to prepare, goods to stow and no time to waste. Every minute counted when early snows might close the mountain passes or freak storms could make shallow rivers impassable for weeks at a time. Many a man had been lost trying to float his team and wagon across a treacherous river. Broken wood and the bleached bones of oxen lying in rifts on the banks were proof.

Faith wished she'd had more sleep during the long, trying night. Between the shooting pains in her side and a lack of rest, she was thoroughly exhausted. In a way, she wished the remainder of her were as numb from the cold as her feet and legs were.

"We'll dismount here," Connell said, swinging easily to the ground.

When Faith tried to do the same, her knees gave out and she crumpled into a heap next to the horse.

In an instant Connell was beside her. There was no use insisting she was fine when he bent to pick her up.

Clearly, she was not. Worse yet, being cradled in his strong arms made her forget Charity and everything else except the two of them and the way his awesome presence was increasingly affecting her.

He tenderly carried her to a hiding place and set her down behind an enormous gray boulder. "You wait here. Take off your boots and rub your feet and ankles to get the circulation back into them. And don't stick your head up. I don't want some overeager meat hunter to mistake you for a drowned prairie dog and take a potshot at you."

"I beg your pardon."

He chuckled. "I forgot. You haven't seen your hair lately. Too bad you lost your bonnet in the storm."

Embarrassed, Faith patted at her head and tried to tuck wisps of mud-matted hair back into the long plait that hung down her back. "I hope Charity recognizes me like this."

"Don't worry about the dirt. It should help prove you're telling the truth," he offered, a softer tone coloring his deep voice.

"I want to go with you."

"No. First of all, I may have to run and you're in no shape to keep up. Secondly, no one knows I'm involved in your troubles anymore, so I can probably ride into camp without arousing much suspicion."

"I suppose you're right," she grumbled.

"You know I am. Sit tight. I'll be back as soon as I can." With that, he mounted Rojo and rode away.

Left alone with her thoughts, Faith used the damp hem of her petticoat to wipe her face and hands as clean as possible. There were some advantages to ladies' abundant garments, weren't there? At least a body had spare rags handy if need be.

Sighing, she contrasted her father with Connell McClain. They both were good men in their own ways. Her father, Emory Beal, had never been as strong or as imposing a figure as the big plainsman was, but she'd loved him in spite of his faults. The hard part was forgiving him for deserting his family to go west to search for gold when he didn't know the first thing about prospecting.

Too bad Papa couldn't have been more capable, like Hawk, she mused, noticing an unexplainable tingle running through her as she visualized her boon companion. Connell McClain was clearly a lot better suited to the rigors of pioneer life than any man she'd ever known.

In the back of her mind she remembered how sure she'd been that she didn't need anyone but the Good Lord to look out for her on the trail. How wrong that notion was. Nobody, man or woman, could hope to stand totally alone. Not out here. Not in these difficult times. And she couldn't think of a single person in whom she would rather place her trust than the big, rugged plainsman.

Clearly, she'd made a mistake when she'd struck out for California by land instead of trying to scrounge enough money to sail around the Horn. It was one thing to trust God for deliverance, yet quite another to tempt Him by making foolish choices, as she apparently had.

Thinking of Little Rabbit Woman, Faith grew pensive. What was life like in an Arapaho camp? she wondered. What would it be like to live there, the way Irene was, only with someone like Hawk McClain? Her cheeks flamed at the thought. Where had that wild, sinful notion come from? A person would think she was as taken with men as Charity was!

She wasn't, of course, so it surely wouldn't hurt to give her reveries free rein for a moment or two. The man was already spoken for. Therefore, he was not available and could pose no threat to her long-range plans.

Closing her eyes, Faith leaned back against the rock and tried to picture herself as a young squaw, relying on her memories of the women gathered at Fort Laramie to imagine a native costume and wondering which tribe was which. Always, the imposing presence of the plainsman lay in the center of her fancies.

Soon a pleasant euphoria overtook her, pressing fatigue won out, the vision faded and she fell sound asleep.

Connell's arrival at the Tucker camp was just as he'd predicted; he rode slowly among the wagons without attracting more than an occasional "Good morning."

Tipping his hat, he noted that most of the men were as wet and grimy as he was, thanks to their extra duties during the night and the early morning.

As he passed, he listened carefully to anyone who happened to be talking about Miss Charity's close call. Few mentioned the fact that Faith was missing.

The Ledbetter wagon stood directly in front of Faith's. Through the canvas cover he could hear the voices of at least three women.

"Now, now, dear. We all know you aren't like she was, thank the Lord. Them that live by the sword, die by the sword, I always say. We all saw that horrid pistol she insisted on wearing."

One of the women began to wail loudly while the others offered emotional support. "Here, take this hanky and blow your nose, child. Cryin' won't help a bit. You're a young thing, but you're a woman, just like the rest of us, and you gotta do as your man says."

The wailing abated slightly, then resumed at a high, screeching pitch. Connell didn't doubt for a minute that he'd located Charity Beal.

Which meant she had company in her misery. It wasn't going to be possible to just grab her, throw her across his saddle and cart her away for a meeting with Faith. Emigrant women tended to do everything in a group, from cooking and cleaning to taking care of their personal needs. Catching one of them alone under normal circumstances wasn't easy. Catching Charity by herself on this particular morning was going to be next to hopeless.

Still, he had to try. A promise was a promise whether he liked it or not. Grumbling to himself and wondering how he'd let Faith talk him into doing this, he left Rojo grazing just outside the wagon circle and made his way to the Beal wagon to wait for Charity to come home.

Personal belongings were stacked as low to the ground as possible to help keep the wagon from tipping over in rough terrain. Bedding was usually spread on top of the trunks and boxes at night, then stored away in the morning before travel resumed.

Connell looked inside the wagon and noted that only one sleeping place remained. It was as if Charity knew Faith was never coming back.

That was when he remembered the old family quilt Faith had mentioned seeing wrapped around her sister the night before. It would be soiled, of course, but perhaps if he could locate it he'd take it to her when he delivered Charity. Poor Faith had precious little else left of the life she'd once lived. Having the quilt would surely give her comfort.

He found the thoroughly soaked coverlet lying discarded on the prairie about twenty-five yards from camp. Picking it up, he squeezed out as much water as he could and took it back to the wagon with him, thinking it might make a good conversation piece when he tried to explain what he was doing there.

Charity was inside her wagon by the time he arrived for the second time. She was fully dressed but still gave a little squeal of fright when he knocked and pushed back the flap. "What do you want?"

In the tight confines of the small wagon he could see she was all by herself. "I came to return this," Connell said, holding up the quilt.

"I don't want it!" Charity's reddened, puffy eyes filled with new tears. "Take it away."

"I heard about what happened to your sister," he went on. "Please accept my condolences."

"We…we shouldn't even be out here in this god-forsaken desert," the girl stammered. "Faith insisted we come. Look what her bossy nature got her." She started to sniffle. "I hate this place. All I want to do is go home."

"Lots of folks feel that way, Miss Beal. I could escort you back to Fort Laramie and you could wait there to join up with an east-bound party."

"It's too late for that, I'm afraid. My husband surely wouldn't like it if I rode out of camp with another man."

Connell's fist tightened on the quilt. "You're married? When?"

"Two days ago. Captain Tucker, Ramsey, wanted us to keep it a secret from nearly everyone. He was afraid my sister would pitch a fit and spoil things if she found out." Charity blinked back tears. "When I came back to our wagon last night I was going to explain it all to her, to prove to him he was wrong, but I never could make myself speak the words." She paused to stifle a sob. "How I wish I'd told her the whole truth before… before she…"

"I am sorry," Connell said. "But wherever Faith is, I'm sure she wishes you only the best."

"Will the Indians hurt her?" Charity blurted out. "I couldn't bear that. I just couldn't."

He didn't dare tell her the true details of the fake kidnapping because she might make the mistake of saying something about it to her nefarious husband. If Tucker began to suspect what had really happened, Charity could be in worse danger than she already was. Instead, Hawk tried to comfort her another way.

"The Plains tribes I know are not vicious and cruel the way the dime novels say they are. We don't always understand their ways because they're so different from ours, but they do have loving families. They care about each other the same way white men do…maybe better."

"Truly?"

"Truly," he said. "I can assure you, if your sister is with the local tribes she will be well cared for."

"If she's alive," the girl added.

"I have a strong feeling that she is," he said. "And I promise to keep my eyes and ears open for any word of her."

The hair on the back of his neck prickled a warning. He turned in time to see Ramsey Tucker headed their way.

"I have to go," Connell said. "But first, tell me. Now that you have a husband, do you still plan to meet up with your father in California?"

"Yes, of course." Charity pushed her mussed blond curls back from her pale cheeks. "Looking forward to the day of that blessed reunion is all that keeps me going."

"Then I wish you the best." Quickly tipping his hat, he dodged around the corner of the wagon, leaped into the saddle with the quilt in front of him and spurred his horse out onto the prairie.

Behind him, he could hear the angry curses and shouts of Ramsey Tucker.

Faith awoke to a gentle calling of her name. Sitting bolt upright, she peered up at Connell expectantly, happily, then looked past him right and left. "Is Charity here? Did she come with you?"

"No. I saw her and she's fine, though. A little weary, and you can see she's been crying, but all in all she's the same as always."

"Oh, I'm so thankful."

He hunkered down beside her. "There's more."

Eyeing him curiously, she saw the regret in his expression and realized that the news he was about to deliver was not going to be good. "Tell me."

"Charity says she and Tucker are already married."

"Oh, no!" Faith's hands flew to her throat. "So fast?"

"Apparently it happened shortly before you were kidnapped. Your sister says she tried to tell you everything but couldn't bring herself to do it."

"What can we do? We have to help her."

Connell shook his head. "As I see it, there's not a whole lot to be done for the present. She says they are traveling on to the mining country to meet your father, just as Ab told us they would."

"So?"

"So, that means he was right about her being safe for the time being. As long as we beat Mr. and Mrs. Ramsey Tucker to California and tell your father the whole truth ahead of time, I think we can safely put off doing anything right away."

"We?" Faith's eyes widened in disbelief.

"Did I say that?"

"You certainly did."

"Then I guess I'd better honor it. Get ready to ride."

Praise God! After all that had gone wrong, all the danger she'd already lived through, Faith could hardly believe the amazingly wonderful offer. "You'll take me with you?"

"If you want to go."

The idea of spending more time with Hawk didn't frighten her nearly as much as the nameless joy she found she was feeling in anticipation of the opportunity to travel with him. Still, her strict upbringing insisted she add, "We hardly know each other."

"Yes, we do. We're like family, already. You feel it and so do I, so don't bother to deny it. Besides, did you think I'd ride off and leave you? Just where do you think you could go all alone out here?"

"I—I hadn't thought that far ahead," Faith answered, wondering absently if he had meant family like kin, or family like man and wife.

"Well, I have. I can't send you back to the Tucker train or you'll probably be killed. And I certainly can't abandon you. If the bandits or the hostile Indians didn't get you, starvation or thirst or cholera probably would."

Kin, she decided. Definitely like kin. "That's not a very comforting list of choices."

Smiling, Connell got to his feet. "Glad you realize that. I was hoping you'd be sensible and see this my way. It'll make the next few months much easier on both of us."

Months? Was it really going to take that long? Reeling and confused by all she'd been through, all she'd learned, fantasized about, then dismissed as the ridiculous yearnings of a silly girl, Faith took the hand he offered and let him help her up without objecting.

The bare, moist ground felt cool and soothing beneath her feet, as if she were meant to go barefoot for the sheer pleasure of being in close contact with the earth. Awed, she clung to his warm, steadying hand and tried to explain to him how different she'd begun to feel since coming to the plains.

"I'm not surprised to hear that," he said when she had finished. "I always did sense a trace of the People in you."

"The People?"

"That's what the Indians call themselves. I've never

met one who wasn't totally in tune with the wildness of the land and the animals."

Faith followed him to where their horses waited, her shoes and stockings in her hand. She gasped with delight when she noticed the old quilt draped across Rojo's withers in front of the saddle.

"Grandma Reeder's quilt! You found it! Oh, thank you."

"You're welcome. It's pretty muddy, but I think it'll clean up all right." He chuckled. "Hopefully, so will you."

Looking down at the horrid red mud clinging to her skirt she could only imagine what the rest of her must look like. "Is it possible I could have a bath and rinse out my dress before I meet Irene? I'd hate to make a bad impression on her." *Not to mention the impression I must be making on you,* she added to herself.

"Maybe." Connell nodded, thinking. "I don't intend to head straight for Black Kettle's camp without making certain it's necessary. First, I'll take you to meet Little Rabbit Woman's people and try to find out which branch of the Arapaho Ab left her with. I'm pretty sure they'll help us. They may even offer to give you something more appropriate to wear in trade for the clothes you have on."

"These rags? Goodness! Why would they want to dress like me?"

"Their interest in the white man's culture is understandable but worrisome. To them we're as fascinating as a new species of animal. I'm afraid their curiosity about us may eventually be their undoing."

"But, surely they realize we feel the same way in regard to them," she suggested.

"Maybe you and I do, Little Muddy Dove, but you have to admit that particular opinion is not a popular one among most settlers."

Faith giggled at his use of the silly nickname. "Little *What?*"

"Don't blame me. You're the one who came up with it in the first place."

"I hardly meant it to become permanent." She was secretly glad he'd substituted the word "muddy" for "soiled," because of the sinful inference of the latter.

"Why not?" He eyed her up and down. "The muddy part certainly fits you lately. And since I'm the Hawk, I think it's appropriate that my traveling companion be a Dove."

Flattered, Faith thought for a moment, then agreed. "All right. I'll be Little Dove. But you have to leave the muddy part out."

"Little Dove Woman it is, then," he said, adding, "It's customary for all Arapaho squaws to have the identifying word, 'woman,' in their full names."

"Like saying 'missus' or 'miss'?"

"I never thought of it quite that way, but I guess you're right." He laced his fingers together to make a cradle for her to step into as she mounted Stuart's sorrel horse again. Then he handed the quilt to her for safekeeping.

Faith slung it over her horse's neck the same way he had carried it, smoothing the fabric as best she could and arranging it in loose folds. "Thank you."

"You're quite welcome. Keep turning it like that to

help it air out so it doesn't mildew. And don't wrap it up in your slicker till you're sure it's completely dry."

"I know that."

He shrugged and smiled over at her as he climbed aboard Rojo and took up the reins. "Sorry. You look so much like a ten-year-old street urchin it's hard to remember how old you really are." He paused a moment. "How old are you, anyway? I never did ask."

"Nineteen last May," Faith said proudly.

Thoughtful, he drew his hand over his neatly trimmed beard and slowly looked her up and down. "I know you won't take kindly to this notion, but I think it would be best if you didn't try to look or act like a capable, grown woman out here. When the question comes up, which it will, leave the explanations to me, even if others happen to be speaking our language."

"What do you intend to say that I couldn't impart every bit as well as you can?"

"Mostly that you're a little crazy in the head," Connell told her. "Indians fear madness. They think it's catching, like smallpox." As expected, his companion didn't seem to relish his honesty or his sarcasm.

Kicking her horse, she urged it closer to him and flicked the loose ends of the reins to sting him on the arm.

"Ouch! Didn't anybody ever tell you that doves are supposed to be harmless?" Laughing, he dodged her second attack.

"Not this dove," Faith declared. "And don't you ever forget it, mister."

"I'm not likely to," he replied. "Just don't get all het up. What I'm really going to say is that you're my long-lost niece. That way, everyone will honor my decisions about what happens to you."

Was he really old enough to be her uncle? she wondered, doubting he could be much more than thirty now that she'd gotten to know him better. Still, if that was how he wanted to think of her it was probably for the best, especially considering the untoward thoughts she'd been battling whenever he was near. *And* when he wasn't.

"What might happen to me? Just for instance, mind you," Faith finally asked. They had fallen into a comfortable, side-by-side canter and were leading the extra horse as they started back to where they'd left Ab.

"Well, for one thing, I don't intend to let any young brave buy you for one of his wives…unless that's what you want, of course."

Faith coughed and sounded like she was strangling. Connell patted her lightly on the shoulder with the flat of his hand while he laughed out loud at the stricken look on her face.

"Wives?" she finally managed to choke out. "Plural?"

"Actually, you're probably already too old and worn-out for most warriors but we can't rule out an old man maybe wanting you, so it's best to be prepared."

At this point, Faith couldn't tell whether he was teasing her or not. One thing she was certain of, however, was that his suggestion she masquerade as his niece and pretend to be family had touched her deeply. In truth, she already felt more genuine affection for the rough plainsman than she could ever remember having had for any man except her father.

As for the rest of the unsettling feelings she was struggling to understand, perhaps they were better forgotten as much as possible, at least until all their other problems were solved.

And there was no time like the present to begin acting the part Hawk had chosen for her. "I'd be pleased to consider you family," she said with genuine affection. "And I promise I will try to comport myself well and make you proud of me, Uncle."

"I already am proud of you," Connell told her.

Faith was so touched by the honestly spoken praise she didn't bother to ask why he felt that way. Having his complete acceptance was enough.

Chapter Nine

Ab was in better spirits by the time they returned to fetch him. At sunup he had managed to locate the shallow grave intended for Faith, drag Stuart's body into it and bury him, but not before stripping the other man of every stitch of clothing and keeping it for himself.

Consequently, the skinny little man was no longer freezing, which helped lift his dour mood considerably even if he did look strange with Stuart's trousers draped over his shoulders like a soggy shawl.

"How far to the Arapaho camp?" Faith asked as she rode along beside Connell with Ab bringing up the rear.

"Not far. Which reminds me, you'd better let me carry your Colt from here on out."

"I thought you wanted me armed all the time."

"That was only to impress Tucker. Where we're going, most women aren't warlike."

"Neither am I," she said, unbuckling the belt and handing the holstered pistol to Connell. "You sure I won't need to protect myself from the Indians?"

He huffed. "If you did, one gun sure wouldn't be enough."

"I suppose that's true." Faith shifted in the saddle. "I'm not used to riding so long. Can't we stop and rest?"

"In an hour or so you'll get all the rest you want." He was scanning the horizon. "We should start seeing the Coyote Men pretty soon."

"The what?"

"They're a guard society of the Arapaho. They dress in white buffalo robes and paint their faces white, too, then stand sentry duty outside the main camps."

"Oh, like in the army."

Connell glared over his shoulder at Ab when the old man snorted in derision. "Not exactly like that. In the cavalry a different man takes over the post every few hours. Coyote Men do their jobs for years. They live in the hills, build no shelter no matter what the weather, and remain totally alone for as long as they continue to hold the office."

"You mean *totally* alone?" She blushed and averted her gaze.

"Yes," Connell said. "They have no families, most especially no wives. Women are considered far too much of a distraction."

Faith was flabbergasted. "I've never known anyone that dedicated to their job."

"It's more than a job to the Arapaho," he explained. "It's an honor. When one Coyote Man decides he's finished, he takes his decorated rifle or war club and personally passes it to the man he has chosen to be his successor."

"Goodness. There is a lot to learn about red men, isn't there?"

Ab was chuckling and trying to stifle the noise by covering his half-toothless mouth with his hand.

"That's another myth," Connell said. "Indians aren't red by nature, they paint themselves that color for certain ceremonies. For instance, when a family member dies, there will be a year or more afterward when mourners who have cut off their long braids for the burial will not try to improve their appearance in any way. Then, when the mourning time is over, an elder will paint their faces and hair with red clay. That signals that they're free to dress and act like everyone else and resume normal life."

"They aren't born red?" Faith continued to be astonished. "But I've read lots of novels that said they were."

"Written by men who had never been west of the Mississippi, I'll wager," Connell said with disdain. "Some of them have darker skin and distinctive features, but that's all that sets them apart. That, and their primitive culture. Many's the time I've thought their ways made a lot more sense than ours."

While he'd been explaining Indian custom, Faith had been studying his strong profile and wondering what he might look like without a beard. There were tiny wrinkles in the outer corners of his eyes, caused undoubtedly by his prolonged exposure to the elements, but she was willing to bet he was a lot younger man than he let on.

"I have an idea," she ventured, hoping to change the subject enough that he at least quit scowling. "Instead of pretending to be my uncle, why don't you be my brother?"

From the rear, Ab piped up, "I vote for that one, mister."

A half smile lifted the corner of Hawk's mouth as he nodded in agreement. "Sounds good to me, too. Only there's something you should know first, Miss Faith."

"What now? Will you be painting me red, too? I know I should still be in mourning for Mama."

"Oh, no, nothing quite so easy to bear, I'm afraid. You see, from puberty on, Arapaho brothers and sisters are not permitted to speak to one another. As my sister, you would be expected to keep totally silent in my presence and not dare to even look at me, no matter what."

"Oh, dear."

Connell's smile grew. "Something told me you wouldn't cotton to those rules. Of course, if you want me as a big brother instead of an uncle I have no objections."

Faith knew he was having fun at her expense, a conclusion that bruised her pride. Granted, she talked a lot but what did he expect under the circumstances? She needed to learn as much as she could before reaching the Indian camp or she might break some obscure Native taboo and inadvertently get them all into terrible trouble.

As for her habit of staring at Connell so much of the time, well, she couldn't help that. Not really. She'd tried to keep from gawking and had succeeded in subduing her yearning only enough to limit it to the instances when she didn't think he'd notice the undue attention.

Obviously, she had not been nearly as surreptitious as she'd fancied.

And now, both he and Ab were laughing at her. Well, let them. For the present she had little choice about anything, including her traveling companions, and it was of no consequence whether or not she was happy about the trying situation. Later, when they had rescued Irene and put Tucker in his place, she'd speak her mind. Until then she intended to play the acquiescent compatriot even if it galled her something awful to do so.

Faith never saw any guards outside the Arapaho camp, which, of course, didn't mean there had been none. The thing that did astound her was the noise of so many barking dogs and the shouts coming from the horde of people who flocked out of the teepees and gathered around them as soon as they entered the camp circle.

Looking down from atop her mount at the hundreds of stern-looking Indians pushing in on them, she found herself much more breathlessly frightened than she had imagined she would be.

As if reading her mind, Connell reached over and patted her hands, taking the reins of her horse from her without protest to lead her farther into the fray.

Faith felt a bent old crone tugging on her skirt and forced a brief smile of greeting, only to be met with a toothless sneer. Most of the men, as well as the children, were nearly naked. For the most part the people were thin and muscular, with the men being taller than those few old women she could see.

In the distance, younger women watched in relative

silence, some balancing babies on their hips or packing them in cradle-boards decorated with brightly dyed porcupine quill designs. The designs looked the same as the ones on the beautiful doeskin rifle scabbard Connell treasured so.

"We should have brought gifts," he called back to Faith. "Too bad there wasn't time to at least hunt on our way here."

Her reply was thin, quavering, in spite of her brave front. "I just hope you know what you're doing."

Without comment, Connell swung down off his horse and began to make hand signals to an impressive-looking man.

Faith took him to be the chief, due to the deference everyone else was paying him and to the larger-sized teepee from which he had emerged.

The entire group of Arapaho stepped back abruptly, leaving Connell and the Indian standing alone inside a tightly packed outer circle of taciturn braves.

Faith was intensely glad she had not insisted she play the part of Connell's sister, because she couldn't have taken her eyes off him at that moment if their lives had depended upon it. He was magnificent! Standing tall and strong, he faced the Arapaho leader as an equal, showing no fear, while he made sign language with his hands.

The surrounding din was such that she couldn't hear whether he was also speaking aloud, although she assumed he must be. The bits and snatches of language she could hear in the background were foreign sounding. Some had a lilting quality that fascinated her, making the hair at the back of her neck prickle in primitive warning at the same time.

The chief finally shook Connell's hand, nodded, then made a sweeping signal with his arm. To her amazement the mob on that side of the camp divided into two halves as obediently as she imagined the Red Sea must have parted for Moses!

Connell made some apparently corresponding motions then returned to stand beside her horse and speak briefly. "Irene was here, like Ab said, but the hunters I talked to were right about her being with Black Kettle now. His camp is over that ridge to the west. We'll have to hurry. All the tribes are getting ready to start their move toward winter quarters."

Faith nodded. Connell's demeanor remained cautious and rather stilted as he mounted Rojo, adding to her already considerable nervousness. He obviously knew the chief to whom he had been talking, yet it seemed as though their relationship was not an overly friendly one in spite of his earlier references to his late wife's people.

She fell into line behind him, with Ab closely following, and they rode through the legion of braves. Waiting till they had cleared the camp, she finally gathered the courage to ask, "Is everything all right?"

"Yes," Connell said quietly aside.

"What about gifts? Don't we need to get some to ransom Irene? And what are we going to do with Ab, drag him along all the way?"

"I should have made you my sister," he muttered.

Faith was not subdued enough by his obviously disapproving tone to give up completely. "I just wondered."

Connell relented. "Ab will be staying with Black Kettle as a willing slave, if the chief will have him— by his own choice, I might add."

She frowned. "Who was that noble Indian we just left? He acted awfully important."

"He is. Chief Bull Bear was my wife's second cousin," Hawk explained, glancing back over his shoulder at the circle of teepees behind them. He was speaking softly, as if the wind might carry his words back to the chief's ears even at that great distance.

"You're considered related to him, right?" The assumption made her feel a lot safer in their present circumstances.

"I was, yes. No one was pleased when Little Rabbit Woman married a white man, but I made enough gifts to the family after our marriage to atone for her supposed sins and they ultimately accepted me as one of their own."

"Then why are you acting so uneasy?"

"Now that my wife is dead, I don't have as secure a place in the tribe as I once did."

"There's more, isn't there?" Faith asked, nudging the sorrel in the flanks to keep up.

"Yes," he said. "Bull Bear knew all about my family history. I had never mentioned having a brother, let alone a niece, so he suspects I lied about you. He's willing to overlook it for now, but there's no telling what he might do to save face if he learned the entire truth about your past, especially regarding Tucker. He hates emigrants. Wagon trains carried cholera to the plains last year. Many tribes saw half their members die of the white man's sickness."

"Oh, dear."

"My sentiments, exactly. Now, if you're through asking questions, let's make tracks."

Trembling, she reined her horse and fell in behind him, praying silently for God's guidance and strength in the trials yet to come.

Faith seldom took her eyes off Hawk's broad back until they were within sight of the second camp.

Hundreds of teepees stood in an enormous circle, their outer walls shimmering and pale beneath the blazing sun as wisps of gray smoke rose through the openings at the peaks.

Off to one side, a group of women had pegged buffalo hides to the ground and were kneeling next to them, removing the last remnants of fat with handheld scrapers of bone and antler. Nearby, little girls were pretending to be busy at the same task as they mimicked their mothers.

Faith looked over at them and smiled, remembering her own childhood and the way she'd wanted to be exactly like her mother in every way. Oh, how she wished she were a carefree child again, at home with her parents, instead of being led through hostile territory into goodness knows what kind of awful danger.

That sobering thought was enough to destroy the brief camaraderie she'd been feeling in regard to the other women and girls and make her once again assess the Indian camp with a critical eye. Many Cheyenne had lifted and tied up the skins lining the lower several feet of their teepees, apparently to take advantage of any cooling breezes. That was certainly sensible, given the weather of late.

Faith sighed. The flat, nearly treeless prairie radiated heat like an iron skillet. Without her slat bonnet or a hat of any kind, she was a helpless victim of the sun. She yearned to raise her hand, to shade her eyes so she could better observe the details of the village, but hesitated sensibly. Any untoward movement, especially one which could be construed as fear or aggression, would be very foolish. She wasn't about to do anything that might trigger an attack response. She and her companions were obviously in enough hot water already.

Ahead, Connell rode slowly into the circle of teepees, his back ramrod straight, and she followed. It was clear that their imminent arrival had been expected. Faith assumed Bull Bear must have sent word to his Cheyenne cohorts, because their little threesome was not creating nearly the furor it had in the other camp, although a few little boys did stop their stick horses and lower their play bows and arrows to watch the unusual party pass by.

Dogs of all sizes and descriptions set up an awful din, some even darting out to nip at her horse's heels, but other than that, very few Cheyenne ceased their daily labors. Nor did fierce-looking warriors seem to be gathering in the numbers she had seen in the Arapaho village.

Maybe Connell had been worried about their situation for nothing, Faith mused, trying to convince herself more than anything. Perhaps he had borrowed trouble simply because he'd felt so uncomfortable facing his former Arapaho relatives.

And maybe the reverse was true, she added with dismay as her thoughts came full circle. Given Hawk's Indian background and his awareness of her stubborn temperament, perhaps he was minimizing their danger merely to keep her from worrying or trying to help. If he felt he had a choice, would he tell her about the inherent dangers of their journey or would he hide them from her?

She knew the answer to those unsettling questions as well as she knew her own name. Hawk McClain would not have told her any details about their shared peril if he had felt there was an alternative way to govern her thoughts, words and actions.

Consequently, they were no doubt muddled in a far bigger predicament than she'd so far imagined and she wished mightily that she had not been quite so quick to figure out the truth.

The question now was, how personally risky was the trouble they were about to face? And what could she hope to do about it, unarmed as she now was—thanks to him—other than pray more fervently than she had before?

Prayer, she concluded, was a *very* good idea.

Chapter Ten

"Black Kettle is generally not warlike, but don't expect him to be as genial to us as Bull Bear," Connell warned aside, preparing Faith for their upcoming encounter.

"You're certain this is where we'll find Irene?"

"I hope so. Black Kettle bought her from the Arapaho. If he didn't turn around and sell her to another chief, she'll be here."

Faith could tell from the set of his jaw and the way his chin jutted out that he was anything but pleased to hear that his future wife had been traded like a prized horse or a bundle of bright cloth. Still, she was alive. There was that to be thankful for.

"What else did you find out?"

"Not much more," Connell said. "I do know she's unmarried, which is a surprise. Apparently she's been living with an old Arapaho medicine man. They say he's the only one who's not afraid of her magic, so Black Kettle bought them as a pair."

"Magic? What magic?"

"Your guess is as good as mine. All Bull Bear would say was that she can make the heavens sing and the earth tremble whenever she wants."

"Dear me."

"I expect I'll be invited to sit and smoke with the Cheyenne," Connell explained, reining in his horse and leaning closer to speak with her more privately. "I plan to refuse to leave you behind with Ab, but there are some rules you'll need to observe no matter what happens."

"Go on."

Her tone was so compliant, so cooperative, Connell raised one eyebrow and studied her expression for a few moments before continuing. "If Black Kettle doesn't come out to greet us in person, that means we'll be taken into the lodge to see him. Just follow my lead and you'll do fine."

Faith was trembling. "What if we're separated?"

"That's not going to happen."

"But what if it does? How will I know what to do, how to act around the Indians?"

"I can't possibly tell you everything you'd need to know in the few minutes we have left."

"Well, try," she insisted. "You'd be surprised how clear my mind is when I'm scared to death!"

Connell smiled slightly as he dismounted and circled the big gelding, patting the faithful horse's rump as he went. Approaching Faith's horse, he gathered up the reins of both mounts and handed them over to Ab for temporary safekeeping before helping her dismount.

He paused a moment to make sure she was steady on her feet before letting go, then whispered, "All right.

There are a few details which might help. Remember to always turn to the right when entering a lodge."

"Why?"

He gave her a stern look. "Do you want instruction, or not?"

"I do, I do. Go ahead. What else?"

"Once you're inside, pause and wait to be invited farther, then do whatever your host indicates. In my case, Black Kettle will probably ask me to sit on the left, which is an honor because it's the family side of the teepee. You stay to the right unless you're told otherwise."

She nodded gravely. "I understand. Go on."

"If you're moving around in there for any reason, never walk between your host and the fire, or between the fire and anyone else, for that matter. Go behind them, even if there's precious little room to pass. They'll lean forward for you."

"Okay. What else?"

He sighed, yet graced her with an amiable smile. "That's enough etiquette for now. Get that much right and you'll impress them plenty, believe me."

Directly ahead lay the largest teepee of the scores Faith could see. Its skin flap of a door was propped open by means of two straight sticks, but the outer walls were let all the way down to ground level. A tall, stalwart brave armed with a feather-bedecked lance and a round, leather shield was standing guard.

Connell received the invitation he had expected and took Faith's hand to pull her along behind him, leaving Ab outside to mind the horses and fend for himself.

Daunted, she walked softly, cautiously, recalling her

brief instructions on proper comportment and wondering what other details she should know that Connell hadn't had time or inclination to impart. Why, oh why, hadn't he used their time traveling between the Indian camps to educate her?

As her vision adjusted to the dim light she saw a dozen pairs of shadowy, narrowed eyes trained on her. In the gentile society from which she'd come, such undue attention might have made Faith embarrassed at her unkempt appearance but it wouldn't have frightened her. Here, it unhinged her almost to the point of wanting to yank free of her partner's hold and try to flee.

Connell must have sensed her distress because he said something to the gathered savages that made them laugh, then physically plunked her down on the ground near the door before proceeding to greet the chief and take a seat beside him by direct request.

Faith tucked her legs beneath her to mimic the posture and demeanor of the other women and tried to keep her ever-widening eyes demurely averted. It was impossible. Finally she gave up fighting her curiosity and settled for feigning submission while she peeked from beneath lowered lashes.

Black Kettle, Connell and several other men began to smoke a long-shanked pipe that they passed around the semicircle with great ceremony. The bowl nearly touched the ground and the long stem pointed to the sky every time a different smoker took a turn.

Far younger than she'd expected him to be, the chief was wearing a leather shirt ornamented with beads and small hanks of hair. Swallowing hard, she shuddered to think where the latter decoration might have come from!

Except for quill and bead adornments, the other braves were bare from the waist up. In spite of their inherent ferocity they were truly magnificent specimens of humanity, Faith thought, blushing, although not one was nearly as appealing looking as Hawk had been when she'd convinced him to strip off his shirt while she cut his hair.

Immediately penitent, she wondered what her prim, godly mother would say if she happened to be looking down from heaven and was able to read her elder daughter's decidedly scandalous thoughts!

The heat inside the tent was stifling compared to the outdoor temperature, not to mention the strong odors of cooking and goodness knows what all else that filled the air. Clouds of worrisome gnats buzzed around Faith's head. If the others had been paying the slightest attention to the pesky insects, she would have shooed them away. As it was, however, she was loath to move a muscle, so she sat and endured the itching, tickling flies, praying, above all, that the tiny bugs would not scoot up her nose and make her sneeze!

One of the Indian women across the tent suddenly arose and began to fill a wooden bowl with bits of roast meat from a skewer. The sight made Faith's mouth water. Food! She was so hungry she knew she could eat almost anything and be truly thankful for it.

With a respectful bow, the squaw offered the bowl to the chief, who took four small pieces of meat and raised them in his clasped hands in what Faith took to be a spiritual blessing akin to her family's habit of saying grace over a meal. The bowl was then passed to Connell and proceeded around the circle of men.

Faith waited. The food bowl never came her way. Instead, everyone was acting as if she were invisible.

Correction, she thought glumly. Not invisible. Of no importance. There was a big difference. Not that she cared one whit about the Indians' personal opinions of her. She just wished they'd feed her something—anything—before the noisy growling of her stomach disturbed the entire gathering.

Connell noticed his erstwhile niece's fidgeting and quieted her with a stern look. The woman who had offered the meat had returned to her place across the tent while a younger and much prettier squaw had been summoned and was bowing before the chief. In moments, that girl ducked out the door and disappeared.

Instinct told Faith a momentous event was about to take place. Her pulse quickened. She couldn't tell much from looking at the faces of the Indians, but Connell's expression clearly held promise. Every muscle in his body was tense.

Long minutes passed. Faith had been so intent on watching Hawk she flinched noticeably when a skinny, bent, old man limped into the teepee. He was leaning on a crutch that was nearly as gnarled as he was and in his opposite hand he carried a small leather pouch.

The old man stopped. A hush fell over the crowd. Everyone turned to look at the doorway.

There stood the most elegant woman Faith had ever seen. Her dress was of softly pliant deerskin adorned with porcupine quills and beaded fringe. The left shoulder of the short gown was loosely draped while the woman's right arm was encased in a sleeve that reached her elbow. Below the calf-length skirt, her legs were hidden by leggings and the tops of her moccasins.

The woman glided forward with the utmost grace, making no noise as she approached Connell. Faith could see from his expression that he was deeply moved. Could this regal Indian possibly be his lost love?

In moments Faith had decided that the newcomer was, indeed, Irene Wellman. The woman's native garb had confused the issue at first, as had the fact that her long, dark hair had been braided and elaborately decorated with beadwork, then wound into coils against the sides of her head, one coil over each ear.

There was little time for Faith to speculate further. The man who had preceded Irene into the teepee handed her the leather bag and stepped aside with a low bow.

Seated where she was, Faith couldn't see everything that was transpiring, but her observations of the Cheyenne told her plenty. They were clearly in awe. Some even looked frightened, although they hid the emotion well.

Irene opened the beaded pouch and reached inside. Someone coughed nervously. Caught up in the mood of the moment, Faith held her breath like everyone else. She believed in the kind of miracles that were mentioned in the Bible but not in magic. What could possibly be in that little bag that could have bamboozled so many Indians so thoroughly?

Irene raised a small, shiny object aloft in her upturned palms and murmured words that sounded a lot like a civilized, Christian prayer. The only other sound was raspy communal breathing.

Heart pounding, Faith clasped her hands together tightly and kept them in her lap, waiting along with the rest of the company for whatever was about to happen.

Suddenly, the silver object Irene held began to whir and jingle, the cacophony of sound heightened by the close confines of the teepee. Every Cheyenne present gasped, some even ducking and cowering against the tent.

The breath went out of Faith's bursting lungs in a loud whoosh of relief the moment she recognized what she was hearing. Papa had once owned a pocket watch with an alarm bell just like that! He had often delighted his daughters by setting it to go off at odd times. Until now, it had never occurred to Faith that anyone might be frightened of the pleasantly interesting sound, yet these people obviously were.

Her eyes bright, her soul comforted, Faith chanced a smile at Connell and was rewarded by the most threatening look he had ever bestowed upon her.

Immediately repentant, she lowered her glance and struggled to control her outward glee. How foolish! Of course she must not show any sign of relief or amusement. To do so might destroy the Indians' confidence in Irene's supposedly supernatural abilities and undermine her position of importance within the tribe.

Cautiously subdued, Faith peeked up at the priestess of the pocket watch long enough to ascertain that the gathered worshippers had not noticed the untoward reaction from their uninvited guest. Good. At least she hadn't jeopardized Connell's plans, whatever they might be.

Sighing, Faith noticed for the first time that she had a splitting headache, which was not at all surprising considering the fact that she hadn't eaten in longer than she could recall. Not that she would really have welcomed dinner from the communal pot the others had shared. She'd heard stories about some tribes' fondness for dog meat and she wasn't all that sure that the Cheyenne didn't partake of such atrocities. Give her a delicious rabbit stew any day.

The ridiculousness of that thought was not lost on Faith. As a child she'd made pets of all the farm animals, much to her parents' regret, and had often refused to consume nourishing food simply because she had known the main course too personally.

Customs being different for various societies, she supposed she had no real right to be shocked by anything the Indians did, any more than they would be expected to understand that the mechanical workings of a fancy pocket watch did not qualify it for deification.

Irene was lowering her arms and bowing before Black Kettle. If she had acknowledged recognizing Connell she had done it in a guileful manner hidden from Faith.

Hawk got to his feet, as did the chief. Black Kettle led the way to the door, followed by Connell, then Irene and her stooped companion.

Faith hadn't been instructed what to do next. She'd not been able to catch Connell's eye for direction either. If she hadn't seen one of his fingers crook slightly as he passed, she'd have been at a loss. Hopefully, it had been his signal to follow rather than a nervous twitch!

Her decision to bolt wasn't a hard one to make. The Cheyenne men had all filed out, but the few women remaining were staring at her as if she were the most repulsive person they had ever seen. The last thing Faith wanted was to remain there with them.

Struggling to her feet, she straightened her clothing and brushed off her skirt as if it had been clean to start with. No one spoke or stepped forward to stop her. She took a tentative step toward the door. *So far, so good.*

If she'd been visiting in the home of one of her friends back in Burg Hill she'd have known the proper way to behave. Here, she could only guess. Surely, some pleasant parting word was in order, if only to make herself feel more normal.

With a slight smile and a nod to the other women she said, "So nice of you to invite me. Sorry I can't stay and chat. Maybe next time."

Their bewildered looks widened her smile. Obviously, they hadn't expected her amiable tone of voice or polite leave-taking.

She proceeded to the door, then paused and turned. "I know you don't understand a word I'm saying, but I am grateful. I doubt anyone I know back home would have welcomed you the way you've welcomed me." The corners of her mouth lifted once again. "I just wish you smiled a little more."

To her surprise, the Cheyenne women not only smiled, they began to giggle.

* * *

Connell hoped Faith had seen his signal and was trailing along behind, as was the custom. He hadn't dared speak to her as he passed or break stride while accompanying Black Kettle on through the camp. To do so could have caused him to lose face, setting him back a long way in his negotiations to free Irene.

He'd figured from the start that he'd have to either buy her or convince the chief she was already his wife and therefore belonged to him. Now that he'd seen how important her so-called skill was to the Cheyenne, however, he suspected he'd have to rethink his plan.

If Irene had been adopted into that Cheyenne band, his task would have been much easier. As chief, Black Kettle was supposed to set an example of benevolence for his subjects, which meant he would take no personal revenge if Irene decided to run off. Moreover, the chief was wearing a scalp shirt, indicating that he bore an even bigger burden to live in peace with tribal members. Both of those elements could work to Connell's advantage as long as he didn't push his demands too far.

Above all, it was critical he find a way to be alone with Irene and learn her exact situation. Then they could work together to secure her freedom. In theory, that sounded easy. In truth, the problem was far from simple. And speaking of solving insurmountable problems, he still had Faith to worry about, too.

Connell altered his even strides just enough for a quick glance back. The sight that greeted him was so comical he nearly burst out laughing.

Black Kettle noticed and paused to look back, too. The men's eyes met in shared good humor.

"She is brave," Black Kettle said.

Nodding, Connell chuckled. "Sometimes too brave."

"The little ones like her."

"True." The plainsman laughed, incredulous. "I hope they don't tear her to shreds proving it."

As he watched, Faith struggled to make forward progress while surrounded by a gaggle of excited children, some barely big enough to walk. He could tell she was speaking to them because she kept bending down, first one way, then another, in response to a tug on her skirt or a tap on her arm. One little girl of about five was holding up a miniature cradle-board with a doll made of deer hide tucked inside.

Faith barely had time to properly admire the doll when another girl thrust a tiny brown puppy into her arms. She held it the same way the child had, like a baby, and rocked it, much to all the children's delight. When the pup started to wiggle then lunged up to lick Faith's face, the entire group burst into riotous laughter.

Eyes twinkling, smile bright, Faith's gaze met Connell's and he was struck by the fact he'd never before seen her look so happy. She was like a child, herself, a carefree girl enjoying an amusing time with friends. Had she been that lighthearted before her mother had died and she'd been forced to take charge of her fool-hardy sister? he wondered. Or had she always been the serious, overly conscientious person he'd helped at Fort Laramie?

Whichever it was, he was glad to see her smiling now. Very glad.

Chapter Eleven

Though Irene and the medicine man went on ahead, Connell and the chief waited until Faith and her playful entourage drew nearer. When the little ones stopped in deference to Black Kettle's authority, Faith did, too.

She was still holding the squirming puppy in her arms and grinning. "Sorry you had to wait," she told Connell. "I would have been here sooner but somebody made me designated babysitter and I have no idea how to quit the job!"

"They're just curious about you," Connell said. "And little wonder. They probably think you sprouted from the earth like a stalk of corn."

"Why would they think that?" His cursory glance at her muddy clothing answered the question. "Never mind. I get the idea. Do you suppose I—?" She'd been about to say *Irene,* and stopped herself in the nick of time. "I mean, would it be possible for me to clean up while we're here? I'd love to be able to wash."

"How about your ribs?" the plainsman asked. "Don't you need them wrapped again?"

"I told you before. They're fine."

"Humph. I didn't believe you the first time you gave me that story and I certainly don't believe it now. Not after the manhandling you got from Stuart."

"I'll be okay," she insisted.

Sobering, Connell turned to Black Kettle and they began to converse in Cheyenne.

When he again faced Faith he said, "We'll be given a lodge for the next two days. After that, everybody will break camp and move north to follow the buffalo for better hunting."

He waited, watching her face until he saw the full portent of his statement register. The moment she opened her mouth, he interrupted. "That's right. One lodge. Don't look so shocked. It's the custom in all the tribes. Families live and work together. In *harmony*."

"But…"

"As my niece, you will be expected to cook and clean and care for the teepee while I go out hunting with the braves." He smiled benevolently. "Actually, it's not all that different from the arrangement we had before."

"You didn't bunk in my wagon!"

"We have no choice."

"Well, I have a choice. I'm not sleeping with you!"

Standing off to one side, Black Kettle began to chuckle, then said in perfect English, "I am glad she is your kinsman, Pale Hawk. Forget what I said about making a trade. I would not have such a prickly pear if you gave her to me with a hundred fine horses."

The lodge they were assigned was on the outskirts of the village. Connell entered first and Faith followed.

In the center, directly below the vent hole at the top, a small fire smoldered. Buffalo robes lay at one end of the room, hair-side down, and folded leather parfleches filled with dried fruit and meat hung like decorated saddlebags from the slanting rafters. The only worn or soiled things in the room were the sparse trappings they'd had with them while traveling, including Connell's rifle scabbard and Grandmother Reeder's quilt.

"This place looks brand-new," Faith marveled.

"It is." He closed the door flap for more privacy. "It belongs to a newly married couple. They'll stay with relatives until we're gone."

"How unfair! We can't let them give up their home."

"We can't refuse. It would be disrespectful. The fact that we were offered this lodge shows we're highly valued guests."

"Oh." She walked slowly around the perimeter and assessed the fine handwork on the parfleches as well as the embroidery on the tent lining. "This is beautiful. Did the bride make all this?"

"Probably none of it," Connell explained. "It's customary for her mother to prepare the lodge and pitch it near her own, then furnish it just as you see it and present it as a gift. Sometimes other relatives contribute things, too, but it's the bride's mother who's in charge."

"Won't she be resentful of us? Most women would be."

"If she is she won't show it," Connell said. "One of the things the white man doesn't understand about the Indian is his sacrifices for the common good. Even though tribes make war with each other, there's very little dissension within the bands. If a man is poor or sick, the others take care of his family's needs without hesitation."

"We do the same back home," Faith argued.

"Really? After the tornado blew your house away, how many of your neighbors offered you another house, or even a bed?"

"They would have if they could have. They'd been hit hard, too. Everybody suffered terrible losses."

"I understand that," Connell said. "But out here another branch of the tribe would have brought all they owned, if necessary, and given it to you with no strings attached. In return, all you'd have been expected to do was try to get back on your feet and someday do the same for another needy neighbor."

"That's like the scripture, 'Do unto others'!"

"Exactly."

"How wonderful."

"Yes, it is. But that isn't all there is to this culture. Rules are strict. Customs can seem harsh. Even cruel. Justice is swift and deadly. Tribal life is not for the fainthearted." He looked at her tellingly. "Or a good place for a lone, unprotected woman."

"I know what you mean. So, how are we going to save Irene?"

Connell snorted. "That's a good question. One I've been asking myself ever since I saw how important she's become to the Cheyenne. I need to know more details, which is why you won't have to worry about me getting in your way tonight, Little Muddy Dove Woman."

She ignored the jest. "Why not? Where will you be?"

"Standing under a blanket in front of Irene's lodge

and waiting to properly court my future bride," he said flatly. "If she plays by the rules and comes out, she'll join me under the blanket and we can huddle together to talk privately—all night, if necessary—as long as we stay in the public view."

"What if she doesn't come out?"

"Then I may have to abduct her."

Faith couldn't help the catch in her breath. "Isn't that dangerous?"

"Not for Irene and me. Even if Black Kettle weren't the chief, he's wearing a scalp shirt. Both dictate his code of conduct. If he came after us he'd be breaking a taboo and proving he's not worthy to remain chief." The plainsman's brow furrowed. "But that doesn't prevent him from getting even another way. You and Ab might have to pay dearly if I left you behind."

"You wouldn't!" she blurted, immediately penitent when she saw the hurt in his eyes. Her voice gentled. "No, of course you wouldn't. I know that. And I'll do whatever I can to help you free your beloved Irene. I promise."

Without a word, Connell nodded, turned and walked out.

In minutes, a girl of about fifteen arrived bringing food, water and a soft, pale deerskin shift. Faith had never been so thrilled to receive new clothes in her entire life. She slipped out of her dress, unwound the chafing muslin strips that circled her torso, and gladly donned the native attire over her bloomers.

The girl showed her how to wrap and tie the leggings she'd brought, then lace moccasins over them.

The completed outfit was comfortable beyond belief. Faith stepped back and twirled to show off the dress.

"Oh, thank you! I love this."

Her words were heartfelt and simple, yet clearly not understood, so she smiled and patted the teenager's hand in a motherly fashion.

Acting shy, the girl held up a small rope.

Faith took it and looked down at her garb. Nothing seemed to be missing. "What's this for?" She chuckled at her own silliness. "Never mind. Of course you can't tell me." Holding it out, she asked, "Show me?"

The Indian girl gestured to her waist, then made a tying motion, so Faith knotted the rope around her dress like a belt, much to her companion's muted glee.

Shaking her head and covering her smile, the girl went to work on Faith's hair with a wide-toothed comb, eventually making long braids, leaving them loose instead of rolling them as Irene's had been. She then led her to the food she'd brought and presented it proudly, using hand signals to urge her to eat.

Faith was so intent on devouring the dried fruit and stringy meat she didn't even bother to protest when the Indian girl gathered her ruined calico into a bundle and ran from the lodge with it.

At dusk, Connell waited patiently outside the door to Irene's teepee. A blanket was draped across his shoulders in spite of the continuing heat.

To his consternation, he wasn't her only suitor. A muscular brave who looked to be about twenty-five, had come to stand beside him. The enmity in the Indian's eyes was as sharp as an arrow point and as menacing as the fangs of a prairie rattlesnake.

Connell's only advantage was that he had arrived before the brave and was therefore closest to the teepee door. If Irene stuck to Cheyenne custom, she would speak to him first, perhaps ignoring the other man entirely. In that case, Connell knew he'd best not turn his back on his rival unless he wanted his hair parted with a war club.

He could hear Irene inside the lodge. She was talking to the old medicine man in a mixture of Cheyenne and Arapaho. Pleased at the sound of her familiar voice, Connell listened. It seemed strange to hear her speaking languages other than English, but he was proud that she'd become so accomplished. Some prisoners never even tried to understand their captors, let alone learned from them.

Neither man moved a muscle when the old Arapaho appeared at the teepee door, paused to tell Irene he was going off for a quiet smoke, then limped away.

Tense, Connell waited for her to come out. Seconds seemed to tick by very slowly. *Like a pocket watch in need of winding,* he reflected. His heart swelled with gratitude that Irene had had her amazing watch with her when she'd been kidnapped, and that she'd had the intelligence to use it to such good advantage.

He could only think of one other woman who would have done as well, and that woman was Faith Beal. Except that Faith would probably have talked too much or acted stubborn and gotten herself into a worse pickle, Connell thought, smiling to himself. She was quite a woman. Unique. With a heart as big as the prairie and courage that would put many a man to shame.

His musings came full circle and his gut gave a twist. Irene was his betrothed, not Faith. Irene should be first in his heart even if they were both merely honoring an old promise rather than being madly in love, so why did he keep thinking of Faith with so much affection? And why had no other woman ever stirred such fervor within him? *Not even Little Rabbit Woman.*

As if summoned by his turbulent thoughts, Irene Wellman left the confines of her lodge to face her suitors.

Connell lifted the front edge of his blanket. So did the brave standing close by.

She hesitated, looking from man to man, and raised her hand toward Connell, palm out, as if urging patience. To his total astonishment, she then stepped into the arms of the Cheyenne brave!

Connell froze. Had his worst fears been confirmed? Was he going to have to resort to the same kind of warlike tactics that had put her in the Indian camp in the first place? He strained to hear what she and the brave were saying, but their words were muffled beneath the wrapped-around blanket. All he could hope at this point was that she'd give him a chance to talk to her, too.

A tug on his buckskin distracted him momentarily. He looked down to see who had had the audacity to break into a courtship ritual. The most unlikely Indian he'd ever seen was grinning up at him.

"Thank goodness I finally found you," Faith said.

Connell scowled. "I should have known. What are you doing here?"

"Looking for you, mostly." She pivoted to display her dress for him. "A sweet girl brought me this. Isn't it wonderful? And so comfortable. Even my sore ribs feel better. She fixed my hair and fed me, too."

He was eyeing her costume. "Who dressed you?"

"The same girl. She didn't understand a word I said and I didn't understand her, either, but we managed just fine."

One corner of his mouth twitched in a repressed smile. "Not entirely."

"What do you mean?"

"Irene can explain it to you," he said, cocking his head toward the blanket where the two still stood, wrapped together from the waist up. "When she's done with him."

Faith lowered her voice. "That's her? Under there?"

He nodded. "Why don't you go into her lodge and wait for us. There's nobody else home right now so it's perfectly safe."

"Are you sure?"

"Positive." He allowed his smile to spread. "I'm sure glad I already warned the tribal council you were crazy in the head."

"Why?"

"Never mind. Just get inside, out of sight, and wait for me."

Faith faced him, hands fisted on her hips, and pressed her lips into a stubborn line. "No. I'm not going anywhere till you tell me what's so funny."

"You won't like it."

"Try me."

"Let's just say, as your *uncle,* I'm disappointed in your upbringing and leave it at that."

"Oh, no," she said, shaking her head. "Talking in riddles won't get you off. I intend to know what's going on around here or else—even if I can't speak the language."

"Okay," Connell drawled, "but remember, I didn't want to do this. You asked for it."

Pausing for effect, he smiled and added, "Little Dove Woman, I regret to inform you…you've tied your chastity belt on the outside of your clothes."

Mortified, Faith had immediately wheeled and run for the privacy of Irene's teepee, fumbling to untie the rope as she went.

Although she'd now had hours to examine the knotted cords more closely, she still couldn't visualize how they were supposed to be applied or what good they'd do.

Her cheeks flamed. No wonder the Indian girl had giggled and looked so embarrassed when she'd mistaken the rigging for a sash!

In retrospect, she felt slightly vindicated, however. Never in all her reading or listening to tales of fellow pilgrims had she heard even a whisper about Indian women wearing such things. On the contrary, more than one emigrant had sworn that promiscuity was the norm for the tribes of the plains.

Was it? Were the Cheyenne that different from all the rest? If so, they must have a terrible time adjusting to living and working beside other groups. No wonder so many of them fought amongst themselves as well as against white men.

With neither pockets nor a reticule in which to hide her humiliating error, Faith wadded the string girdle into a ball and stuffed it beneath the edge of a buffalo robe, then sat down on the robe to wait for Irene and Connell.

The soft background hum of the camp blended into a slumberous blur. Weariness encroached on her mind, urging much-needed rest. She gave in only enough to lie back on the soft skins, fully intending to remain awake. Her lids grew heavy, her aching body finding the respite it so desperately craved.

The next thing she knew, the rumble of Connell's voice was pulling her back from a dreamless sleep.

"She's game," he said.

A woman answered. "Young."

"Yes. And all alone, thanks to Ramsey Tucker."

"We must take her with us."

"I was hoping you'd say that. I've already promised to escort her to California."

Connell came across the room and stopped. Faith could sense him standing over her. She tried to keep totally still, but a flutter of her lashes gave her away.

"I think she's awake," the woman said.

"Yes, I am." Faith opened her eyes and sat up with a yawn and a languid stretch. "Sorry. I didn't mean to doze. It's been a long day." She smiled up at her companions. "Actually, the last couple of months seem like a lifetime."

The woman smiled sweetly. "It is easy to lose track of time out here, even if you have a pocket watch." She offered her hand. "I'm Irene Wellman. Connell tells me your name is Faith Beal."

"Yes. It's an honor to meet you, Miss Wellman. I've heard a lot about you."

"Please, call me Irene." Grasping Faith's outstretched hand, the older woman pulled her to her feet. "How would you like to sleep here with me, tonight?"

A terrible weight lifted from Faith's conscience. "Oh, could I? I don't know all the rules and I'm so afraid I'll make another dreadful mistake if I don't have a woman to ask for advice."

Irene looked puzzled. "Advice about what?"

"Everything!" she interjected, hoping and praying that Connell would be gentleman enough to refrain from explaining her most recent cause for embarrassment. It was bad enough that he'd noticed the belt in the first place. Bringing it to her attention in public like that was an inexcusable breach of etiquette.

Faith's cheeks burned as if she'd just spent another week under the scorching sun without her bonnet. Yes, she knew she'd pressed him, even threatened him, but that didn't mean he'd had to *listen* to her.

"I think I'd better be going," Connell said with a low chuckle, "and let you ladies talk privately."

"What about the old man? Where's he?" Faith asked.

"Walks With Tree is going to stay in Connell's lodge. It's all been arranged. You and I will have this one all to ourselves."

"Praise the Lord!"

Irene laid a hand lightly on Faith's arm. "It would be best if you didn't mention our God quite so loudly. The Cheyenne are tolerant of other people's beliefs, but this teepee is considered sacred because I keep the watch in here most of the time. I have to be very careful."

"Sorry." Faith pulled a face. "That's what I mean. I need advice. *Lots* of it."

"My pleasure."

In the background, Connell huffed with derision. "I hope she takes directions from you better than she has from me. Little Muddy Dove Woman can be as hard-headed as a bull buffalo."

Laughing, Irene repeated the Indian name, then asked Connell, "What made you call her that?"

Faith answered instead, rather than give him the chance to explain that her ruined reputation on the wagon train had been the initial reason for the nick-name. "And mud seems to follow me wherever I go. I washed up, but I'm afraid my hair is far from clean."

"I'll help you work on that."

"Oh, would you! That's wonderful."

Irene glanced at Connell. "Weren't you leaving?"

"I sure was. When two women start to sound off like a gaggle of geese I'd just as soon skedaddle."

Raising his hands, he ceremoniously folded his arms across his chest, each fist coming to rest at the point of the opposite shoulder. All teasing ended, he bowed slightly and said, "Good night," before ducking out the door.

Faith's breath caught. No one had to tell her that the sign he had made in parting was one of affection. Its meaning had been evident, both from his manner and his expression when he'd looked at Irene.

I was right here, too, Faith's pride insisted. *He could have meant it for me, as well.*

She would have loved to convince herself of that but she knew she was only making believe, just like the Indian children who had pretended that darling puppy was a real baby. Connell belonged to Irene and Irene belonged to Connell. End of story. Except…

Faith looked over at her doeskin-clad hostess. "Can I ask you a personal question?"

"Of course. You and I should have no secrets."

She steeled herself for the disavowal she was certain would come. "Who was that man out there under the blanket with you?"

"Ah. That was Red Deer." Irene's eyes misted. She sighed. "I will miss him terribly. He and I were planning to be married as soon as the first snow fell. He loves me—in spite of the fact that I'm almost seven years his senior."

Faith could hardly believe her ears. "Married? What about your promise to Connell?"

"I'd been assured he was dead. I thought I'd never see him again," Irene said sadly. "Ramsey lied to me about that, too."

"Perfidy seems to be his keenest skill."

"So I've learned." She mellowed noticeably. "Connell is amazing, isn't he? Imagine him locating me after all that's happened. When my so-called husband tried to do away with me, I should have presumed Connell was still alive and would keep searching till he found me. He was always very tenacious, even as a boy."

"How long have you known him?"

The older woman signed. "Forever. Our families were neighbors when we were children. After Connell's mother died, he and his father argued all the time. His father used to get drunk and beat him terribly. He ran away several times and came to our house for refuge. I think he was about thirteen and I was nearly seventeen when we pledged our troth."

"That's a long, long time ago," Faith offered innocently.

Irene smiled. "Not *that* long."

"I'm sorry. I didn't mean to imply you were old. It's just that when I think about my life when Mama was alive, it seems like years and years have passed."

"How long have you been on your own?"

"About three months. I've kind of lost track since I left the wagon train."

"Connell says your sister is still with the Tucker train."

Faith made a sour face. "Unfortunately. She told Connell she'd married the captain. There's nothing I can do for her as long as she insists on believing Ramsey Tucker's lies instead of listening to her own kin."

"How about you? Is there no special boy waiting back home for you?"

"I shall never marry," Faith insisted, thrusting out her chin for emphasis.

Irene merely laughed. "We'll see about that, Little Dove Woman. I hear there are many lonesome men in California yearning for a good wife."

"Well, it won't be me. I've learned plenty since I left Ohio. Men can be nasty and cruel. Look at Tucker. And Ab. And Stuart. Mr. Ledbetter was nice, but I couldn't even count on him for help when I needed it. I want nothing to do with the likes of any of them."

"Not all men are so unfeeling," Irene cautioned. "For

instance, I happen to know that Connell admires you greatly."

"He does?" Faith's heart leaped like a frightened jackrabbit and landed in her throat.

"Yes. And I'm sure that if you can't find your father, Connell will be happy to take his place and make sure you get a good, honest, hardworking husband."

Faith's jaw dropped. If she could have thought of anything to say in reply that didn't sound unkind or ungrateful, she would have spoken. Unfortunately, assailed by such conflicting emotions, she had no adequate words to express her consternation.

Instead, she bit her tongue and prayed silently for God's forgiveness for the thoughts whirling wildly through her mind. It wasn't Irene's fault that they were all victims of such a complicated dilemma. Blame lay at Ramsey Tucker's door. Faith knew that.

She was also positive that whatever Connell's eventual place in her life became, she would never be able to see him as anything like a father figure. Never.

Chapter Twelve

Morning in the Cheyenne camp came early. It seemed as if Faith had barely closed her eyes when she heard Connell in conversation outside Irene's teepee. He was probably speaking in Cheyenne, although it could just as easily have been Arapaho or any of the other odd languages she'd heard of late and she'd not have known the difference.

The timbre of his voice sent shivers dancing over her skin and skittering up her spine to tickle the fine hairs at the back of her neck. After the conversation she and Irene had had the previous night, she was even more confused. Faith didn't know exactly what she wanted Connell McClain to be to her, now or in the future, but she was certain she didn't need another daddy. Or an uncle, for that matter.

Then what? she asked herself. What was he? Rescuer? Friend? Cohort? Boon companion? Her guardian in buckskins? He had been all that…and more. When she looked at him her heart raced. The sound of his voice made her tremble. Mere thoughts of his gentle touch stole her breath away and left her yearning to seek him out, to be near him once again.

"Foolish, foolish, foolish," Faith muttered, disgusted with the flight of fancy her imagination had taken. It was one thing to appreciate the big plainsman as a heaven-sent blessing, yet quite another to let her thoughts imbue him with characteristics beyond the norm. He was simply a man.

Ah, she mused, *but he is so much more!*

"And I am crazy," she grumbled as she got to her feet. *"Lock me up in the woodshed and hide the ax crazy."*

From the doorway Connell said pleasantly, "If you say so."

Faith jumped. "Oh! You startled me."

"Sorry. I heard you talking and I was afraid Walks With Tree had sneaked past me."

She quickly scanned the empty lodge. "No. I'm alone. I was having an argument with myself."

"Oh? Who won?" he teased.

"I did, of course." Faith couldn't help grinning at him. "I couldn't hardly lose, given the lack of an intelligent adversary."

That candid observation made Connell laugh aloud and shake his head. "Has anybody ever told you how naturally funny you are?"

"Not as a compliment."

"Well, consider this to be one. If I wasn't so worried about our current situation you'd have me in stitches all the time."

"Thanks. I think."

"You're quite welcome." He stepped back while

holding open the door flap. "Come on. We're having a powwow in my lodge. I'd like you to be there."

Faith followed his orders without hesitation and fell into step beside him. "Will Irene be there, too?"

"Of course. She's waiting for us. We'll need her help if we expect to get out of this mess and keep our hair."

Scurrying to keep pace with his much longer strides, she made a sour face. "That sounds awful."

"Sorry. I didn't think. I'll try not to be so blunt."

"No, no," she said, laying a hand lightly on his arm. "I don't want to be coddled. I'm a part of all this and I need to know everything, just like the rest of you do."

"You're sure?"

"Positive. In spite of what everybody seems to think, I'm not a child. I'm a grown woman."

The muscles of his arm flexed beneath her fingers as he said, "I'm more than aware of that, believe me."

"All I have to contribute is Rojo," Connell told the group, "but if I have to give him up, I will. Black Kettle had never seen a canelo before. I know he fancies the red color."

Faith had folded her grandmother's quilt into a small bundle and was sitting on it instead of the buffalo robe. "I wish I still had the money Anna Morse gave me so I could donate something," she said, "but it's with Charity in our wagon."

Both Connell and Ab shook their heads. The plainsman explained. "Out here, the best currency is on the hoof. A swift, sure-footed horse can carry a hunter after buffalo or a warrior after his enemies. It's worth its weight in gold."

"That's right," Irene said. "Horses are used as a dowry, or payment of a debt, or as a reward for heroism…lots of things. A husband even has to give one to his mother-in-law if he wants to talk to her face-to-face. She can't even go visit her daughter unless she's sure her son-in-law is not at home."

Connell smirked, "Now that's a habit a lot of men would like to see spread to every culture."

"Very funny," Faith countered, making a face. "That rule was obviously made by men."

"Perhaps," Irene said. "But in many ways our women have more rights than you do. For instance, the horses given to a bride's father by her husband-to-be become her property and the whole herd stays with her even if the marriage breaks up. She also remains within her own tribe and he joins that one, instead of the other way around."

"Oh, my." Faith was surprised to hear the older woman seem to identify so closely with the Indians, but since no one else had noticed that Irene had referred to the Indians as "our" women, she made no comment. *Poor Irene.* It was getting easier and easier for Faith to push aside any niggling envy and feel sorry for her. After all, the woman had loved Connell and believed he was dead, then married a skunk like Tucker and almost lost her life because of it.

Being sold into slavery to the Arapaho or traded to the Cheyenne sounded like solace after having endured all that other grief.

Except what about Red Deer? Faith added, keeping her thoughts to herself while the others continued to discuss various options relating to barter with Black Kettle. How sad it was that Irene had found true love, only to be forced to abandon it. Still, she had been reunited with her betrothed. Some women never had even one chance at happiness, yet here was Irene, so blessed with men who loved her that her heart was torn between them!

I will not be jealous, Faith insisted. *I will not covet her good fortune.*

Furious at the difficulty she was having living up to those noble declarations, she felt like stamping her foot and shouting, *I won't, I won't, I won't.*

How adult. How ladylike. How stupid, she told herself wisely. The others were never going to accept her as their equal unless she took control of her emotions. It was high time to stop thinking with her heart and start relying upon her wits again.

It would also help her mature image if she quit running around with her Cheyenne garb tied around her waist, she added, blushing. Now that Irene had explained how the knotted cord was supposed to be tied and that its presence was more symbolic than functional, it was easy to see what the Indian girl had been trying to explain with her confusing hand signals.

Lost in thought, Faith worried a loose thread in the quilt hem with nervous fingers. Every time she recalled her encounter with Connell from the previous evening she was mortified all over again. If she lived to be a hundred years old, she didn't think she'd *ever* be more embarrassed than she had been the moment she'd fully comprehended her openly scandalous error.

* * *

No one asked Faith's opinion during the impromptu powwow so she offered none. When the group broke up and Connell left to meet with Black Kettle, she was the only one who chose to remain in the teepee to wait for him.

Upon his return his countenance was grim. She managed to allow him a few moments of peace before her curiosity and impatience got the better of her and she blurted out the questions that had been nagging her.

"Well? Did you make the trade? Can we leave soon?"

"Yes, I've arranged for Irene's freedom. And, no, we can't leave right away."

"Why not?" Faith's imagination immediately saw many possible scenarios—all of them bad.

"Because Black Kettle wants to hold a special feast in our honor."

Her breath left in a whoosh of relief. "Oh, is that all? When?"

"Tonight. That's when the exchange will take place and Irene will confer her supposed spiritual powers on Walks With Tree."

"Can he be trusted?"

"As long as he sees an advantage for himself, yes."

"What if he pretends to go along with your plan, then changes his mind and tells Black Kettle the truth?"

Connell regarded her with concern. "He won't."

"But what if he does?"

"Let's worry about the things we can control and leave the other stuff to the Good Lord, okay?" He stopped looking so somber and smiled encouragingly. "If you want to help, I suggest you spend the afternoon praying that our plan works and that nobody gets hurt in the process."

She pulled a disgusted face. "Maybe you should do the praying for both of us. I'm afraid God isn't very happy with me right now."

"Oh no? What terrible sin have you committed, Little Dove Woman?"

"I keep breaking a commandment and I can't help myself."

"I find that hard to believe." There was growing mirth in his eyes, in the lopsided quirk of his mouth.

"Don't make fun of me."

When he came closer and laid his hands lightly on her shoulders, Faith felt his controlled strength, the warmth of his palms, and imagined that he caressed the strip of bare skin where her Cheyenne dress had left the curve of one shoulder exposed.

Surely, he couldn't have done so. Connell loved Irene. They were still promised to each other. Faith looked up into his smoky-colored eyes and saw them glistening.

"I would never make fun of you," he said earnestly, quietly. "Never."

At that moment, if he had asked her what sin she was battling, she could not have kept from confessing her covetousness. To her relief, he didn't press for an explanation.

Instead, he said, "I'm sure God understands what's in your heart, Faith. You want to do the right thing. But you're human. We all make mistakes. God's grace and forgiveness take care of that."

"Only if we repent and stop doing the same thing over and over," she said in a hushed voice.

Connell drew her into his embrace. "It'll be all right. You'll see. You'll feel much better when you're back with Charity and we find your father."

The moment he'd pulled her close, Faith's arms had slipped around his waist as naturally as if they'd done the same thing a thousand times.

Clinging to Connell, drawing on his strength, she listened to his heart pound in unison with her own racing pulse. Truth to tell, if he hadn't brought up her estranged family she wouldn't have thought of them at all. Not now. Now when she was so dizzy with excitement, so taken with his nearness, that there was no room in her consciousness for anybody or anything but him.

Could she *love* him? she wondered in awe. Was that what these turbulent feelings were?

Why not? her conscience answered. Of course she cared for Hawk. It was perfectly normal to be grateful for all he'd done and all he'd promised to do when they finally got to California. She'd be lost without him, both literally and figuratively, and when the time eventually came to part, she was going to miss him terribly. The thought of never seeing him again brought unshed tears.

Long minutes passed in silence. When he finally did ease his hold on her, Faith was reluctant to let go.

Connell once again grasped her shoulders, but this time it was to put her away from himself and say, "I'm sorry. I shouldn't have done that."

"I didn't mind. Really."

"Still, it was wrong. It won't happen again."

The fact that he was obviously determined to keep

that vow was underscored by the squaring of his shoulders, the jut of his chin.

Faith's pride reared up and took control of her tongue before she could stop it. "Fine. Don't touch me. Don't even act like my friend if it pains you so. Just get me out of this horrible camp, point me toward California and forget about me. I can look after myself."

Taken aback, Connell scowled down at her. "Who put the burr under your saddle?"

To her utter dismay her lower lip began to quiver. "Nobody. Go away. Leave me alone."

Instead, he reached out and gently cupped her cheek. "I won't desert you, even if you try to get rid of me. Don't cry."

"I'm not crying," she insisted.

His large thumb intercepted a tear on her cheek and whisked it away. Then, with a hoarse groan he once again pulled her close. Holding her as if he never intended to let go, he laid his cheek against her hair and murmured, "I'll keep you safe, Little Dove. I swear it."

Touched by his sincerity and warmed all the way to her soul, Faith was about to answer when he whispered one more thing just before he broke away and strode quickly from the lodge.

She couldn't be certain, but she thought he'd said, "Even from myself."

Chapter Thirteen

Faith didn't see Connell again until evening. The day had seemed endless. Bored, lonely and growing more fidgety by the hour, she'd thought of offering to help the Cheyenne women with their chores. If they'd seemed more amiable when she'd approached them she might have tried.

Some of the young warriors, however, were a different story. They'd acted much *too* friendly when she'd left the meeting lodge and started to walk back across the encampment toward Irene's teepee. Rather than stir up more trouble, Faith had decided to be discreet and had reversed direction, determined to stay out of sight until Connell called for her.

Several shy little girls had peeked in at her by getting down on their knees and peering under the raised outer edges of the teepee. Then they'd run away giggling when Faith had tried to talk to them. Other than that, and the occasional passage of a rangy dog, she'd remained totally isolated for the rest of the day.

Shadows lengthened. A cooling breeze wafted beneath the vented skirts of the teepee, bringing Faith welcome respite from the stifling heat. Outside, the camp was coming alive. People called to each other, women sang, children shouted, and somewhere not far-off somebody was playing a flute.

The sound of passing hoofbeats drew her to the door. She moved the edge of the flap just enough to see out. Several mounted Cheyenne were driving fresh horses into the circle and exchanging them for ones that had been staked in front of various teepees during the day. The men rode in such harmony with their horses it was as if they and the animal were a single entity. Little wonder the U.S. Cavalry had found the Plains Indians to be such formidable foes.

Though weary from relentless pacing, Faith couldn't force herself to rest. She'd been almost ready to throw caution to the winds and make a mad dash for Irene's when Connell finally appeared. He ducked inside and let the door flap fall closed.

"Oh, thank goodness! I thought everyone had forgotten me," she said, hurrying toward him.

His raised hand stopped her. "Simmer down. I just came to check on you and tell you to stay put. I'll send for you later. When it's safe."

"Safe? Here? How can any of us be safe in this camp? You should have seen the way those Indians leered at me when I tried to go find Irene!"

"You went out? By yourself?" He muttered an unintelligible expletive. "No wonder."

Faith was sorry he was upset, but she wasn't willing to accept the blame for his foul mood. "You never told me to stay inside," she argued. "As a matter of fact, you didn't bother to tell me anything before you went off and left me. What was I supposed to do? Sit here and twiddle my thumbs all day?"

"It would have been preferable to attracting attention. Have you looked outside our door lately?"

"I watched a herd of horses go by about half an hour ago," she said with a scowl and a glance past his shoulder. "Why? What's out there now?"

"A Cheyenne with a flute. Didn't you hear him playing?"

"I heard some unusual music. Is that important?"

"To him it is. The flute and the special tune come from a medicine man. Hearing it is supposed to make you fall in love with whoever plays it."

"Me?" Eyes wide, she gaped at Connell. "That Indian expects me to fall in love with him?"

"He sure does."

"Oh, dear. What should I do?"

"Well, for starters, don't get close enough for him to throw his blanket over you. If you do, he'll take it as a sign you're willing to be courted."

"You mean like Red Deer and Irene?" The moment the words were out of her mouth, Faith rued them, wished she could call them back, but the damage had been done.

She saw Connell's jaw clench, his spine grow rigid. "No," he said. "Like Red Deer and Singing Sun Woman."

"Who's that?"

"That's the name the Arapaho gave Irene. After tonight she'll become Irene Wellman again and Singing Sun Woman will cease to exist."

Faith wasn't so sure. It seemed inconceivable that Irene could just forget the past year and go back to being the same person she'd been before coming to live with the Indians. A lot more had changed than just her name. And speaking of her name…

"I can see why they'd think the watch was singing, but how did they come up with the sun part?" Faith asked.

"The pocket watch has a gold case. Maybe it looked like the sun to them."

"That makes sense." Puzzled, she thought of the few descriptive Indian names she knew. "What about Walks With Tree? Did they call him that because he was born crippled and needed a wooden crutch?"

"Probably not. Children aren't given permanent names when they're little. Sometimes they do something special to earn their adult name. Other times they'll be presented a name as a gift. An older warrior may admire a younger man and give away his own good name as a kind of blessing."

"Wouldn't that get confusing? Two people would have the same name?"

"It doesn't work like that. Once a name is given away it's treated like any other gift. The one who had the name before chooses a different new one for himself."

"Gracious. I'd be totally befuddled."

"Not if you were used to it."

"I will never get used to all this," she said, sweeping her arm in an arc that took in the whole teepee. "How much longer must we stay here?"

"We'll leave tomorrow," he said. Then he smiled

slightly and added, "Unless you go wandering again and get yourself engaged to be married before morning."

When the same girl who had brought her clothes and food the previous evening returned, Faith was so glad to see a familiar face she felt like hugging her. How she wished the young woman spoke English so she could properly thank her for her kindness. Still, she reasoned, there were some emotions that lent themselves well to pantomime, graciousness being one of them.

Faith grinned as she reached for the girl's hand and said, "I'm so glad to see you again." Genuine tears of thanksgiving misted her vision. "I'm going to be leaving soon. I want to thank you for letting me wear your beautiful dress."

The girl tried to pull away. Faith resisted. "Don't be frightened. I want to be your friend." A barely perceptible hesitation on the girl's part encouraged her. "That's right. Friend," Faith repeated.

She let go to use both hands for gesturing, sweeping her hands from herself to the other and back again while continuing to nod and smile. "Friends. You and me. Good friends. Yes?"

The girl finally nodded.

Faith was thrilled to have spanned their language barrier, however minimally. She pointed to her own chest and said, "Little Dove Woman," then gestured toward her companion, eyebrows raised questioningly.

The Cheyenne said something in her own language, then translated it. In English it became, "Spotted Fawn Woman."

Feeling like a teacher who had just broken through

to a difficult student, Faith could tell her companion was as proud of their progress as she was. Encouraged, she caught up folds of her soft deerskin dress as if about to curtsy and tried again to make herself understood. "My dress? Where is my dress?"

Spotted Fawn shook her head and took a cautious step backward.

"It's okay," Faith cajoled. "Don't go. You can give it to me later."

Again came the shake of the girl's head, this time a lot more insistently and accompanied by a wave of her hands.

Faith frowned. "What's wrong? I don't know what you're trying to tell me."

Whirling, the young Cheyenne made a dash for the door, only to be stopped by running into Connell's broad chest with a dull thump.

He caught her neatly. Held her fast. His gaze shot to where Faith stood. "What's going on?"

"I don't know. I thought we were becoming friends, then she suddenly got upset and tried to run away."

He spoke calmly to the girl. Her answer made him smile. "She thinks you want your old dress back."

"I do." Faith continued to scowl. "I'll need it to wear when we leave here."

"That's not how this works," he explained carefully. "Spotted Fawn Woman offered you the best she had. When you accepted it, you agreed to a trade."

"She wants my old calico? It's a mess."

"Is it the best you had?"

"It's *all* I had," Faith said.

"Then she's happy with it. If you insist on trading

back you'll be insulting her skill. She made what you're wearing with her own hands. It probably took months of her spare time just to do the beadwork."

"Tell her it's the most beautiful thing I've ever owned and I wouldn't dream of parting with it." Faith spoke to Connell, but her tender regard rested on the Indian girl. "I'll treasure it always. And please say I wish I had something better, something prettier to give to her besides my old dress."

Watching closely, Faith could tell when he'd conveyed the full message because Spotted Fawn's expression softened and her winning smile returned.

"You do have one other thing," Connell reminded her. "The quilt."

For an instant Faith's heart rebelled. Then she got control of her selfish desire to keep her grandmother's handiwork and nodded at Connell. "You're right. That will be perfect. I'll get it."

Lovingly displaying the quilt in her outstretched arms, Faith presented it to the younger woman. "Tell her I want her to have it," she said sincerely. "To go with the dress."

He spoke, then said, "She wants to give you something else in return."

"No. This outfit is already an unfair trade. We don't know what's ahead for us. Anything could happen. I'd like to know my grandmother's quilt is safe and treasured, as it should be."

Tears sprang to Spotted Fawn's eyes when Connell translated the presentation of the gift. That emotional reaction was all the thanks, all the confirmation, Faith wanted or needed.

It was wonderful to be so positive she was doing the right thing for a change. She knew there was a time, not long ago, when she would have clung to her last possession, seeing it as the most important element in her life. Yet, now that she'd been stripped of every concrete tie to her past, she felt liberated.

Faith's eyes also filled with unshed tears when the girl accepted the quilt and clasped it close to her heart as if it were the most precious gift she'd ever received. Giving it was certainly the most rewarding thing Faith had ever done.

Being able to part with the quilt and be truly glad to have given it away felt like a direct answer to her prayers for deliverance from covetousness. Seeing how happy she'd made the girl doubled Faith's blessing and she silently thanked the Lord that she'd been allowed to atone for her sins so perfectly. So conclusively.

This is going to be the first of many more selfless decisions I make, she told herself proudly, *beginning with not being jealous of Connell's relationship with Irene anymore.*

To her consternation, that thought doused her jubilance like a bucket of water poured over a roaring campfire. Though a remnant of joy remained, it was overshadowed by a sense of loss that was just like the way Faith had felt when she'd realized she was going to have to put aside her own desires and leave the place she loved in order to keep the promise she'd made to her mother.

This recent promise to eschew jealousy was even more binding, she realized with chagrin. It had been part of a prayer, so it was a vow directly to God.

Faith was still scuffling with her inner self over that judicious reasoning when Connell said, "That was a real nice thing to do. I'm proud of you, Little Dove Woman."

She huffed in self-deprecation. "You'd best keep calling me a dirty dove for a while longer. I haven't quite got the hang of keeping my thoughts pure yet."

The surprised look on his face was bad enough. Watching him erupt into laughter a few moments later was worse.

"I think you'll do just as you are," he said when he finally stopped chuckling enough to speak.

"Ha!" Faith made a face, said aside, "I hope the Good Lord agrees with you. Somehow, I doubt it."

Before she left the lodge, Spotted Fawn Woman carefully combed and braided Faith's thick, dark hair once again, this time also rolling the plaits into spirals, one on each side of her head, and fastening them there with leather thongs trimmed in beads and small, colored feathers. It wasn't until the girl was leaving with the quilt that Faith realized she had stripped the decorations she'd used from her own hair.

Standing alone in the center of the teepee, every nerve in her body taut, Faith listened. She could only imagine what was going on outside. Most of the individual calling and conversing had died down. Chanting and the syncopated beating of drums had taken their place. Everything vibrated in unison, as if the camp itself contained a living, throbbing, human heart.

Instead of the noises lulling her, as before, this cacophony raised gooseflesh. Where was Connell? He'd promised to return for her as soon as he could. Suppose something awful had happened to him? Suppose he'd been hurt? Attacked? Even killed! That notion was enough to spur her into action.

"If he's not back by the time I count to a thousand I'm going to find him," she muttered. "One, two, three…"

The tent flap swung back. Faith gasped, then took a ragged breath of relief. It was Connell.

"Thank heavens! Where have you been?"

"Busy," he said. His glance traveled over her from head to toe and back again. "I wish you didn't look quite so pretty tonight."

"Thanks, I think. Would you like me to rub some mud on my face again?"

"Too late for that." Turning, he started through the door. "Follow me. And don't say a word. Is that clear?"

"Of course, but—"

He stopped only long enough to scowl down at her and say, "Hush. If you don't do one other thing I tell you the rest of the way to California, do *this*. Understand?"

Faith nodded solemnly, lowered her eyes and fell into place behind him like the subservient person she was supposed to be.

It was not his plea for silence that made her comply, it was the glitter of warning in his stare, the threat of menace underlying his tone.

She didn't think for a minute that Connell would harm her if she disobeyed.

But what the Cheyenne might do if they discovered

Irene's subterfuge in displaying the so-called magic of the watch was quite another matter. One Faith didn't even want to consider.

Chapter Fourteen

Flames from the communal fire in the center of the camp bathed the gathered throng in a shimmering aura. The aroma of roasted meat mingled with more earthy odors, swirling toward the heavens in smoky eddies that both tantalized and repulsed Faith.

Connell must have sensed her uneasiness, because he glanced back to tell her, "You're doing fine. We're almost there."

In passing, Faith was able to pick out Spotted Fawn among the dancers primarily because the girl had the familiar quilt draped over her shoulders. Trancelike, the Cheyenne followed one another around the fire with a shuffling, bobbing gait, paying no heed to anything but the drums and their own repetitive steps and chants.

No wonder Connell had wanted her to stay inside the lodge! Getting too close to this ceremony could undoubtedly be dangerous as well as foolhardy, especially for someone who knew almost nothing about tribal lore. Clearly, her experiences with Spotted Fawn Woman, although fascinating and rewarding, had imparted a sense of security where none existed.

Faith shivered imperceptibly. She might be dressed as a Cheyenne, but she was still an outsider. It would behoove her to remember that, especially if she didn't want a hank of her own hair added to Black Kettle's scalp shirt!

She chanced a brief look at the chief. There he was, big as life, wearing the proof of people he'd killed like so many war trophies.

Which was exactly what they were, she reasoned. Those scalps were his medals of valor. They might be more grisly than the ribbons or stripes the soldiers at Fort Laramie wore, but they stood for exactly the same thing. What a sobering thought!

Studying Black Kettle from a distance, Faith was struck by his departure from the amiable nature he had displayed before. Here and now, he was the unquestionable ruler of all he surveyed; a force not to be trifled with. Everything about him, from his proud posture to his defiant expression, insisted that he be obeyed.

In Faith's eyes, the only person more formidable looking was Connell McClain. Praying silently for his deliverance, she watched him stride forcefully toward the chief and the tribal council. He never faltered, not slowing until he stood eye to eye with Black Kettle.

Frenzied chanting and drumming ceased. Even the dogs seemed to sense a momentous event in the offing, because they stopped yapping.

Faith was sure anyone standing near her could hear the wild thumps of her heart. *She* certainly could. She held her breath as Connell began to speak. Though she couldn't understand what he was saying, his voice came across strong, his confidence in himself and his cause evident. Irene couldn't have asked for a better champion.

And speaking of Irene, where was she? Faith wondered, scanning the crowd.

That question was answered quickly. Connell swept his arm in a grandiose arc and pointed. Irene was approaching on foot, accompanied by Walks With Tree. Between them they led a magnificent horse. Bunches of feathers and beads were tied in the horse's mane; a blanket was draped across his back and he was decorated with war paint. That was why it took Faith a few seconds to realize she was looking at Connell's horse, Rojo!

Overwrought on behalf of the plainsman, she had to clamp her hand over her mouth to keep from protesting.

The assembled Cheyenne closed ranks behind the little procession and pressed in on their chief and his captive medicine woman.

Faith edged closer, too, wanting to keep Connell and Irene in sight, but she was far too short to see over the heads of those in front of her. Determined to follow the drama, she circled around to the opposite side of the campfire where a group of wide-eyed youngsters had gathered to watch the show. Their smiles of remembrance warmed her heart. One little girl even reached up and took her hand.

"Hello again," Faith whispered.

The child tugged her to sit beside her on the ground.

"Okay." How Faith wished she could educate this dear child, could tell her the truth about the so-called magical watch without risking everyone else's life. She didn't dare, of course. Too much was at stake. Yet it seemed so unfair to let the impressionable girl go on thinking a mere pocket watch held spiritual significance. Perhaps someday, after they'd rescued Charity and found Papa, she'd be able to return to the Cheyenne as a teacher or a missionary or both and set things right.

That notion took her totally by surprise. Before she could pursue it further, however, Irene held up the watch. On cue, the alarm sounded.

Children gasped. So did many of the adults. The little girl who had befriended Faith ducked beneath her arm to hide.

Faith pulled her closer and leaned down to offer quiet reassurance. "It's okay, honey. Don't be afraid. It won't hurt you. I promise."

She thought she'd spoken cautiously enough to keep from being overheard, yet in seconds two sinewy warriors appeared in front of her, grabbed her by the wrists and yanked her to her feet as easily as if she weighed less than one of the children she'd been sitting with.

Shock overrode any modicum of remaining restraint. "No!" she screeched. "Let go of me. I haven't done anything!"

They ignored her protests and dragged her through the assembled throng while she writhed and kicked like a rabbit caught in a snare. The child left behind began to wail.

Faces passed in a blur. Angry faces. Hostile faces. Shouting faces. The braves delivered Faith to the chief and dropped her in a heap at his feet, then shoved her facedown into the dirt.

Spitting and struggling, she tried to right herself but was immediately forced prostrate once again. They pushed her so violently this time she could hardly catch her breath.

Over the sounds of the surrounding melee she heard Connell shout something in Cheyenne. His voice held so much pathos she needed no translation to know he was pleading on her behalf. She covered her face with her hands and lay very still, too shocked to think straight let alone pray rationally.

More nearby voices joined in expressions of rage. Faith's head was spinning. This was all wrong! She was innocent of any crime. If only she could explain and apologize, surely they'd see she'd simply been trying to comfort a frightened child and had meant no harm to anyone.

She suddenly remembered that Black Kettle spoke English. He'd understand what she was trying to convey.

She pulled her knees under her, preparing to rise, but before she could even look up, Connell gave a guttural shout and threw himself over her as a human shield, knocking her back down and keeping her there.

His mouth was inches from her ear when he rasped, "Don't move."

"I—"

"And don't say another word."

Faith bit her lip so hard she tasted blood mixed with the gritty dust in her mouth. Poor Connell! What had she done? She clamped her hands over her ears and squeezed her eyes shut tight. So much shouting was going on all around them it would have been impossible to tell who was saying what even if everyone had been speaking English. At this point, all Faith was certain of was her own precarious position—in more ways than one.

A lance tip had cut through Connell's shirt to pierce his back near his left shoulder blade. He knew the quick thrust had been meant to warn, not to kill. Yet.

Every muscle in his body readied for defense while his mind insisted that such resistance was futile. What could one man do against hundreds of armed braves? More importantly, how could he hope to save Faith Beal when so many were now calling for her execution?

Reality hit him squarely. The truth was, he couldn't save anyone. Especially not now. He'd shown his true allegiance when he'd thrown himself between Faith and the warriors' weapons, thereby sealing his own fate. It was going to take a lot bigger influence than Irene's watch could provide to get any of them out of this predicament alive. It was going to take genuine Divine intervention. The kind that came from only one source.

Connell hadn't consciously, purposely, talked to his God since Little Rabbit Woman's death. To pray now, when he was about to join her, seemed sacrilegious.

A surprising calm descended upon the plainsman. If he must die, he would face that fate with honor. With courage. With few regrets except his inability to deliver on all his well-intentioned promises.

Hunched over beneath Connell, Faith sensed a change in him that gave her hope. As soon as she figured out what he planned to do, she'd gladly cooperate and they'd all get out of this mess in one piece. Together. Just as originally planned. In the meantime, she wished somebody would say something in English so she'd have a little idea of what was going on.

As if in direct answer, Connell again warned, "Don't move," and began to slowly lift his upper body off her while remaining on his knees before Black Kettle.

Faith almost disobeyed his command when she heard his muffled groan of pain. It was only with the utmost effort that she kept her eyes covered, her posture submissive.

Head already bowed, eyes closed, she turned to silent prayer. *Dear Lord, please help Connell. Help us all. I know You sent him to help me and I disobeyed You when I didn't listen to his advice. I'm so sorry. Please, please forgive me. And tell me what to do now, Father.*

Above her, she heard courage in the plainsman's voice as he said, "Black Kettle is a wise chief. A brave warrior. Will he make war on a crazy woman who knows nothing of the ways of the Cheyenne? Will his ancestors honor him for her death? If he must have another scalp, let him take one from a brave fighter who has proved himself in battle. Let him take mine."

Faith's heart leaped to her throat and choked off her breath. Was she doomed simply because she'd spoken out of turn? It seemed impossible. Yet Connell obviously thought so or he wouldn't have offered himself in her place.

No, God! No! her soul screamed. *There must be another way. There must be. Please!*

A hush fell over the crowd. Tempted almost beyond

her strength to resist, Faith yearned to rise and somehow defend her champion.

Reason prevailed. That was exactly the kind of rash behavior that had thrust them into this fiery furnace of wrath in the first place, she reminded herself, contrasting her current dilemma with the biblical deliverance of Shadrach, Meshach and Abednego.

I trust God like they did. I do, she insisted. *So where is God now? Where's the answer to my prayer for deliverance?*

Had God forsaken her because she'd been unable to overcome her jealousy even after she'd recognized it as a sin? Or was He expecting her to bravely declare her Christian faith and become a martyr? It wasn't hard to admit that that particular prospect didn't appeal to her one bit. It had been a lot easier to think of God as master of her destiny when she hadn't been facing the final precious moments of life. Yet what better time for total commitment?

Faith took a deep breath as she raised her head and looked straight at Black Kettle. Their gazes locked. A barely perceptible tilt of the chief's head was all the warriors needed to tell them to move Connell off her and keep him out of the way.

No longer encumbered, Faith got to her feet, spread her hands wide and bowed before the Cheyenne chief to say, "The child was afraid. I comforted her because I have the heart of a woman, of a mother. If I must die for showing a woman's kindness, then I am ready."

She straightened, proud and unwavering, her shoulders back, her chin raised. She didn't know if Black Kettle was surprised at her unusual boldness and reasoning or not, but *she* was certainly shocked by the wisdom that had just popped out of her mouth! Moreover, she had absolutely no idea where those erudite thoughts had originated. They certainly hadn't been rehearsed, nor had she planned to do anything but apologize profusely when she'd gotten to her feet in front of the chief.

Silence reigned. Any other time, Faith would have continued to babble, to try to add to her appeal, but absolutely nothing else came to mind. It was as if any connection between her brain and her lips had been severed.

Finally, Black Kettle spoke. "You have the courage of a warrior, Little Dove Woman. If your tongue did not wag all day and all night like the tail of a hungry dog I would buy you from your uncle and make you my fourth wife." He chuckled to himself and waved her off. "Go with Pale Hawk and Singing Sun Woman and leave us in peace."

"Yes, sir!" Faith's grin was so wide her cheeks hurt.

Backing away, she glanced over her shoulder to locate Connell. The braves had released him, too, and he was standing near Irene. Walks With Tree now held the precious alarm watch and was hunched over it, muttering.

Faith skirted the old medicine man and went directly to Connell. She yearned to ask him if he was all right but decided that query could wait. The only serious question she had at present was in regard to their future mode of transportation since he'd obviously given his horse away. Surely, he didn't intend to walk the rest of the way to California!

Sidling up to him, she waited for him to pay her

heed. When he continued to ignore her she gave a light tug on his sleeve, expecting him to lean down so she could whisper to him privately.

Connell slipped an arm around her shoulders. Instead of bending an ear, however, he crooked his arm just so and placed his large hand directly over her mouth! Holding her thus, he nodded to the chief who laughed heartily.

Faith struggled in vain to dislodge the plainsman's firm grip. It was no use. She couldn't even pry his fingers loose by using both hands. Disgusted, she stopped trying.

Leaving her hands clamped over Connell's, she watched the tableau unfolding by the fire. If Walks With Tree intended to impress everyone with his skill as guardian of the magic watch, he was going to have to hurry because the crowd was beginning to stir impatiently.

The old man held the watch aloft just as Irene had. Nothing happened. He lowered it, held it to his ear, then nodded sagely before speaking aside to Black Kettle.

Listening, the chief began to frown. Was Irene going to have to stay behind after all? Faith wondered. Worse, if the old man couldn't make the watch work, were they going to be made the scapegoats for his failure? Irene must have explained the alarm to him. Could he be too uncivilized to understand how to set and then secretly trigger it?

When Black Kettle stared at Connell with skepticism, Faith felt the plainsman's arm muscles clench. Whatever was going on, Connell was jittery about it. She held very still, hardly breathing, and watched the parade of emotions on the chief's face. Finally, he shook his head and barked an order to his guards. Two saddled horses and a laden pack animal were immediately led into the circle.

Connell boosted Faith aboard one saddle and helped Irene mount the other while Walks With Tree began a vigorous chant over the watch. Still, it remained silent.

Then Rojo was brought forward. Black Kettle took the horse's reins and handed them ceremoniously to Connell. Everyone paused, waiting and listening expectantly. Mere seconds dragged by like hours.

Faith's stomach was knotted, her heart racing. The mount beneath her sensed her apprehension and shifted its feet, uneasy.

Patience had never been one of her virtues and she was about to come to the end of what little she had left when the bell inside the watch suddenly began its noisy clamor.

The shock jolted everyone, including the horses. Faith's jittery mount probably would have unseated her if Connell hadn't still had hold of its bridle. Even steady Rojo flinched and snorted.

Connell mounted quickly and wheeled the big gelding to lead the way out of the camp. It wasn't until they'd passed the final perimeter lodges and sentries that he hesitated long enough to pass the reins of their horses to the women.

Faith had been about to burst. "You've been hurt. There's blood on the back of your shoulder!"

"I know. It burns like fire," he replied, "but we can't stop now. Not yet. Irene can take care of it when we camp for the night."

Irene. Faith had to bite her lip to keep from commenting adversely. Of course Irene should take care of it. After all, he was planning to marry her. And she had been living with the old medicine man, Faith added, so she probably did know a lot about wounds and such. Still, the idea galled. It shouldn't have, but it did.

"What happened? When did you get hurt?" Faith pressed.

The older woman spoke up. "He took the spear thrust meant for you."

"Oh, no. Oh, Connell, I'm so sorry."

"You'd be a lot sorrier if he hadn't shielded you the way he did," Irene said harshly. "You two almost ruined our whole plan. Walks With Tree kept his head or we'd be in deep trouble right now."

"What happened?" Faith asked. "About the horses, I mean. When I saw Rojo all decked out in feathers and paint I was sure Black Kettle was going to keep him."

"He was," Connell answered, "until Walks With Tree convinced him the magic wouldn't work unless he released us and our horses, too."

"How clever. And how nice of him."

Irene snorted. "Don't give the old fox too much credit for altruism. He's no fool. He knew the less we left behind, the stronger his own position would be."

"And he wanted to make sure we put plenty of distance between us and him as soon as possible," Connell added. "That's the only way he could be sure the Cheyenne would continue to see him as indispensable. To do that, we needed good horses."

"I'm glad you got your beautiful red horse back," Faith said. "He really is magnificent." She sighed audibly. "I just wish I'd been able to rescue Ben from Tucker."

"Who's Ben?" Irene asked. "I thought your only relative on the train was a younger sister."

"Yes. My sister, Charity," Faith said with a wistful smile. "Many's the time I'd have gladly considered trading her for another faithful friend like Ben. Not that I'd actually do it, mind you, but the thought certainly has appealed to me from time to time."

Connell laughed quietly to himself, then explained to Irene. "Ben's a mule. One of those big Missouri ones that can pull all day without giving out."

"Mercy sakes," Irene said. "The way you were talking about him I figured he was a person."

"He almost is. He's been my dearest friend for most of my life," Faith said solemnly. "I'd trust him a lot longer than I'd trust most people, especially lately. It was poor Ben who first showed me the rotten side of Captain Tucker."

Irene was clearly interested. "How? What did he do?"

"Well, he didn't want the captain to get near me, for starters. Kept stepping between us whenever he could. Then I caught Tucker beating him one night and that was the last straw. I didn't even think about what I was doing or how dangerous it might be. I just grabbed the first whip I could lay my hands on and lashed at Tucker the way he'd been whipping Ben."

"You didn't!"

"Oh, yes, I did. And the captain backed off. But he'd been shamed in front of the other men. After that he never missed a chance to make my life miserable." Her shoulders slumped. "And now he's not only got my sister in his clutches, there's no one left to defend Ben."

"Then we'll steal him for you," Irene said brightly.

Connell coughed. "We'll *what?*"

"Steal him. It won't be hard. All we have to do is locate the train and watch till the drovers take the stock out to graze. Then you and I can create a diversion to distract the guards and Faith can creep in to fetch her mule. We do it all the time."

"We?" Connell's eyebrows arched quizzically.

"I mean the Cheyenne do it," Irene said, blushing slightly. "Besides, the mule truly does belong to Faith. All we have to worry about is hiding the fact that she's still alive. It'll be simple." She grinned over at the younger woman. "Even her sister wouldn't recognize her in that getup."

"She wouldn't, would she!" Faith was caught up in the plan. "I might even be able to sneak close enough to get a look at her myself. I've been so worried. Charity was always the baby of the family. I don't know how she's managing to cope after all that's happened to her. She's never been strong, like me."

Connell laughed cynically. "We agree on that. I doubt there's one woman in a hundred who would have the courage to stand up to a war chief the way you did, Little Dove Woman. Maybe not one in a thousand."

"Thanks." Gratified by such high praise, Faith glanced over at Irene, expecting her to concur, and found her scowling. She quickly added, "Don't forget what Irene did. It must have taken great heroism to fool so many savages for such a long time."

Instead of the appreciation she'd anticipated, Faith

was taken aback when Irene said, "The Cheyenne are far less savage than many whites I've met. When a warrior makes a vow he keeps it, no matter what it may cost him to do so."

"I meant no offense," Faith told her.

Irene nodded. "Nor did I. I simply speak the truth. If a liar like Ramsey Tucker were a Cheyenne he'd have been thrown out of the tribe or executed for his crimes long ago instead of having so many chances to repeat them and hurt more people."

Tears of frustration clouded Faith's vision as she visualized that kind of swift, sure justice. "I wish…" she began before her voice trailed off, leaving the unacceptable thought unspoken.

Connell finished it for her. "You wish that were the case right now, but you feel guilty because your Christian upbringing argues that it's wrong to take personal revenge. I can understand that. Just remember, wanting to even the score is a normal human reaction to injustice."

"Murder is a sin, no matter what the reason," Faith said. "'Vengeance is Mine, I will repay, sayeth the Lord.'" She looked from him to Irene and back again while struggling to gain control of her whirling emotions.

"What about your sister?" the older woman asked. "Wouldn't you like to see her freed from that awful man?"

"Of course I would! But killing him isn't the answer. Think. There are only three of us against fifty or more armed men on that wagon train. As long as they all believe Tucker's lies, we wouldn't stand a chance of escaping. All we'd do if we went after Tucker is get ourselves shot. Then who would be left to bring him to justice?"

"White man's justice is too slow." Irene's eyes were sparking with hatred.

Faith laid a hand of consolation on her arm. "Try to be patient. With your help I know we can prove his guilt and see that he's held properly accountable when we reach California. It's the right thing to do. This is hard for me, too, you know. Very hard." She managed a slight smile. "Be patient? Please?"

"Faith's right," Connell said. "Even if we did manage to do away with Tucker we'd be hard-pressed to get Charity away from the others. Plus, we'd be draining their precious resources. They'll need every ounce of fortitude they have left to make it across the desert. Innocent folks will die if they waste their energy chasing after us."

Watching Irene's face, Faith saw eventual signs of resignation. What she didn't see was compassion for the emigrants who were about to embark on such a difficult leg of their long, arduous journey.

Chapter Fifteen

Connell had serious misgivings about bothering with the mule. He could have thwarted the plan by simply pretending he couldn't locate the Tucker train. That idea had occurred to him—more than once. Trouble was, the emigrant track across the high plains was spread so wide, its path of desolation so evident, a child could have easily found and followed it by day.

Not only had the passing wagons left behind deep ruts and trampled vegetation, there were so many household items discarded along the trail it looked like a parade of drummers had passed by dropping off samples of their goods. Had those travelers who came later not been in the same dire straits as their predecessors, they could easily have provisioned themselves many times over—with anything but food and water.

Connell knew that choosing between heirlooms or survival became easier and easier as the westward migration progressed. The first things to go were usually those special niceties the women had insisted on bringing along, such as mirrors and pianos or trunks crammed with fancy frocks.

By the time the overland trail reached the Sierra Nevada, travelers were more than ready to let go of the last vestiges of their past lives in the hope of enduring long enough to see a future. Any future.

Connell held up his hand to bring his little party to a halt on the crest of a ridge. Irene rode up on his right. Faith took the opposite side. The trail lay in the barren valley below, accentuated by a long, snaking column of dust that partially obscured a wagon train.

"Is that them?" Faith asked. She strained to see. "I can't tell from here."

"I think so. The timing is about right," Connell said. "The wagon boss will call a rest near here so the stock can gather strength and the men can load extra fodder and water to get them across the desert. When he does, I'll ride closer and see if I can spot Tucker or some of the others we know."

"It looks to me like they're already in a desert," Faith said, worried.

"It gets a lot worse west of here." He pointed. "There's a good forty-mile stretch of nothing but dry sand between the Humboldt Sink, where the river disappears underground, and Carson Pass, when the trail starts up over the Sierras."

"Oh, dear." She shaded her eyes, stood in her stirrups. "I don't think I see my wagon. Maybe this is the wrong train."

"Wagons break down, draft animals give out and families have to combine their resources," Connell reminded her. "I wouldn't be surprised if Charity isn't back with the Ledbetters so Tucker doesn't have to bother with her."

"Oh, do you think she could be? That would be wonderful! I've been so afraid…." Faith's voice trailed off again. She couldn't bear to think or speak of her naive sister sharing that horrible man's bed.

"If she kept on wailing the way she was the last time I talked to her, it's certainly possible. Tucker needs her alive and well when they meet up with your father, so we know he'll make sure she's well cared for. I just can't see a man like him putting up with her hysterics for very long. Not when he could farm her out and let someone else deal with the buckets of tears instead."

"And she can't cook a lick," Faith offered, spirits rising. "Never tended to the animals, either." She grinned over at him. "She's useless! Isn't that wonderful?"

Her enthusiasm made Connell chuckle. "In Charity's case, it may be." Reining the canelo around, he started down the back side of the ridge, away from the wagon train. "Come on. We need to find a good place to make camp before dark. Somewhere far enough away that the smoke from our fire won't be spotted. I'll come back later and do some more scouting."

Irene followed obediently.

Faith held her horse back with a jerk on the reins. "Whoa. Wait! We can't leave yet. We're not even sure that's the Tucker train. What if you're wrong? What if it isn't? What then?" She noticed Irene's disdainful smile, arching brows and the way her eyes darted to Connell to assess his reaction.

Instead of answering Faith, he smiled at Irene. "Do you think it's too late to go back and sell her to Black Kettle after all?"

Irene huffed. "I'm afraid you'd have to pay him to take her, not the other way 'round."

"Oh, well in that case," he said with a chuckle, "I guess we'll have to keep her. I doubt there are enough good horses in the territories to make Black Kettle change his mind."

"Very funny," Faith grumbled.

The ensuing mutual laughter of her companions didn't amuse her one bit. Gritting her teeth, she watched them ride away for a few dozen heartbeats, then kicked her horse in the sides and followed reluctantly.

For once, she actually missed having another woman like her sister to talk to. Charity might be self-centered but at least she thought and acted in ways Faith was used to. Irene, on the other hand, was a lot more like an Indian than Faith had imagined she'd be.

As she rode behind her companions, she was able to observe them without blatantly staring. Connell sat his horse straight and strong in spite of his injured shoulder and Irene rode beside him as naturally as if they'd been a couple all their lives. Perhaps they had.

All the more reason to believe they were ideally suited to each other, Faith reasoned. If she were truly honest with herself she'd have to admit that the best thing she could do for Connell McClain was to drop out of his life for good. As soon as possible. That notion stuck in her throat and burned like a dose of Grandma Reeder's homemade spring tonic.

Alone with Irene after Connell left on his scouting mission, Faith tried several times to breach the gap between her life and the other woman's by making small talk. Her efforts were to no avail. When Irene did deign to speak, her conversation was terse and strictly to the point instead of chatty as Faith had hoped.

By the time Connell returned, she was about ready to start talking to clumps of inanimate sagebrush.

"Well?" she blurted as he dismounted and started to loosen the canelo's saddle girth before reporting. "What did you learn?"

He paused, turned to give her a patient look. "Your wagon broke an axle about fifty miles back. After that, the Ledbetters and the Johnsons took what they could carry of Charity's stuff and left the rest behind, wagon and all."

"Then we did find the right train!"

"Yes. And a more demoralized bunch of folks I've never seen. A quarter of their party split off back at Fort Bridger. The rest are complaining about all the hardships of Sublette's Cutoff, even if it did save them a week of travel. If they think that was bad, this next patch of rough country is going to really wake them up."

"Is Charity okay? Did you see her? Talk to her?"

"I saw her. From a distance. Didn't see any reason to stir things up by bothering her. She's a little the worse for wear but otherwise fine. Looks like she's had to learn to do chores since you left. She was tending a cooking fire while a couple of other women fussed at her."

"Thank heavens." Faith sighed with relief. "But what about Ben? If we don't have a wagon anymore, what are they using my mules for?"

"Nothing, at the moment," Connell said. "I spotted

Ben and one of your other mules. They're a little gaunt but not sickly or broken down like some of the horses. That's a good sign. If we can liberate the old boy before he's driven across the desert with the rest of the herd he'll have a better chance."

"Then let's do it! What're we waiting for?"

Irene shook her head, clearly concerned. "Is she always this enthusiastic?"

"Most always," Connell answered. "She goes off half-cocked more often than a worn-out flintlock."

Faith faced them, hands fisted on her hips. "I do not. I just want to get my mule and be on our way, that's all. I keep expecting to see a bunch of Indians riding after us."

"She has a point there," Irene said. "Walks With Tree is an old man. If something happened to him, Black Kettle might decide he wants me back again."

Not to mention what Red Deer wants, Faith thought. The virile Cheyenne brave had stared daggers at Connell as their party had ridden out of camp and she wouldn't have been a bit surprised to see him sneaking through the brush, readying an arrow. There had definitely been times lately when she'd felt as if someone or something was watching them, following them. It wasn't the same kind of sensation a person got from knowing they were being looked after by a benevolent Providence, either. It was more like what she imagined an antelope might feel at its first glimpse of a mountain lion lying in ambush. A shiver followed the conclusion that their invisible nemesis might indeed be a lion or other dangerous denizen of the wilderness.

"All right," Connell said, breaking into Faith's

thoughts. "We'll use Irene's diversion idea since I haven't been able to come up with a better one. She and I will cause a stir so you can sneak into the herd to get Ben." He scowled at Faith. "Just Ben, mind you. If other mules follow him we'll have to take them, too, but I'd rather not. The less fuss the better."

"Right." She unfastened her braids to let them hang free. In answer to Connell's questioning look she said, "Since I don't have my bonnet and Ben's not used to these clothes either, I want him to know it's me. He's smart. Too smart. There's no way I can catch him if he doesn't want to be caught."

"Take one of the horses," Connell ordered. "Ride him close enough to spot Ben, then decide whether or not to approach on foot. We'll leave that up to you. Just get in and out as fast as you can. If nobody spots you and gives chase, come back here to camp. If you're followed, head west. We'll find you."

Faith pulled a face. "Ha! The way you two have been talking about getting rid of me I'm not very comfortable being separated."

Chuckling, Connell patted her on the top of the head. "Don't worry. I imagine by now you're a regular legend in the Cheyenne camps. If they did pick you up again you'd be treated well as long as you kept your mouth shut and minded your own business."

"Yes-sir-ee," Faith drawled cynically. "I'm about the quietest, most harmless little dove there ever was. Have to live up to my Indian name, don't I?"

"I should have named you Babbling Brook or Squeaking Wheel Woman," he countered, amused though also worried about her participation in their mule-theft plan. "If there was any other way to be sure we'd be able to get to Ben without being noticed, I'd leave you behind."

"You can't. You need me," Faith said flatly. "We all agree on that. So, are you going to stand around jawing all evening or are we going to go after my mule?"

"We're going to go after your mule," he said. "If you can't sneak close enough to safely nab him tonight, we'll wait till daybreak and try again when they drive the livestock to water."

"I'll get him tonight," Faith vowed. "I'm not giving Ramsey Tucker any more chances to hurt him. I just wish there was some good way to make off with my sister, too."

"We've already been over all that. You said it yourself. The men would form a posse and hunt us down if we kidnapped her."

"I know, I know. And they won't miss Ben the way they would Charity. Especially since he's not being worked. I understand that. I was just wishing things could be different, that's all."

Irene nodded sagely, soberly, and surprised Faith by saying, "I know *exactly* how you feel."

The country was open. Flat. Faith couldn't very well show herself to the emigrants while still clad as an Indian, so she dismounted, left her horse behind and crouched low to approach the weary herd.

The closer she got, the worse the livestock looked. Innumerable flies buzzed around oxen's eyes and dotted their backs, especially where the yokes had rubbed their hide raw. The poor beasts were so exhausted they barely flinched from the biting insects.

Their suffering touched Faith's heart. If only she had some of her homemade tansy-and-sulfur ointment to put on those wounds. But that precious tin of salve, as well as personal belongings like the mourning pendant she'd worn in memory of her mother, had probably been abandoned when her wagon was left behind.

An enormous brown and white ox lifted its head to glance at her as she came closer, then went back to wrapping its tongue around tufts of coarse grass and yanking it out by the mouthful.

Faith laid a steadying hand on its withers and kept the large animal between herself and the wagon train so she wouldn't be visible if anyone chanced to look her way.

Speaking calmly, she soothed her four-legged concealment. "Hello, old boy. That's it. Keep eating. I hear you're going to need every bite."

There had been a time, early in their journey, when even the most placid ox or mule would have resisted the touch of anyone who might place it back in harness before it was sated. Now, however, the animals were too tired, too sore-footed, to fight any longer. They seemed as resigned to their fate as their human owners.

With barely an occasional twinge left to remind her of the injury to her ribs back at Fort Laramie, Faith felt guilty to be enjoying renewed well-being when there was so much suffering, man and beast, all around her.

Well, better to help one poor traveler than none at all, she reasoned. She hadn't come to rescue the wagon train from the harrowing trek. Only God could do that.

Her task was to locate her faithful mule and spirit him away undetected.

That was plenty, considering the size of the herd and the waning daylight. Men would soon return to gather the draft animals and drive them inside the corral formed by the circled wagons. If she didn't get to Ben before then, they would have to wait till morning, as Connell had warned.

She crept closer and closer, hoping to catch a glimpse of Charity while continuing her search for Ben. Sound carried well over the tranquil prairie, but she was unable to pick out her sister's voice above the general hum of the camp. Still, that much background noise would help to mask her summons if she shouted to Ben. With time growing short, she decided it was a chance worth taking.

"Ho, Ben," she called, beginning softly as a test.

Peeking over the oxen's broad back, she stood on tiptoe to see if Ben—or anyone else—had heard. To her amazement, she was now the only two-legged creature remaining on that side of the wagon circle!

On the opposite side, however, a hue and cry was rising. People were running to and fro, waving rifles and pointing at two mounted figures silhouetted by the glow of the setting sun.

Faith smiled to herself. Clever Connell. He'd put himself and Irene directly in front of the sun so no details about them were discernible. All they had to do was sit there like Indian scouts and wait to be spotted. The imaginations of settlers who had already faced more than one raiding party since leaving St. Jo would do the rest.

Freed of remaining inhibitions, Faith stepped out from behind the ox, cupped her hands and started working her way through the herd shouting, "Ben! Here I am, Ben. Ben," over and over.

Darkness was falling. She was just about to give up and sneak back to where she'd left her horse when a soft snort at her elbow startled her. Her old friend had come!

She wheeled, grinning, and opened her arms to hug his neck the way she always had. "Good boy!"

Unsure, the mule tossed his head to escape her grasp then went back to sniffing her Cheyenne outfit.

Faith settled for scratching the bridge of his nose and spoke to calm him. "That's right. It's me, boy. Sorry I don't have any apples for you."

She hadn't thought to bring a lead rope either. Thankfully, she didn't need one. All she had to do was turn and start off with a quiet, "Come on. Let's go, Ben," and the mule followed her through the herd like an oversize, obedient pup.

They were almost in the clear when a distant shout went up. "Indians! Quick, boys. Mount up. They're after the horses!"

Faith's initial reaction was to freeze and look around her for the threat. In another instant she realized that *she* was the Indian they were hollering about!

If the emigrants caught her, Tucker would find out she was alive. Then there'd be no escape for sure! But how was she going to elude capture? She'd left her riding horse ground-hitched at least a half mile away, maybe farther. Making a run for it and reaching it without being overtaken was not feasible. But what other choice did she have?

Think. Don't panic. There must be a way!

If she were astride Ben, escape might be possible, she reasoned. The trouble was, she was short and he was sixteen hands at the shoulder. That put his back far above her leaping ability.

Lacking stirrups for a quick boost she cast frantically about for something to stand on. A rock or a stump would do. Anything. As a child at home she'd always led Ben over to the edge of the back porch where he'd stood patiently and waited for her to clamber aboard. Unfortunately, there weren't any handy porches in the middle of the prairie!

If only she could vault from the ground onto his back without aid the way she'd seen the Indians do it. Then again, they'd had their horses' long manes to grab hold of while Ben's had been roached short and bristly, leaving nothing except one little lock of longer hair right at the base by his withers.

The old mule sensed her fright and tossed his head. "Easy, boy. Come on, Ben," she pleaded. "We've got to stick together till we find something for me to stand on."

She broke into a trot, dodging sagebrush and trying to keep the clumps of long grass that the herds had not yet decimated between her and her pursuers. Here and there, the bones of long-dead animals lay scattered, cleaned by scavengers and sun bleached. The largest of the lot was the skull of a bull buffalo. Maybe it would be enough.

Faith stopped and motioned to Ben. "Here, boy. Over here," she gasped. "That's it." She knew that if he didn't trust her implicitly, the sense of death surrounding the bones would keep him away.

Head down, treading cautiously and blowing through his nostrils, he came.

Thrilled, Faith could hardly contain her nervous energy long enough to let him step into proper position. She grabbed hold of the lock of mane before she jumped onto the skull and began her leap of faith. It was now or never.

Momentum carried her in a forward arc toward the mule's side. His big head came around fast, almost as if he wanted to help. That additional swinging movement gave her just enough boost to manage to plant the inside of her right foot and ankle on his backbone!

Thanks to her leather moccasins, her foot didn't slip back off. Inching along and finally hoisting herself the rest of the way to sit astride was easy compared to making that initial leap.

The moment she straightened, a rifle shot cracked. Faith ducked to lie closer to the mule's back and pressed her cheek against the side of his neck, then urged him forward with a prod from her heels and a familiar, "Let's go, Ben."

She was certain the settlers wouldn't want to risk hitting valuable animals by firing too low so she figured as long as she kept her head down and Ben kept moving she'd be safe enough.

Logic quickly countered by reminding her that anyone who came after her on horseback might manage to get a clear shot. Worse yet, one of the undisciplined drovers might decide to sacrifice the mule in order to down a real Indian.

That sobering possibility was enough to spur her to more drastic action. Tightening her knees against the mule's sides and holding on for dear life, she kicked him as hard as she could and let out a war whoop that would have made Black Kettle proud!

All around her, animals shied and scattered. Only Ben remained steady. Without a single buck or lunge, he changed gaits and gained speed until he was covering the ground at a gallop faster than most horses could equal.

It had been years since Faith had ridden the mule without a saddle, let alone raced him. At that moment she cared less about where he took her than she did about keeping her tenuous balance. Later, she'd worry about where they were. Right now all she wanted to do was escape in one piece, together with Ben.

Thankfully, she and the old mule seemed of the same mind.

Chapter Sixteen

From his vantage point on the ridge opposite all the commotion, Connell saw what was happening. He wheeled his horse and raced after Faith without pausing to explain anything to Irene.

After reaching the flatlands, he skirted the milling herd, staying in their dust to hide his passing. He needn't have bothered. No one was paying the slightest attention to him. All they wanted was to catch the so-called Indian they thought was making off with one of their mules.

Frightened oxen were lining out and starting to run in spite of their fatigue. Connell saw his chance to solve everyone's problems at once. Riding straight at the advancing animals, he waved and shouted, turning them back. Others followed the leaders, creating a whirlpool of stampeding, panting, wild-eyed livestock.

Trapped in the midst of it were the mounted settlers who had started in pursuit of Faith and Ben. Tucker was among them. Spurring his horse mercilessly, the wagon boss worked his way out to where Connell was patrolling the perimeter on Rojo, preventing breakouts.

"What the blazes do you think you're doing?" Tucker shouted.

"Saving your bacon," Connell yelled back. "You almost had a stampede."

"Bah! Nothing me and my boys couldn't handle." He stood in his stirrups to scan the distance. "I should hang you fer lettin' that Injun get away like that."

"What Indian? All I saw was a bunch of dumb critters fixin' to run themselves to death. That what you wanted, Captain?"

"'Course not. You tryin' to tell me you didn't see nobody out here stealin' horses?"

"Not one single brave," Connell said. He was proud of avoiding a blatant lie and wondered if Faith was going to appreciate his effort at veracity. She might, especially if he made a joke out of it when he told her about putting one over on Tucker.

"You was pro'bly in cahoots with 'em." He started to swing his rifle barrel toward the plainsman.

Connell reached out and tore the weapon from his hand, then reversed it and pointed it back at its owner. "I'd watch my mouth if I were you, mister. There's plenty of folks sick to death of your meanness. Bet they wouldn't mind a bit if my finger slipped and I accidentally pulled this trigger."

"You wouldn't."

"You're right," Connell said, sizing up his adversary, "I wouldn't. But not because I'm so forgiving. You've made this trip before. You're the only guide these folks have, sorry as you may be. They need you. I won't take that away from them."

Ramsey Tucker obviously wasn't a man who understood altruism. "Ha! Wouldn't surprise me if you wanted my job."

"If I thought I could get these wagons through better than you can, I'd take your place gladly," Connell said. "Let me put everybody on horseback instead of in wagons and I might try it. But I don't know enough about managing settlers and all their gear, especially through the Sierras. That's rough country up ahead."

"Well, stopping a few cows from running off won't get you another job on my train," Tucker said, gesturing at the herd. "The Beal wagon is long gone and so is Miss Faith. We've got no place for you here anymore."

"Pity." Connell touched the brim of his hat. "In that case, I guess I'd better ride."

"Where you headed?"

The plainsman smiled. "California. Same as you." His grin spread. "Maybe we'll run into each other out there."

"Not likely," Tucker countered, eyeing his rifle. "You ain't gonna ride off with my gun, are ya? I need it for protection."

"I'll leave it on down the trail a ways. If nobody steals it before you get there, it'll be waiting."

"What about the Injuns?" Tucker sounded incredulous.

"You'd better hope I'm right and there aren't any Indians hereabouts. If you were imagining them, your rifle will be right where I put it. If not, well, there's nothing I can do about that."

"You could hand it over right now."

"And give you a chance to shoot me in the back when I ride away? Not hardly."

"You don't trust me? Why not? What did I ever do to you?"

Connell wasn't about to let himself be drawn into a conversation that might make him so angry he'd accidentally reveal too much and thereby put others in more danger.

He turned Rojo quickly and rode away as additional men joined the wagon boss.

It vexed Connell to have to travel the emigrant trail to dispose of Tucker's gun. He'd chosen that route simply because Faith had headed in the opposite direction. The longer he kept Tucker and the settlers distracted, the better her chances of escape.

The last time Connell had seen her she'd been clinging to that mule's back as if she was part of it, going like the wind. Since she wasn't using a bridle, he hoped she'd have enough control to keep her mount from instinctively circling back to rejoin the familiar herd.

If the rider in question had been anyone but Faith Beal he'd have doubted that feat was possible. In her case, however, he'd learned never to underrate her capabilities. If anybody could convince an old mule to behave, using nothing more than voice commands and a few firm nudges, Faith could.

It was a sight he wished he could stick around to see for himself instead of having to hightail it west on account of Tucker. Oh, well, Irene could tell him all about it when he rejoined her.

Irene!

Taken aback, Connell realized he hadn't even remembered to bid his future bride goodbye when he'd ridden off so abruptly. All his thoughts, then and since, had been of Faith. All his concern had been only for her.

His gut twisted with remorse, yet he couldn't help feeling continued apprehension for the young woman whose bravery, wit and compassion had earned her a special place in his heart.

There was no way to make amends until he went back to camp, either. Fortunately Irene was a mature, sensible woman. Surely she'd understand his actions, if not his motives.

Did he understand those motives? Did he want to? That was an excellent question, one he was not ready to consider, let alone answer too honestly.

He slowed his horse, tossed Tucker's rifle to the ground and sped away. There was no time to waste. Wherever Faith was, she needed help. His help. He'd rescued her before and he'd keep doing it as long as necessary. It was impossible to imagine himself not caring, not looking after her, no matter where she went or what she did.

That thought plunged into his consciousness like raindrops splashing onto the surface of a river to instantly become part of the flow. How could he and Irene marry as they had promised when they were little more than children, while he continued to shepherd Faith through life's trials? Even the most tolerant wife would wonder why her husband took such an inordinate interest in another woman.

And she wouldn't be the only one wondering, Connell told himself. He'd been pondering the same question lately.

His life, his thoughts, his heart, had become so entwined in Faith Beal's dilemma he couldn't imagine ever breaking free. The question was, did he even want to try?

Fingers cramped, muscles throbbing, Faith didn't know how much longer she'd be able to hang on…or how many more miles Ben was going to travel. Though he'd slowed to a stiff trot as he picked his way through the unfamiliar landscape, he was still making good time. She could hear him snorting, feel his sides heaving with every breath.

By listening carefully she decided no one was pursuing them. At least there was that to be thankful for. Speaking of which, she'd been lax in giving proper thanks for her deliverance. Again.

It was hard to enunciate clearly with the mule's gait bouncing her around, but she did manage to string together a simple, heartfelt "Thank…you… Father!" by inserting one crisp syllable between each stride.

The unexpected sound of her voice after she'd been quiet for so long must have startled the old mule. It shied, pranced sideways for a few yards, then kicked out at an invisible nemesis before continuing forward.

Had Faith been riding with a saddle, or even just a bridle, she wouldn't have had trouble staying aboard. Riding bareback was another story. She was already slipping off the right side of Ben's back when his unexpected lunge pitched her forward. Instead of falling all the way to the ground, she closed her arms around his upper neck and hung on for dear life.

Straddling his mane, her face nearly between his big ears, she wondered what in the world to do next.

Ben took any decision from her by lowering his head and proceeding to shake her off like a pesky insect.

All Faith had time to do was yell "Be-e-e-e-n! Whoa!" before she landed in a heap at his feet. If he hadn't been so seasoned and wise he might have run right over her. Instead, he carefully sidestepped, stopped and waited, looking about as sorry and disconcerted as a traveling preacher who'd misplaced his only hymnbook.

Faith sat there in the dust for a moment, making a mental and physical assessment of the parts of her that hurt. Two hands weren't nearly sufficient to soothe all her bumps and bruises, not to mention wipe the dirt out of her eyes or check the scrapes she'd gotten when she'd slid to the ground.

She'd decided no bones were broken and was getting to her feet when she heard a female voice say, "Nice dismount."

"Irene?" Faith's head snapped around. Her mouth gaped. Not only had the other woman managed to follow her through the twilight-dim wilderness, she'd also picked up Faith's riding horse and brought it along. "You startled me. I didn't hear you coming."

"You're not supposed to. That's one reason our ponies aren't shod."

"You mean Indian ponies, don't you?" Faith asked, frowning slightly.

"That's what I said."

"No, you said *our* ponies. You may not realize it, but you talk like that all the time. It's as if you identify more with the Indians than you do with your own people."

Irene nodded. "I suppose I do. This was my second summer with the Cheyenne. They treated me with respect and made me a part of their tribe while I learned their ways. It's going to take me a while to get over those influences."

Faith was dusting off her doeskin skirt as she spoke. "I guess I can understand that. Right now I'm glad I traded my calico for this dress. If I'd been wearing a cloth outfit when I took that fall just now I'd probably have been torn to ribbons."

"Are you all right?"

"I think so."

"Then we'd better be going. Connell is going to wonder where we are."

"Humph. That makes two of us," Faith said, scanning the countryside with a puzzled frown. "All this land looks the same to me. I'm sure glad you showed up. I have absolutely no idea how to get back to our camp."

"It isn't too far. We'll have to pick up and move if the men from the wagon train come looking for you. I haven't seen any sign of them so far, but they may change their minds." She held out a rope. "Here. Throw a loop on your mule like you should have in the first place and let's ride."

Faith was already beside Ben, meticulously checking him for injuries. "In a minute. I'm almost done."

"You'll be *done* all right, like a roasted Christmas

goose, if you don't mount up and follow me. There's not much moon tonight and the desert gets very dark once the sun sets all the way. That can work to our advantage if we're smart."

"What about Connell?"

"He could track an antelope blindfolded if he had to. Don't worry. He'll find us wherever we go."

Faith put the rope around Ben's neck and tied it off, then took the reins of her saddle horse. She was about to mount up when an odd noise caught her attention. She froze, listening. "What was that?"

"I didn't hear anything," Irene insisted. "Come on."

"Well, I did." Faith paused long enough to see if Ben had noticed, too. Not only was he acting more alert, his ears were pricked and he was staring in the same direction she thought the sound had come from. "And so did he."

"All the more reason for us to keep moving," the older woman cautioned. "You can either come with me or stay here and fuss about some will-o'-the-wisp. It's up to you."

"I'm coming, I'm coming," Faith said quickly. Keeping hold of the mule's lead rope, she climbed into the saddle, kicked her horse and fell into line behind Irene without further discussion.

Bringing up the rear, Ben snorted and blew condensation through his flared nostrils as if making his own comment.

Faith glanced back at him. She could tell he was uneasy, as was she. Whether the third member of their trio believed it or not, she and Ben both sensed that something was amiss.

Faith might have believed she'd merely been imagining things if her mule hadn't echoed her nervousness. She shivered and peered into the distant dimness, straining to sort out the sounds of the desert at night.

It was totally peaceful. Too peaceful. That wasn't how other evenings had been. Normally, birds called and insects chirped, even in the darker phases of the moon. Tonight, absolute quiet reigned.

The only sounds Faith was able to discern, no matter how hard she tried to hear, were the soft clumping of the horses' hooves and the pounding of her own heart.

Chapter Seventeen

Circling wide to pick up Faith's trail without being seen by anyone from the wagon train took Connell the better part of an hour. By the time he did find her mule's tracks they had been joined by those of a pair of Indian ponies.

He'd been hoping Irene would see what was needed and take appropriate action. Assuming those particular hoofprints didn't belong to renegade Indians, she'd done just that and was currently shepherding Faith back to their campsite. Good. He'd have had a terrible time keeping track of both of them if they'd remained separated.

Thinking of the two women at the same time pointed up many contrasts. Irene was steady. Predictable. Sensible to a fault. He might have attributed those characteristics to her maturity had he not known her when she was a mere girl. Even back then she had been the sober, rational type, wise beyond her years.

Faith, on the other hand, was anything but prudent. She viewed life as one grand adventure and conducted herself accordingly. Where another woman might have collapsed in despair or fright, Faith Beal had trudged bravely on, head held high, spirits unflagging. When they'd first met, at Fort Laramie, she'd denied the pain of her injuries until her body had rebelled and forced her to pay heed. Now that she'd mended, it was even easier for him to appreciate her fortitude. Too bad it wasn't tempered by more discretion.

Rojo's head suddenly came up, his ears swiveling forward. Since their campsite lay only a few hundred yards ahead, Connell wouldn't have worried if a shiver hadn't pricked the nape of his own neck at the same instant.

He reined in the big gelding and dismounted. The camp was dark. Because of lingering danger from the wagon train, he hadn't expected to see a fire. He did, however, think someone should have noted his approach and called to him by now. Irene would remain wary, of course, but Faith didn't know the meaning of caution. *Not* hearing her voice made him more uneasy than he would have been if she'd shouted out a greeting—or a warning.

There was no way he could sneak closer when Rojo was with him so he let go of the reins to leave the horse ground-hitched, then dropped into a crouch and started to circle the tiny encampment. Irene's horse's tracks had led straight there, so where was she? Moreover, what had become of Faith and her mule?

Before Connell had time to ask himself any more questions he heard three telltale metallic clicks. Somebody had just cocked the hammer of a revolver! He froze.

To his soul-deep relief, the sound was not immediately followed by a bullet. Instead, he heard a sharp intake of breath, then a smothered gasp.

A lone figure arose out of the darkness. His subconscious recognized Faith in time to keep him from acting on instinct and forcefully defending himself. Relieved, though still on alert, he started to straighten slowly, cautiously.

Faith uncocked her pistol, holstered it and launched herself at him with a squeal of delight. "Connell!"

Her arms were open wide, her enthusiasm overwhelming. The plainsman caught her as she barreled into him, but her momentum carried them both to the ground and temporarily knocked the wind out of him.

"Oof."

Faith didn't seem to notice. "Oh, Connell. Praise God!" she blurted. "I've been so worried!"

"Thanks. I think."

He gave her a wry smile, then asked, "Do you mind?" before clasping her waist and bodily moving her to one side. Once he'd regained his feet he gave her his hand and pulled her up, too.

Faith was blushing, flustered. "I'm so sorry. I didn't mean to knock you over. I was just so glad to see you. I've been terribly nervous, out here all alone."

Connell stiffened, fully alert and scanning the darkness beyond. "Alone? Irene isn't with you? Why not? I followed your tracks."

"She was here. She took Ben and the horses to water."

Reassured, Connell began to relax. "Then everything's okay. She wouldn't have left you if she'd thought there was any danger. How long has she been gone?"

Faith's words tumbled out like water through flood-gates. "I don't know. It feels like forever. I was sup-posed to wait right here by the fire—only we didn't light one—and tell you not to worry, that she'll be back shortly. She swore she never gets lost. I didn't know what else to do. After she went away, I began hearing things prowling around in the dark so I got out Papa's gun. Oh, Connell! I might have shot you. I'm so glad I didn't. You shouldn't go sneaking up on me in the dark. I mean, what if I'd...oh, my."

Connell let her babble on till she'd run out of things to say, then reassured her with a soft chuckle. "Hey, you didn't shoot, so stop fretting."

"I suppose I should have, shouldn't I?"

He rolled his eyes. "Shot me? No."

"No, not *you*. I mean whatever else is out there. I know something is. I can feel it. Ben sensed it, too."

"Probably coyotes." Connell noticed she was trem-bling and put his arm around her shoulders for com-fort. "You should never shoot at anything unless you can see it clearly and be sure it's really what you think it is." He gave her an amiable squeeze. "If you'll re-member that one rule you won't blow holes in your friends by mistake."

He'd intended to raise her spirits with the silly com-ment. Instead, Faith stared at him for a second, then buried her face in her hands and burst into tears.

"Hey, enough of that. The scary part's over. Every-body came through safe and sound, even the dumb kid who jumped on her mule bareback and started a stampede."

Faith sniffled, wiped her damp cheeks with the backs of her hands and looked up at him wide-eyed. "I—I did?"

"You sure did."

"What happened? I was so busy trying to get away I never looked back."

"Let's just say that Ramsey Tucker was good and bamboozled by the whole thing. He rode up after I got the stampede stopped and wanted to know what I'd seen. I swore I hadn't seen one single Indian brave."

"You lied?"

"Nope. He didn't ask me about seeing any squaws. My conscience is clear." Connell's smile grew. "I knew you'd be proud of me for telling the truth."

Faith slipped one arm around his waist and leaned into him to take full advantage of the way he was still hugging her shoulders. "I'd be proud of you no matter what. I can't believe anyone would offer to take my place the way you did when Black Kettle was so angry."

"I can't believe I did it, either. It wasn't planned."

"That doesn't matter. You did it. That's what counts. I'm so, so grateful. And I'm so sorry you were hurt."

Turning slightly to fully face him, Faith put her other arm around his waist and clung to him with a fierceness that surprised her while she choked back sobs. She hadn't meant to weep anymore, but her emotions were overwhelming.

"Hey, there's no need for that," he said, closing his arms around her and gently rubbing her upper back. "It's all over now."

"No it isn't. It'll never be over." Faith was afraid to let go, to stop drawing courage from his solid strength.

"Sure it will." Connell wished he could honestly say that her trials would soon be at an end, but it wasn't fair to lie to her, even if the truth was painful. "Look, we've come this far in one piece so we must be doing something right. Your problems will all work out for the best. And I'll stay with you till everything is settled."

"You—you will?"

"Of course I will. That's what friends do."

"We are friends, aren't we?" she asked, swiping away the last of her tears and looking up at him. "I'm sorry I've been acting so silly. I don't usually fall apart like this. When I stop to think about everything that's happened, I just can't seem to keep from crying." She managed a smile. "I don't want you to think I'm like Charity."

"Not a chance," Connell assured her. "I already know you're one of a kind."

"I am?"

"Oh, yes," he drawled, nodding. "When the Good Lord made you, I imagine He realized He'd outdone himself so He stopped right there. One Faith Beal was enough."

Silently, Connell added, *And in my case, one is probably one too many.*

Faith would have gladly stood in the man's tender embrace for hours if she hadn't felt him suddenly tense. She looked up. "What is it? What's the matter?"

"I don't know. I heard something out there."

"Maybe Irene is bringing the horses back."

"Maybe." He grasped her shoulders to set her away from him. "In which case I don't suppose she'd be all that thrilled to find us acting like a couple of Cheyennes standing under a blanket."

"We weren't!"

"No, we weren't. But it might have looked like we were, which is bad enough." He turned to scan the prairie beyond their camp. "It's a new moon so there isn't much light. You stay right here. Keep your head down."

Faith made a grab for his sleeve. "Wait! Where are you going?"

"Out there," Connell told her quietly. "Keep your papa's pistol handy while I'm gone but, for heaven's sake, don't pull the trigger unless you're positive you're not shooting at me or Irene."

"Or the horses."

That comment made him chuckle in spite of the tension in the air. "I figure you can probably tell the difference between a fella like me and a critter like Ben, especially if you think hard about it. Just remember, he's the one with the long ears."

Watching Connell disappear into the dimness of the desert night, Faith thought about his parting remarks. His ears might be smaller, but he was every bit as stubborn as her old mule. And strong. And just as faithful.

"You're all I have left. I love you both," she whispered with soul-deep honesty. "More than anything else in the world."

Embarrassed by the admission even though no one had heard her make it, Faith blushed. She didn't know how the plainsman would feel about being compared to a mule, especially when that comparison gave equal favor to both man and beast, but she'd meant it to be the highest of compliments. There wasn't a single person on the whole of the earth that she trusted the way she trusted Connell McClain. Nor was there another mount besides Ben to whom she wanted to assign her future well-being. Now that she had him back, nobody was ever going to wrest him away from her again.

A stick broke beneath a footstep somewhere in the dark. Faith started. Crouched. Picked up her father's Colt pistol and held it at the ready.

"Don't shoot," a man's voice called. "It's us."

Breath left Faith is a whoosh of relief. "Connell. You found Irene?"

He came closer. "Yes."

"Is everything all right?" The expression on his face was muted by the night, yet Faith thought he looked disturbed, maybe even angry.

"Everything's fine. There wasn't any watering hole close by after all. We'll take the horses and Ben to find food and water at daybreak. They'll be fine until then."

He glanced at Irene, who was following with their mounts, and told her, "I left Rojo a ways out. I'll go get him. You stay here with Faith." There was a long pause in which nothing else was said before Connell added tersely, "Is that understood?"

Irene merely nodded. As soon as he'd walked away, she went to work hobbling the other horses by tying short strips of rawhide between their front legs. Trussed up that way, they could take short steps to graze yet were prevented from running off.

"I'll leave Ben for you to take care of," she said,

straightening and facing Faith. "Unless you're sure he'll stick close no matter what, I'd tie him, too."

"He won't leave me," Faith assured her.

"If you say so."

"I do. I know him very well. We grew up together."

Irene made a soft sound of disgust. "Believe me, just because you've known him all your life doesn't mean he won't start to think and act differently if his circumstances change."

"Are we still talking about me and my mule?" Faith asked. "Or have we started talking about you and Connell?"

Irene retained her stoic Cheyenne expression. "If you want your mule to be here in the morning, Miss Beal, you'll take my advice and tie him."

"You didn't answer me. I've been getting the feeling that something's wrong ever since we left Black Kettle's camp. What is it? Why is Connell acting so funny?"

With a cynical laugh, Irene said, "You don't have much experience with men, do you?"

"Of course I do. I had a father. And I managed to outwit Ramsey Tucker."

"Only because Connell intervened. If he hadn't, you'd be long dead by now."

Faith had to admit she was right. "Okay. So I had help. You did, too. Ab was supposed to kill you, you know, but he went against orders and sold you, instead."

"I know."

Sadness colored the other woman's countenance, making her shoulders slump, her voice sound tremulous. It was the first time since Faith had met her that Irene had shown any sign of being downhearted.

"Then cheer up. You should be giving thanks to our Heavenly Father. We both should," Faith urged. "We were spared. There must be some good reason, some special deed we were meant to accomplish, perhaps even together." She was warming to her subject as more and more truth dawned. "Think of it. You and I were strangers until a benevolent Providence united us in the midst of all our troubles. Isn't that wonderful?"

Irene looked askance at her. "Wonderful? Do you actually believe that what's happened to you—or to me—is *good?*"

"It can be. If our faith is strong enough we can triumph over any evil. You'll see. Everything will turn out for the best. All we have to do is keep our eyes on the Good Lord and our minds open to His plans and we'll persevere."

"Life isn't that simple." Irene stared off into the distant emptiness, her vision unfocused. "And this isn't the Garden of Eden."

"I suppose not." Faith sighed. "There are times when I've thought it was beautiful enough to be, though. This country has a stark, unique beauty. Sunsets out here seem to last forever. When the sky turns all pink and orange, it takes my breath away."

At that, Irene nodded agreement. "Mine, too. In the spring, the Cheyenne and Arapaho hold a dance to honor the sun. I was traded to Black Kettle during one of those celebrations."

"That must have been awful."

"If Walks With Tree hadn't already befriended me by then it would have been worse." She smiled slightly at the memory of the kind old man. "He was very quick-witted. I suspect he realized right away that my so-called magic was a trick, but he never hinted that I might be faking."

"Because he wanted a share of your glory."

"Not entirely. Now that I've had time to think about it, I know he could have gained just as much prestige by revealing my charade. The fact that he chose not to, leads me to believe he genuinely admired me, as I did him."

"I still can't imagine having to live that way every day, among all those Indians, with none of your own people to talk to or confide in."

"Funny," Irene answered. "I'm having trouble imagining living anywhere else."

Chapter Eighteen

Faith had decided to keep Irene's confession to herself, though she had mulled it over a lot during the two days they'd rested while Ben and the horses gained strength.

By the third day, when Connell gave the order to resume their westward trek, Faith had made up her mind that his increasingly dour mood must have its roots in Irene's melancholy. It was more comforting to blame his bad disposition on the other woman than it was to entertain the notion that she, herself, might be a contributing factor.

Faith kept remembering Irene's words as their party rode toward the Sierras. It had seemed strange to hear anyone say they preferred to live with Indians rather than return to life among the settlers. Still, Faith supposed that was a natural result of a long stay in the Cheyenne camp.

In her mind, Faith likened Irene to a formerly tame riding horse that had become accustomed to living with a herd of wild mustangs. That same horse could be recaptured, and even broken to ride again. But it was never the same. No matter how well it was treated or how obedient it seemed, it always kept looking into the distance as if wishing for the freedom to rejoin its former companions.

People, of course, had sense enough to realize they couldn't do that. Irene knew where she belonged. Though she might pine for the life she'd temporarily led among the Cheyenne, she'd realize she could never go back.

Truth to tell, neither could Faith, though she had often wished she could return to Ohio and resume her life exactly as it had been before her mother's untimely death. That was an impossibility, of course. Pretty daydreams couldn't wipe away harsh reality. Right now, her only concern had to be surviving the remainder of her trek without succumbing to thirst, hunger, accident or Indian attack. Judging by the signs of failure littering the trail, success had been the exception rather than the rule for far too many preceding travelers.

Worried, she urged Ben ahead and reined him in next to Connell. "This is awful. Just look at what people had to throw away. And their poor animals. Some of their bodies are still in harness, like they're lying right where they fell." She covered her nose. "What a terrible stench."

"I told you this was going to be a hard crossing. If we hadn't let our horses rest back at the meadows, they'd be giving out by now, too."

"I can see why you didn't want to travel during the worst heat of the day." She drew the back of her wrist across her damp brow. "It's beastly out here."

Connell frowned. "You're right. You need a hat. I should have thought of that."

"I'll be fine. I'm just not used to such bright sun, that's all. I know it must be my imagination, but it feels more intense out here than it ever did back home."

"You're not imagining anything. Part of the heat comes from the reflection off the ground. With no grass or trees to break it up, it bounces back and cooks us from all sides, like venison on a spit."

Talk of the oppressive heat was making Faith a bit woozy. She did her best to keep any unsteadiness from showing but saw Connell eye her with a frown.

He held up one hand and announced, "This is far enough for now. We'll stop here and rest. Drink a little water and give some to your mule while Irene and I see to the horses. Don't let him have too much. We don't want to waste it."

"How much farther to the Carson River?"

"Far enough."

Faith swung her right leg over Ben's rump, leaned against the side of the saddle and kicked loose with the opposite foot so she could slide the rest of the way to the ground. Landing, she hid the unsteadiness of her aching legs by keeping one hand on the saddle horn and leaning on the mule for support. To her relief, Connell was concentrating on the horses and didn't appear to notice.

What she would have liked to do was pour the contents of her canteen over her head and revel in the coolness. The mere thought sent a shiver skittering along her spine. What a delicious idea—and one she would someday carry out. Now, however, was not the time to indulge a silly fantasy. Not when every drop of water could mean the difference between life and death.

She raised the canteen and put it to her parched lips. One, two, three swallows of precious liquid slipped over her tongue and down her dusty throat like quicksilver, yet they felt more like rocks when they landed in her stomach. Clearly, that was enough for now. It was Ben's turn.

The moment Faith cupped her hand to make a watering trough she realized how inefficient that method was. Ben was sure to spill most of his water the minute he thrust his big muzzle into her palm and tried to drink.

Noting that Connell had inverted his leather hat and was using it to water the horses, Faith knew she could wait her turn and do the same. She would have, too, except that Connell had assigned her only one chore and she was determined to complete it on her own.

Casting around for a suitable receptacle, she scanned nearby necessities left behind by previous travelers. Surely there would be something there in which she could offer Ben water.

Vultures circled above them, mute testimony to the seriousness of her task. Ben might be terribly thirsty before this trip was over—they all might be—but as long as Faith had water to give him he'd survive. She'd see to it.

She kept a tight hold on the mule's reins and led him toward a wagon that lay about fifty feet off the main trail. The rig looked as if its owners had merely climbed down and walked away after the axle had broken. Except for fraying of the loose flap that served as a door, the canvas covering was intact. Roofs of many other wagons were either gone or badly damaged. Therefore, Faith reasoned, this rig had been deserted recently and was more likely to contain whatever she needed.

The cautious mule balked at the odor of death all around them. Faith calmed him with her voice. "It's okay, boy. That's it. Come on."

She continued to grasp the makeshift rope reins as she stood on tiptoe to peer into the abandoned wagon. The interior was as pristine as the outside. If she didn't know better, she'd guess the family had merely stepped away briefly and would soon return. They wouldn't, of course. No one took an extended respite in the midst of a desert. Which meant that whatever they'd left behind belonged to whoever came along later and needed it.

Faith spied a deep iron pot, heavy but perfect for her needs. It banged against the back of the wagon and startled Ben as she dragged it out by its looped handle.

"Easy, boy, easy. How about some water? Would you like that?"

She carefully poured precious water into the pot and waited in the shadow of the wagon while the old mule dipped his nose and drank.

Heat shimmered off the bare ground, making even that small patch of shade nearly unbearable. Faith sagged against the tilted tailboards. How any animal— or human, for that matter—could stand this unrelenting torture for long was beyond her. It was a wonder that any survived the crossing.

Connell joined her. He was alone. "Ben okay?"

"Fine, considering."

"How about you?"

Faith huffed, then smiled. "Fine, considering."

"Good. We won't be able to rest long so make the most of it." He eyed the abandoned wagon behind her. "Did you find yourself a hat?"

"I never thought about it. I was looking for a pot to water Ben. That's as far as I got."

"I'll see what I can do," Connell said, passing her and clambering easily into the leaning wagon bed. "I'd like to find regular clothes for you and Irene, too. Time will come when it'll be a lot better if you look like city women instead of refugees from an Indian camp."

"We are refugees from an Indian camp."

"My point, exactly. Once we reach California, it'll be easier to find your father if we don't have to keep explaining who and what we are."

"When you figure out who I am, let me know, will you? I'm sure not the same person I was a few months ago."

Connell's voice was muted inside the wagon, but Faith thought she heard him mention Irene.

She peered in at him. "What?"

"I said, I think Irene feels the same way. Crossing the plains changes everyone, and the two of you have really been through some harsh trials. You're bound to have grown in the process."

"Or dropped dead," Faith said cynically. She stared at the distant purple-tinged hills. "I didn't know there was such a godforsaken place in the entire world."

"It isn't the place that's to blame," Connell explained. "Giving up is in the heart. The folks who pass through here bring their faith, or lack of it, with them. I'm just coming to understand that. Bad times can push a man either way. In my case, I guess I'd turned away from the God of the Bible long before Little Rabbit Woman was killed."

"Yet you blamed Him?"

"Exactly."

"That's foolish."

"I know that now." Connell poked his head out of the wagon and squashed a straw farmer's hat on her head, then passed her a bundle of colorful fabric. "Here. I couldn't find a bonnet so that hat'll have to do till we come across something better. Next time we camp, you and Irene can fight over which dresses you want."

"Fight? Why should we fight?"

"Beats me," he said, climbing down. "Irene's been acting about as agreeable as a badger with a toothache. That's not like her. I about fell over when I came back to camp after we'd gotten Ben. I couldn't believe she'd gone off and left you there by yourself."

"That's not my fault."

"Nope. But I never have figured you out, either, so I'm not about to get myself between you two, no matter what else happens."

"Meaning?" Faith was scowling.

"Meaning, I'll still guide you to California, just like I promised, but you'll have to make your own peace with Miss Irene Wellman. I'd have figured she was just jealous of you if she wasn't acting like she hates everybody, me included."

This was the opportunity Faith had been waiting for, praying for. Nervous, she licked her parched lips. "Maybe…maybe she doesn't want to go back to her old life."

One eyebrow arched and Connell snorted his disbelief. "Why would you think that?"

"Because she seemed to be happy with the Cheyenne, for one thing. She did have a beau."

"Only because she thought I was dead," he argued. "Once she found out I was alive, she told Red Deer about our old arrangement."

"Arrangement?" Faith's voice was rising. "If that's all it was—or is—then I pity you both."

That said, she stomped away, leaving Connell staring after her, dumbfounded.

Little was said for the remainder of the afternoon. Conversation took energy and there was none to spare. Mouth dry, Faith licked her cracked lips and kept her head tipped so the brim of the oversize hat would offer a smidgen of shade. She knew there'd be no relief, no cool respite, until they reached the foothills of the Sierras. How soon that would be was irrelevant. The only thing that mattered was staying alive.

Too weary to pray, Faith merely closed her eyes and let the gentle rocking of Ben's walk lull her into an internal awareness of the Lord's presence. In Bible stories, many a man had been shepherded safely through the wilderness. Strong faith was the key to survival, just as Connell had said. That, and putting her complete trust in those who had been ordained to deliver her. Surely, McClain was such a man. Meeting him had been a wonderment, considering how many other travelers had been nearby when she'd been injured. The fact that he'd been the one to come to her rescue was proof enough that he was special. Heaven-sent.

Her heart swelled with gratitude—and more—taking her imagination on a flight of fancy. She pictured herself in his arms, her cheek lying against his broad chest as she listened to his heart beating rhythmically like the thudding of her own pulse in her ears, at her temples. Soft cadence. Drumming. Humming in her veins. Dulling the unrelenting assault of heat on her exhausted body and soul.

She swayed in the saddle. Flashes of light sparkled behind her closed eyelids like a night sky filled with millions of stars. At the periphery, blackness waited to envelop her, to rescue her from reality.

In the deepest parts of her mind, Faith knew she must be falling, yet her only sensation was one of floating. The desert disappeared from her consciousness, as did all her suffering and thirst. Empty, welcome blackness took its place.

When Faith came to, she was lying in the shade of a scrubby tree. Connell was bathing her face with a wet cloth and fanning her with her straw hat.

She opened her eyes and reached for his wrist to stop him. "Don't waste water."

"It's all right," he said softly. "We made it. There'll be plenty to drink from here on out."

Faith tried to sit up. He held her in place with a hand on her shoulder.

"Just lie there and rest," Connell said. "You've had a rough time of it."

"What...what happened?"

"You passed out."

"I don't remember." When she tried to moisten her

lips, she realized how dry and cracked they were. "I'm so thirsty. Are you sure there's plenty to drink?"

"Positive. Irene's gone to water Ben and the horses." He cradled Faith's head, lifted it and held the canteen to her lips. "Here. Drink. Just don't overdo it or it's liable to make you sick."

She swallowed all he'd allow, then sat up and thanked him. "I don't think I'll ever quench this thirst."

"Sure you will." A relieved smile lit his face and crinkled the outer corners of his eyes. "You're looking better already. Had me worried there for a while, though. I was beginning to think you were going to quit on me."

"Never." Faith smiled as far as the cracks in her sore lips would allow. "You're stuck with me, mister."

"I'm glad to see your feisty attitude is intact, too. I kind of missed it."

"Probably not nearly as much as I did," she quipped. "I think I must have been hallucinating part of the time. I imagined I was..." A blush rose to her already reddened cheeks.

"What?"

Faith looked around to see if Irene was near before she told him. "If you must know, I was dreaming I was—we were, um—I mean, well, sort of hugging. Like back in camp after I almost shot you. Remember?"

"I remember all right. You weren't dreaming. I caught you when you started to fall and carried you till we finally found water. I didn't think you'd mind, especially since the alternative was to sling you over a saddle like a pack."

"That's what Ab did to me," Faith said. "I didn't like it one bit, thank you. Especially with sore ribs."

"How are you doing now? I haven't asked lately because you weren't favoring your side at all."

"I hardly know I was hit. Either my ribs weren't broken in the first place or I heal fast. Or both." She gave him a lopsided grin. "Of course, if these were biblical times I'd say it could also have been a miracle."

"The amazing thing is that we managed to make it this far in spite of all that's happened," Connell said, getting to his feet. "You rest. I'll go see what's keeping Irene."

"Wait! There's something you should know. Something that's been nagging at me. I can't quite put my finger on what's wrong with Irene, but I'm sure something is. I can feel it." Faith could tell by the look on his face he wasn't taking her seriously.

"Intuition?"

She shook her head soberly. "More like a sense of foreboding."

"Now you *are* imagining things." One eyebrow arched. "As a matter of fact, Irene mentioned the same notion about you. I suspect you're jealous of each other."

"Over what? You? Don't be silly. I know you're only helping me because you got stuck with the job. And I know you're the kind of honorable man who doesn't make a vow unless he intends to keep it."

She sighed, then went on, "It's not *your* motives I'm worried about, it's hers."

"You don't have to fret about Irene," he said. "She's as reliable as anyone I've ever met. I know she's been through a lot in the past year or two but you can trust her completely. I do."

"You trust her with your life?" Faith asked quietly, cautiously.

"Of course. And so can you."

Nodding, she bowed her head as he walked away, waiting until he was out of earshot before whispering, "I'm afraid I'm not so sure."

Chapter Nineteen

The trip through the high Sierras was rigorous beyond belief. By the time Faith and the others reached the western side of the range, she was in awe of any and all who had braved the difficult trek. Wrecked wagons that bespoke lost dreams and perhaps lost lives framed the steep, rutted trails and littered the canyons.

Though the sight saddened Faith it was hard for her to continue to grieve for nameless strangers when she was feeling such a sense of success. Every day for the past week she'd asked Connell, "How much longer," and every day he'd answered, "Soon."

Now that the higher elevations were behind them the weather was warm again, though not nearly as uncomfortable as it had been in the desert. When Connell called a halt and suggested the women bathe while he set up camp and prepared an evening meal, Faith was more than glad to oblige. Though she'd loved the comfort of her Cheyenne garb, she was ready for a change of clothes. And the doeskin was definitely ready for a scrubbing. The thought of lighter-weight calico over a cotton chemise and drawers absolutely thrilled her.

Irene remained silent and waited as Faith gathered up the dresses and personal items they'd procured back at the Humboldt Sink. Together, they made their way downstream from where Connell had placed their camp.

Without hesitation, Irene plunged into the waist-deep water, clothes and all.

"Isn't that cold?" Faith asked.

Irene didn't answer. Crouched down up to her neck, she was stripping off her leather garments and rinsing them in the current.

Following Irene's sensible example, Faith waded in. Icy rivulets crept inside her leather moccasins and leggings, chilling her immediately. Shivering, she gave a high-pitched "Ooh!"

"Hush," Irene warned. "Get down into the water, like this, and be quiet, before you draw every bandit and renegade Indian in the territories."

That thought sobered Faith. She ducked and scanned the brushy riverbank, imagining menace in every shadow, behind every tree. "Sorry. It's so beautiful here I forgot to be cautious."

"Women can't afford to forget," Irene told her.

Faith sobered even more. "Was it very bad?"

"What?" Irene continued to tend to her washing without looking up.

"Living with savages."

"Savages? You mean Ramsey Tucker?"

"I wasn't referring to him, but I do see what you

mean. I suppose savageness or civility is all in whatever point of view a person holds, isn't it."

"You are learning," Irene said quietly.

"Do you really wish you could go back to the Cheyenne?"

Irene ducked under the running water for a moment before surfacing and swiping a hand across her eyes. "I refuse to dwell on what cannot be."

"But what do you really want to do?"

She heaved a deep, sorrowful sigh. "If I had any choice, I'd go back to being a carefree girl in love with the young man my family befriended after his mother died. Then I'd run away with him like he wanted me to do many years ago and we'd start a new life."

"Connell?" Faith's throat tightened at the thought.

"Yes. We imagined we were in love. Maybe, in a childish way, we were. I don't know."

"Why didn't you go away with him?"

"Family obligations. I felt those came first and he had a terrible urge to see the Territories, so we were at an impasse."

"What made you change your mind and come west?"

"My parents' deaths, mostly. When my excuse was gone, I wrote to Connell at the last address I had for him, in Sacramento City. I never dreamed he'd still want me after all the time that had passed."

"It's a wonder your letter even reached him."

"I know. I was actually surprised when he answered. He told me he was lonely, and why. So was I. It seemed the most sensible thing in the world to renew our old promise to marry."

"And then you met Ramsey Tucker."

"Yes."

Again Irene ducked beneath the rippling water but not before Faith glimpsed the shimmer of unshed tears. As soon as she came up for air, Faith said, "It's not your fault. None of this is. Tucker lied to you the same way he's lied to my sister. He's very accomplished at getting his way."

"I know."

"Maybe we can procure a settlement from him, on your behalf, when we liberate Charity."

"Money, you mean? Oh, no. Not money." Faith saw Irene's eyes spark, narrow and fill with malevolence. "All I want from Ramsey Tucker is his mangy scalp. It would pleasure me greatly to lift it myself."

"You're not serious!"

Irene stared straight at her and said with unmistakable conviction, "Oh, yes, I am."

Faith knew she should quote the scripture where God said vengeance belonged to Him, but she feared that if she did, Irene's anger would focus on her as well, so she kept silent.

Irene didn't tarry long at the river. Left alone to rue her temporary timidity, Faith prayed for greater strength, wisdom and the courage to express her faith no matter whose displeasure or what obstacles she had to contend with in doing so.

Shivering, she undid her braids and let the river rinse her hair clean the way prayer had cleansed her conscience, then climbed out and followed Irene's example by donning the settlers' clothing they'd brought from the abandoned wagon.

Now that they weren't facing imminent death, Faith could think of other amenities she wished she'd had the presence of mind to pick up when she'd had the chance. Not the least of those was a hairbrush or comb.

She leaned to the side and twisted her long tresses to remove as much water as possible, then looked around for something with which to fasten her hair back. Irene had laid their Cheyenne clothing over brushy lower limbs of trees to dry before starting back up the hill toward their campsite.

Lagging behind, Faith realized she'd lost the colorful ties the young Cheyenne girl had used to hold her rolled braids in place. She was about to give up and forget about doing anything with her hair when she spied a narrow strip of beaded leather tied to a branch beside their old dresses. It was just what she needed. It was also not hers.

Faith opened her mouth to call after Irene for permission, then remembered the older woman's sensible admonition of silence. Surely, it wouldn't hurt to borrow the decorative tie. After all, if Irene had wanted to wear it herself, she'd have done so.

Without further qualm, Faith undid the knot, slid the leather thong under her hair at the nape of her neck and tied it. Having been braided until now, her hair wasn't as tangled as she'd expected, especially considering all she'd been through. She smiled, patting and smoothing the sides. Probably just as well she didn't have a mirror. Some things were best imagined rather than seen.

Besides, she thought with derision, who cared what she looked like? Certainly not Connell McClain. He had

Irene. If any man was a perfect match for poor Irene Wellman, it was the plainsman.

"So why does it bother me so to see them together?" Faith muttered. She started to argue the point with herself, then stopped. It was true. She knew she should be exhibiting Christian charity and thanking the Lord that her rescuer had found his betrothed, yet she couldn't help wishing otherwise. It wasn't the right attitude to harbor. It was simply human.

Faith smiled and muttered, "Well, well. What do you know? One character flaw after another. I guess that's what I get for praying for more wisdom."

Connell had a simple meal almost ready by the time Faith returned to camp. His future bride was sitting sideways on one of the saddles while he squatted by the fire, turning a makeshift spit to finish cooking a rabbit and several small game hens.

Faith grinned. "That smells wonderful. I didn't know how hungry I was till just now." When he looked up at her, his eyes widened and his eyebrows arched, much to her delight.

She twirled to display the calico frock. "Do you like it? It's almost a perfect fit."

"I'll say." Straightening, Connell stared. "Looks like it was made for you."

"Maybe it was. I wish I had a proper ribbon to match." She touched her hair and gave Irene a quick glance as she added, "This was the best I could do. I found it down by the river. I hope you don't mind."

Before Faith could react, Irene leaped to her feet,

screeched in Cheyenne and began to claw at the beaded thong, grasping handfuls of hair with it.

Confused, Faith fought off the attack as best she could. If it hadn't been for Connell's intervention she might have been seriously hurt. He held the struggling Irene at bay while Faith untangled the thong and handed it back to its owner.

"I'm sorry. I didn't think I was doing anything wrong."

"You weren't," Connell replied. Keeping Irene at arm's length, he stared down at her. "What was that all about?"

She twisted out of his grasp without answering, fisted the tangled tie and ran back toward the river where they'd left their Indian garments.

Rubbing her scalp, Faith turned to Connell. "I *told* you she was acting funny. Do you have any idea what's going on?"

"No."

In spite of his denial, Faith was certain she'd glimpsed more than concern in his expression when he'd looked at the object Irene had coveted so. Either it was of special significance by itself or it bore markings that identified it as belonging to a certain person or tribe. Possibly both, she concluded. Although their garments themselves were unique, perhaps the tie was even more so. Perhaps it had belonged to Red Deer.

Faith's breath caught. Suddenly feeling her senses prickling in warning, she stared after Irene. What if the thong had been tied to the branch for some reason other than to dry it? What if it had been placed there as a sign, a marker for someone who was following?

That thought was so bizarre she gawked at Connell, slack jawed and speechless. There was thunder in his expression, lightning in his eyes. Could he be thinking the same thing she was? Was he finally ready to listen to reason and take precautions?

Faith closed her mouth and let it twist with sarcasm. He was already certain she was insanely jealous of Irene, which wasn't far from the truth. Any accusation against Irene, coming on the heels of their tiff over the hair tie, would sound like nothing more than another foolish manifestation of female rivalry.

What could she do, short of knocking Connell over the head and forcing him to pay heed to her concerns?

The more she pondered all the strange things that had occurred since they'd liberated Irene, the more Faith was certain the other woman was up to something. It was beginning to look as though her rescuer was going to need someone to stand firm beside him, and there was only one person in a position to offer support. Her.

She made her way to where her saddle and gear were piled and strapped on her papa's Colt. The holster and enormous revolver looked incongruous atop her new dress but she didn't care. Unlike Charity, she'd decided long ago that self-preservation was far more important than fashion.

Resting a hand on the pistol grip, Faith stood straight and faced Connell, daring him to disagree with her decision to once again travel fully armed.

Instead of the argument she'd expected, he merely nodded thoughtfully and said, "Good."

* * *

Faith watched Connell as they ate, noting his growing unease. His gaze kept darting in the direction where they'd last seen Irene as if expecting her to reappear.

Finally, Faith asked, "Do you think I should go after her and apologize?"

The plainsman shook his head. "No. She'll come back when she's ready."

"Are you sure? I don't mind going."

He got to his feet. "You stay put. Keep the fire built up. I'll go fetch her. The last thing I need is to have both of you wandering around in the hills getting into trouble."

"Do you think she's in trouble?"

"Not till I catch up to her." He sighed. "Irene's as good at wilderness survival as I am, thanks to the Cheyenne. I'd just feel better if I knew exactly where she was."

Faith huffed. "Me, too. I know you don't want to hear this, especially coming from me, but I can't help thinking she's up to something."

"What makes you say that?"

"No one big thing," Faith replied. "Just lots of odd little things that don't add up. Can you honestly say you haven't noticed?" She saw his expression close, his eyes narrow.

"We'll talk about this later," Connell said flatly. He paused beside Rojo and swung his saddle onto the horse's back. "I'm going to mount up in case she's gone farther than the river. You keep track of Ben and the other horses. Make sure they don't disappear while you're sleeping."

"Sleeping?" Faith was on her feet in a heartbeat. "Aren't you coming right back?"

"That's my plan, unless I have trouble finding Irene."

"I should come with you then."

"You'd just slow me down."

"Thanks a heap, mister. Have I slowed you down so far?" She pulled a face. "Never mind. I know I have and I'm sorry. I just don't feel right letting you go out there all alone." Without conscious thought she rested her hand on the butt of the revolver, realizing belatedly that her actions were amusing him.

"I promise to let you protect me some other time," he gibed with a cynical smile. "Right now, I want you to concentrate on looking after yourself." Finished tightening the cinch, he swung into the saddle. "And one more thing. This river feeds straight into the American. Remember that."

Faith frowned up at him, wondering why he felt the need to be so specific until he continued with, "You can find Beal's Bar by sticking to the riverbank and following it downstream. Understand?"

"I understand your directions," Faith said. "What I don't understand is why you're telling me this. Are you trying to scare me? Because if you are, it's working."

He wheeled Rojo in a tight circle while the horse pranced with eagerness. "Just stay alert. I'll be back as fast as I can. I promise."

"Wait!" Faith hurried closer and reached out to him. In an instant he'd bent down and lifted her off the ground, holding her close while she threw her arms around his neck and kissed him soundly.

Just as quickly he put her down, backed his horse away and galloped into the night.

Unsteady, Faith pressed her fingertips to her tingling lips and blinked to try to clear her head. There had been a desperate quality to Connell's goodbye kiss. A yearning that echoed all the pent-up emotion she'd been trying to deny in her own heart.

Realizing their shared feeling lifted Faith's spirits.

It also scared her silly and piled enough guilt on her heart to make it ache.

Chapter Twenty

It was nearly dawn before Faith yielded to fatigue and closed her eyes. The campfire had burned down to glowing embers by the time she stirred again. Except for Ben and the two horses the Cheyenne had given them, she was alone.

How long should she wait for Connell? she wondered. If he'd found Irene, he would have returned as he'd promised. Therefore, he must still be searching. Unless...

Breath caught in Faith's throat. Unless he'd been hurt. Or worse. The notion was so dreadful, so unacceptable, it made her heart race and her head throb.

Every instinct told her she must search for him. Logic countered by reminding her she had no idea where he'd gone. Nor did she know where *she* was. Her only clue was Connell's instruction about following the river's course to Beal's Bar. Clearly, he'd wanted her to proceed in case he didn't make it back, but how could she leave the area without knowing what had happened to him?

She stood, forlorn in the midst of the vast Sierra range, and looked toward heaven. "This isn't right. It isn't fair, Father. I can't leave him. I can't."

Yet, if she didn't go on alone, Charity and Tucker might reach the mining camp ahead of her. Then her innocent father and sister would be in terrible jeopardy. Only Faith knew the whole truth. Only she could save her family from Tucker's planned perfidy.

She had no choice but to break camp and head downriver. Heart heavy, she doused the campfire, packed their supplies aboard one of the horses and saddled Ben. It occurred to her to leave a sign or an arrow to guide Connell but she decided against it. He already knew which way she was going. There was no use giving anyone else a clue to her whereabouts.

And speaking of not leaving behind any sign, she had one important task left. Leading her mule, Faith headed toward the river to pick up her deerskin dress. It was still draped on the bush where she'd left it to dry.

Irene's Cheyenne clothing, however, was gone. So was the beaded tie that had caused such an uproar.

Praying and hoping and wishing, Faith continued to follow the river as Connell had instructed, even after she lost sight of the clear trail of Rojo's prints along the bank. Either the man had ridden his horse into the water or she'd somehow missed some trace of him on the rocky ground. Whichever it was, she was truly on her own.

Too bereft to form coherent plans and too numb to recall comforting scripture verses the way she wanted, she let Ben pick his way along while she thought of

Connell and prayed randomly for his safety and well-being.

"And for his happiness," Faith added. "I do want him to be happy, God. Honest I do. I just don't understand all this. Why did I have to fall in love with him when everything is so hopeless?"

Just then, Ben blew a noisy snort and Faith thought she heard a horse nicker a soft reply. She reined the mule in. "What is it, boy? What's wrong?"

His ears pricked, head turning slowly. Faith stood in her stirrups, straining to see into the distance. There didn't seem to be any reason for the mule's concern, yet he was growing more and more agitated. Behind her, the horses she'd been leading were equally nervous. Suddenly, one bolted, jerked the lead rope out of her hand and galloped off. The other followed.

Shouting "Whoa!" had no effect on either of them and Faith had no clue as to the equivalent Cheyenne word. She was, however, sorely tempted to use some of the colorful language she'd heard more than one so-called gentleman shout in similar circumstances.

"Well, pooh," she finally said, talking to the mule and patting his neck. "At least I've still got you."

He blew another loud snort. This time, Faith knew she heard a horse or mule reply. Urging Ben forward, she took her bearings on the river behind her and went to investigate.

In minutes, she realized her prayers had been answered. Or had they? She stifled a shout and slid from Ben's back.

Connell lay sprawled on the rocky ground, face-down. Rojo stood guard over him. There was blood on the fancy beaded rifle scabbard hanging from his saddle and a nasty-looking cut on the horse's foreleg.

Dropping to her knees beside the prostrate man, Faith touched his shoulder with trepidation. "Connell?"

To her relief, he stirred, moaned.

"Oh, thank God. You're alive!"

He sat up slowly, with effort. "What happened?"

"Don't you know?"

One hand explored his bloody forehead. "Maybe Rojo stumbled. Is he okay?"

"I think so." Faith helped the plainsman stand. "He's cut, but he seems to be putting weight on that leg. How did he fall?"

She saw Connell stiffen and reach for his pistol. It was no longer in its holster. His rifle was gone, too. All he had left was the knife he used for skinning. No wonder he was suddenly on full alert. If his horse had merely fallen, Connell wouldn't have lost both his guns. It didn't take a genius to figure he'd been assaulted and robbed.

"We have to get out of here," he said.

Faith easily adopted his attitude. "Now you're making sense. Let's go. You can ride Ben till we make sure your horse isn't badly injured."

"No. You mount up and ride. I'll follow when I can."

"In a pig's eye, mister. I came to rescue you and that's just what I intend to do."

"You *what?*"

"You heard me. I'm saving your sorry hide. Now stop arguing and get on that mule before I get really upset."

"You don't know what you're saying. It's too danger-ous. Whoever knocked me out might still be around."

"Oh?" Faith cocked an eyebrow. "I thought you got that knot on your head when your horse fell." She could tell she'd bested him, at least for the present.

"Never mind how I got hurt. Just do as I tell you."

"If I'd followed your orders and stayed by the river you might still be lying in a heap with your poor horse bleeding all over you. Now, are you going to do this my way or do I have to sit myself down right here and wait for you to come to your senses?"

Muttering to himself, Connell nevertheless agreed. "All right. Mount up. I'll ride one of the other horses. Where did you leave them, anyway?"

Faith didn't think this was a good time to tell him she'd lost the spare horses so she merely smiled and said, "Give me a boost and swing on behind me. Ben can carry us for a short way and Rojo can follow till we have time to sort everything out."

To her relief, Connell went along with her plan. If she hadn't been so worried about meeting up with who-ever had attacked him, she'd have spent more time fret-ting about how to explain her careless loss of the extra horses.

The throbbing in Connell's temple was the least of his concerns. Even if Rojo had been sound and he'd still had all his weapons, he'd have had to decide which of the two women to help first. Both of them were special to him—Irene because of their long history of friend-ship, and Faith Beal because she needed him and…

He paused, dismayed by the clarity of his mental

ramblings. Faith was special because he not only admired and cherished her, he loved her! She was intelligent as well as the bravest, most virtuous woman he'd ever met.

What a sobering conclusion. The qualities he most admired in her were the very ones that would preclude his ever revealing his deep affection. Honor and righteousness meant everything to Faith. He knew she would never consider marrying a man who had broken his vows to another woman, even if he could bring himself to do so. Which he couldn't.

After all the trials Irene had suffered attempting to join him in California he couldn't just turn away from her. She was like a frightened, wounded animal in need of healing, of the comfort a faithful husband could offer. He'd had his chance at the lighthearted romance of youth with Little Rabbit Woman. It was time to settle down and fulfill his vow to Irene, as he'd promised so long ago.

Still riding with Faith, Connell rested a tender gaze on her shoulders. Ever since he'd foolishly given in and mounted Ben behind her, he'd had to fight the tendency to wrap his arms around her and pull her back against his chest.

He could still taste the sweet kiss they'd shared when they'd last parted. It had been so spontaneous, so right for that moment, he hadn't stopped to think about what he was doing until after the fact. Now, he was beginning to worry that he might have altered the way Faith viewed their relationship. If so, he had some serious atoning to do.

He lightly touched her arm. "Faith?"

"Yes?"

"This is far enough. We'll be safe here. Stop and let me down so I can check Rojo."

She reined in the mule. As soon as Connell swung a leg over and jumped to the ground, Faith dismounted beside him.

"We need to talk," she said quietly.

"That's what I was about to suggest."

"Really?" He'd already started to walk away so she dogged his steps. "You figured it out?"

"Figured what out?"

"About the other horses. I tried to hold on to them but they spooked and ran away. There was no way Ben could catch Indian ponies running scared so I let them go."

"You what?"

"I let them go. What did you expect me to do, go galloping all over the mountains after them and get myself good and lost?"

"No. I expected you to hang on to them."

"I tried to. I don't know what scared them but something sure did. They took off like they'd been shot."

Connell's gaze narrowed.

"Well, they did," she insisted, hands fisted on her hips. "I'm glad I was riding Ben instead of one of them."

"So am I." He glanced past her to scan the hills. "All right. What's done is done. It's obvious I can't leave you alone under the present circumstances so I'll escort you the rest of the way to Beal's Bar. It shouldn't be far. Once you're there, your father can look out for you."

"What about Irene?" Faith saw his jaw muscles knot.

"That decision's been made for me. I can't track her far on foot and I won't ride Rojo till I'm sure he's okay. I'll pick up a spare horse when I drop you off."

"Drop me off? Just like that? I thought you were going to stay and help me get even with Tucker."

"That's all changed. I have to find Irene."

"I know you do. I just thought…" Faith's voice trailed off. "Oh, never mind." She didn't like sounding petulant so she added, "Do whatever you feel you must. I understand. I just wish you could be there to see Tucker taken down a peg. I thought Irene wanted to be in on it, too."

Suddenly, Faith brightened. "I know! Maybe after you find her you can *both* come to Beal's Bar."

Before she finished speaking Connell was shaking his head slowly, soberly. "No, Faith. As soon as Irene and I are back together I'm taking her to my ranch near Sacramento City. She deserves a home of her own and the life I promised her years ago."

"Of course." Though Faith turned quickly away, she feared Connell had glimpsed the tears she was fighting to subdue. When she felt his gentle touch on her arm once again and heard the pathos in his voice, she was certain.

"I'm so sorry," he said. "All I wanted was to rescue you, to do you good. I never meant to cause pain. Please don't cry."

"I'm not crying," Faith insisted. "I just got something in my eye, that's all."

Connell turned her to face him, his hands softly caressing her upper arms through the sleeves of her calico. "If things had been different, I…"

She reached up and placed her fingertips on his lips to silence him. "Don't. Don't say nice things. I can't bear hearing them." Blinking back emotion, she was about to go on when the nearby snap of a dried branch made her gasp and hold her breath.

Connell instinctively reached for his missing pistol, then drew his knife, instead, and placed himself staunchly between Faith and the noise.

Less than fifteen feet away, an Indian woman stepped into the clearing. She was chuckling and shaking her head. "It's a good thing for you two that I'm not hunting scalps."

Together, Faith and Connell shouted, "Irene!"

He started toward her. "Where have you been?"

"Following you two," Irene said. "I spotted our Cheyenne horses grazing back a ways and brought them along." She eyed Connell's forehead. "What happened to you?"

It surprised Faith when his reply was gruff, his attitude off-putting. "Never mind. Where have you been?"

"Out here, same as you. Only it looks like I've been a lot more careful." She pointed back the way she'd come. "I also came across your Hawken rifle. I left it with the horses, over there a ways, when I followed the sound of your voices."

"And the packs? The supplies?"

"All there," Irene said.

"Then go get them. I need medicine to treat Rojo's cut before we go any farther."

The last thing Faith wanted was to interfere, so she volunteered to fetch the horses, assuming he'd be glad to get rid of her. With a bright "I'll do it," she took a step in the direction Irene had indicated. To her surprise, Connell stopped her.

"No. Stay right where you are. She'll bring the horses." He glared at his Cheyenne-garbed betrothed. "Won't you?"

"Of course," Irene answered flatly.

Faith's gaze bounced back and forth between her two companions as she tried to decipher the tacit undercurrent. Something more was going on than that which was evident and whatever it was had made Connell irate and wary. Irene's mood was more difficult to label. Her closed yet cautious expression reminded Faith of the Cheyenne.

That was it! Even in settler's clothing, Irene Wellman had carried herself with the proud aura of a Cheyenne. And now that she was once again dressed as one, she wore her off-putting attitude like a badge of honor.

"Stay here with Rojo," Connell told Faith. "Having Ben nearby will help settle him so he doesn't move around too much and open up that cut again. I'll go with Irene and bring back the horses." He started to leave, then paused. "And don't get careless. Keep your pistol handy."

"You are coming back this time? For sure?"

"For sure," Connell said.

She watched him stride purposefully after the already disappearing Irene and heard him shout, "Slow down. I don't want you out of my sight. Understand?"

Irene's answer was faint but Faith did manage to hear Connell say angrily, "What in blazes is going on?"

That, Faith agreed, was a very good question.

Chapter Twenty-One

Faith had hoped that her companions would have settled their personal differences before they returned with the horses. Instead, they had apparently argued to the point where they were no longer on speaking terms.

Tired of their childishness, Faith stroked Ben's velvety nose and talked aside to him. "Can you believe it? Look at them. Grown folks acting like spoiled brats. And they're fixing to get married. Imagine that."

The old mule lowered his head and nudged her gently. Faith smiled. "Sorry, old boy. I'm fresh out of apples. You'll have to wait till we get to Papa's and see what treats he's got for you."

She looked to Connell and raised her voice. "How far are we from Beal's Bar, anyway?"

"My guess is about half a day," he replied.

"Is that all? Well, what are we waiting for?"

"I don't want to push Rojo. We can make camp here, rest up, and still have plenty of time to get there ahead of Charity and Tucker."

"You're sure?"

"Positive. Even with our side trips—" he glanced daggers at Irene "—we're ahead of schedule."

"I could ride on ahead," Faith suggested.

Connell was adamant. "Not alone."

"Why not? It's sure not very enjoyable keeping company with you two. Besides, if I hadn't followed Ben's instincts and left the riverbank, I'd be by myself right now anyway."

"But you're not, are you? I'd think even you would have figured out that the Good Lord intends for me to keep looking after you."

"Oh really?" Faith fisted her hands on her hips. "And I get no credit for rescuing you? Seems to me you're the one with the short memory, mister. Besides, I thought you were anxious to get rid of me."

"I never said that."

"You most certainly did. You told me you were going to drop me at my father's, then turn right around and take Irene home to your ranch."

Irene had been listening quietly. Now, she spoke. "No."

Connell whirled. "What do you mean, no?"

"I'm not going anywhere with you, or anyone else, until I've seen Tucker get what's coming to him."

Faith recalled what Irene had said about taking justice into her own hands. The memory made her shiver. Yes, she wanted to see justice done, but she didn't want to be a party to another murder. Standing over her own grave and knowing it contained the body of the man who had planned her demise had made her painfully aware of the heinous consequences of such an act.

Being a Christian meant she believed she'd go to be

with the Lord when she died, would greet her mother and other loved ones again in heaven, but it didn't mean she was eager to depart immediately! Or that she was willing to send another human being on his way to eternity.

There had been a time when, consumed with irrational anger, she'd wished for the chance to end Ramsey Tucker's life with her own hands. That time had passed. There was no goal more important than rescuing Charity and making her see the folly of her ways. Once that was accomplished, the problem of Tucker should solve itself, unless Irene interfered and killed him before Charity realized what kind of man he really was.

Now that Irene was again garbed as a Cheyenne, Faith found the woman's countenance threatening. In order to muster the courage to speak her mind, she had to keep reminding herself that as a Christian she was clad in the whole armor of the Lord.

"Irene wants to kill Tucker," Faith announced. "We mustn't allow that. He needs to be unmasked and properly punished by the law so my sister can see him for what he is, a thief, liar and murderer. Behaving like him will only undermine our position of truth."

Connell nodded. "I agree. However, if the wagon boss manages to talk his way out of this mess, he'll be free to repeat his crimes against other innocent women. We can't allow that either."

"Of course not." Pacing, Faith pressed her fingertips to her throbbing temples and took a deep, settling breath before she continued. "I just want you to promise—both of you—that you'll work with me, not against me. I know my father will help us, too."

"Assuming we locate him," Connell said. "If not, once Charity and Tucker are away from the protection of the men on the train, we may have to kidnap her for her own good."

"I don't object to doing whatever is necessary to rescue my sister," Faith said, "but it's my fervent hope that we can best Ramsey Tucker at the same time."

"In other words," Connell drawled, smiling, "you want the impossible."

She returned his smile. "Why not? This whole trip west has been one improbable event after another."

"One disaster after another, you mean."

Faith shook her head. "No. The tornado that killed my mother was a true disaster, but even that's been used for good. Think about it. If Charity and I hadn't been forced to travel west when we did, you and I might not have met at Fort Laramie and you'd have had no reason to join Tucker's party and travel with us. If you hadn't, you might never have met Ab and Stuart and finally located Irene. See? It all works together, just like the Good Book says."

"Ha!" Irene huffed in disgust. "That's easy for you to say. You weren't married to a heinous man like Tucker and sold into slavery. If God is so good, why did I have to suffer all that?"

"I don't know," Faith said with evident empathy. "But I have thought about your situation and come to one important conclusion. You need a man like Connell, a man who understands Indian culture and is comfortable with you, just as you are. Just as you want to be."

Her gaze traveled over the older woman's outfit, pausing at the toes of her moccasins before returning to her dark, sad eyes. "He'll be a good husband for you. I know he will." If emotion hadn't choked off her words she'd have added, *Please, be a good wife to him*.

She turned away to hide her gathering tears as she thought, *The kind of good wife I would be, if he were free to love me the way I love him*.

Rising at dawn, Faith was dressed, mounted and ready to travel as soon as the others were. Though they were about to enter a populated area, Irene had chosen to continue dressing like a Cheyenne, Faith noted. All the more reason for the woman to fit comfortably into the life that awaited her. Faith's mind was convinced Connell and Irene belonged together. It was her stubborn heart that kept arguing the point.

Looking for distraction, she urged Ben ahead of Irene's horse and trotted along beside Connell. Seeing such a big man mounted on the scruffy Indian pony instead of his magnificent canelo made her smile.

Grinning, she said, "Hello down there, mister. How much farther?"

He gave her a taciturn look. "Maybe an hour. Maybe less."

"How can you be so sure? We don't have a map."

"I know where the Feather River joins the American. Your father's camp is supposed to be just south of there. As soon as we hit the river there'll be plenty of men to ask, which reminds me," Connell said. "I don't think you should identify yourself unless you have to."

"That's exactly what I was thinking," she said, smiling. "If we can get to Papa without the whole camp finding out who I am, maybe we can keep my survival a secret and catch Tucker unaware." It pleased her to see appreciation in Connell's expression.

"Smart girl."

Girl? I'm a woman, she wanted to screech. *Grown and madly in love with you, you big idiot.*

Instead of uttering such a revealing retort she merely said, "Thank you," nudged Ben in his sides and rode on.

Faith was about fifty yards ahead of the others when she heard Connell and Irene start to argue.

"What happened to the dress I got you?" he asked. To which Irene replied, "I like this one. It's better suited for riding."

"Fine. So tell me again where you found my rifle."

"I already told you. On the trail."

"What were you doing behind me?"

"Who said I was?"

"I do."

"Okay, so maybe I was on my way back to camp."

"That still doesn't explain how you managed to catch the horses Faith lost."

"They're Cheyenne. They came right to me. Probably recognized me."

"Who else is supposed to recognize you?" Connell demanded. "And who knocked me off my horse? Was it you?"

"Don't be ridiculous," Irene said flatly. "Rojo stumbled and you fell, that's all."

"And my rifle? Did it fall, too?"

"I suppose so."

"Then maybe you'd like to explain how you managed to locate it? Faith and I looked all over. It wasn't anywhere near the place where she found me. Am I supposed to believe some stray coyote dragged it off like a dog with a bone?"

"How should I know? Maybe you were groggy and wandered around after you were hurt. Maybe, maybe…"

Faith couldn't quite hear the rest of Irene's excuse. She didn't have to. It had been plain for some time that the other woman wasn't being totally forthcoming. What that might mean, however, was yet to be seen. Living as a captive had left poor Irene as wary as a rabbit in a snare, which could mean she was merely being cautious and circumspect out of habit, not necessarily dishonest by choice.

If I could talk to her alone, woman to woman, maybe I could get closer to the truth, Faith reasoned.

Given their current traveling arrangements, however, she couldn't imagine an opportunity to do that until after they'd arrived at Beal's Bar, and by that time, it might be unnecessary. By then, Connell might have spirited his bride away to their new life, negating any reasonable cause for concern.

But I'll still care about him, Faith told herself. *No matter where he goes or what he does, I'll care for the rest of my life.*

Nothing in the newspapers back home in Ohio or in her father's few letters had prepared Faith for the perilous final approach to the mining camp. Beal's Bar lay at the bottom of a barely accessible canyon. If she hadn't been aboard Ben and trusted his sure-footed gait she doubted she'd have had the nerve to attempt the steep, narrow trail. Yes, she trusted in God's protection—but she also knew it was wrong to test Him by behaving foolishly when she knew better.

Connell led the way, entering the trail after a brief conversation with a scruffy miner who had just come up from the valley. Trembling, Faith was glad she was last in line during the descent. Showing fear was unfitting, especially since neither of the others seemed at all nervous.

As they neared the river at the end of their precarious trek, Faith relaxed enough to appreciate the beauty of the sparkling water that snaked through the gorge. It rippled over and around rocks in a random pattern that made it look like quicksilver seeking a path through scattered mountains of glistening gravel.

In the midst of it all, atop a rough rise that looked low and insignificant enough to be inundated at any moment, lay the makeshift buildings of Beal's Bar. There were tents, wooden structures, and various cobbled-up combinations of both. The largest edifice was almost completely canvas-covered, roof and all. Someone had painted "Majestic Hotel" across the front, an arguable conclusion if she'd ever seen one.

Wide-eyed, Faith scanned the motley group of men that had begun to gather at their approach. Most of the miners were dressed similarly in flannel shirts, pantaloons with the legs tucked into boots, and black felt hats with wide brims that shaded the only parts of their faces that weren't covered in whiskers.

Where shade and beards left off, dirt took over. Considering that the town was situated practically in a riverbed, their lack of attention to personal hygiene seemed strange to her until she peered into some of their eyes. In spite of all the shouted greetings, whistles and grins, she recognized the same hopelessness she'd felt while crossing the desert. If this was truly the land of milk and honey, someone had failed to convince these poor folks.

Connell stopped his horse and waited for her to ride parallel before he said, "Stay close. Most miners aren't used to having decent women in camp. I'm not sure how rowdy they'll get."

"Nonsense." Faith rested her hand on the butt of the Colt. "I can take care of myself. All I intend to do is ask directions."

"All right. You and Irene wait here while I go make some discreet inquiries."

Before Faith could object, he dismounted and strode through the crowd into the makeshift hotel. Not about to take orders when her own father was involved, she started to follow, then thought better of it. There were other mules around but none as big and impressive as her Ben. It wasn't wise to leave him unattended.

Instead, she spoke to the nearest miner, a bearded derelict in tattered clothing whose skin was as weathered as the cracked leather of his boots.

"Excuse me, sir, we're looking for Mr. Emory Beal," Faith said. "Do you know where I might find him?"

"Mebbe." He spit into the dirt. "What's it worth to ya, pretty lady? A little dance, mebbe?"

She drew herself up, back straight, chin jutting proudly. "I'm certain Mr. Beal will reward you for your information if he feels remuneration is called for."

"Re—what?" The man guffawed. "Well, aren't you a puffed-up little prairie chicken. All right. If'n you're not interested in staying in town and keepin' us company, how's about her? She ain't bad lookin'—fer an Injun."

A quick glance at Irene told Faith her companion was thinking about eliminating that miner's need for future haircuts. Permanently.

"I'd mind my manners if I were you, sir," she warned, smiling slightly. "My Cheyenne friend has a short temper. Now, are you going to give us directions or not?"

He spit again, pointing. "It's that way. The cabin on the rise at the end of this here trail. But ol' Emory can't give ya what me and some o' these other boys can, lady. My claim's rich. Beal's diggin's played out months ago. I hear he's nigh busted. Wouldn't surprise me to see him hightailing it up to the Feather to try his luck there, if he ain't left already."

Others in the crowd were nodding agreement. Faith looked to Irene, then at the hotel door, then back to Irene. "I don't see any reason to sit here and stew, do you?"

"None. If we can find the cabin, so can he."

"Right. Then let's go."

Wheeling Ben, Faith led the way up the canyon in search of the father she hadn't seen in well over a year.

Chapter Twenty-Two

Connell dashed out of the so-called hotel in time to see Faith and Irene riding off without him. He cursed under his breath. If it wasn't one of them causing him grief, it was the other. And now both. No telling what they'd said or done while he was inside. Probably given the whole situation away, he thought, disgusted.

He'd left them so he could quietly inquire about the overall circumstances in town, including whether or not anyone had seen Faith's fool sister. Thankfully, nobody had, which was the first good news Connell had heard in some time. Next stop was the Beal cabin.

He swung onto the Indian pony, grabbed Rojo's lead rope and rode off amid jeers, laughing and calls of "Lose something, mister?" and "Hey! Where's your women?"

The long, narrow valley left few choices of travel. Connell knew approximately where the Beal cabin lay, thanks to the bartender in the hotel. Judging by the direction Faith and Irene had headed, they'd found out, too. All he needed to do was follow them, the quicker the better, and hope he got there before they made any more stupid moves. If Emory Beal was half as impulsive as his eldest daughter, he was liable to grab a shotgun, blow a hole in Tucker without considering the consequences, and hang for murder instead of the other way around. That was not the kind of retribution Connell had in mind.

Emory was coming out of the one-room cabin as Faith and Irene rode up. Hardly able to contain her excitement, Faith grinned, waiting for him to realize who she was. Seconds ticked by. Emory was apparently so concerned about the presence of an Indian woman he wasn't paying heed to anything else, including the once-familiar mule.

Little wonder he didn't know her, Faith decided, fidgeting. Her face was half-hidden by the brim of her borrowed hat and although she was wearing a calico dress, she'd had no boots or shoes so she'd kept the moccasins the Cheyenne had given her. Besides, unless her sad letter had reached him, Emory thought she and Charity were still back in Ohio—with Mama.

Sobering, Faith slid to the ground beside Ben and threw the reins over his head. When she said, "Papa!" there was such pathos in her voice, her father's jaw dropped.

He stepped forward. "Faith?"

"Yes, Papa!" She flung herself into his arms, clinging like the child she once was.

He was weeping with her. Faith leaned away to wipe her cheeks. "You didn't get my letter?"

"There's been no mail from home for months." He

looked past his daughter to the other rider. "Who's that? And where's Mama and your sister?"

"It's a long story, Papa," Faith said. She kept an arm around him as she turned toward the cabin door. "I think we'd better go inside to talk."

He resisted, staring at her with evident dread. "No. Tell me right now. Where's your mama?"

Pausing, Faith took a deep breath and prayed silently for strength, for the right words. There was no way to soften the blow. Nor was there any way for her to escape being the messenger of tragedy.

"Mama's gone to Glory," she said simply. "There was a tornado. The whole house collapsed. There's nothing you could have done, even if you'd been there."

She watched as his shock and disbelief were replaced with soul-deep sadness. Anger would come later. It had for her. And then she'd finally stopped blaming God and had moved on with her life, just as Connell had after his own losses.

Pulled back into the present by thoughts of the plainsman, she glanced down the slope and saw him approaching, tall in the saddle, leading his prize canelo because of its injury.

"The Good Lord has watched out for me," Faith told her father. She pointed. "That's Connell McClain. We owe him my life."

"Charity, too?"

"I pray so," Faith said.

She waited while Connell and Irene dismounted, then made formal introductions. Emory didn't question the way Irene was dressed or hesitate to greet the rough plainsman, yet he did seem befuddled, in a fog.

Faith kept hold of his thin arm while he showed everyone to the corral at the rear of his cabin. As soon as they saw to the needs of Ben and the horses, he invited the party into his home, made them welcome and offered to share a meal while he listened in awe to their tales of the harrowing journey.

Hearing her own words, Faith was struck anew by the awesomeness of her deliverance. It was getting a lot easier to see how God had worked for her good than it had been at the time she was going through the trials. How simple life would be if only she knew exactly what her heavenly Father wanted her to do next.

By the time Faith had finished telling her story and had shared her candid opinion of Charity's dilemma, all she wanted to do was bury her head in a soft pillow and sleep for days. She also wanted to give her father a chance to be alone with his grief, yet she knew there was no time for either. Her sister might arrive any day. There were preparations to make. Plans to agree upon.

"Ramsey Tucker wants your gold, Papa," she said. "The men in town told me your claim's played out. Is that true?"

Emory nodded slowly. "Yes."

"Then what are we going to do?"

"I'd give everything I have to see you and your sister safe and well and happy," he answered. "But since I have nothing of value to offer, we'll just have to make Charity's husband understand."

"It's not that simple," Faith explained. "Tucker doesn't take kindly to bad news. He probably won't believe you're penniless no matter what we tell him."

"I'm not. Not exactly," he said. "I'd saved out a few nice nuggets to show your mama." Eyes misty, he went to a tin sitting in plain sight on a shelf beside his bed, opened it and removed a yellowed white handkerchief.

He handed the small bundle to Faith. "They're yours, now, Faith. Yours and Charity's. I never want to see another fleck of color. Never. It's all been for nothing."

"Oh, Papa, don't say that. You did what you thought was right. I know you wanted to make a better life for all of us. That's not wrong. It just didn't work out the way you'd expected. Mama knew you loved us. That's why she made me promise to come west and find you."

"It's a wonder you did. Many's the man who disappears for good in the diggin's," Emory said, sighing.

Irene had been silent during most of the conversation. Now, she spoke up. "Where Tucker is concerned, it's mostly his women who are never heard from again. How can you all just sit there, talking about that man as if he were less than evil?"

"It's not like that." Faith sought to placate her. "We have to prove his character to Charity as well as make him pay for his crimes." She scowled a warning at Irene. "And I don't mean take the law into our own hands."

"Why not? The minute Ramsey Tucker sees you and me he's going to know his evil doings have been exposed. Then what? We can't let him walk away with your sister, even if she won't believe us. She's a witness. Once she puts two and two together, she'll be in terrible danger."

Holding the handkerchief containing the gold nuggets, Faith fingered their hardness through the fabric.

"Maybe we could trade?" A smile lifted the corners of her mouth. "Suppose Papa offered to trade Tucker his valuable mining claim in exchange for his daughter's freedom? We all know he'd accept. And that would certainly show Charity her husband's true colors, wouldn't it?"

Connell laughed. "It sure would. I like the way your mind works, Little Dove Woman."

"And then what?" Irene demanded.

Faith had a ready answer for that question, too. The whole plan was suddenly coming together brilliantly in spite of her weariness. "Papa can keep our presence secret while he deals with Tucker. Nobody in town knows who we are so we'll be safe enough. I don't think the Good Lord will mind a temporary falsehood in order to right a wrong."

"You? Lie?" Connell chuckled. "It's okay with me, if you think your conscience can stand it."

"I'll live," Faith retorted cynically. "While we get things ready here, you backtrack up the canyon and see if you can spot Tucker coming so we won't get caught unawares."

"I might be persuaded to do that for you." Connell glanced at Irene. "If my future bride doesn't mind waiting a bit to see her new home."

His innocent words tore into Faith's heart and left it bleeding, empty. She averted her gaze rather than chance seeing anyone's unspoken query into the reason for her pain. She thought she'd die when her father said, "You know, there's a traveling preacher due here in a few days. He could marry you. We might even be able to come up with a regular dress for the lady from the Kentucky gal down at the Majestic. I know I've seen her wear a pretty one."

Faith wanted to scream. To wail. To jump to her feet and confess her love for Connell in spite of Irene's presence. She opened her mouth, but all that came out was a croak any frog would have been proud of.

Irene, however, had no trouble stating firmly, "No."

"No?" Connell looked puzzled.

"No." Standing proud, Irene addressed everyone, Faith included. "You all seem to forget. I'm already married to Ramsey Tucker. Until that problem is resolved, one way or another, I'm not free to marry anyone else."

Faith breathed a relieved sigh. In all her mental ramblings regarding Irene and Connell, she'd never once thought of the problem that Irene's marriage to Tucker was still binding. He didn't think of it that way, of course, because he believed Irene was dead. They all knew better. And the proof was standing right there in front of her, very much alive.

Truth dawned. She gasped. "That's right! Charity *can't* be legally married to him. Isn't that wonderful?"

"For you, maybe," Connell said flatly. "But it sure puts a serious crimp in my future plans."

Faith watched her father closely for the next several weeks. Some days he seemed almost normal. Other times, no matter how he tried to hide it, she could tell he was dismally unhappy. She understood how he felt. Every time she thought of Connell she experienced a jolt of awareness, a sense of abiding love that warmed her all the way to her soul. Those blissful thoughts were always spoiled by an imaginary picture of him standing beside Irene, reciting wedding vows.

Except for an occasional foray out to check on Ben and the horses, Faith had kept to the cabin. Her father had explained to his friends that his wife's cousin and her traveling companion were visiting and no one had doubted the story. In the Territories and those few states west of the Mississippi, men didn't ask questions, nor did they welcome being queried about their own past lives. It was a place to start again. To take a new name, if necessary, and leave behind the failures of the past.

Seated by the small stove in one corner of the room, lost in thought, Faith was suddenly overcome by the realization that nothing could ever be as she remembered it. In a vague way she'd sensed that truth when she'd first set eyes on her father and his simple cabin. It wasn't only that their family home in Ohio had been leveled by disaster, it was knowing that none of them could go back to the kind of life they'd once shared.

They'd all changed. Grown. Faith especially. She'd been forced into taking charge and as a result had found a fortitude within herself she'd never dreamed existed. The carefree child she'd been such a short time ago was merely a fond, distant memory.

And now?

Faith sighed. Her duty, once all was said and done, was to her father, just as Irene's had been when she'd chosen to take responsibility for her elderly parents rather than marry Connell and accompany him to the wilderness. Funny how history repeated itself, wasn't it?

The sound of an approaching horse and Ben's answering bray drew her from her reverie. She jumped to her feet to greet Connell with a grin as he burst through the door.

"They're coming!" he shouted. "About ten minutes out. Is everything set?"

"Yes." Faith hurried to the tin box. "I have the nuggets right here. Papa's been spreading the word he's made another big strike. We're as ready as we'll ever be."

"Good." Connell scanned the room. "Where's Irene? Is she okay?"

"She's fine. She's gone down to the river with my father. He's showing her how to find gold with a Long Tom." *And I'm fine, too, thanks. Real tickled to see you,* Faith added, deriding herself for being so excited that Connell was finally back in Beal's Bar.

"Well, don't just stand there. Let's go. We have to warn the others and plant those nuggets."

"Right." Faith followed him out the door. "I'll go saddle Ben."

"There's no time for that," Connell said. "Take my hand. We'll ride double."

"You're sure Rojo is well enough to carry the extra weight?"

Chuckling, the plainsman grabbed her arm and swung her up behind him in one fluid motion. "Don't worry. He's all healed up. Hardly even a scar. Besides, even a lame horse wouldn't feel the little bit you weigh."

"I'm so glad he's okay."

"Me, too. In case I didn't remember to thank you, we owe you a lot for coming to our rescue."

"You didn't remember," Faith said, adjusting her

skirt as best she could while the horse pranced and shifted beneath her. "But you're quite welcome."

"Good."

He wheeled the big gelding, pointed his nose down the slope toward the river, and kicked him into action.

Straddling the apron of the saddle behind him, Faith knew if she was to keep her seat she had no choice but to wrap both arms around Connell and hang on for dear life. She couldn't help smiling. There was nothing like necessity to overcome inhibitions, was there?

All her good intentions, all her promises of self-control, fled the moment she touched him. Arms around his waist, Faith pressed herself against him, held tight and closed her eyes.

Their trip was over in moments, but she nevertheless thanked the Lord for giving her that one last chance to be so near the plainsman, to innocently lay her cheek against his warm, broad back and dream of what could never be.

Moving quickly in spite of her whirling emotions, Faith dismounted, helped Emory place the nuggets in the narrow, wooden race of the Long Tom, then stood back. By shading her eyes with her hand, she was able to watch Charity and her villainous husband descending the steep trail toward the river.

"They'll be here soon. Time for the rest of us to hide," Faith said, giving her father a peck on the cheek. "Will you be okay, Papa?"

Emory nodded. He hadn't taken his eyes off the nuggets since they'd laid them in the shallow, sandy water. His white-knuckled grip on the lever that kept the sluice from rocking gave Faith pause. Though he'd claimed gold had no effect on him anymore, clearly he was deluding himself. Then again, those few nuggets were the only bait they had for their trap. Losing them would be catastrophic.

"Remember, Papa, Charity thinks I'm dead," Faith reminded him. "You can't let on otherwise until Tucker has made his move or we'll lose our advantage."

Emory agreed. "When she finds out you're alive she'll be so happy I know she'll forgive us for holding back. A few more hours and we can tell her everything."

"I hope it's that quick."

Connell tapped her arm to get her attention. "It'll be even quicker if you and Irene don't skedaddle. Take Rojo and hide him behind the cabin with Ben. I'll stay close to your father, just in case." He eyed Emory's fisted hand. "The way he's shaking, it'll be a wonder if he lasts long enough to convince Tucker he's found the mother lode."

Faith couldn't argue with that. Emory's complexion had grown so ashen she'd been thinking the same thing. "All right. Since you've shaved your beard off he may not recognize you anyway, especially without your horse."

"True." Drawing his fingers slowly over his jaw, Connell smiled at her. "I wondered when you were going to notice the change in me. Were you surprised?"

Surprised? More like thrilled, Faith thought. The urge to caress his bare cheek had been so strong the first time she'd seen his handsome face sans whiskers, she'd barely managed to control her desire. Only the presence of Irene had stopped her from making a fool of herself.

"You'll do," Faith said, trying to sound uninterested.

She'd have been convinced she'd succeeded in misleading him if Connell's roaring laughter hadn't continued to echo up the valley from the sandbar long after she and Irene had reached the cabin.

Chapter Twenty-Three

Real windows were a luxury few dwellings in Beal's Bar enjoyed. The two-story Majestic Hotel had three genuine glass panes which, according to Emory, had been packed in from Marysville at the exorbitant cost of forty cents a pound!

Emory's cabin had one small window in the front, beside the door, which was covered with thin cotton cloth in the summer and blanketed securely come winter. It was easy for Faith and Irene to stay out of sight by simply remaining with the horses and Ben. Conversation inside the cabin echoed up the stovepipe like a megaphone, much to Faith's surprise and delight.

The sound of her sister's voice brought tears of relief to her eyes. Charity had survived! And she was mere feet away, on the other side of the wall. Unfortunately, so was Ramsey Tucker.

"My wife and I thank you for your hospitality," Tucker said. "I'm glad to see you're doing so well. Naturally, since her poor sister met with such a sad end, Charity has been beside herself."

"Of course." There was a choked sound to Emory's voice. Faith hoped Tucker would assume the telltale emotion was due to something other than perfidy.

"Charity was never strong like her sister," Emory said. "I can see she's in need of nursing to get her strength back."

Faith heard the younger woman begin to sob inconsolably. She chanced a peek inside by lifting a lower corner of the fabric-covered window opening and saw Charity in their father's tender embrace, her pale blond curls a stark contrast against his dark vest. Ramsey Tucker stood back, his lips curled in a sneer, watching the family tableau unfold.

"If you'll make me a partner in your mine I might consider letting her stay here with you—until she's well, I mean," Tucker said smoothly.

With an arm around her shoulders, Emory gently led his younger daughter aside before he asked, "Would you like that, Charity? Would you like to stay with your papa?"

Nodding, she burst into another wave of loud weeping.

As her father turned back to the wagon boss, Faith saw fire in his gaze. *Not yet, Papa,* she thought, praying he'd be able to hold his tongue and control his temper. *Wait till we finish carrying out our plan.*

As if in answer to her thoughts, Emory schooled his features. "I haven't been well, myself," he said. "It's dark and dank down here in this narrow valley and winter's coming. I need to recuperate where the sun shines and there's no more cold water soaking my boots. There are times, standing in that icy creek all day long, when my bones ache and I think my poor feet have frozen clean off." He smiled slightly. "I wonder…no, never mind. It's silly."

Tucker rose to the bait. "What?"

"It was just an old man's folly," Emory said. "For a minute there I thought of asking you to take over the mine for me while Charity and I moved to Sacramento City."

"You going to make me a partner, like I asked?"

"No. That wouldn't be fair to you, doing all the hard work while I sat back and got rich." He reached into his vest pocket and withdrew the handkerchief in which he'd wrapped his supposed new find, then handed it to Tucker. "You saw me take these out of the Long Tom when you rode up so you know my claim is a good one. Would you be interested in purchasing the mine?"

"The whole thing? No partners?"

As planned, Emory vacillated. "On second thought, I don't know. I've worked awfully hard here." He looked to his red-eyed, travel-weary daughter. "And I wouldn't want to come between you and your wife."

With that, Charity began to howl like a coyote caught in the steel jaws of a fur trapper's snare.

Tucker guffawed. "Me and the wife aren't gettin' along that well, as you can see. I only married her so she could stay with the train after she was left alone. You want her back, old man, she's yours. I give her to ya. Consider it payment for your claim."

Emory snorted and shook his head. "Nice try, mister, but as much as I love my girl she's not payment enough for a claim as rich as mine." He named an exorbitant price.

"I'll give you half that and not a penny more," Tucker

said flatly. Faith held her breath. Behind her, she heard Irene's sharp intake of breath. It was almost over.

"I'll think on it," Emory said. "You got that much money with you?"

"I can get it."

"Sorry. We can't wait for you to ride all the way to a bank and I won't take scrip," Emory said. "Winter's comin'. Pretty soon the trail up the pass will be too icy for horse or mule. Guess we'll just have to leave my claim for the winter and hope it's okay till spring."

Muttering a curse, Ramsey Tucker said, "Wait here, old man. I'll be right back with your money." He started for the door, then paused and wheeled around, hands balled into fists. "And shut up that squawlin' woman, will ya, or I'll shut her up myself."

Outside, Faith sensed her mule's unrest and calmed him with a hand on his neck. She stroked his velvety nose. "Easy, Ben. Easy. He's not coming after you. I won't let him hurt you ever again. I promise."

Irene was ministering to the canelo, as well. Faith smiled. Any woman who'd make the effort to soothe a helpless animal was okay with her, even if she was a rival for Connell's affection. Given some of the other choices the plainsman could have made in his travels, Irene would make a fine wife. She was probably a lot like Little Rabbit Woman, his late Arapaho mate, which was all the more reason to be happy for him.

Faith made a wry face. Think it often enough and she just might start to believe it. Eventually.

Emory sat Charity in his only real chair, a rocker where he'd whiled away many an hour of loneliness, and patted her hand. "Stay right here, girl. And stop crying. Your daddy's fixin' to make everything up to you. But you've got to trust me, you hear?"

She nodded. "I'm so sorry."

"Nothin' to be sorry for." Having no handkerchief, he handed her the corner of her apron. "Dry your eyes and watch. You're about to see a comeuppance the likes of which you've never dreamed."

"But Papa—"

"Hush." He straightened, shielding her with his body as Ramsey Tucker returned carrying a small poke.

He slammed it on the table with a vengeance. "There. It's gold coin. Count it if you want."

"There's no need. I trust you," Emory said.

"Good. Then I'll be having the deed to all this, including your claim. Put it in writing. You may be the trusting sort, but I'm not."

"We should both sign," Emory said. "So there's no misunderstanding."

"Fine with me. I can read, so no trickery."

"You're buying my cabin and my diggings, is that correct?"

"And all your tools. Be sure to spell it out. I don't want any questions after you leave."

"Of course." Emory took out the stub of a pencil and wet it with his lips while he opened a small notebook. "Let's see now, the date is around October twenty-ninth, I think. That's close, anyway. We just heard California became a state, so I know for sure it's late October."

"Fine, fine. Get on with it."

Emory's hand was shaking. He finished writing, tore

the paper from the book and handed it to Tucker. "That look right to you?"

Tucker read it and shoved it back at him. "Sign."

"You, too. Here. I made a copy."

"All right, all right. Whatever you say." Grinning, he signed and immediately spit on the dirt floor. "Since this is my house now, take your useless daughter and get out."

"In a minute," Emory said. "First, there's some folks I'd like you to meet."

"I got no truck with any of your friends. Gather up your clothes and skedaddle."

Passing the table, Emory pocketed the poke Tucker had given him, took Charity's hand and led her to the door. When he opened it, Connell was waiting.

Tucker gaped. "What in blazes…?"

"I believe you already know Mr. McClain," Emory said.

Connell entered, glaring at Tucker, then stepped back to clear a path for the women.

Faith was first. She came into the room, head lowered, her hat brim shading her face and hiding her features. When she raised her eyes and looked straight at the wagon boss, there was vindication and triumph in her expression.

Before she could speak, however, her sister gave a high-pitched shriek and fainted dead away. If Connell hadn't been expecting such a reaction and stationed himself close by, she'd have hit the floor. As it was, he managed to catch her before any damage was done.

He looked to Faith with a grin. "I seem to be good at keeping the Beal women from keeling over, don't I?"

"That, you do."

Tucker had recovered his self-control enough to say, "She's no Beal, she's a Tucker, like it or not."

"Oh, I don't know about that," Faith drawled. "It seems to me you have one too many wives, Captain."

On cue, Irene stepped through the door. There was no smile on her face. Her spine was stiff, her gait halting. Hate sizzled in her dark eyes.

The astonished look on Tucker's face was so comical Faith had to giggle. "That's right," she said. "Your dear wife, Irene, is alive and well. Isn't that wonderful? You know what that means? It means my sister can't possibly be your legal wife. You were still married when you forced her to wed, you, you..."

Words failed her. She'd expected Tucker to show some redeeming emotion: remorse, fear, maybe even relief at seeing that another of his wives had survived. Instead, he began to grin maliciously.

"You can't prove a thing," he boasted. "I don't care what that crazy woman says. Every man in the company knew Indians took her, just like they took you. If she survived, so be it. I was never legally married to her, either. I have a wife waiting for me back in Missouri, the stupid cow. Now, all of you, get out of my house!"

Faith wanted to pummel him with her fists, to wipe the smug grin off his ugly face. Judging by the look Irene was still giving him, she wanted to do much worse.

That was all it took to convince Faith that a strategic retreat was in order. Taking the older woman's arm, she tried to urge her toward the door.

Irene balked. Faith felt the muscles of her arm bunch beneath her touch just before she jerked free.

A knife blade flashed.

Faith wasn't braced well enough to stop Irene's attack. The woman raised the knife over her head, gave a guttural scream and lunged at Tucker.

Though he defended himself, a red slash appeared on his cheek. Blood trickled down his face. With a howl he flung himself at Irene and they landed in a heap on the hard-packed dirt floor, barely missing the small table.

Tucker had one meaty fist clamped on her wrist, stilling the knife. With the other he began to batter her mercilessly.

In two strides Connell was beside them. He passed the unconscious Charity to Emory.

Everyone was shouting, Faith the loudest. She leaped atop Tucker, hoping to slow his assault on Irene.

She might as well have been a flea on a dog's back for all the attention he paid her. Nevertheless, she resisted when Connell tried to pull her off.

"Get out of the way," he ordered.

It took several seconds for his command to register with Faith. In those moments, a cut opened on Irene's temple. Frantic, Faith filled her fist with the wagon boss's hair and yanked. Irene was like family. She couldn't step back and let him do her any more damage.

Gripping Faith around the waist, Connell lifted her, kicking and screeching, off the pile of struggling humanity. He grabbed the captain's shirt collar and jerked him away from Irene, who scrambled to the side, stunned.

Faith hurried to her, steadying her and keeping her

from rejoining the fray. Clearly she was in no condition to continue her fight. Tucker was twice her weight and mean as a rattler. Enraged, there was no telling what he might do.

Obviously concerned for Charity, Emory had carried her out the door. Faith tugged Irene and followed. They stumbled around to the rear of the cabin where Emory placed Charity on the ground by the corral.

"What about Connell?" Faith shouted.

"I'm going back to fetch my Colt and help him," her father answered. "You stay here."

"No. I'm going with you!"

Before her father could argue, Ramsey Tucker appeared, armed with a pickax. Empty-handed, Faith placed herself between him and the other women, praying Connell was hot on his trail.

Her breath caught. Her heart sped. Where was Connell? Could he be hurt? Maybe even mortally wounded? That thought tore her apart, made her knees weak and her head swim.

Fighting to maintain an air of defiance and fortitude, she prayed silently, fervently, for deliverance. After all they had been through together, was their quest going to end like this, with their entire party slaughtered by the madman they had vowed to destroy? It was unthinkable!

Suddenly, the tall, robust figure of a stranger appeared. He was clad in deerskin breeches and naked to the waist. In one hand he carried a lance. In the other was a shield decorated with eagle feathers and familiar images. Faith couldn't decide who frightened her more—Tucker or the Cheyenne brave.

Irene pushed past. She threw herself at the Cheyenne, shielding him. The arm he encircled her with was striped with wounds in a geometric pattern that could only have been self-inflicted. Faith had seen similar scars while in the Indian camp but never the fresh wounds of the blood sacrifice.

Her heart broke for the couple. It didn't take a genius to deduce that this must be Red Deer, Irene's betrothed. Had he followed them all the way to California? He must have. No wonder Faith had kept sensing an unseen menace! All those times Irene had disappeared into the night finally made sense.

Confusion in Tucker's expression gave Faith hope. While he was distracted, perhaps someone could disarm him. But who? Why didn't one of the men act? Connell would have.

Her glance darted to the now silent cabin. For all she knew, dear Connell could be lying dead inside, a victim of Tucker's malice. Her heart wrenched with actual physical pain.

No one moved. Red Deer seemed content to shield Irene. Emory was in place to defend Charity. That left only Faith.

She lowered her head like a billy goat and plowed into Tucker, blindsiding him and hoping against hope that her efforts would be enough to snap the others out of their apparent stupor and bring them to her aid.

The attack caused Tucker to drop his weapon. It also staggered Faith. Reeling, she fell back, barely cognizant of her vulnerable position.

With a guttural roar he went for her. Backing away, she tripped. When he lunged, she rolled beneath the rails of the corral where Ben and the horses were shuffling nervously.

Tucker followed without hesitation.

Screeching for help, Faith tried to regain her feet but her skirt tangled around her legs and she floundered in the dust. Eyes wide, she saw stout hooves stomping the ground beside her, barely missing her head.

In a heartbeat, Tucker was towering over her. Though he was now weaponless, his grimace declared his deadly plans more clearly than any words.

Helpless, Faith closed her eyes and raised her arms to shield her face. She was beyond prayer, beyond hope.

Above her, Ben snorted. Just when she thought the mule might come to her aid he wheeled, apparently fleeing. Tears stung Faith's eyes. Her heart broke. Even Ben, her staunchest ally, was forsaking her in the face of the captain's wrath.

Time stood still. Tucker loomed. Irene screamed something in an unknown tongue.

Faith peeked between her folded arms. An animal snorted. Hooves flew above her. Ben! He hadn't deserted the fight. He'd simply turned to aim his kick!

The force of the mule's hooves lifted Ramsey Tucker off the ground and sent him flying into the rough-cut rails of the corral. He hit with a crack that sounded as if the wood had split. His back and neck arched unnaturally.

Faith rolled out of the way as Ben charged. His lip was curled, his teeth bared, his long ears laid back against his lowered head.

As Tucker made his final slide to the ground, the

mule bowed his neck, stiffened his legs and came down on the body with both front feet. Hard.

Faith could tell that the last assault was unnecessary. Tucker had died the moment his back had snapped. It was over.

She struggled to her feet just as Connell rounded the corner of the cabin. A more blessed sight Faith had never seen. Though he was holding his side and walking unsteadily, he was alive. That was enough for her.

She glanced at Irene and Red Deer. Their decision was plain. They were a couple. There was no question about it.

Connell saw it, too. Nodding, he passed them by and went straight to Faith. "Are you all right?"

She caressed his cheek and nodded. "Yes. You?"

"I've been better," he said. "I saw what happened. Guess old Ben finally got even for all the abuse."

"Yes." Soberly, Faith considered her loyal mule. "They remember cruelty, sometimes for years. Ben was always gentle with me but the captain was a different story. I know it's not a very Christian attitude, but I think he got exactly what he deserved."

"They say the Lord works in mysterious ways."

Agreeing, Faith glanced at Irene. Red Deer had assumed a defensive stance, clearly ready to do battle for his chosen wife if need be.

Connell shook his head and managed a smile. "She's all yours," he said. "I release her from her promise to marry me."

Irene evidently translated, because as soon as she'd finished speaking the Cheyenne eased his stiff posture.

"Where will they go," Faith asked Connell. "She can't go back to Black Kettle, can she?"

"No, but the Arapaho will take her in again because she once belonged to them. Even if she were Cheyenne they'd go to live with her mother's tribe instead of staying with Black Kettle's band."

"So, Red Deer will be safe, too?"

"Yes." Connell chuckled. "I owe him for one of the knots on my head but I'll forgive him—as a wedding present to Irene."

"He is the one who was following us, who knocked you off Rojo, isn't he?"

"I'm sure of it."

"You're not angry?" Faith remained close to him, sighing when he slipped his arm around her waist.

"How can I be?" Connell said softly. "He brought you and me together and solved Irene's problems, too. What more could I ask?"

Faith gazed up at him. "Together? Us?"

"If you'll have me," Connell said. "The Sacramento Valley is lush and rich, good for cattle and farming. And I'll build you a new house if you don't like the one I already have."

"What about my family?"

Connell looked to Emory, who was still in the process of reviving Charity. "May I have the honor of marrying your daughter, sir?"

"This one or that one?" Emory jested.

"This one. Definitely this one." Connell gave Faith a light squeeze and winced. "As soon as my ribs heal a bit. Right now, I think I'd better sit down."

Epilogue

The traveling preacher stood in the rear of the Majestic, Bible in hand, while the miners crowded around.

Faith had managed to piece together a presentable frock from some calico Connell had found for her and was radiant. He stood beside her in his buckskins, beaming from ear to ear, while the preacher made them man and wife.

A raucous cheer went up as the ceremony concluded. The prospectors had come from all walks of life, all parts of the country, yet were united in a celebration of joy not often seen in the gold camps.

"I wish Irene could have stayed long enough to be a part of this," Faith told her new husband, "but I understand why she and Red Deer felt they should go. I hope they're as happy as I am."

"I'm sure they are," Connell said. "And so is your sister. We'll be lucky to get her to come to Sacramento City with us after all the attention she's getting from these lonesome miners."

"Papa will see that she behaves herself. He's anxious to leave here as soon as possible. It's a wonder the winter weather has delayed as long as it has."

"I know. Are you packed and ready to travel?"

Faith nodded, her eyes filling with admiration, thankfulness and unshed tears. "Yes. And this time I'm not a bit afraid."

"Because Tucker's dead?"

"No," she said, sliding her hand through the crook of her husband's arm. "Because you're here. I can face anything with you as my guide."

Connell patted her hand and chuckled. "Just as long as you don't confront any more chiefs like Black Kettle and scare me to death, I'll be content."

Faith giggled behind her free hand. "Do you really think I'm a legend?"

"If you aren't already on account of Ab's or Walks With Tree's tall tales, you soon will be," he said with conviction. "By the time Irene—Singing Sun Woman— and Red Deer have told our whole story over and over in the camps it'll be common knowledge that Little Dove Woman is a force to be feared and admired."

"Just so long as my husband feels the same way," she teased, giggling nervously. "I think I'm more afraid of disappointing you than I was of any wild Indian. I just hope I can be..."

"Kiss her!" someone yelled. A chorus of similar suggestions swelled.

Connell smiled as he bent to do as the crowd wanted. An instant before their lips met he whispered, "I believe I've finally figured out how to stop you from talking out of turn."

"Well, it beats a spear in the side," was all Faith managed to say before he silenced her with a kiss.

She slipped her arms around his neck and kissed him back. After all they'd been through, she guessed she could allow him to think he had the upper hand. At least for a little while.

* * * * *

Hannah Alexander is the pseudonym of husband-and-wife writing team Cheryl and Mel Hodde (pronounced "Hoddee"). When they first met, Mel had just begun his new job as an ER doctor in Cheryl's hometown, and Cheryl was working on a novel. Cheryl's matchmaking pastor set them up on an unexpected blind date at a local restaurant. Surprised by the sneak attack, Cheryl blurted the first thing that occurred to her: "You're a doctor? Could you help me paralyze someone?" Mel was shocked. "Only temporarily, of course," she explained when she saw his expression. "And only fictitiously. I'm writing a novel."

They began brainstorming immediately. Eighteen months later they were married, and the novels they set in fictitious Ozark towns began to sell. The first novel in the Hideaway series won the prestigious Christy Award for Best Romance in 2004.

Books by Hannah Alexander

Love Inspired Suspense

Note of Peril
Under Suspicion
Death Benefits
Hidden Motive
Season of Danger

Love Inspired Historical

Hideaway Home
Keeping Faith

Visit the Author Profile page
at Harlequin.com for more titles.

HIDEAWAY HOME

Hannah Alexander

We wish to honor our loved ones
who risked everything for our country's freedom
in World War II: Ralph Hodde, Larry Baugher,
Irwin Baugher, Loy Baugher, Cecil James,
Leonard Wesson and Glen Jones.

Acknowledgments

We're so grateful for our editor, Joan Marlow Golan, and her exceptional staff, and for our agent, Karen Solem, who help us make our books the best they can be.

We thank Lorene Cook, who helped us establish the authenticity of our story and patiently answered late-night calls with questions about "the way it was back then."

Ray Brown, Barbara Warren, Lee McCormick, Soni Copeland, Mike Hemphill and Jackie Bolton shared their memories, their knowledge, their expertise and their historical material for this story. We will always be grateful for their generosity.

Chapter One

Something was wrong. The news hadn't reached California yet, but Bertie Moennig knew something had happened. She couldn't pinpoint when she'd decided she wasn't jumping to conclusions, but her instincts had never failed her. She would have to wait and see.

It frustrated her no end, because she didn't like to wait for anything. Still…in the midst of this wretched war, she'd grown accustomed to it.

Bertie paused in the noisy workroom of Hughes Aircraft to untie the blue bandana from her head. Her hairnet had ripped this morning, too late for her to get a replacement, and there were strict regulations about keeping long hair restrained.

Now, half of her bun had fallen down over her neck and shoulders. As if this plant wasn't already hot enough! Folks liked to chatter on and on about the wonderful weather in Southern California; those folks must've never worked in a busy, noisy aircraft plant on a sunny day.

Another trickle of perspiration dripped along the side

of Bertie's face, and she rubbed her cheek against her shoulder while fiddling with the bandana. She'd take a summer afternoon on the farm in the Missouri Ozarks over working in the heat of this plant any day.

Not that she disliked California. She loved it most of the time—the weather, the ocean, the mountains—but it could be a challenge for a country girl to get used to the crush of people and traffic, even after living here for eight months.

In Hideaway, Missouri, Bertie would've ridden her bicycle the three miles to work, but here she saw more cars passing by the apartment than she would see in a year back home. The crazy pace of Southern California had shocked her upon arrival and—

"Hey, hillbilly!"

She winced at the sound of the barrel voice approaching from behind her. Looking around, then up at the department supervisor, Franklin Parrish, she braced herself for yet another earful of complaining.

"Yessir?"

"Get back to work. And get that hair up," he snapped, looming too close, as he always did. He eyed the blond hair that fell around her shoulders, then his gaze wandered.

Even though he mocked her Ozark accent and figures of speech, he made no secret of the fact he liked her figure well enough.

She tied her hair back on top of her head. "A man in your position should mind his manners, Mr. Parrish," she said quietly, wishing Edith Frost, her roommate, was here. She'd have an extra hairnet.

Franklin leaned closer to Bertie, his face flushed like that of a child who'd been caught snooping in his mother's purse. "And you'd better mind who you're talking to, hillbilly. I can turn you out of here by signing the bottom line of a little sheet of paper."

Bertie met his gaze, trying hard not to show her irritation. After three hundred hours of instruction in St. Louis, she'd been sent here as a trained machinist at the company's expense. If he fired her for no good reason, he'd have to answer for his actions.

"You want these parts to pass inspection, don't you?" she asked. "We still have a war to win against the Japanese, and I aim to help win it." She knew she should smile to take the bite out of her words, but she held his gaze, straight-faced.

Franklin glowered. Bertie nipped on her tongue to keep it from getting her into deeper trouble. Franklin grunted and walked away.

Bertie sighed. Someday, she'd go too far, but she didn't think that day had come yet. Years ago, her mother had tried to tell her that a woman could get more accomplished with honey than with vinegar, but Bertie had found that the two mixed well together. That was especially true for a woman working in a man's world.

Besides, Mom never had depended strictly on honey to get what she wanted. When she was alive, Dad used to brag to the other farmers down at the coffee shop that his wife was full of more sass and vinegar than any plow mule in the county. Just recently, he'd accused Bertie of taking after her mother a little too much.

Those words had made Bertie proud, and it had given her courage to know that she had some of the same strength of character as Marty Moennig.

She felt a pang of homesickness. She missed her fa-

ther and couldn't stop worrying about him. She'd tried
to place this dread in God's hands several times last
night and this morning, but her mind kept grabbing it
back again. *Where was he?*

She also missed Red Meyer like crazy, and thinking about him raised her anxiety even more. Though
Red was somewhere in Italy, cleaning up after the surrender of the Germans last month, she knew she would
feel closer to him if he was back home in Hideaway.

Of course, if Red was back in Hideaway, she'd be
there, too. So many memories…so much she missed.
She wanted to be able to step out of the house and stroll
around the victory garden in the backyard. Had Dad
even been able to plant one this year? He was all alone
on the farm, with so much work to keep him busy.

Fact was, she worried about both the men in her
life. News of Red hadn't come often enough to suit her
lately. He'd stopped writing to her. Just like that, the
letters had quit coming. She was pretty sure the Army
hadn't suddenly stopped sending soldiers' mail home.

Charles Frederick Meyer didn't like being called anything but Red. With a head of brick-colored hair and
a blue gaze that looked straight into the soul, he was
strong and kind, and quick with a smile or a joke.

Bertie could usually spend much of her workday
thinking about him, dreaming of the time they would
be back together again. That was easier to do now that
the war with Germany was over.

But if he was out of danger, why wasn't he writing?

Red Meyer stared out the train window at the lush
Missouri Ozark landscape, nearly lulled to sleep by the

gentle rocking of the passenger railcar. The train took a curve, and he got a better look at the cars ahead of him. Four cars forward, one lone figure with the straight, stiff posture of the military, made his way to the rear exit.

Looked like at least one other person on this train was as restless as Red, but he didn't have the luxury of pacing along the aisles from railcar to railcar.

Instead, he tugged one of the envelopes from his left front pocket and pulled two folded pages from the raggedly slit top. Gently, he unfolded the sheets and looked at the handwriting.

He didn't read the words right off. He didn't need to. He practically had this letter memorized—maybe not every single fancy swirl and dotted *i*, but he could see an image in his mind of Bertie Moennig leaning over her stationery, chewing on the end of her pencil, eyes narrowed. It had been her first letter to him, and it was well nigh three years old. The smudges and worn corners of the pages showed how often he'd handled them.

Dear Red,

I'm sitting here at the station in Hollister, watching your train pull away, trying hard not to get the paper wet with my tears. If you ever show this letter to anybody, I'll make you pay when you get back home.

He'd laughed at that when he first read it, but he'd not been able to see the page very well for a few lines, himself.

I already miss you so much I want to run after the caboose and hop on, the way we did ten years ago. Remember how much trouble we got into when the train didn't stop until it reached Springfield?

Red nodded to himself. He remembered. Gerald Potts

had had to drive up to get them, and then all the way home he'd lectured them about the stupidity of risking their lives for a lark. Neither of them had ever told Gerald that his own son, Ivan, was the one who'd dared them to hop that train in the first place.

We've been friends for so long, Red, I can't imagine going on without you. You can make me feel better no matter how bad things are, even with Mom's funeral only weeks past. I don't know how I'd have gotten through it without you.

He squeezed the pages between his fingers and stared out at the passing countryside. He couldn't remember a time when Bertie wasn't in his life, whether she was socking him in the mouth for picking on her in their Sunday school class, or kissing him goodbye twelve years later at the train station, chin wobbling, eyes promising more than he'd ever dared ask of her. A future.

He looked back down at the letter, swallowing hard as he recalled her face, her voice, the love he'd held on to for so many long, hellacious months.

Red, you remember that talk we had on our first real date? You should, since it's only been a couple of months. You told me you'd always thought you'd end up a bachelor, because you never thought you had anything special to offer a woman in marriage. But you are somebody special, and don't let anybody ever tell you different.

His eyes squeezed shut. He'd never loved her more than he did right now. She'd been so true to him all this time. Her letters…they'd been his lifeline. Her love was what kept him going and kept his determination strong to do the right thing by her, though it was the hardest thing he'd ever have to do.

I've heard they treat soldiers rough in the Army, but you're strong enough to take whatever they throw at you. Don't you forget you're more of a man than most men ever even dream of being. You've got more heart in you than anybody I've ever known, and you'd make a fine husband. The woman who marries you will never be sorry. Just make sure you get home alive to get married.

I'll be waiting here for you, and I'll be writing so much you'll probably get tired of reading my letters. If anything happens to you, it'll be happening to me, too, so you'd better take care. You have both our lives in your hands.

If he'd smiled at all during these past three years, it had only been because of her. Oh, sure, he'd let himself joke with the guys, or at least chuckle at their jokes, but it was because thoughts of home kept him going— thoughts of Bertie.

He didn't pay any attention to the man in Marine uniform coming down the aisle, until that man plunked himself down in the empty seat next to Red.

"On your way home, soldier?" came an awfully familiar voice.

Red's head jerked up. He looked with surprise into the face of his good friend Ivan Potts, in the flesh.

Before Red could say anything, Ivan had him in a bear hug and was thumping him on the back so hard it felt like Red's spine might snap in two. The man had the muscles of a plow horse.

"I didn't know you were on this train 'til I caught

sight of your face in the window when we went around that last curve." Ivan's grin showed the contrast of his white teeth against dark-tanned skin. "Thought it was you, anyway." He rubbed his knuckles over Red's scalp. "Can't miss this color, Charles Frederick."

"Well, if this don't beat all." Red tucked the letter back into his pocket, trying not to let it catch Ivan's attention. He shoved the cane out of sight beneath his seat with his foot. Happy as he was to see one of his closest friends alive and whole, he wasn't ready to do any explaining. Not yet.

Chapter Two

Red grinned at his old buddy—the first time his face had felt a smile in days. He almost expected to feel his lips crack, but they held firm. It was good to see Ivan all decked out in his uniform, with medals aplenty, some as golden as the hair on his head.

"Man, oh, man, I've missed you," Red said.

"Same here. Heard you won the war on your side of the world," Ivan said, clapping Red on the shoulder. "Now come and help us with ours. The Pacific's still hot."

Red felt his smile slip. "You're not home for good?"

"How I wish!"

Red's stomach clenched with fresh worry. He'd been relieved when he first saw Ivan, alive and well. "You're home on leave, then?" That wasn't what he wanted to hear.

Ivan nodded. Something seemed to darken in the deep brown of his eyes. "One week, then I'm back in the trenches."

"Maybe we'll have won the Pacific by then."

The grin returned. "Isn't going to happen without my help. I want to make sure the blue star my folks have in the window at home doesn't get exchanged for a gold one."

"I think you're too ornery to die," Red said. "But you'd best take care, anyways." It might destroy Gerald and Arielle Potts if anything happened to their only child. They'd always doted on him.

Ivan had been the most rambunctious of Red's friends throughout their school years, leading the gang when it came to childish pranks, overnight hunting parties and outhouse tipping. He'd given his poor parents a lot of grief. Red recalled one night when Ivan had sneaked a cow from the barn of a local farmer into a high-school classroom. It wasn't discovered until the morning—along with a big mess.

"I've made it this far." Ivan's voice snapped Red from his memories. "I plan to make it through this war alive."

Once more, Red eyed the decorations on his friend's chest. Ivan Potts had a right to be proud of the medals he'd earned. He'd proven himself to be a man in this war, and his parents would be more than proud.

Red's medals were packed away in the duffle under his feet. He wore his regular uniform instead of military dress, and he had kept his head down most times on the trip home, hoping nobody'd notice him and start asking questions. The last thing he wanted to do was talk about the war. Or talk about anything, for that matter.

War sure changed people.

All his life, Red had started conversations easily with strangers, never running out of something to talk about. But that had been a different Charles Frederick Meyer.

Ivan glanced out the window. "We're getting close."

Red nodded, rubbing sweat from his forehead as the sunlight beat down through the window. "It's nice to be nearing home, sure enough." The hills got a little taller, the valleys deeper in the southwest part of Missouri.

"I can't wait to be back for good," Ivan said. "How about you, Red? Are you coming home to stay, or do they have plans for you over on our side of the world? To hear Bertie tell it, the Army can't do without you."

Red warmed at that but he didn't know what to say now. "War's over for me, probably." He couldn't bring himself to explain why.

It'd be easy for a man in his shape to think he wasn't worth much of anything anymore, since he probably wouldn't even be able to do the work that needed doing at home now, much less help tidy things up after the ruin of a whole continent. He'd wanted to be there still, liberating the prisoners and helping set things in order again.

He squeezed his eyes shut against the June morning sun, but he opened them again quickly, and caught Ivan watching him.

"I don't think the war will ever be over for us," Ivan said, his voice suddenly soft. "It follows a guy wherever he goes."

Red nodded. The nightmares...

"Thanks to Bertie and her friends, I've kept up with your whereabouts most of the year," Ivan said. "How's Italy?"

"Hardly anything there anymore," Red said. "Except the mud and rubble of wrecked buildings. Always the mud. Heard you took Iwo Jima."

Pain crossed Ivan's features, and Red knew he'd said

the wrong thing. Would life ever get back to the way it had been, when everyone didn't have to tiptoe around minefields of conversation?

"You don't have to answer that," Red told him.

Ivan nodded slowly. He swallowed and met Red's gaze with a fierce stare. Then he looked down and swallowed again.

"We were landing on the beach," he said, his voice so soft Red had to strain to hear. "Next thing I knew, the night sky seemed to explode all around us."

Red winced. He knew what that meant.

"Five of my best buddies were killed before I could move." The words seemed to spring from Ivan—fast, hard, his voice low—as if he'd been bottling them up inside.

Red studied his friend, but didn't see any signs of damage, no Purple Heart. "But they didn't get you."

Ivan shook his head. "Sometimes I think it would've been better if I'd gotten a bullet, too."

"No, it wouldn't." But Red understood.

Ivan glanced at Red, eyes narrowing. "What's your worst memory?"

Red couldn't tell him. He could probably never tell anybody. So he pulled out another recollection. "German soldiers surrounding our fire support team."

The surprise didn't show in Ivan's eyes as much as it did in the sudden jutting of his strong chin—as if bracing himself for details. "You were captured."

"It's been a couple of months." Even now, Red could picture in his mind the grim, white faces of his captors. He could feel the fear licking at his insides, almost feel the rough hands shoving him and Conner and Beall through fields of mud.

"When?" Ivan asked. "Why didn't I hear about it? Bertie would have told me about it in a letter." He looked at Red's uniform for the first time. "Where are your medals?"

Red shrugged. "It don't matter. I'm alive. Before word could be carried back home that we were prisoners of war, we escaped in the middle of the night."

Ivan gave a low whistle. "If that doesn't beat all."

"Just in time, too. I got the impression, picking up on some of their words, that they'd planned to kill us soon."

"You speak German?"

Red nodded. "I learned some words from my pa years ago. I hadn't even realized I remembered them until I listened to our captors talking to one another. There were five of them and only three of us. I thought we were goners."

"How'd you get away?"

Red shrugged. He couldn't talk about the whole thing. "The fifth night, after a long day's march, we got loose from our bonds." He couldn't go into more detail without explaining more than he wanted to.

Ivan waited, eyes slightly narrowed in confusion. "Just like that?"

Red nodded. He'd never thought much about the humanity of the enemy. That wasn't something they talked about in the foxholes or on the scoutin' trail. All they did in the foxholes was curse the enemy, and do everything they could to make sure he died.

The rattle-clack-rattle-clack of the train filled the si-

lence for a few long moments as the two men sat steep-
ing in the ugliness they'd seen.

"Don't mention that bit about the massacre to my parents," Ivan said softly. "Why worry them about something that's already happened? They've worried enough
about me in the past three years."

"Reckon there's lots our families are never gonna
know about."

"Sometimes it seems the farther I get from the war,
the more I remember," Ivan said.

Red knew what he meant. All that loud commotion
clattered around in his mind, along with pictures of
mangled or dead friends. He still felt the pain of his own
wounds—both in his flesh and in his heart.

"Maybe we have to remember," Ivan said. "A man's
got to stay on the alert."

Red agreed, but he couldn't help wondering if he was
already going soft. Since he was a German by blood, he
couldn't hate his former countrymen.

It was hard not to hate them when he heard about all
those concentration camps, the awful things they did to
other human beings. Torture? Gas chambers? Trying
to stamp out a whole race of people? Genocide, it was
called. Devilish. Straight out of the pits of hell.

As the thoughts started tormenting him once again,
Red did what he always did to take his mind from them.
He patted his shirt pocket, thick with letters.

Ivan, of course, knew without asking what was in
Red's pocket. "You still writing to Bertie?"

Red grimaced. "She's been doin' most of the writing." Especially the past few weeks.

His sweet Bertie had a heart as tender and beautiful

as spring violets, a face to keep a man alive through the worst of war, and a voice as warm and spicy as hot apple cider.

But he couldn't keep thinking like that…not about her bein' *his*.

"That little gal had a regular letter campaign going, you know," Ivan told him. "She had all her friends writing to me, and any time I'd mention a buddy who hadn't received mail in a while, sure enough, in a week or so he'd get a note from some stranger out of Culver City, California. Our Bertie's all spunk. If she was president, this whole war would already be won."

Red felt a quick rush of pride. "She's kept me going, that's for sure."

"How's Miss Lilly been getting on without you?"

"You know Ma," Red said. "She says she's doin' fine, but it's hard to tell 'cause she never complains."

Ivan chuckled. "Strong as a Missouri mule and the best cook in Hideaway."

Red returned his attention to the scenery sliding past the window. Now that Ivan had brought up the subject, Red remembered that he had someone else to fret about.

Until he was called up, he'd helped his mother run the Meyer Guesthouse in Hideaway. It had been a family operation since his pa's death.

Lilly Meyer never let on about how hard it was to keep the place going without Red's help—but he knew business must've gone slack without him to serve as fishing guide, hunting guide and storyteller, along with all the other chores he'd done for her every day.

Fishing along the James River had been a popular sport among their best and wealthiest customers, many

of whom returned to Lilly's guesthouse year after year
for the fishing. These guests had gotten the Meyers
through the depression.

But how much of the work could Red do now?

Ma's letters were mostly filled with the goings-on in
town, until this last one. Even the handwriting seemed
to lack her usual pizzazz. Kind of shrunk in on itself,
hard to read.

Red couldn't quite figure it. Seemed like Ma was trying to avoid the subject of Hideaway altogether. Maybe
Drusilla Short was telling tales again. That woman was
the orneriest old so-and-so in the county, exceptin' for
her husband, Gramercy. Last time Red had been home
on leave, Mrs. Short had the nerve to spread the rumor
that Red was AWOL.

Ma, of course, had nearly come to blows with the old
gossip about it—and Ma wasn't a fighter, unless someone tried to hurt one of her kids. Then, she could whup
a mad bull, and she was big enough to do it.

Red glanced out at the peaceful countryside, at the
cattle grazing in a valley. Pa had actually taken on a
mad bull twelve years ago—and lost. That ol' bull had
been raised on the farm as a pet, but then had turned
mean, and caught Pa in the middle of the field where
he couldn't get away in time.

Ma had been left to raise Red and his brother and
sister alone.

What was up with Ma now?

And how was Red going to break his news to Bertie?

Chapter Three

Bertie thought about her father as she held the fine sandpaper to the gear shaft turning in the lathe. She moved the paper back and forth to wear the metal of the shaft to smooth, even perfection—to ten thousandths of an inch of the final recommendations.

She couldn't help feeling, again, that something wasn't right back home. At seven o'clock, on the second Sunday night of every month since she'd come out here, she'd telephoned Dad. If she couldn't reach him right away, he would phone her, and every time except once, he had been sitting beside the phone, waiting for her call. By the time their short talks were over—long distance cost too much to talk more than a few minutes—half of Hideaway knew what was happening in her life.

Everyone on their telephone party line got in on the call. It aggravated Dad half to death, and he wasn't always polite to the neighbors. But that didn't stop the townsfolk from picking up their phones, even when they knew the specific ring was for Dad and not for them. They were always "accidentally" interrupting the conversation.

Last night Bertie had tried four times, with no answer from Dad. He never called back. She'd talked to the Morrows, the Fishers and the Jarvises, but not to Dad. Nobody seemed to know where he was. Mrs. Fisher did tell Bertie that a couple of Dad's best cows and five of his pigs had gone missing two weeks ago. Bertie had heard Mr. Fisher in the background, telling his wife that if Joseph Moennig wanted his daughter to know about the lost animals, he'd tell her himself.

Mr. Fisher was one of the few people in their Hideaway neighborhood who believed in minding his own business. His wife, poor thing, held a dim view of her husband's antisocial behavior.

Why hadn't Dad mentioned the animals in his letters?

Mr. Morrow didn't have much to say about the matter, which struck Bertie as unusual. He'd never lacked for opinions before.

If Bertie didn't know better, she'd start getting a complex. First, no letters from Red Meyer for six weeks, and now even her father wasn't answering her calls.

She'd written Red's mother, but though Lilly Meyer's reply had been chatty and filled with news, she hadn't given Bertie any useful information about Red, except that he was "takin' a few weeks of rest from the battle."

But where was he doin' his resting? And if he was getting rest, why couldn't he write to her? Was he having so much fun on his rest that he didn't want to waste time on her?

Bertie heard news about the war from everyone but Red.

Until VE Day last month—Victory over Europe, May 8, 1945—which would always be a day of celebration, Bertie and Edith had kept up with the news from the European front through their favorite magazine, *Stars and Stripes*. They had especially loved war correspondent Ernie Pyle, who'd informed readers about all the things Red never wrote about—such as the living conditions of the men who were fighting so desperately for freedom.

How she missed those articles now that Ernie was dead. How the whole country missed him!

"Roberta Moennig, you know the boss is tough on daydreamers." Emma, the utility girl, came by with more parts to work on the lathe.

Bertie's hand slipped, fingers rapping against the shaft, and she yelped when she accidentally did a quick sanding job on her fingertips.

"Hey, you all right?" Emma asked.

"Yes, I'm fine." Bertie had too much on her mind right now. She'd developed too much of a worry habit.

Emma hefted the parts onto Bertie's table. "What's got your goat? Keep this up and Franklin Parrish'll be chucking you out the door."

Bertie grimaced and picked up a shaft. She placed it in the lathe, tightened it in, and started polishing it. Today her concentration was about as sharp as a possum hanging from a tree limb.

"Got another letter from my soldier last night," Emma said, leaning her elbows on Bertie's worktable, obviously of a mind to gab a while, in spite of the whine of the lathe's motor, and her own just-issued warning about Franklin.

Bertie nodded, wishing Emma would leave it at that, hoping the noise of the lathe would keep the conversation short.

"You heard from that man of yours lately?" Emma asked, raising her voice.

Bertie frowned. "Not for a few weeks. You know how the mail gets bundled up for days at a time, then a bunch of letters comes at once." Even to her own ears, the excuse sounded overly bright.

Emma gave Bertie a narrow-eyed look. "Red's never gone this long without writing to you, has he? He still a scout with the Army?"

Bertie suppressed a sigh and turned off the lathe. "He's called a fire support specialist."

"I thought it was a forward observer."

Bertie released her pent-up breath. How many times had she corrected Emma about Red's title? She didn't want to sound boastful, but she *was* proud of Red and what he did. He'd received several commendations for his skills—and his bravery. It was the bravery that worried her something awful.

Emma stepped closer, her pinched face and mousebrown eyes sharpening with concern. "You don't think he's… I mean…you think he's—"

"Hush, now." Bertie gently patted Emma's thin arm. "Honey, you know we can't start thinking that way. Gotta have some faith that God's in charge. Our men are helping to win this war. Besides, bad news always seems to travel faster than good these days. If something had happened to him, we'd know by now. I got a letter from his mother a few days ago."

Emma's eyes narrowed even more as she nibbled on her chapped lower lip. "That man that got killed? You know, that reporter out in the Pacific? He wasn't even a solider, Bert! It's dangerous all over, and men are being killed every day, and what with our own president dying, it feels like everything's out of control."

"Nothing is out of control," Bertie assured her. "President Truman knows what he's doing. He's a Missourian, born not too far from my hometown. He'll see things through. We Missourians are made of tough stock."

Emma didn't seem to hear her. "Lives can be cut short just like that," she said, snapping her fingers. "It could happen to anybody."

Bertie shook her head. She didn't need to hear this kind of talk right now. "It could even happen to you or me if Franklin catches us chatting instead of working," she said with a wink to keep her words from sounding too harsh. "He's already threatened to fire me once today."

To Bertie's relief, Emma nodded, sighed and returned to her cart. Bertie turned on the lathe again, which she shouldn't have turned off in the first place; there was no standing around talking except at break time.

At least once a week, poor Emma got all perturbed about her soldier. Every time, Bertie prayed for them both. She'd offered to pray *with* Emma, but that seemed to be going too far.

As it was, Bertie often felt overwhelmed with the amount of work she and Edith Frost had volunteered for these past months. During her free time, Bertie signed people up for war bonds, and she and Edith helped with the blood drive, which included giving their own blood as often as they could.

So many of her hometown friends had left for the war as boys and had returned as men. Three men from her hometown had returned in caskets.

She switched her attention back to the shaft in her lathe, trying her hardest to shake off the worry that Emma had helped stoke like the cinders of a woodstove.

Red sat with his feet planted firmly on the floor in the swaying railcar, growing more and more conscious of the cane he'd shoved beneath the seat and the attention of his friend, Ivan Potts.

It would be easy to reach down and pull out the cane and show it to Ivan. Everyone in Hideaway would know about it by tomorrow, anyway, so why not show it first to someone he knew he could trust?

But something kept him from it. It was almost like another bad dream—if he kept pretending the problem wasn't there, maybe it would disappear.

Like the war?

Ivan peered out the window, then stood and gestured to Red. "Why don't you come up to my car with me? I've got to collect my things before we get off. Dad said he'd be waiting for me at the station, and I bet Mom will be with him. You can catch a ride with us."

Red hesitated for a few seconds, then declined. Ma would want to pick up Red herself, so they could spend the long ride back home catching up, just the two of them.

"Thanks, but I've got a ride," Red said. "Ma told me she'd see to it I got picked up."

Ivan nodded, then grinned. "Lilly probably cooked your favorite meal, knowing you were coming back today."

"If she had time. She's been awful busy."

"But if I know your mother, she'll have her famous chicken and dumplings waiting at the table for you as soon as you walk in the door." Ivan licked his lips. "And blackberry cobbler with enough butter in the crust to make a grown man cry."

Red couldn't help grinning at his friend. "Could be." Ivan loved a good meal, and though his mother was brilliant and kind and an excellent hostess, her finger pastries and cucumber sandwiches didn't exactly stick to the ribs.

"Think Lilly could be persuaded to set an extra place at the table for me?" Ivan leaned toward Red, looking like a hound about to tree a coon. "My mom has a party planned for my homecoming tonight, but man, oh, man, Lilly's chicken and dumplings for lunch would make the whole ordeal worth enduring."

Red sometimes kidded Ivan that he was not his mother's son. Arielle Potts was a cultured lady—an accomplished hostess, who loved to entertain. She was a savvy political wife who enjoyed helping her husband campaign for mayor of Hideaway—not that there'd been much campaigning to do. Gerald Potts's only opponent had been Gramercy Short, who likely didn't get more than a total of ten votes, all from his relatives, and there were probably at least two dozen Shorts in Hideaway.

Ivan, on the other hand, would rather go huntin' with

Red and his coon dogs any night than socialize with the town's high and mighty.

"Sure," Red said, "come on over. Even if Ma hasn't made chicken and dumplings, the meal's bound to be good."

Ivan nodded. "I'll do it."

Ivan had the kind of face that revealed his thoughts several seconds before he spoke them. And he always spoke them. He didn't believe in keeping things to himself. As long as Red had known him, there was most often a hint of humor in Ivan's eyes, not quite mischief, but almost.

As Red watched, all humor left Ivan's face, and the darkness entered his expression again. Red didn't have any trouble knowing what was going through his friend's mind.

"Red, the war's taken something from us that we might never get back." He glanced up and down the aisle at the other passengers.

Red waited without speaking. This wasn't the time to talk about it. Not now. Not on this train with other people listening. Besides, he couldn't help thinking that if he spoke aloud what had been on his mind the past few weeks, it would make everything that happened over on those deadly fields too real.

"I think it's hit you harder," Ivan said at last. "Hasn't it?"

Red swallowed. "Not sure what makes you think that. We've all been through a lot."

Ivan leaned closer and waited until Red met his gaze. "Because I know you, buddy. You bury things down deep inside. Me, I sit by myself and write my poetry and get it out of my system. You should see the stack of poetry in my duffle bag. I've probably sent poems to half of Hideaway, and several of Bertie's friends in California."

"You oughta try to get them published. You'll be rich."

Ivan laughed out loud at that. "You think there's money in poetry? My Daddy taught me how to make a living, don't you worry. And don't change the subject."

"Thought the subject was poetry."

Ivan sobered. "You've lost something, Red." His words were soft and gentle, but they felt like broken strands of chicken wire digging into Red's heart. Ivan didn't know the half of it. "It's like all the laughter's dried up inside of you."

Red didn't know what to say. He'd not seen much to laugh about.

"Find some way to get this war out of your system," Ivan told him. "Don't let it keep you down."

Red nodded toward the window. "We're getting close. Better get your things. I'll see you for dinner."

Ivan frowned. "Lunch, Red. Noon meal is lunch."

"Not where I come from."

"You come from here, same as me."

"Your mother comes from Baltimore."

Ivan chuckled and gave Red a playful sock in the arm. It was one of their favorite arguments.

To Red's shame, he felt only relief when Ivan shook his head and walked back up the aisle toward the door that led to the forward car.

Chapter Four

Thoughts of Red once more filled Bertie's mind as she struggled with a misshapen part. She tossed it to the side so Emma could pick it up to send back for repair.

Time to switch the lathe to a higher gear and get some of these parts finished. Hurriedly, she turned off the machine, released the tension on the v-belt, and reached down to move it to a larger v-pulley. Her hand slipped. The belt which hadn't come to a complete stop, grabbed her forefinger. Before she could react, her finger was snatched into the pulley.

Pain streaked up her arm. She gritted her teeth to keep from crying out as she jerked her hand back.

Blood spread over and down her fingers, and for a moment, because of the pain, she thought all her fingers had been mangled. She closed her eyes and breathed deeply to keep from passing out, then turned to look around and see if anyone had noticed what had happened.

No one looked her way.

She reached for the bandana on her head. Her hot

hair once again fell over her shoulders as she tore off a strip of the cloth and dabbed away the blood. To her relief, only her index finger was torn.

Maybe she could take care of this herself, without going to First Aid.

But she discovered she would have no choice. The blood kept flowing from a fair-sized cut over her knuckle. There was no way to deal with it on her own.

She used what was left of the bandana to tie her hair back into a ponytail, her movements awkward.

Reluctantly, she went to find her supervisor for permission to go to First Aid. She'd catch an earful this time.

Red peered out the window at the passenger cars curving along the track in front of him. He thought he saw Ivan's blond head in one square of window, but it was too far away to know for sure.

He couldn't say why he was relieved that Ivan had gone back to his seat. It'd been good to see his friend, to know there was someone else, someone he knew, who could understand what he'd gone through.

But then, looking into Ivan's face, Red had been able to recall the war that much clearer, when what he really wanted to do was forget it, not be reminded of every detail, every death. There were too many.

Rubbing his fingertip across the corner of one of the envelopes in his pocket, Red resisted the urge to pull them out again. He knew what the letters said. He had most every word memorized. He could see Bertie Moennig's face against his closed eyelids—her sweet, saucy smile, her thick, fair hair, and turned-up nose.

The letters he'd gotten from her were nearly falling apart, he'd read them so often. The latest ones, of course, were full of questions, full of worry and wondering why he hadn't written. Those were the ones that ate at him.

He remembered one letter he'd gotten last year, soon after he returned from leave. It had been even harder than leaving the first time, and it'd apparently been hard for Bertie, too.

I've made a decision, the letter had said. *I'm going to learn how to be good at waiting, because I know there are some things—some people—worth waiting for. Dad and Uncle Sam are urging me to take some training and work in one of the defense plants, and I think I'll do it. I want to do all I can to help win this war, and get our men home again. Write me soon, Red, and let me know you're okay.*

He'd written to her then, telling her how much he already missed her, how proud he was of her. He'd written more during just one week of war than he'd done all through school. Bertie had always been so good for him.

Problem was, he didn't know what to write now. Whatever he told her, it wouldn't be something she'd want to read. And she didn't *need* to know. Not yet.

He'd even told Ma not to let Bertie know about his injury. What good would it have done? Ma, of course, had argued, but he knew she'd done what he'd asked.

Thing was, he'd seen too many hearts broken already in this war. Too many of his buddies had died, leaving wives alone to grieve as widows, leaving mothers brokenhearted over their dead sons.

He'd also seen too many friends going back home

as damaged goods, to wives who'd have to take care of them the rest of their lives. He couldn't do that to Bertie.

Nosiree, Joseph Moennig had a good farm that needed running, and what with his son, Lloyd, off in Kansas with a wife and family, his only daughter Bertie would be the one to take over the farm someday. She'd need a husband who was whole to help with that. A woman like her wouldn't have any trouble finding someone.

Red closed his eyes and tried to think of something else, because the thought of Bertie loving another man almost made him sick to his stomach.

Bertie watched the suture needle prick the skin of her knuckle in the first stitch. She jerked, in spite of her determination not to. How embarrassing! All this time she'd followed all the safety rules, been so careful about every single movement. And now this.

That was what happened when a person got in a hurry. She'd known better.

"That hurt?" asked Dr. Cox as he tied the stitch.

"Not at all. You do what you have to do."

"Are you left-handed?" He started the next stitch.

"No, sir."

"Good, because I would have to warn you against using your finger any more than necessary. Flexing that knuckle will make the healing time longer."

"I'm glad it didn't come to that. I have letters to write."

He worked quickly, his fingers moving with precision. He was the company doctor, and had probably done this a lot. "You have a beau in the war?"

Bertie hesitated. Was Red her beau? She nodded. It was how she thought of him, even if he couldn't seem to write now that he was on leave.

"Is he from Missouri, too?" Dr. Cox asked.

Bertie blinked up at him, her attention distracted from the needle. "How'd you know I was—"

"I pride myself in my ability to pick up on an accent within seconds of meeting someone. Southern?"

Bertie stared into his kind eyes. "You mean Southern Missouri? Yes, Southwest, almost into Arkansas."

"Ozarks, then. Your beau is from the Ozarks, too?"

"He sure is." Bertie felt herself relaxing. "We grew up in the same town along the James River." How she wished for those times again. "We went to school together and were close friends for as long as either of us can remember."

The doctor smiled. "Think you'll get married once this war is over?"

Bertie felt herself flushing at the thought. She'd considered it a lot. In fact, the thought of marrying and settling with Red was one of the things that had gotten her through her homesickness, her worry, her fretting. Until now.

"My father wouldn't mind," she told the doctor. "Red comes from a good, solid family. Dad knows Red real well." There were times Bertie had felt as if Dad preferred Red's company to her own. "He's already like a son to Dad." She grimaced. "Why am I telling you all this? You don't want to hear my life story."

Dr. Cox chuckled. "Sure I do. It keeps your mind off what I'm doing, and when you're relaxed, I can work better."

"Do you see many more patients now that so many doctors are helping in the war?"

"I sure do. Two of the other doctors with offices in this building are on hospital ships somewhere in the Pacific." He looked at her. "I love hearing stories from my patients, especially those involved in the war effort. Now," he said, fixing her with a pointed stare, "you were telling me about Red?"

She smiled at him, relaxing further, enjoying the chance to talk about her favorite subject. "Before Red's father died, the Meyers had two hundred acres of prime farmland along the James River. After her husband's death, Mrs. Meyers sold off a parcel of land every couple of years to the town, which was expanding and needed more room."

"To help get her family through the depression?" the doctor asked.

"Yes, even though Red warned her not to sell. He feels they could've gotten by without selling. It would've been worth more with the James River becoming part of a new lake, with a dam south of a tiny burg called Branson. That would've made her property lakefront. Now I guess it doesn't matter, though, since they had to put the plans on hold for the dam when war struck."

"Sounds as if Red is a smart man."

"Yes, but he comes by it honest. Lilly, his mother, opened their big house to paying guests. She did so well with it she was able to help send her two older kids to university in Kansas City."

"What about Red's education?" Dr. Cox asked.

Bertie shrugged. "He didn't go to college."

"Why not?"

"He knew his mother needed help with the guest-house. He loves working with livestock, and he's won blue ribbons at the state fair for the cheese he cultured from their cows' milk."

"So he gave up his opportunity to go to college to help with the family business," the doctor said. "He sounds like quite a man. It looks to me as if you and your young man are a perfect match."

She shrugged, studying the neat work the doctor was doing on her hand.

Dr. Cox paused for a moment, frowning at her. "Am I detecting some hesitation about him?"

She shrugged. "We only started dating a few weeks before he went off to war."

"Maybe it took the war to show him how much he cared about you."

Then why had Red stopped writing now that the war with the Germans was over? "I know why everyone suddenly wants to see stardust," she said. "Life's too scary right now. When all this began, a body didn't want to think he might go off to some strange land and die without ever knowing if someone besides his folks could love him. Later, when he comes back alive and whole, he might change his mind. He might find someone he likes better."

Dr. Cox placed salve over the sutured wound, then gently wrapped gauze around her finger. "I like my theory better."

Bertie looked into the doctor's sincere gray eyes. "I hope you're right." But he didn't know enough about Red to judge.

"There you go, Roberta," he told her as he finished

bandaging her finger. He gave her final instructions for sutures to be removed in ten days.

She thanked him and walked back out to the waiting room, where she found Connie, the company nurse, reading a magazine and chuckling at a "Joe and Willie" war cartoon.

Connie looked up at Bertie and grimaced at the bandage on her finger. "Guess you'll be put on special duty."

"No need," Bertie said. "I'm right-handed."

Connie got up, shaking her head. "You don't know Franklin Parrish, kiddo. Last gal who cut herself was transferred out of his department. He's about as easy to work with as a porcupine. You may find that out soon enough."

Chapter Five

The train slowed at a long uphill curve, and Red saw Lake Taneycomo gleaming in the sunshine out his window. Not much farther now. He started watching for familiar landmarks: the big cedar that'd been hit twice by lightning and lost most of its branches, but kept on thriving; the rocky cliff that looked like half a huge teacup—one of the area's bald knobs, where it was rumored that the old vigilante gang, the Bald Knobbers, sometimes met when preparing to raid a farmer's land.

He remembered riding the train to Springfield with his mother and listening to stories from old-timers about the places along the tracks that had been raided by that gang, the owners forced from their land with threats of beatings or burned homes—or death.

That had happened just before the railroad came in. It had become evident later that the vigilante gang had had inside knowledge about its course. Many men became rich when they later sold their ill-gotten land to the railroad.

Red closed his eyes, wondering when his mind would

stop wandering to brutality and the ugliness of human-kind. When he looked again, the first buildings of the tiny burg of Branson came into view.

The train continued toward the Hollister station, a short jaunt south. He wasn't sure what kind of a ride his mother would've arranged, what with the gasoline rationing and so few cars in town, anyway. Could be she'd come for him with the horse and buggy, unless she was in a hurry to get back to the house, and was able to convince one of the neighbors to take a car out of hibernation long enough to drive her.

Lilly Meyer always said one of the big draws of the Meyer Guesthouse was her horse and buggy. In this new world of modern cars with all their speed and fancy buttons and gadgets, Ma believed her guests returned to Hideaway year after year because they wanted to be taken back to a time when life wasn't so hectic.

Red knew how it felt to be lulled into a sense of peace by the clopping of horse hooves instead of a smoking tailpipe.

Many who did have automobiles in Hideaway had followed Lilly Meyer's lead and parked their cars for the rest of the war. They rode their horses or bicycles to town when they needed to shop or have a haircut or deliver goods. The gasoline was left to the farmers in the rest of the country, who needed to supply food to the troops.

Most farmers around Hideaway still used mules as their power source for plowing and wagon pulling, cutting hay and reaping corn. This way they didn't have to fret about the shortages as much. They could save for other things.

Red had discovered just how well-off he and his neighbors had been in Hideaway by talking to other soldiers who'd come from farms across the Midwest. His hometown had five hundred and fifteen of the best people he'd ever known. That was why the population had doubled in the past ten years, smack dab in the middle of the depression, and that was why it would keep growing long after the war ended. Why, he could even see it doubling again in time, maybe to a thousand or more.

The train stopped at the Hollister station. He looked out the window for signs of his ma. Other men in uniform left the train, including Ivan, who glanced back in Red's direction and waved. They'd see each other soon enough. Ivan could never resist Ma's cooking.

Red waited, watching happy reunions taking place on the train ramp. Two soldiers and an airman stepped off, uniforms proudly decorated, as Ivan's was. Many were probably home for good after the victory in Europe.

Home. It was the one thing everyone in the field dreamed about and talked about most.

Until now, Red hadn't been any different. He slid his left hand down the side of his thigh to his knee, where shrapnel had ripped into the muscle and bone. He'd been held in the stateside hospital for three weeks, with daily injections of some new drug called penicillin that was supposed to kill the infection.

He didn't know how well it had worked. The surgeon had told him the bone looked good, the infection gone, but for some reason his brain didn't seem to be getting the message he was healed. He couldn't put all his weight on his left leg yet. Smart as the surgeon was, he wasn't God.

Red still didn't see his mother or anyone he recognized who might be here to pick him up. And so he stayed put, the darkness of the past few weeks haunting his thoughts.

Dark and heavy. Dark and hopeless.

Here he'd been thinkin' that Bertie would be better off without him, but wouldn't that be the same for everybody else, as well? Nobody needed a lame soldier taking up space, Ma least of all, with all the work she needed done.

The last of the passengers disembarked, and the crowd on the platform began to thin. Red looked on glumly as Ivan greeted his parents in the parking lot.

Ivan's father, Gerald, broad-shouldered and smiling—teeth gleaming so brightly Red could see them from where he sat—gave his son a bear hug. Both men towered over the fair Arielle Potts, whose Swedish coloring Ivan had inherited.

Ivan gestured toward the train, and they all glanced toward where Red sat watching them from the shadows. He didn't think they could see him, looking from the bright sunshine into the darkness of the railcar, but he waved back.

The three of them climbed into a shiny black Chevrolet.

After most others had left the train, Red hefted his duffle over one shoulder and reluctantly grabbed the cane, forcing away his brooding thoughts. He dreaded seeing the look on his mother's face when she saw him with his cane for the first time.

Sure, Ma knew about the injury, but to see her youngest hobbling on a cane like an old man? No mother should have to witness that.

Finally, out of the window, he saw Lilly Meyer come riding up in a buggy pulled by the big bay gelding Seymour, and Red felt a rush of relief.

Ma's broad, sun-reddened face showed him she'd spent a lot of time outside in the vegetable garden—one of Red's jobs when he was home. She guided Seymour carefully through the crowd in the parking area, waving to several acquaintances along the way.

Even before the gasoline rationing of the war, Lilly Meyer had held with her horse. She wasn't afraid of cars. She wasn't afraid of anything. She just always loved her horses. Pa had tried to teach her how to drive when he was alive, but she would have nothing to do with it. She didn't mind people thinking of her as a little backward.

In fact, Ma was the envy of the town with a business that had thrived through the depression and kept going during the war.

Hay and oats weren't rationed here because the farmers raised their own. Neither were garden vegetables or milk from their own cows, or meat and eggs from their own stock. In his travels, Red saw what the rest of the country had had to do without. He couldn't believe how blessed he'd been all those years.

Red grabbed the metal soffit over the door and tried his hardest not to grimace. As he stepped down, he saw his mother look at his cane, then his leg. The pain in his leg was nothing compared to what he felt when he saw the look in her eyes.

"Now, Ma, don't you go worrying about me," he greeted as he rushed to hug her. Ordinarily, he'd pick her up and twirl her around—well, maybe that would be called lumbering her around. Lilly Meyer was, after all, nigh on three-hundred pounds. He couldn't lift her now, but he wrapped his arms around her bulky form and was grateful for her strength.

She clung to him for a long few seconds, and this surprised Red. Their family'd not been much for shows of emotion.

She drew back at last, and he saw tears on her cheeks. She patted the moistness on his uniform collar with alarm.

"Now, look what I did," she said.

"It'll dry, Ma." His mother didn't cry. Even at Pa's funeral, she'd been as strong as a man, setting the example for Red and his older sister and brother, Agnes and Howard, not to show a trembling lip or damp eye. The Meyers wore brave faces for the rest of the world, no matter what.

Her double chins wobbled as she looked up into his eyes and brushed her fingers across his cheek, like he was a little boy again. "It's going to be okay now. My hero's home." She glanced around them. "And none too soon, either, from the looks of things," she muttered.

"What're you talking about?" he asked. "The war's half over."

"Germans aren't exactly the best-liked people in Hideaway right now, especially since we're hearing about all those death camps."

"But we're not German, we're American, Ma."

"We're German enough for somebody to hate us."

"Who's been snubbing you?"

She sniffed once more, then composed herself. "That ol' Drusilla Short says I'm a Nazi sympathizer. Thinks I oughta surrender and be locked up and my guesthouse shut down."

"Since when did anyone ever listen to that woman's opinion?" Red patted Seymour on the nose and received a welcoming nudge that knocked him off his stride.

"Since two nights ago when someone threw a brick through our window that nearly conked poor John Martin on the head when he was reading the paper," Ma said.

"John!" Red paused before he climbed in beside his mother. "He okay?"

"Fightin' mad, but other than that he's just got a mark on his noggin from some flying glass. Tough young buck."

Red clenched his hands into fists as anger streaked through him. "Who do you think did it?" If he found out, he'd hobble out and bang some heads. They'd never try to hurt his mother again.

"You know bullies are cowards," she said. "They don't show themselves. And our house ain't the only target for mischief. It's been going on a couple of months. Mildred went missing last month."

Red stared at his mother. The loss of one of Ma's two milk cows would've been a huge blow to her. "You never told me that. You never found her?"

"Nope, but Joseph Moennig loaned me one of his. Said he's got his hands full with all the farm work now that Bertie's in California." She nodded. "That Joseph is a good man. But he paid for his goodness two weeks ago. Some of his own stock went missing."

"His cattle?"

"A couple of cows and some pigs, and you can bet they were taken off to market and sold. He'll never see them again, and they were the best of his stock." She shook her head. "I'm tellin' you, Red, this place is in for troubled times. Want to know why I was late gettin' here?"

"I figured you had a good reason."

"Somebody decided Seymour needed to be let out of his corral sometime last night. If he wasn't such a homebody, no tellin' where he'd be by now. As it was, I found him washing his feet down by the river. I saw a chalk mark on the side of the shed. It was that broken cross the Nazis use."

"A swastika?"

"That's the sign."

"Anything else?"

"Nope. Don't you think it's too much of a coincidence that ol' Dru Short's been hurling lies about us, and now we've got bricks through our window and Nazi signs on our stable?"

"Is the sheriff doing anything about the thefts?"

"Not that I've seen. Mayor Gerald says he'll not let 'em get away with this, but he can't stop it if he don't catch nobody." She patted Red's arm. "Not to worry now. You'll take care of it. You'll find out who's doing this, if anybody can."

Red climbed into the buggy, glad for the sturdy handles he grasped to pull himself up. He felt more helpless than ever. What was happening in Hideaway?

Chapter Six

On the short ride back to the plant with Connie, Bertie slid Red's last letter out of her purse. She'd studied it over and over when she'd received no new letters, thinking maybe it held a hidden reason why he hadn't written again.

Sometimes she nearly convinced herself he'd met someone else—not that there was much chance of meeting a woman in the muddy trenches where he'd been stuck for so many months. Still, she'd heard there were women aplenty in the towns where the men went when they were on leave.

In all his letters, Red had never made any promises to her about the future. What if he'd met some Italian beauty off in that foreign world? From what she'd read in letters from other soldiers, a man could get mighty lonely, mighty desperate in the midst of war.

She carefully unfolded the letter written nearly six weeks ago. It was two pages of awkward words that had gripped her heart and convinced her for sure that she loved him and he was the only one for her.

Bertie, you keep asking me if I've gotten a chance to see Italy. I've seen more of this place than I've ever wanted to see of any country, anywhere, anytime. I've seen whole orchards battered to kindling wood. I've seen people living in bombed buildings, starving, begging us for food.

I see your face every time I close my eyes, and can almost hear your voice every time I pull your picture out of my pocket.

Funny, ain't it? I always thought of all Italians as dark haired, dark eyed. That's not true. Some are as blond as you are, with skin like yours. I've been into some towns a few times, and I can't tell you how often I thought I'd seen you in the crowd on the street, and I'd run toward you and call your name, and when I got there, I'd find a stranger watching me like they thought I was about to shoot them.

She looked up from the words, as the warmth of them flowed through her. Instead of the California highway, she saw the lines of Red's smiling face—he was most always smiling or laughing at something—never at someone else, most times at himself.

She wanted to cry over his loneliness for her. And yet she felt reassured. A woman couldn't read such heartfelt words and doubt a man's love for her.

Straightening the fold in the page, she read on.

These people aren't the enemy. They were dumb, maybe, and weak when they should have been strong, but how can I say what I'd have done in their place? They're defeated now, you can see it in their eyes, and especially in their land.

There's times I can hear your laughter or your voice

in the middle of the night when the shells are whizzing through the sky, and that voice keeps me from going plumb out of my mind.

Bertie, if I get home alive, it's because of you. I feel like I have somebody waiting for me. I feel like I have a future. So many of my buddies've gotten their Dear John letters—their women didn't want to wait around. All this time, I keep on getting letters from you. I never expected different, but I want you to know something. If I don't make it home, it's not because you didn't pray hard enough, it's because the evil caught up with us, after all, and the old devil won a battle. Like you keep reminding me, he won't win the real war.

You take care out there in California. You never know what could happen in a place like that, so close to the ocean. The enemy can reach you better there than he can in Missouri. Don't let that happen.

If anything happens to me, I want you to be happy. Marry somebody you know I'd approve of, settle and have that passel of kids you've always wanted. And know that there was one soldier who went to his reward fighting for the best gal in the best country in the world.

I kinda like you.

Your Red

She folded the page and slid it back into her purse, and felt the sting of tears in her eyes. No promises, for sure, but he never "kinda liked" anybody else. He'd always been good at understatement. But she knew Red Meyer better than most anyone except his mother. He never made a promise until he knew for sure he'd be able to keep it. And then he kept it.

Just because he hadn't written in the past few weeks didn't mean he'd forgotten about her.

This letter was filled with his affection for her, his abiding friendship. She'd read love letters received by her friends at work that didn't show as much love as this letter did.

Could the man who'd placed his life in her hands stop writing because he'd met another woman he liked better?

She knew things were different now, and she couldn't help worrying about how lonely a man could get. But Red wasn't the type to lead one woman on with letters while courtin' another. It wasn't his nature. He was constant, steadfast, not a ladies' man at all. He was a man any lady would be proud to marry, who would put a lot of joy and laughter into her life—as he had always done in Bertie's.

She couldn't help smiling when she remembered how Red had changed after he'd first asked her out on a bona fide date more than three years ago. Always before, he'd seemed as comfortable with her as he was with his old bluetick hunting dog. Then, suddenly, when he came to pick her up with the horse and buggy for a drive down to the lake, or when he and Ivan double-dated with her and Dixie Martin, John's sister, and went to the cinema in Hollister in John's tan Pontiac, Red got all tongue-tied. He didn't know how to talk to Bertie.

He opened doors for her, paid for her meals and movie, treated her like she was someone special, but he stumbled over his words and his face flushed more easily.

His awkwardness touched her. She felt honored that he thought that much of her.

"We're here," Connie said, interrupting Bertie's thoughts. "You want me to walk back to the department with you in case Franklin decides to strangle you?" She grinned. "That way I can administer first aid quicker."

"I can handle him," Bertie assured the nurse.

She wasn't so sure of herself once Connie left, but if Red could depend on thoughts of her to get him through the horrors of the battles he'd fought, she could keep him in her heart as she tried to deal with Franklin.

Red took the reins from his mother and guided Seymour toward the road that followed the course of the White River back to Hideaway. It would be a long ride.

"Let's check on Joseph on our way home," Lilly said.

Red looked at his ma. "He sick or something?"

"Nope, I'm worried about him, is all. I didn't see him outside anywhere on my way here, and Erma Lee Jarvis called out to me from the garden as I passed their house. Joseph didn't answer Bertie's calls last night."

"Calls?"

"Four times, according to Erma Lee."

"He never misses her calls."

"That's what I'm saying. Something could be up."

Red flicked the reins to urge Seymour forward at a quicker walk. "Why didn't the Jarvises check on him last night?"

"You know how tetchy Joseph can be when a body tries to coddle him. Besides, he gets tired of the neighbors always listening in on his calls with Bertie. He can be sharp at times, you know."

Red nodded. Yep, Joseph could be that. Bertie called him grumpy, but she knew better. Joseph tried hard to be a tough ol' farmer, but he was a man with a soft spot for those he was closest to.

Red remembered when one of Joseph's prize milk cows took out after Bertie for petting her new calf. That poor ol' cow got sold so fast, she never saw it coming.

"It'll be good to see Joseph again." Red cast his mother a quick glance. She looked worried. "He been around in the past day or two?"

"I saw him at church. He was lookin' forward to his daughter's call." She shook her head. "That's another reason it's so strange he never answered. Hope he's not had any more trouble with cattle rustling."

Red flicked the reins again, and Seymour broke into a trot. Red tried not to worry, but worry seemed to've become a part of him since going off to war.

Joseph had always seemed partial to Red, and taught him a lot about being the man of the house, looking out for his mother, taking on a lot of the workload. He'd shown Red everything from stacking firewood the right way to handling newborn calves to plantin' a garden.

Joseph had also written to Red at least twice a month all the time he was in Europe. Nobody would take Pa's place, of course, but Joseph Moennig came the closest. He had to be lonely with Bertie out in California.

Red cast another curious glance at his mother. Well, maybe Joseph wasn't always lonely. Ma would see to that. And it didn't seem she'd mind all that much.

"I can't do much right now to help him on the farm," Red warned her.

"He won't care none about that, he'll be worried

about you." She sighed and shook her head. "Can't deny it'll be a relief to share the load a little."

"What load's that?" Red asked.

She jerked her head toward his leg. "Since you didn't want Bertie to know about your injury, I couldn't tell nobody about it. Somebody'd have blabbed for sure. You're gonna be a shock to all our Hideaway friends, Red. Nobody even knows you got shot."

He nearly groaned aloud. Why had he done that to his poor mother? "I didn't get shot. I got hit by shrapnel. They'll know soon enough."

"Guess that means you need to have a talk with Bertie before long, because you're sure not going to keep this thing a secret now. You're back in the States, you can pick up a phone and call her. She's really gonna be hurt you didn't tell her about this right off."

"I couldn't, Ma. I didn't know how it'd all work out, and you know how she worries."

"You can tell her now."

Red nodded. "Guess I could."

"You know, I never did like keepin' this thing a secret from her, especially when she asked about you time and time again."

"I know, and I'm sorry."

"I've never been a liar, and keeping this from her felt like I was lyin'."

He sighed. "I know, Ma. I know."

"And you never did tell me why you did it."

"She's gone through a lot, Ma. Her brother moved away, then the war hit, then her mother died. And now she's all alone in California without any kin nearby."

"And now her beau's stopped writing to her," his mother said, giving him a pointed look.

"I'd rather have her wonder about a few missed letters than know about this." He tapped his leg.

"It's gonna heal fine," Ma said.

Red didn't argue, but he couldn't agree, either. That'd be lying. For the past few weeks, he hadn't believed anything would be fine again. But no reason to try to tell his mother that.

Still, she was right. He had to tell Bertie about this leg. He dreaded doin' it, because it would change everything. Could be that was why he hadn't said anything about it yet—pure selfishness. As long as Bertie didn't know there was anything wrong, in her mind, at least, they were still together at heart.

But when he told her about the leg, he'd also have to tell her his decision about the two of them. He still didn't know how he could bear it.

"So you might as well get it over with," Ma said. "She's hurtin' out there in no-man's-land, all alone, thinkin' her man's done dropped her like a hot biscuit."

Red started to speak, and he couldn't. He swallowed hard, feeling his mother's sharp gaze. "I will, Ma. Soon as she's had time to get home from work tonight, I'll call her and tell her all about it."

From the corner of his eye, he saw his mother nod, saw her mouth open to speak, and he cut her off.

"I heard tell you've cooked Joseph a meal or two lately." He hoped she would let him change the subject.

When he glanced at her, his eyebrows nearly met his hairline at the sight of the blush that tinted her face.

"Bertie tell you that?" she asked.

Red nodded. Bertie had written a lot of things in her letters that he'd never realized before—about her dreams of living on a farm and having kids, of maybe someday having her own guesthouse like his mother's.

He'd also learned how much Bertie admired Lilly—and Red. It was a funny thing about Bertie—when they were growing up, Red had treated her about the same way he treated all his buddies. Like a guy. Never took much notice of her any other way until they were nearin' high school. Then he'd struggled for years to come to terms with his feelings.

Even when the war hit, spurring him to finally ask her out on a real date, they'd never talked about feelings and such, not the way she wrote about them now. They'd talked baseball scores and fishing, and, of course, they'd talked about the war.

"Joseph never says anything about how he's doin' alone out on the farm," Lilly said. "Used to be he wouldn't even let me bake him a pie, but lately, he's helped me out with a few things—like when Mildred got lost—and he hasn't minded when I cooked a few things up. He's still as stubborn as a mule."

"His daughter has some of his stubbornness," Red said, unable to keep his thoughts from settling on Bertie, same as they'd done throughout the war—same as they'd done for nigh on twelve years or so.

"Soon as he heard about the brick in the window, he came to town and helped shore up the hole," Ma said. "Then he went looking for signs of the scoundrels."

"Maybe he's figured something out by now," Red said.

"Could be the two of you need to put your heads together." She nudged him. "Seeing as how he's practically your father-in-law."

Red noticed that his mother's teasing grin didn't reach her eyes. She was worried about that, he could tell, and he could almost hear her unasked question.

Joseph Moennig and his daughter weren't the only stubborn ones. Ma could be hard to live with when she wanted something she couldn't get. Like a certain young lady for a daughter-in-law.

Also, that brick and the missing cow had scared Ma worse than she would let on, but Red knew if he pushed, she'd clam up. Best to talk about other things for a while. And so they did, throughout the hour-long ride back to Hideaway.

Chapter Seven

The dirt road to Hideaway from Hollister skirted the southern ridge of hills that formed bluffs above the James River. Simply named the Hideaway Road, it continued on from Hideaway to Cape Fair, where it was called the Cape Fair Road. The Moennig farm was barely a quarter mile from Hideaway.

Being near town was the reason the Moennig place had electricity, while most of the farms in rural Missouri didn't. For the last few years, the Moennigs also had indoor plumbing and hot and cold running water, another rarity around these parts. Before that, they'd pumped their water out back of the house, heated it on the wood cookstove in the kitchen, and bathed in a tin washtub, like most other folks out in the country.

As Seymour kept up a steady trot down the road, Ma chattered about the young men coming back home from the war, about who'd been discharged early, and hinting that some of the discharges hadn't been honorable.

"You mean like Hector Short?" Red asked. No wonder Drusilla was so mean. Her own son was a scoundrel, bringing embarrassment to the family.

"I've seen neither hide nor hair of him around here," Ma said. "If I had, I'd've suspected him of throwing that brick through the—" Her voice broke off. "Would you listen to me? I'm getting as bad as Drusilla. I need to wash my mouth out with lye soap."

Red turned Seymour in at the Moennig driveway and kept going until they reached the corral gate. Then he stopped the horse and frowned.

"The gate's open. Did you notice that when you came by earlier?" he asked.

"Nope, you can't see this gate from the road." She gestured back toward the tall hedge around the front of the yard. "That isn't like Joseph, even if he didn't have cattle in the corral."

"Hello!" Red called as he reached for his cane. This time of day, Joseph would usually be out in the field, working the hay, or in the garden.

Ma gasped, then put a hand on Red's arm, gripping him hard. "Charles Frederick."

He turned to her, startled at her use of his full name. She was staring at something out in the cattle lot behind the barn. Red saw a patch of blue. A human shape, redchecked shirt and blue overalls.

Red tossed the reins to his mother and scrambled from the buggy, then reached back for his cane. Without a word, Ma pulled it from beside her on the wagon's running board, passed it to him, then gripped the railing beside her to get out.

"You stay right here," he said.

For once, she did as he told her.

As he hobbled along the rutted driveway toward the back fence, he felt chilled to the bone. If only this was just another nightmare he'd wake up from any minute.

But it was real. He'd seen too many images like this.

He felt sick as he stepped into the cattle lot and got a close look of Joseph Moennig. The side of Joseph's face was so white it seemed to reflect the hot, late-morning sun.

Red dropped awkwardly to his good knee next to his friend and gently rolled him to his back. Joseph stared without sight toward Heaven—his new home.

"Roberta Moennig."

Bertie caught her breath, and looked up at Franklin.

"Yessir," she said, taking care to turn off the lathe and keep her hands away from the moving parts. Her wound was beginning to ache as the pain killer wore off.

Franklin's broad face didn't have the usual scowl she'd come to know and dislike. When she met his eyes, he looked away. Then she realized he'd called her by her real name instead of hillbilly.

"You want something?" she asked.

"Your injury doing okay?" he asked, his voice still gruff, but sounding almost sincere.

"I'm fine."

She started to return to her work, but then he spoke again. "You need to report to the front office. Talk to Charlotte."

She stared at him as a chill traveled across her shoulders and down her arms. "What's she want to see me for?"

He avoided her look. "You've…got a call."

"What kind of a call?" Had he actually followed through with this morning's threat to dismiss her?

It couldn't be. Franklin enjoyed firing people, didn't he? Right now, he didn't look as if he was enjoying himself too much.

"Just get to the office," he muttered, turning away.

She nodded and left her worktable. She refused to beg. If she got fired, she'd find another job easily enough. Hughes Aircraft wasn't the only place in town that could use a trained machinist.

Still, she wished she'd watched her mouth a little closer with Franklin this morning. Sass and vinegar weren't always a good thing.

Minutes later, she stepped into the business office, abuzz with so many typewriters clattering and telephones ringing. Most folks in the plant wanted an office job, but not Bertie. Give her a machine over a typewriter any day. Machine work made more sense to her, and she loved operating a lathe, forming the parts that would be used to build the airplanes that would help win the war. She felt she was doing something useful. Of course, the people working in the office were useful, too.

If she couldn't work with machines in the shop, give her a barn full of milking cows rather than a typewriter in a stifling office. In fact, she'd pretty much prefer anything over being cooped up in an office all day.

A woman with dark hair tied severely away from her face was the first person Bertie encountered when she walked through the door. The woman didn't stop typing, didn't even look up, when Bertie approached her desk.

"Help you?" the woman asked.

Bertie paused, waiting for eye contact.

When the woman finally looked up, her fingers continued their clattering across the typewriter keys. "What do you need?" she snapped.

"I'm Roberta Moennig, and I was told to report to Charlotte. You care to point her out to me?"

The woman's eyes widened, and she stopped typing. The sharpness vanished. "I'm Charlotte," she said in a voice suddenly gone soft. She paused, eyeing Bertie. "Why don't you have a seat, Roberta." She pointed toward the chair in front of her desk, then picked up a telephone receiver from the desktop and handed it to her.

"I'm so sorry," she whispered, placing a hand on Bertie's shoulder before rising from her chair and walking away.

Bertie stared after her in confusion, aware that others in the office had stopped their work and shot glances toward her. Something wasn't right.

She closed her eyes and took a deep breath. "Hello?" she said into the telephone receiver. "Who is this?"

"Bertie? It's me. It's Red."

Her mouth dropped open, and she gasped. It was him! Here she'd been thinking about him and…"Red! Where are you? I've not heard from you in so long I was beginning to wonder if you were okay. What's… why are you…" She frowned. "*Are* you okay? Why are you calling me in the middle of the—"

"I'm…home." His voice was gentle, uncommonly soft. "I'm back home in Hideaway."

"For good? You've been released?"

"I've been discharged."

"I wondered if they'd send you home after Germany's

surrender, but since I never heard a word from you in six full weeks, I couldn't help wonderin'—"

"Bertie, we'll have a long talk about that later, but I didn't call to talk about me right now." He paused. "Ma picked me up at the train station, and we stopped by your Pa's place to check on him." Another pause.

Bertie leaned forward. She hated the solemn sound of Red's voice. "What is it? Is Dad all right? Is he sick?"

"Bertie, I'm sorry. I…" He cleared his throat. "I found him…he's gone."

Chapter Eight

For a moment, Bertie didn't grasp what Red meant. She was dreaming—or this wasn't really Red. It was some kind of practical joke.

"I don't understand," she said, hearing the tremor in her own voice. "H-how can you find him if he's gone?"

"I found his body."

She shook her head, unable to let the words sink in. It couldn't be... She'd been worried about him last night when he didn't answer her call, but this?

"Bertie? You there? You okay?"

She closed her eyes and swallowed hard. "I'm sorry, Red, I didn't—"

"Your father's—he's dead," Red said. "I found him myself, out in the cattle lot behind the barn."

She gasped, and her vision went dark for a moment. She became aware of someone standing beside her with a hand on her shoulder, placing a glass of water on the desk in front of her. She looked up to see her friend and roommate, Edith Frost, looking down at her, dark hair mussed, dark eyes narrowed in concern.

"What's the water for? And what're you doing here?" Edith should be home asleep. Her shift wouldn't begin for a few more hours.

"Charlotte called me," Edith whispered. "She wanted me to be here for you."

"Bertie?" Red said, his voice growing gruffer. "You okay?"

"Yes, I'm… I'll…"

"What's happening out there?" he asked.

"Would you just…give me a minute?" She closed her eyes. "Oh, Dad," she whispered.

It was true. It must be. But reality clashed hard against denial. "No, this can't be," she whispered. "Not Dad. He wasn't fighting in the war."

"He's been fighting a war, all right," Red said.

"How?" she asked. "What happened to him?"

"I wish I knew for sure."

"What do you mean? Was he sick? What happened?"

"There looks to be a…an injury to the side of his head."

She frowned. "And he was in the cattle lot? Could be the bull got him, but ol' Fester's never been a mean—"

"Not Fester. Not an animal…not a four-legged one, anyway. It looks like…like something small hit him in the side of the head, Bertie."

Bertie nearly dropped the phone. "Something like what?"

"I'm not sure yet. The sheriff's out there now, along with the mayor."

She heard something in his voice, some thread of doubt, as if he was hiding something from her, unwilling to say what was on his mind.

"You're saying somebody killed my father?" she heard her own voice, loud with shock, saw the surprised faces of the people standing around her, and felt as if the floor was buckling beneath her.

"I'm not saying anything yet."

"Oh, yes you are. That's what you're thinking, I can tell."

"Now, don't go putting words in my mouth. I'm gonna find out what happened," Red promised. "You hang on out there, you hear?"

Bertie took a few deep breaths and managed to keep her hands from trembling. "What are you thinking, Red? Talk to me!"

Edith slid a handkerchief into Bertie's hands and placed an arm around her shoulders, but Bertie wouldn't let tears fall.

"Don't you worry, Bertie," Red said. "We'll see to it your father has a good, Christian funeral."

She took a few more breaths. "Red Meyer, what aren't you telling me?"

"I don't know, yet, okay? I don't know what happened. Give us time to figure things out on this end, and I'll call you. You stay put, though. You don't need to be traipsing back here. We'll take good care of your pa's body."

"Don't make any plans until you know how soon Lloyd and I will be able to get there. I'll have to call him right away." Her brother would be working on his in-laws' family farm in Kansas this time of day, but someone should be able to get to him.

There was a short silence, then Red cleared his throat. "Bertie?"

Again, the tone of his voice alerted her. "What?"

"I don't think you oughta come to Hideaway right now. Lloyd neither."

"Of course I'm coming. You can't call and tell me my father is dead, then think I'm not coming home as soon as I can get there."

"I'm not saying you shouldn't grieve, Bertie, I just think you need to do it out there in California. It's safer there."

Her grip tightened on the telephone receiver. "What do you mean, safer?"

"I already told you, I can't say for sure what happened to your father, but it might not be safe here right now for you or Lloyd, not until we know for sure what happened."

She waited for him to continue.

"Could just be my own reaction to the war," he said, "expectin' trouble when there isn't any, but I can't help thinking the war's brought out some enemies we didn't know anything about, even here in Hideaway."

She felt a chill down her spine. She wasn't sure she wanted him to explain more, wasn't sure she could take much more information today. *Oh, Lord, someone might've killed my father?*

"You hear what I'm saying?" Red asked. "You stay put and stay out of trouble right where you are."

"I can stay out of trouble, but I'll be in Hideaway while I'm doing it," she said. "That's where I'm going to be as soon as I can get there, and don't you try telling me different. I'm not some helpless little thing who can't take care of herself."

There was a quick grunt of irritation over the line,

then, "Bertie Moennig, you might cause more trouble than I can handle if you come traipsing into town right now. I never said you was helpless, but don't be daft, either. Stay put!"

The sharpness of his words pierced her anger. But even though part of her could see the wisdom of his words from his point of view, she wasn't him. She couldn't do what he wanted her to.

"Don't you worry about a thing, Red Meyer. I won't be a burden to you."

"Now, Bert, you know that isn't what I meant, I was only trying to—"

"You'd better give me some space *when* I get there, because I'm comin'. Don't you dare treat me like I don't belong." She returned the phone receiver to its base, and pressed her forehead to the cool desktop for a few seconds.

A hand touched her shoulder. "Are you okay, sweetie?"

Edith's voice was soothing, but it also cautioned her. Sorrow and self pity too often formed a partnership, but it wasn't going to happen this time. Not with Bertie Moennig. She couldn't afford that weakness.

The door opened, and she looked up to see Franklin walk in, his beefy shoulders grazing the sides of the door frame. For once, his presence didn't threaten her.

"I won't be back to work today," she told him, bracing herself for an argument.

"I know. I've already got someone on your job." He glanced around at the office workers who hovered near. Though he wasn't their supervisor, they scattered back to their desks.

He crossed the room and leaned over Bertie. "I'm sorry about your father. Are you going to be okay, hillbilly?"

The sudden, unfamiliar note of gentleness in his voice surprised her. "Thank you. I'll be fine, but I have to catch a train to Missouri."

He nodded. "Any idea how long you'll be gone?"

She hesitated. She may not be back. Yes, she was needed here, but she would be needed on the farm at Hideaway with Dad gone. Cows would have to be fed and milked, the crops gathered, and she couldn't expect Lloyd to leave his in-laws in the lurch so he could tend to everything.

"Hillbilly?" Franklin said sharply. "When do you think you'll be back?"

"I'm not sure. I've got a farm to run now, and the troops need food as badly as they need airplanes."

"Not sure I can keep your job open for you."

"I'm not askin' you to."

He ran a thick palm across his forehead. "I'll tell you what, you give me a call when you decide."

She gave him a wry look. "I thought I was about to get fired today."

A hint of a smile touched his mouth, and his eyes wandered downward. "That's what I wanted you to think. You work better that way." He gave her a wink, then turned and left, his thick shoulders grazing the sides of the door frame once more.

Edith stepped up beside Bertie. "Well, what do you know? That slave driver might have a heart, after all."

Bertie allowed herself to be distracted. "Don't count on it. He just knows good help when he mistreats it."

"Are you sure you're going to be okay?"

A quick swallow, a deep breath, and Bertie regained control of her emotions. There were things to do. "All I need is a train ticket to Missouri."

Edith nodded. "We'll make that two tickets. I'm not letting you go by yourself."

"You have a job to do," Bertie said.

"I have a friend to sustain, and that is more important to me than my job right now."

"You have a war effort to support," Bertie repeated. "I'm going alone. Don't you argue with me, Edith Frost."

She had to make arrangements to get home to Hideaway.

Chapter Nine

Red stared at the telephone receiver, then replaced it in its holder on the wall of the dining room. Curious paying guests returned their attention to their noontime meals at the long table. He'd tried to keep his voice down, but it hadn't worked very well.

Most of the guests were lodgers for a day or two, maybe a week at most. Two he recognized from years past, four of them he'd never seen.

Then there was John Martin, a good friend who'd been lodging at the Meyer Guesthouse for years, ever since he'd started teaching school in town. On weekends he went to the family farm several miles out, to help his father and fifteen-year-old brother work the fields while his older brother, Cecil, fought in the Pacific Theater. With school out, John continued to work in town during the week, helping build new classrooms.

Ivan Potts was also at the table. He and John had both been so shocked to see Red's cane and his limp, their reactions would have been almost comical if Red was in the mood to laugh. He wasn't.

After a couple of short words from him, both John and Ivan knew better than to ask about his injury in front of the guests.

It was awkward trying to take care of business with strangers hearing everything he'd said to Bertie over the telephone.

Ma was working in the kitchen, pulling dessert out of the oven. She hardly ever sat and ate with the lodgers and other customers. No time. No help. As soon as she got all the food on the table, it was time to start cleaning up.

The guests showed a sudden interest in their chicken and dumplings. They were almost convincing. This meal was Ma's specialty, with thick chunks of chicken in the creamiest gravy and lightest dumplings this world had ever tasted.

These people didn't fool Red, though. They were hungry for more details of his conversation with Bertie, in spite of the fact that their meal was late in coming because of all the awful activity after finding Joseph's body.

"Bertie's coming back home, isn't she?" asked John from his seat halfway down the table.

Red nodded. "I don't know how I could've made it more clear that she needs to stay away."

"Me, neither," John said. "But you know Bertie. She's going to do what she wants to do, and you'd better not get in her way. I bet you made her cry, didn't you?"

Red cast his friend a glare. "No."

"You aren't that great with women, are you, Charles Frederick?" asked Ivan, who sat at the far end of the table.

Red glowered at him. "You're not making this any easier." Ivan never hesitated to speak his mind, but he might be in danger of a tongue lashing if he didn't mind his manners, war hero or not.

The six other lodgers kept their heads down and ate in silence. Red might've been gone a long time, but he sure didn't remember ever having a quiet dining table before.

Ma bustled out through the kitchen door and gave Red a warning look. She never liked airing private matters in front of paying guests, and though his call to Bertie within hearing of everyone had been unavoidable, further talk was not.

Red got the message. He took a few bites of his food, but could barely swallow. He didn't have much of an appetite, even though his ma's chicken and dumplings were his favorite food, and she had prepared it special, just for him.

He couldn't get his mind off Joseph. Who could have done something like this to him? Those lifeless eyes... Bertie had her father's eyes.

A widower, all alone on the farm. Everybody knew there was no truer man in Hideaway. Joseph had helped his neighbors when they needed help, and he worked hard to keep his farm going.

He had been the first person in the county to learn that this soil was ideal for raising tomatoes, and so he had planted fields of tomatoes, and encouraged others to do the same. Could be his wisdom had saved the community from a lot more loss during the depression.

His death didn't make sense, and Red felt especially

helpless—particularly since he'd been told by the sheriff to stay out from underfoot.

Underfoot! Old Butch Coggins was the one underfoot. He wouldn't know a crime scene if he stumbled over a murder weapon and saw the victim bleeding to death in front of him.

Red grabbed his plate in one hand, his cane in the other, and left the table. If he stayed, he'd for sure shoot off his mouth about something he shouldn't. Ma would forgive him for his rudeness in leaving the table. Eventually.

Right now he couldn't force a smile, couldn't make friendly conversation.

He hobbled through the large living room, past the fireplace, and turned into the front parlor. He used the cane to close the door behind him, then stood for a moment, still holding his plate of dumplings as he stared out the big picture window toward the river. He had a bad feeling that life in Hideaway was about to change even more drastically than it already had. He hated the thought.

A fella was bound to expect the worst after seeing the things he'd seen in Italy.

He'd heard too many tales about the way Japanese Americans had been treated here in America during the past few years. They'd been driven from their homes and forced into detention centers, often losing their property, their friends, their jobs. Men had been separated from their wives and children, and sometimes had been forced to return to their native country—where they were now considered the enemy.

He'd also heard rumors about Germans being treated

the same way, though he wasn't sure if there was any truth to it. Wild stories flew through the Army as fast as bullets.

"Wasn't this war enough, God?" he whispered, half angry, half pleading. "Does it have to be brought right here to our own doorstep?"

Edith Frost turned from the telephone ten minutes after she'd picked up the receiver, her dark gaze lingering on Bertie's face, concern evident. "Well, sweetie, we've got tickets for early tomorrow morning unless we get bumped by servicemen coming home or being called out for duty."

Bertie nodded her thanks. "I could've made the arrangements myself."

"Hush, now, and let me pamper you a little. It's not much, considering how much you've done for me the past months. I told the clerk this was a funeral trip, but she wouldn't budge. We'll still have to wait to know for sure until the last minute."

Bertie put her hands on her hips. "You mean she wouldn't let both of us travel for bereavement. I bet *she'd* let me go by myself, *unlike* a certain person who doesn't think I'm capable of traveling alone across five states."

"Six."

"Missouri doesn't count. We're barely inside the state line by fifty miles."

"Seventy."

"Not in a straight line."

"From what I hear tell, there aren't any straight roads in your part of Missouri."

"Edith, you need to stay here. How long have you waited to work on this new project?"

Edith waved her hand. "The Spruce Goose project won't get off the ground, and no pun intended." She shook her head. "Wood and glue? Howard Hughes must have lost his mind when he decided to fund that contraption."

Bertie shot a glance around at the secretaries, who had returned to their typing. "You shouldn't talk about him that way. He's dedicated to the war effort."

"This war effort is making him plenty of money."

"Edith, what's changed your mind? Last I heard, you were gung ho for that project. You begged for weeks to be transferred, and now that you are, you—"

Edith took Bertie's arm and glanced at the others, then the two of them walked out the front door. The bright Southern California sunlight touched their faces and seemed to settle beneath the surface of Bertie's skin. She closed her eyes, wondering if she would ever feel this west coast warmth again, smell the air, enjoy this clearness that she had only experienced in California.

It was like honey to the soul.

Edith waited until they were out of earshot of the office, then said, "What's changed my mind is you, Roberta Moennig. You don't need to be alone right now."

"What makes you think I'll ever be alone? The trains will be packed with servicemen coming home, and Hideaway is filled with friends. I know I'll be in your daily prayers."

"How will I know how to pray for you if I don't know what kind of mischief you're into?" Edith asked.

"I don't get into mischief, and if I ever do, I'll be sure to call you," Bertie said dryly.

Edith shook her head, resolute. "I spent too much time alone after Harper got killed at Pearl Harbor. I don't want that to happen to you."

In spite of herself, Bertie was touched by the admission. Edith hadn't spoken much about losing her husband, and at times it seemed she stayed especially busy for the sole purpose of avoiding thoughts of her loss.

"You heard what I told Franklin," Bertie said softly. "I may not be back. In fact, the more I think about it, I know I probably won't be, not with Red back home." Hearing the tremor in her own voice, she realized again how much she'd come to love this place in such a few months.

And yet… Hideaway was home.

"It's too early to know what you're going to do," Edith said. "So don't go making plans."

"Don't lecture me," Bertie said. "My brother, Lloyd, is working for his in-laws on a huge ranch in Kansas. He can't leave them and move back home to take care of things. There's no one but me."

"Farming's no life for a single woman," Edith said.

"But the farm's still there, and it can't be left to manage itself."

"You aren't the only person in the world who can run a farm."

"I can't sell off what Dad worked so hard to build."

Edith shook her head. "Nobody's asking you to. Look, I'm sorry, I shouldn't have brought this up. You're already overwhelmed. Give yourself a chance to grieve your father's passing. I had a pastor tell me not to make any big decisions for at least six months after Harper died." She shrugged. "Thing is, it's been three and a half years, and I still don't have any plans."

Bertie closed her eyes. "If I'd only known, when I came out here, that I'd never see Dad alive again… I wouldn't've left Hideaway."

Edith put her arms around Bertie and drew her close. Bertie hugged her back, but still she refused to cry. If she did—if she started thinking about how much she'd lost—she'd be stuck in despair.

Chapter Ten

The parlor door swung open and Red turned to find Ivan Potts and John Martin filing in, both solemn, heads bowed.

Ivan sank into the wingback chair beside Red and gazed outside. John sat on the sofa. None of the men spoke for a few moments. They didn't need to. The three of them had known each other well-nigh all their lives.

"I can't believe Joseph's gone," John said.

"Me neither," Ivan agreed. "Bertie's got to be hurting bad."

"Especially after Red yelled at her," John said.

Red scowled out the window. "I might as well have called from the coffee shop, so's half the town could've gotten into the conversation."

"For pity's sake, Red, she's just lost her father," John said. "You're not going to keep that little gal long if you can't learn to treat her any better than that."

Ivan frowned at John. "In case you hadn't noticed, my friend, Bertie's been loyal to Red for three years. I was in the service for barely six months when your sister decided she wanted to up and marry Eugene Arthur."

John scowled. "Dixie never promised to wait for you."

"I never asked her to." Ivan turned to Red. "Did you ask Bertie to wait for you while you were off fighting for our freedom?"

Red shook his head, suddenly uncomfortable. They needed to change the subject.

Ivan nodded to John, as if Red's answer had proved a point. "There you go. Right now Red's the only man here who's even got a girlfriend."

"That could be due to his not being around to run her off," John shot back.

John Martin had a full head of dark brown hair and the tanned skin of a farmer, deep now with summer's glow. He'd tried three times to enlist in any branch of the service that would have him, but he had flat feet and a partial deafness in one ear. He'd been told to help out on the home front.

John was an elementary school teacher in Hideaway. His brother, Cecil, had been a high-school science teacher before joining the Marines.

"How'd Bertie seem to be holding up when you talked to her?" Ivan asked Red.

"Good as can be, I s'pose." Red had never been sorrier for the way he'd spoken. Bertie'd lost her father, and, like John said, he'd practically yelled at her, and for sure scared her half out of her wits, hinting about ugly deeds afoot in Hideaway.

What had gotten into him?

Of course, he knew. It was the same thing that had gotten into everybody—this awful war.

But he'd needed to make Bertie listen, and what he'd said hadn't been a lie. Joseph's death looked suspicious to him. Bertie didn't need to worry about that on top of everything that'd happened to her.

Red had been surprised by the depth of his own grief for Joseph, so he could imagine how Bertie was faring right now.

"Something's wrong," Red said. "It's just wrong. I don't think this was any accident."

"The sheriff's checking things out," John said.

"Dad's out there with him," Ivan reminded him. "As mayor he'll make sure everything's done right. They're looking over the house to see if they can come up with any clues. Maybe they'll find something."

Red gave him a sideways glance. "Butch is not going to get by with brushing this death under the rug just because he doesn't know how to investigate it, or because Joseph had a German heritage."

"Might not have anything to do with Joseph's heritage," John said. "The whole town's filled with Germans and even a few Italians somewhere in the mix, I'd suspect."

"But Joseph hailed from the old country," Red said. "He wasn't born here. You know about the brick through Ma's window."

"I'd say I do." John brushed his hair back, demonstrating how close the brick had come to his head. There was a small gash on his forehead from the flying glass.

"And Ma's German," Red said. "To me, that smacks of prejudice."

"Old Butch has never had a murder in these parts," John said. "He doesn't know what one looks like."

"That's because he turns a blind eye to most meanness," Ivan said.

Red thought about that a minute, then looked at his friends, leaning forward, glancing toward the door. He kept his voice low. "Think this time Butch might be part of the meanness?"

Ivan and John looked at each other, and the silence in the room filled Red's ears before talk and laughter reached him from the dining room. Chairs scraped across the wooden floor, and voices drifted into the living room.

"I know you've never been too crazy about the sheriff," Ivan told Red. "But do you really think he could be behind this?"

"Well, now, just wait a minute," John said. "Butch and Joseph never have seen eye to eye about anything. And I overheard Butch a few weeks ago telling a bunch of the men down at the coffee shop that there weren't enough detention centers in this country to place all the folks who don't belong here."

Red sighed. "I don't mean to accuse the sheriff of something like that, but it seems to me Butch has always been less interested in keeping the peace than in using his position to con favors from the citizens." Hideaway didn't have a police force. The town wasn't big enough. He'd heard tell that some churches in big cities were larger than Hideaway.

That was hard to imagine.

"Well," Ivan said, "at best we have to say the sheriff

doesn't know what he's doing. He could use some help, whether he asks for it or not."

"Red, you're the tracker," John said. "What your daddy didn't teach you, the Army did."

"You saying a crippled man oughta run for sheriff?" Red asked.

"You oughta take the lead on this investigation," John said.

"*We* ought to take the lead," Ivan said. "We've been in Hideaway longer than Butch has. We know the people. Red and I know how to hunt for the enemy."

"I can do my share," John said.

Lilly Meyer bustled through the French doors, deftly holding a tray with three dishes of blackberry cobbler straight from the oven. "Pardon me for eavesdropping, fellas, but you can start right out there in our backyard, Charles Frederick. Whoever threw that brick at John might well be the criminal we're looking for."

"That's where I aim to start," Red told her. "You got a room for Bertie? I guess you heard she's comin' to town, and she sure oughtn't be staying out on the farm."

"There's always room for our Bertie, even if I have to give her my own bedroom," Lilly said. "You boys just be sure to find out what happened to Joseph."

Red didn't plan to stop until he had the job complete.

Bertie pulled her best skirts and blouses from the tiny closet on her side of the bedroom. If only she had some idea about how long she'd be in Missouri—or if she was even coming back here. She was tempted to pack light, but then she reached beneath her narrow bed and pulled out a box of letters from Red. Just thumbing through them, she discovered many tiny, pressed blooms of some of her favorite flowers—picked by Red for her when they were dating just before he left for boot camp.

The memories suddenly cascaded over her, and her eyes blurred with tears. She pulled another letter from the pile.

Dear Bertie,

I won't tell anyone you cried, if you won't tell everyone I sleep with your picture in my pocket, close as I can get it to my heart.

Did I tell you that the guys here don't believe in baths? Some kind of superstition, I guess. One soldier—didn't get his name—said I washed too much. It erases the mud that gives me some camouflage. All I got to say about that is I'd rather be shot than stink like these folks do.

A fella doesn't have to live like an animal over here, most of them just want to.

Another buddy of mine got a Dear John letter yesterday. I'll send you his name and address, and maybe you have another pretty friend who could write to him, make him feel not so alone.

Don't know what I'd do without these letters, Bertie. It's so easy for a man to give up hope altogether, seeing the pain and death that stalks these fields.

When we both get back home to Hideaway, I don't ever want to leave the state again. I just want to settle and stay. Give it some thought.

I kinda like you.

Your Red

She'd reread this one two or three times a week, and

had pressed a lilac between its pages, because that was Red's favorite flower, and this letter was the closest he'd ever come to proposing to her. He'd skirted all around the issue, making hints, letting her know he might be interested, but never committing.

To tease him, she'd ignored the subject altogether in her reply to him, hoping he might write something a little more romantic the next time.

The next time, there was nothing about settling. Months passed, and nothing even close to that subject came up again.

What was she expected to do, ask *him* for his hand in marriage? She smiled at that thought. Maybe she could ask Red's mother for permission to ask him. What a laugh that would give Lilly.

On a whim, Bertie packed all the letters, placing them neatly in the bottom of her heavy old carryall. On top of them, she folded her work jeans and boots, and then her dressier clothes for the funeral, church, and entertaining company after the funeral.

In spite of all that had happened, she wanted to look her best when she saw Red for the first time in a year. Dad would have understood.

Chapter Eleven

Late Monday afternoon, Red felt the burn of the sun on the back of his neck, tellin' him the summer heat had already begun to rule the season. Humidity was just as uncomfortable as the heat, settling back in after a short relief from the rain the area had gotten yesterday evening.

He didn't look up when he heard the squeak of the back door, but continued to study the grass and packed mud along the back fence. Someone had been this way recently, taking care to stay on the grass for the most part—but not taking care enough.

He watched where he stepped, as well, not only to avoid possible tracks, but to keep his shoes free from goose and chicken poop. Ma hated when that got tracked into the house.

"I wouldn't let nobody but Joseph Moennig out in the backyard since the brick shot through the window," Lilly Meyer called across the half-acre yard she'd planted with roses and irises, along with cabbages, lettuce, okra, tomatoes, green beans, carrots and potatoes, and a half dozen other vegetables.

Red glanced at her over his shoulder. His mother had once been almost as good at tracking as his father. In fact, back in their younger days, she'd been better at following the coon dogs.

It hadn't set well with Pa.

"You check for any prints before the rain?" Red asked.

She nodded. "Found a few. Looked to be a couple different people, but a couple of the prints matched shoes belonging to our boarders." She pointed toward one set farther along the fence line. "See that gash in the heel of the left shoe?"

Red nodded.

"That one don't belong to any boarder."

Taking care not to step on the tracks he'd found, Red followed the line of the white picket fence, and soon discovered where someone had climbed the old hawthorn tree.

"See this?" he called to his mother. "The grass must've been pressed into the mud here where somebody stepped. It's straightened since, but the mud dried on it."

She pointed to the lowest limb of the tree. "Some of the mud got smeared onto the wood, here. Young hoodlums, maybe?"

"Could be." He wasn't convinced.

"Kids climb trees," she said, obviously reading his mind.

"They're not the only ones. I've seen soldiers on both sides of the war climb trees when they had to."

"You think this has something to do with the war, then," she said.

"I'm not saying that. Did he mention anything about someone causing him trouble?"

"Only the missing livestock. His neighbors lost some, too. But I'll tell you one thing—if someone was causin' Joseph grief, he'd have fought back."

Red agreed. Joseph was never one to back down from a fight.

"Why don't you ask Bertie when she gets here?" Lilly asked. "He might've said something to her about a problem."

Red gave his mother a sharp look. "She call you back after lunch today?"

"Sure did. She's on her way, if she can catch the train tomorrow. Should be here by Thursday, in plenty of time for the funeral on Friday."

Red sighed, leaning against the tree limb. "Ma, you don't need to be encouraging her about anything. We can't stop her from coming, but she oughta get back on that train as soon as the funeral's over and head on back to California."

Lilly gave him a look that expressed her opinion of his advice. "You're sure in a hurry to get rid of her."

"I already said it ain't safe here. Why won't anybody listen to me?"

"Could be 'cause I happen to think she's as safe here as she is anywhere in the world. She's got friends and neighbors to protect her. There might be some villains in this town, but the good folks outnumber 'em." Ma's eyes narrowed. "I think there's some other reason you want her gone from here."

Red looked away. "I don't know that you two oughta be getting so close."

"Don't you go tellin' me who I can and can't be friends with. Bertie and I have always been friends, long before the two of you started your romance. Why are you suddenly so worried about it?"

"Because you've got plans in mind that won't ever come to pass now."

"Why don't you let me mind my own plans? I'll be friends with Bertie no matter what happens between the two of you, though I'd for sure love to have her as my daughter-in-law."

He sighed, a heavy sigh that he knew his mother would probably read well. "Ain't gonna happen, Ma." He turned and held her gaze.

Her thick red eyebrows lowered over large blue eyes. "You two have a fallin' out besides the one on the phone today?"

He shook his head.

She nodded at his leg. "That got something to do with it?"

He didn't answer, but returned his attention to the tracks again.

"You can't let something like that change your life, Charles Frederick," she said. "You can't let it ruin what you got goin' with Bertie. That's too special."

He glanced at the garden. "I might not make such a good husband like this, but at least I can help you with the gardening." It was once his job to keep the vegetables in good supply, keep the chickens fed, the cows milked, and till and harvest the plot of rich farmland between the house and the riverside.

Sure, with the war on, the boarders—especially those who knew Lilly Meyer's circumstances—sometimes helped with household chores. Havin' a little help now and then wasn't anything like having her own healthy, strong son at home.

"You know anything about that G.I. bill they voted into law last year?" she asked.

"I might."

"It means the people who served our country in the war can have their college schoolin' paid for by their country."

"Yep."

She placed her hands on her broad hips. "So why don't you tell me which college you plan to attend? I don't need you here underfoot all the time when you could be gettin' a good education, learnin' a good trade that'll keep you going through your whole life."

"I don't need to learn farmin', Ma. Nor fishin', nor huntin'. Don't fix what ain't broke."

She sighed. "You can't have it both ways. You don't seem to think you can farm with that leg like it is, so you'd better start planning for something else. You're smart, you can learn something new. Accounting, maybe, or teaching, or even doctoring." She grinned, sighing theatrically. "My son, the doctor. Wouldn't ol' Drusilla Short turn green over that? What this town really needs is a good—"

"Think you could give me a day or two before you ship me off to school?" He kneaded his aching thigh.

She watched him in silence for a moment. "The doc say it was your muscle causing you the most trouble?"

"That's what seems to be the problem now."

"Bertie might be able to help you with that."

"Think we could get off that subject for a while?" He didn't want to keep being reminded about what he needed to give up. His own thoughts of Bertie were enough to keep him awake at night.

"Her ma taught her all she could about those medicinal herbs she used on folks who didn't like to leave Hideaway to go to the doctor."

Red sighed. As usual, his mother had ignored his request. Some things the war didn't change. "Bertie's got enough to worry about," he said sharply.

His mother gave him a wise look. She let the silence fall between them, just as she always used to when he sassed her, giving him plenty of time to think about what he'd said.

"Don't treat me like a little kid now, Ma."

"You didn't say anything to her about your leg when you called her."

"How was I gonna do that? Tell her, 'Sorry, Bertie, I found your father dead out in the cattle lot. Oh, by the way, I've got a war injury that's changed everything?'"

"I'm not saying that, but you can't let her come all the way here and see you without warning her first."

"I don't know what else I can do about it now."

"You should've told her weeks ago," Ma muttered. "I should've told her and gotten it over with."

"She'll know soon enough, I guess," he snapped again, then leaned hard on his cane on the way back to the house.

"Still got some of your pa in you," she said loudly enough for him to hear. "Stubborn old cuss had a little too much o' that male pride. It wasn't pretty on him, either."

"Don't talk ill of the dead, Ma. It's bad luck," he called over his shoulder.

"Yep, and it's not respectful, but you're not dead," she called after him. "Leastways, you're still up and movin' around. Don't give up on life until it gives up on you."

He kept walking. He hadn't given up on life, had he? Maybe life had given up on him. Or maybe God had.

Could be God had given up on the whole world, not just him? Everybody who'd seen the mass of war scars on Europe had reason to wonder. Now everybody was counting the loss of lives. They weren't done counting yet, but it was many millions, that much they knew.

And still people trusted in God?

Lately, he'd been wondering a lot about whether God had turned His back on the whole lot of the earth. Maybe they had disgusted Him to the point that He had finally decided to leave them to their own orneriness. They would be allowed to destroy one another without His interference.

Judging by the death and killing Red had seen on the front lines, he couldn't say he'd blame God.

Chapter Twelve

Late Thursday morning, Bertie slowly stood from her seat on the train, stretching her arms and rubbing achy back muscles. Worn to a bare nubbin from the constant movement of the railcar in which she and Edith had ridden for the past two days, she yawned as she reached for her carryall and turned to look at her friend.

Edith looked fresh and pretty and well rested. Bertie's head ached, her legs were stiff, and no matter how much she stretched, she couldn't work out the kinks.

"After sleeping on these hard, rocking beds for two nights, I have a feeling it'll be a while before I can walk without wobbling," she muttered.

Edith grinned at Bertie, her dark brown eyes filled with a little too much wide-awake cheer. "You'll be fine in fifteen minutes."

"Sure, you can say that. You slept last night."

"I knew you were having trouble. That's why I didn't wake you first thing this morning. Didn't you get any sleep at all?" Edith asked.

"Not until the wee morning hours."

Edith frowned as she studied Bertie's face. "You've been fretting more and more the closer you've gotten to home. I'd have thought you'd be relieved to get here."

Bertie shrugged. What kind of welcome would they find here? Or would they even get a welcome? "Lilly promised she'd make sure we had a ride home from Hollister, but I can't help wondering what's going to happen when we get to Hideaway."

"It's going to be fine," Edith assured her.

Bertie wasn't so confident about that. She'd had two long days to think about Red's words, to compare them to what the sheriff told her about the case when she called him from a stop in Albuquerque. According to Red, danger was afoot. According to Butch Coggins, the town was fine, nothing was wrong and Dad had been in a little farming accident. It happened.

She wanted to believe Butch so badly that, until about the middle of last night, she'd been reassured. But the more she thought about it, the less likely it seemed that Dad had been that careless. Joseph Moennig was one of the most careful men Bertie had ever known. To have the sheriff—who wasn't even a citizen of Hideaway—say such a thing about her father had begun to gall her.

And then she'd begun to wonder if Red hadn't reacted the same way. Red loved Dad almost as much as he'd loved his own father. Maybe he'd simply resented Butch's casual dismissal of Dad's death. Or maybe, being among men from all over the country, he knew something more about what was happening to German Americans in this country. Suspicions ran high at times like these.

Edith looped her arm through Bertie's. "Care to tell me what's working through that mind of yours?"

"I think I know what Red's worried about."

Edith raised her eyebrows as other passengers bustled past them to the exit. "Care to share?"

"You've heard about the internment camps, same as I have," Bertie said.

"What does that have to do with you and me arriving in Hideaway?"

Bertie lowered her voice. "The Meyers and the Moennigs are German Americans. Red and I are both children of German immigrants. It isn't just the Japanese who've been forced into those camps."

"The Meyers and the Moennigs didn't qualify for those camps any more than most other Americans of German descent," Edith said. "Besides, the camps here in America are nothing like the concentration camps we've heard about in Germany, or even the detention camps in Japan."

"I still don't have a hankerin' to go there." Though Bertie knew Edith was probably right, it didn't stop her from worrying. Folks did all manner of hideous things to one another during times of stress. Though the war could bring out the best in some, it could bring out the worst in others. Hideaway was no different than any other town in America.

Of course, her government had taken men—even whole families—to internment camps. That was a long way from stealing cattle and then killing the owners.

A very long way.

Bertie allowed the porter to help her down the steps of the passenger car, then moved aside for the rest of the passengers disembarking. The moist warmth of mid-June surrounded her as the brightness of the sunlight hurt her eyes. The faint smell of smoke from the train engines permeated the air.

She knew she probably looked as tired and gritty as she felt.

She glanced around the crowded station, saw no familiar faces, and slid her tiny hand mirror from her purse.

Ugh. Puffy eyes. Limp, stringy hair. A streak of black on the collar of her blouse—dirt? Grease? She didn't know. All she knew was that she didn't want Red to see her this way after being apart a year—and especially since the last time she'd spoken with him on the telephone, she'd hung up on him.

She'd felt badly about that ever since. Red was just worried about her, and here she'd lashed out at him as if he was the enemy.

By this time, she was so tired of travel that she shouldn't care how she looked, as long as she didn't have to climb back onto that train.

She tugged at the sleeve of her red-checked blouse, knowing it wouldn't help with the wrinkles or the dirt, but glad she wasn't wearing something in a solid color. Prints didn't show stains or wrinkles as badly. She wished she'd thought to pack more than two dresses. Her denims were practical—and a lot more comfortable than the formfitting skirt she had on—but according to Lilly, there would be quite a few townsfolk wanting to see her as soon as she arrived in Hideaway.

Still, she'd be busy on the farm. She would need the work clothes more than dresses.

Foremost on her mind, however, was her father and the questions that she couldn't stop from churning in her head.

Why had she lost so much in three years? First Mom, now Dad. And her brother? She'd discovered, after calling Lloyd on Monday night, that he was too sick to travel home for the funeral. He had been taken to the sanitarium in Mt. Vernon, Missouri, with a possible diagnosis of tuberculosis. The test results wouldn't be final for several weeks, and until then, he would be kept isolated from his family. Typical of Lloyd, he had decided not to call Bertie or Dad about it until he had the results.

Instead of coming to Dad's funeral, Lloyd was being forced to grieve alone.

Bertie could only pray the final diagnosis was negative. If it was positive, her prayers would be that her sister-in-law, Mary, and her little niece and nephew, Joann and Steven, hadn't contracted the horrible disease from him.

How much was one family supposed to take?

She felt Edith's arm around her shoulders. Edith was such a comfort, always knowing when Bertie needed to have her mind distracted from painful thoughts.

But even Edith's presence didn't cheer Bertie when she caught sight of two familiar faces in the small crowd waiting to board. She should be glad to see people she hadn't seen in nearly ten months. Instead, she avoided their gazes.

She couldn't bear to see the sympathy in their eyes. Even worse, what if those gazes held accusation of her German heritage?

The thought stunned her, and she swung away quickly. Where had *that* come from? Was she really that consumed by the fear that her own country could turn against her, dragging her, the daughter of a German immigrant, off to some internment camp? What nonsense!

There was something else going on here. Her government wouldn't have murdered Dad.

If that was even what had happened to him. How was she supposed to know for sure?

A wave of loss smacked her hard yet again, as it had numerous times since she'd left California. Home would never be the same, because she wasn't coming home. Family was home. How could Hideaway be home without her loved ones there?

She turned and scanned the crowd for Red's brick-colored hair and broad shoulders, but instead she caught sight of someone hailing her from the parking area in front of the rail station.

Heavy arms flapped in the air as Lilly Meyer waved to her from the open window of a shiny black Chevrolet pulling into the lot.

Bertie stood on tiptoe and waved back, relief washing through her.

"You know that woman?" Edith asked.

"Red's mother." Bertie looked at the driver. He was bent over, and all Bertie could see was a head of short blond hair. Not red. She looked into the backseat of the car, but it was empty.

The enormity of her disappointment surprised her. Red hadn't come. All those letters about how he'd missed her, and yet when it came right down to the moment of truth, he didn't show up to meet her.

Why not?

She picked up her suitcase and carried it toward the car. "Looks like Red decided he didn't have time to meet us." The bitterness in her voice surprised her. What an ugly trait in a lady. But what an ugly act for a man not to appear when the woman he'd sworn to be missing all these years was finally arriving.

He'd had the chance to see her get off the train, to greet her and let her know how glad he was to be with her again, to hold her in his arms. But he hadn't found the time for that.

"Don't you let a man get you down," Edith said. "You've got more important things to…" her voice trailed away and her steps slowed.

Bertie looked up to see what had distracted her friend's attention, and saw her staring at the car's driver, who was rushing around the front toward the passenger door to help Lilly out. Lilly, however, was already making her own way out.

"If that isn't Red, who is it?" Edith asked.

"Lilly's obviously gotten someone else to drive her." As they drew closer, Bertie recognized that muscular frame and that characteristic grin, and felt another rush of relief. Ivan Potts was home from the war. When had he arrived?

"How long ago did you say Red's father died?" Edith asked.

"Twelve years."

"And his mother still doesn't know how to drive?"

Bertie shook her head. "She always said that if she

needed to get anywhere farther than her horse could take her, she'd better get her head examined."

Edith chuckled. "Sounds like quite a homebody."

"She is," Bertie said, admiring the car. So Gerald and Arielle Potts had followed through with their promise to buy Ivan a new car when he arrived home from the war. From the looks of it, they'd gone all out. Of course, that couldn't be a brand new car, since no new cars had been manufactured since 1942. Still, a three-year-old Chevrolet was the newest thing out there.

Nothing had ever been too good for Ivan, according to his parents.

"Remember I've told you that we folks in Hideaway live at a little slower pace than you've been used to in California," Bertie said.

"Sounds good to me." Edith's gaze remained on Ivan as they approached the car. "That's a friend of yours?"

In spite of all, Bertie felt a grin spread across her face. How good it was to see Ivan again! Her old friend seemed to have matured. With his broad shoulders, short, golden hair and dark brown eyes, he could pass for a star of cinema.

"You've already been introduced, silly," she told Edith. "You've even written to him a few times. I've known Ivan Potts since first grade. His father, Gerald, is the mayor of Hideaway."

"So that's the eloquent Marine with the neat handwriting and the heart of a poet."

Bertie grinned. "I'd've never thought that about Ivan. I'm surprised he didn't tell me he was coming home." She glanced at Edith. "In fact, I'm surprised he didn't tell you, if he's writing you poetry. Come and let me introduce you to Ivan and Lilly."

Edith linked her arm through Bertie's once more. "That's my girl. Now you're talking."

Chapter Thirteen

The ripe odor of the Moennig's barnyard filtered around Red in the warm sun as he knelt beside the closed gate. Curious cows and calves snuffled at his head. He paid them no mind. He'd found what he was after—footprints that matched those in the backyard at home. Leastways, he was pretty sure of it.

He'd discovered quickly that he'd get no help from the sheriff on Joseph's case. There was no case, according to Butch Coggins. As it had turned out, the hole in the side of Joseph's head wasn't made by a bullet, but a nail in a piece of wood. Butch decided Joseph had simply had an unfortunate accident and fallen on it.

Red knew Joseph would never have kept anything like that in the cattle lot, because it could have injured one of the animals. No farmer in his right mind would be so careless, and certainly not Joseph. Cattle were a precious stock, always had been, but especially now, when most of the beef was being sent to the armed forces to help keep their fighting men well fed.

The lot itself, where Joseph had fallen, was useless to

show tracks. The animals had destroyed anything Red might've found there. But he did pick up on some dried mud on the wooden gate, where someone had climbed over. From there he had followed tracks through the grass and into the woods south of the house. They led him downhill to the James River and then disappeared.

Had whoever it was left by boat or swum across?

Red knelt again in the mud at the edge of the woods, and reached for a layer of bark he'd peeled from a tree. With another piece of thin bark, he gently dug and lifted the dried mud around the shoe impression, until he placed the whole, unbroken print into the makeshift holder.

Back at home, he could make a plaster impression of the print, trace it on paper, and quietly make some comparisons.

He didn't doubt someone in this town was up to no good. He'd find out who the dirty rascal was before anybody else was hurt, or his name wasn't Charles Frederick Meyer.

He might not be able to return to the war, but he could still fight in his own special way. The war had come to his home turf. He'd have to turn it away as best he could.

Bertie sat in the backseat of the car behind Lilly Meyer on the drive back to Hideaway. The backseat wasn't as comfortable as the front seat, and though Lilly had tried to convince Bertie to take the front, Bertie wouldn't hear of it.

"I've been reading about how busy you girls have been out in California," Lilly said. "Makes me almost wish I was the kind of gal to go out there, myself, helping with the blood drive, working on the very airplanes that might win us a war. I'm so proud of what you've done."

"You're doing plenty," Bertie said. "You've kept up the business with everyone gone. And a son in the Army."

"Yes, but you know how backward we are out here in our own corner of the world. Never catching up with the news of the war until a day or so after the rest of the country already knows about it."

Lilly seemed to have put on some weight since Bertie left for California, but she was as kind as ever, and as pretty. Her red hair was more golden than her youngest son's, and her clear blue eyes often shone with the same good humor that characterized Red. Lilly's eyes also frequently glinted with her own special brand of wise observation, which she seldom kept to herself. But there wasn't much evidence of brightness in her expression now. Her sorrow about Joseph and her tender compassion for Bertie shadowed her face.

Lilly Meyer was a strong woman who Bertie had always admired. After her husband's death, in the middle of the Great Depression, she'd refused to ask for help. Though neighbors had tried to do as much as they could, Lilly stood firm in her self-sufficiency.

She cared for her children the best way she knew how, with her garden and guesthouse, her innate business savvy and other talents.

Lilly could cook like a dream, and she kept her house spotless. Her guests ate like kings and queens, and the many entertaining activities she offered in her establishment brought the same folks back year after year from all over the country. That was how she'd supported her kids.

Though Red had seemed content to remain at home and help Lilly after his brother and sister flew the coop, Bertie guessed he simply could not bring himself to leave his mother without good help at the house.

"I've got a room ready for you at my place," Lilly said. "Had a traveling couple move on this morning, and—"

"That's very kind of you," Bertie said, "but I need to get home and settle in. I'm sure there's work that needs doin' around the place, what with—" To her embarrassment, her voice cracked.

"No problem there," Lilly said, gesturing toward Ivan, whom Bertie had caught watching Edith in his rearview mirror. "Ivan and Red plan to do those chores themselves. They're no strangers to hard work, and after what they've been through in the war, a little farming won't tire them out."

"But I know how to farm," Bertie said. "I've not forgotten how to work."

Ivan and Lilly exchanged a glance in the front seat. Bertie narrowed her eyes.

"Bertie, I sure could use your help at the guesthouse for a few days," Lilly said. "The men know all about farm chores, but they don't know how to bake. That's what I need help with right now."

Bertie gave her a suspicious glance.

"Those black walnut cakes of yours've won plenty of blue ribbons at the fair," Lilly said. "And we have guests right now who are a might too demanding for me." She slung her heavy arm over the seat and turned to pin Bertie with a long look. "Think you could do that for me, just this once?"

Bertie knew she was being had, but she couldn't argue with Lilly. She didn't have the strength. "Not sure what I could bake that you couldn't do better."

"I've got me some black walnuts I held over from last year. We've got honey and molasses aplenty, though there ain't much sugar. Don't guess you'd have much trouble baking without sugar, knowing what a good cook your mother was."

"I have a recipe for molasses oatmeal cookies with black walnuts."

Lilly nodded. "Sounds like it'll work."

"It's at the farmhouse, so I'll have to go get it."

"What say we stop in there on our way to town?" Lilly suggested. "I know you want to make sure everything's being cared for, anyway. 'Sides, Red's out there, doin' him some huntin', and we could give him a lift back to town."

Bertie stiffened. "Hunting?" He'd rather go hunting than greet her at the railway station? "What's in season this time of year?" Didn't he care any more than that?

She felt Edith touch her arm, and she pressed her lips together. She couldn't let on how much it hurt that Red didn't seem to want to see her.

Again, Ivan and Lilly looked at each other across the front seat—a serious look of shared understanding.

Bertie leaned forward. "Is there something going on you two oughta be telling me about?"

Ivan sighed. "Well, I guess you could say some of us are taking the law into our own hands."

"What?"

"Red's huntin' tracks," Lilly explained. "Around your farm. Just seeing what he can come up with."

"What kind of tracks?"

"Human ones, Bertie," Ivan said, giving her a troubled look over his shoulder. "He's not let up since he got home and found your father on Monday."

She sat back in her seat, lips parting. "Oh." Some of her bitter disappointment eased, to be replaced by that tightening in her stomach that she'd felt so many times in the past two days. "He still thinks somebody killed Dad."

"He's not ready to agree with the sheriff that Joseph's death was some clumsy accident," Ivan said, then nodded toward Lilly. "Neither are we."

Edith placed an arm around Bertie's shoulder, protective and comforting.

"I called the sheriff yesterday from the train station in Albuquerque," Bertie said. "He told me he didn't find any evidence that would make him think there was foul play."

"I know what Sheriff Butch Coggins said." Lilly's tone told everyone in the car what she thought of the man. "Some folks in Hidcaway have got other opinions, and I happen to be one of them."

"That's right," Ivan said, glancing over his shoulder at Bertie and winking at her. "You let us take care of things, buddy. You've gone through enough for a while. You've got friends here who are going to help you."

Bertie bit her tongue, touched, but at the same time frustrated by Ivan's attitude. Did he think she was so delicate she couldn't take the truth? Why couldn't they tell her plainly what they'd found?

But she let it go. There'd be time to get to the bottom of things after she got settled in. And she had to admit that she didn't feel quite up to facing much more today, though she wouldn't let on about that to anyone, not even Edith.

She would corner Red soon enough, and he would tell her what she needed to know, or she'd know the reason why.

Chapter Fourteen

Red frowned at a small mess of limbs scattered at the edge of the Moennig's wooden front porch. Joseph never placed his firewood next to any buildings, and he especially would not allow a stack beside his home. He'd taught Red that termites got into houses that way.

Besides, when Joseph stacked wood, whether it be kindling or chopped logs, he did it with the kind of precision Red had only ever seen before in the military. These limbs looked a mess, sticking out every which way, slender hickory switches too green to use for kindling.

He kicked one of the branches with the toe of his shoe, and then frowned. Hickory switches. Something about those little limbs…

He remembered feeling the sting of a hickory switch on his backside a few times when he was a kid. There was never any damage done, but it sure hurt.

There was something else hovering in his mind that he thought he should be gettin'. Some sign…some message…but for the life of him, he couldn't pin down what that could be.

He searched through the house for any clue about what might've happened, then walked around the yard again, in case he'd missed something.

Though Joseph Moennig took good care of his fields, his garden, his livestock, Red didn't figure Bertie's father had given up a lot of time to cultivate a green lawn—and there was not a lot of space left for a lawn after the heap of gardening Mrs. Moennig had always done. With the mature shade trees surrounding the house, the grass grew awfully sparse in some patches.

The Moennigs were practical. They'd used their cattle and mules to mow the lawn when the grass grew too tall. That made for some good fertilizer, too, and recent rains had caused what grass there was to shoot up in lush clumps.

In one patch of dirt a couple of feet from Joseph's bedroom window, Red discovered part of a heel print. Someone had been standing out here, watching Joseph.

If Red wasn't mistaken, the print matched one he'd found at the edge of the barnyard and in the backyard at home.

He didn't bother to collect this one. He had enough to convince himself that Joseph's death was not an accident.

Red stepped around the rear north corner of the house and stopped. Something pop-pop-popped through the trees, softly at first, like the wings of a moth flitting against the window on a summer night. Then it grew louder, more insistent.

Red's breath caught. He froze, clutched by fear as

surely as a rat in a trap. He knew that sound. It was familiar, close and threatening. Snap-pop, snap-pop…the sound of distant artillery fire… It was drawing closer….

His hand lost its grip on the cane. He hit the ground quick as a burned cat, and tasted the grit of dust between his teeth, felt the pain in his leg as he rammed it into the ground, preparing to fight, even though he had no weapon.

The Germans couldn't have found him here, not in the middle of America. They'd surrendered. This didn't make sense.

He closed his eyes, waiting for the thud-crack of incoming enemy fire, waiting for the agony of metal slicing through him.

But as he lay paralyzed, his mind swarming over all sorts of things a soldier should do at a time like this, the sound began to change. Now it wasn't quite right.

He lay with his cheek pressed against the earth, unable to stop shaking, as he listened to that sound, which grew stranger as it grew louder.

It was still familiar, but not artillery fire at all. No, not at all.

It was the sound of rubber tires rolling slowly along the rocky road, a sound as recognizable to him from the war as it was here at home. The roads in Italy were dirt and rock—barely roads at all until they'd been worn down by the hundreds of tires of advancing troops.

He looked up and saw the black hood of Ivan Potts' Chevrolet skimming above the hedge of sumac growing along the roadside.

Before the car could reach the clearing and all the passengers could see him lying in the dirt like a whimpering cur, he scrambled to his feet. Shaken by his reaction, he brushed as much of the dust as he could from his clothes, then limped quickly toward the front porch.

How could he have lost his senses so totally? He'd heard stories of shell-shocked men coming home from the war, but he'd never realized how completely convinced he could be that he was back in Italy, like that bad nightmare coming back to tap him on the shoulder in spite of the sunlight streaming from the sky.

He was standing on the steps, watching the road, when the car came into view. His gaze shot to the shining blond hair of the woman in the backseat.

Bertie. His beautiful Bertie. He couldn't look away.

Even when she stepped out of the car, he couldn't do anything but stand there staring. She wasn't a figment of his imagination this time—not wishful thinking. Bertie was here. He'd thought about this moment, longed for it, ever since he'd seen her last, crying at the train station.

He wanted to run to her and touch her face, catch her in a hug, tell her she was even more beautiful than he'd told the guys. He wanted to tell her that she'd saved his life. She was the reason he'd fought so hard to stay alive. She was what kept him going. Her faithfulness. Her sweet letters. Just knowin' she was there…he wanted to tell her all that, but he just kept staring.

She looked up at him, her face filled with all the spirit she'd written into her letters to him, and her hand raised in a wave. She took a couple of quick steps to circle the car, her eyes filled with sudden, wild joy.

Then her gaze dropped to the cane in his left hand. She gasped, and looked back up into his eyes, her own eyes widening. The joy vanished, and the expression that replaced it stabbed at him. The disappointment was obvious. The hurt. Her lips parted, and he heard a soft cry.

Bertie grabbed the car fender and held on to keep herself from falling over. That cane! Red wasn't just holding it, he was leaning on it. Heavily.

Dozens of thoughts leapt through her mind, and to her shame, some of them were not sympathetic. She realized those thoughts were plain on her face, because she saw Red wince.

Fancy that. A man who had experienced the horrors of war for three years made anxious by one small woman with hurt and anger in her eyes.

This was why he hadn't written? Would he have ever contacted her again if not for her father's death? No one had even told her he was coming home.

Was she nothing more than a goodtime girl to him? The fears she had confessed to Dr. Cox, had they come true? Maybe Red didn't want her hanging around now that things had gotten tough. Maybe he didn't think she was woman enough to handle it.

All this time, she'd thought she meant more to him than that.

Stop it, Roberta Moennig. He's been wounded. Think about someone besides yourself.

And yet…when had he been wounded? Why had no one told her about it?

She shot a look over her shoulder at Lilly and Ivan through the windshield of the car. Neither could hold her gaze. She looked at Edith, and found strength in her calm dark eyes, encouragement in her gentle nod.

Bertie nodded back at her friend, who was silently communicating with her eyes: *You can do this. This is why I came with you.*

Bertie had never known a dearer, more stalwart friend than Edith Frost. As the world seemed to shift and crash, Edith understood because her own world had crashed three and a half years ago.

Odd how those folks Bertie had known and trusted the longest had let her down, while someone she'd known for only eight months could be so solid for her now.

But that wasn't the whole story. It couldn't be. Bertie knew she was overreacting.

Just yesterday, as they sat watching the countryside go past them on the train, Edith had said, "Grief's a strange beast, Bertie. Sometimes you'll think you're through with it, that all is well and you've dealt with your loss sufficiently, and then it will come back, stronger than ever."

"Well, we won't have to worry about that yet," Bertie'd said. "I don't feel recovered in the least. Fact is, I feel smothered with sorrow, wonderin' if it'll ever end."

Problem now was that the sorrow just seemed to expand to include everyone in her life.

Gripping his cane, Red stepped down from the porch and came toward her, limping, leaning hard on that metal support. She could see the pain in his expression, but she didn't know if it was physical, or emotional, because he felt exposed, walking in front of her like this—she, from whom he'd tried so hard to keep this secret. But why?

Except for the cane, he almost looked like the old Red, in his worn blue-denim overalls and red-and-gray plaid shirt. Work clothes, covered in dust. No sign of the Army uniform.

She ached to run to him, to put her arms around him, to ask what had happened—but since he hadn't told her about it, he obviously didn't want to talk to her about it.

Even after all their years of friendship, she wasn't an important enough part of his life to be told about an injury. He could tell her how much he missed her, and talk about home all the time, but he couldn't share this.

He drew closer, his steps awkward. The lines of fatigue in his face, the circles under his eyes, became more evident.

She swallowed hard when he reached her. She hadn't seen him in a year, and even at that time they'd had only short stolen moments together each evening, busy as he'd been helping his mother around the guesthouse, busy as Bertie'd been helping her dad with haying and tending the cattle, garden and house after her regular job at the Farmer's Exchange.

As she studied Red closer, he seemed…hardened somehow, his physique more corded with tight muscles. There was a new darkness in those blue eyes she'd caught only glimpses of last year. Here was no farm boy. There was no boyishness left in this man.

She searched his eyes for the twinkle she'd always known. It was gone, as if it had never been.

"Hi, Bert," he said.

She swallowed again, nodded, suddenly unable to find any words, unwilling to look at the cane.

"Hi, Red." Her voice betrayed her, quivery and hoarse. She knew anything she said would make it sound as if she pitied him. He'd hate that.

"Done with your hunting, Charles Frederick?" Lilly called through the window, her voice a little high-pitched, revealing tension.

Bertie glanced over her shoulder at the woman, and saw the concern in her eyes. Of course, Lilly had read Bertie's reaction. Who could miss it? What must Red be thinking?

But what was he thinking when he decided not to tell her? She didn't believe she'd've been more stunned if he'd backhanded her across the face.

Overreacting. I'm overreacting. This is the shock over Dad's death that's influencing my emotions. I've got to get over it.

"Got all I need for now," Red told his mother.

"Well, then, why don't you sit in the back with the ladies and ride to town with us?" Lilly said.

"Wait," Bertie said. "I have to get the recipe I promised you." She swung around Red like she was changing partners in a square dance and rushed toward the front porch.

Though she heard Red's uneven steps behind her, she didn't slow down, but barreled ahead and pushed through the front door into the living room, where her footsteps echoed through the house. Strange to be pushing through an unlocked door. Usually, she and Edith kept the doors to their apartment locked at all times. In Hideaway, though, few doors even had locks.

In the middle of the room she stopped and caught her breath, overwhelmed by the scents that sharply recalled her father's presence: his pipe tobacco, the lingering aroma of onions, potatoes and ham, which was what he cooked most often when he was by himself.

Her father should come walking into the living room from the kitchen any moment.

The room smelled dusty, too. Dad never dusted, so it would have built up for the past eight months, mingling with the smoke and ash from the woodstove.

She sniffed the scent of old wood smoke as she closed her eyes. *Oh, Dad. How could someone take you away from me like this?*

Chapter Fifteen

Red tried not to make noise as he entered the front door of the Moennig home behind Bertie. How many times had he done this over the years when he and Bertie were growing up? Of course, most times he and Ivan and John had come through the back door with Bertie, like family.

Cecil and Dixie Martin, John's brother and sister, were usually with Bertie's brother, Lloyd, and all together they formed a rowdy gang of kids who loved to play in the Moennig barn because it was bigger than the others and far enough from town so their yells and screams didn't bring out a posse of parents. The hay was always deep in the Moennig barn, perfect for kids swinging from rafter to floor on the rope that Joseph had hung for them.

Bertie's mother, Marty, always had enough cookies and candy to feed the army of youngsters who flocked to their farm.

Red closed his eyes, choking up at the memories. Sometimes this place had seemed more like home than his own, where he had to keep his things picked up and his manners polite because of the lodgers. There were times a fella just needed to be himself, without all the strangers to consider.

He glanced at Bertie, who stood in the middle of the room, her shoulders slumped—Bertie's back was usually ramrod straight. Her hands covered her face.

The front door, its wood swollen from recent rains, thumped against the frame as it attempted to close behind him. Bertie stiffened, half-turning, her face pale.

Red cleared his throat. "I shouldn't've yelled at you over the telephone."

"No, you shouldn't have." Her voice was still quivery, hoarse.

"I could've kicked myself ten ways to Christmas for doin' that," he told her.

She straightened her shoulders.

"But you shouldn't've hung up on me without giving me a chance to explain," he said.

Her lips pressed together in a firm line. She turned to face him as she caught and held his gaze, her eyes narrowing.

He stared back.

She spread her hands out to her sides. "Well?"

He blinked at her. "Well what?"

"There's still time to explain, if that's what you've a mind to do. What's going on around here? Nobody wants to tell me anything, like I'm some weak sister who doesn't have a brain in her head and will fall apart with one wrong look or word."

He sighed. "Nobody's sayin' you're weak, Bertie. You're one of the strongest people I know."

"Then treat me like it."

"But I had good reason to want you to stay away for a while." If only she knew how badly he wanted to protect her, how it tore at him to see her hurtin' like this.

"Because you didn't want me to get in your way while you were investigating *my father's* death?"

The woman sure knew how to rile him. "You think you can do it all yourself?"

"Did I say that?" Fire shot from her eyes. "Stop putting words in my mouth. I think I can help."

"The sheriff isn't even letting me help. I'm doin' this on my own. I don't even know what I'm gonna do next, much less how you can help."

Her gaze burned into his, but the annoyance gradually faded from her expression. For the first time he noticed the darkness beneath her eyes, which was more noticeable because of the paleness of her face. Sorrow replaced her irritation.

"And you might not think it's important," she said, "but I had to be here to say my final goodbye."

Red swallowed hard. Why couldn't she understand that it might not be safe for her here? "Funeral's tomorrow at noon, so you'll be able to say it then. Farm's being taken care of, and the sheriff won't be helpin' anybody investigate Joseph's death, since he don't think there was anything suspicious about it."

"I know that much." She glanced quickly at his leg, then away, as if looking at his injury was painful to her. Havin' her see it was sure painful to him. Was she seein' him as a cripple?

"Then I don't know what it is you think you can do about it," he said. "Bertie, you need to catch the train out of here as soon as you can and go on back to California. It's the best place for you right now." It was the safest place, too. For both of them.

Red could stick to his resolve more easily without her nearby, muddying up the waters, making him wish for something he shouldn't have.

She set her hands on her hips, and he could tell what she thought about his advice. "What would you say if I told you I didn't want to go back to California?"

What would he say? He wanted to tell her to stay, to never leave again. But he couldn't do that. She had too much power over him.

He scowled at her. "My mother said something to me the other day that stung, but she was right, and you could use a good dose of her wisdom."

Bertie matched his scowl with one of her own. "What did she say?"

"Something about how stubborn pride ain't a pretty sight. She oughta know, because she knows me. But it isn't any prettier on a pretty woman than it is on a stubborn, ugly ol' red-headed soldier."

She blinked at him, and her eyes suddenly glimmered with moisture. With another quick glance at his cane, she turned and walked toward the kitchen.

Red wished then that he could've kept his mouth shut.

She would not cry. She *must* not cry. She pulled the recipe drawer out and fumbled through the messy stack of handwritten notes until she found the black-walnut recipes. Several of them. If Lilly wanted black-walnut desserts, she'd get enough to feed the whole town.

While Bertie was working on the desserts, she'd copy each recipe down for Lilly so she'd have her own set.

The front door opened and closed in the other room. Red had obviously left the house. After telling her again to leave, then insulting her, he'd left the house without another word.

She shoved the drawer shut, hugging the recipes to her, staring around the large kitchen. The long oak table had seen so much laughter and happiness in the past. Bertie and Red and their friends had spent so many hours at this table, eating Mom's cookies, laughing, playing games and teasing each other.

She had thought, when they were growing up, that she'd known Red so well. How could she suddenly feel as if she didn't really know him?

All this time—three years—she'd thought she was falling in love with one of the sweetest, kindest, funniest men in the state.

She'd shared her heart with this man. She had thought she would be willing to share the whole rest of her life with him, and now it had come to this.

"Oh, Red," she whispered into the empty kitchen—to that long ago memory of his smiling face at the dinner table, "What's happened to us? Didn't we promise each other we'd never let anything break up our friendship?"

For one moment she considered stepping to the front porch and waving for Ivan to drive on to town without her. She had a perfectly good bicycle in the barn, and it would take only a few minutes to ride it to Lilly's guesthouse. It would mean she'd have her own transportation. She wouldn't be dependent on anyone.

Then she looked down at her skirt, and shook her

head. Of course, that would be unthinkable. Down deep, she knew the real reason she didn't want to ride in Ivan's car was because she would be sitting beside Red. She'd wanted so badly to throw herself into his arms and kiss him and tell him she loved him.

How far different her dreams were from reality.

She walked back through the house, her footsteps echoing on the hardwood floors, through the only home she had ever known—the home no one wanted her to return to.

By the time she reached the car with recipes in hand, Red was sitting in the middle of the backseat. She slid in beside him, noticing that his overalls and shirt had a thin layer of dust over them, as if he'd been rolling in the dirt. She wondered why.

She swallowed hard and forced her voice past the growing lump in her throat. "Been gardening?"

"Not today." His deep voice held a new quality that she'd never heard in it before. There was a sharp edge, almost of anger, or some other deep emotion.

She glanced at his shoes. "Herding cattle?"

"Nope."

She looked up into his tight face. He wouldn't meet her gaze. She studied the curve of the cane at his side, resenting his attitude.

Not everything about him had changed. He was still the same Missouri mule when he wanted to dig his heels in about something, and he obviously wanted her gone.

She could be just as stubborn.

Red sat staring straight ahead, miserable and not knowing how to fix things. Maybe he shouldn't try. She was mad at him now, and maybe she needed to stay that way. Thing was, he'd never figured on losing a friend when he decided against the romance. This wasn't what he'd had in mind.

Ordinarily, Bertie would be nagging him about getting his wound seen to by a doctor or demanding he take one of her treatments with crushed onions or tree leaves or some other such concoction that she believed would help him heal.

Not this time. She hadn't even mentioned the cane, just looked at it—and at him—with pity. So on top of her anger, there was also pity. What could be worse?

An ugly voice told him she was avoiding the obvious subject of his injury because the Red Meyer who wasn't whole and healthy wasn't the Red Meyer she wanted.

But why should that bother him, since he'd been thinking the same thing himself?

"Your mother has talked Edith and me into staying at the guesthouse a couple of days," Bertie said.

He looked at her, nodded, looked away. At least she was being sensible about that, not staying at the farm.

"I'll walk out to the farm later," she said. "After Edith and I get settled in and I change my clothes. I need to get my bicycle out of the barn so I won't have to depend on anyone else to get where I want to go."

Ivan glanced over his shoulder at her. "I'd be glad to drive you wherever you want to go."

Red scowled. Good ol' Ivan, always helpful to a lady in distress.

"Thanks," Bertie said, "but I've got two strong legs, and I need to—" Her voice broke off. As if against her will, she glanced at Red's leg, and color crept up her neck and into her face.

If it hadn't been so awkward, he'd have laughed. If it hadn't been so painful, he'd have at least smiled. He could almost see the pity forming in her eyes.

"I'll be fine," she said quietly. She looked so sad all of a sudden. She leaned forward and touched Lilly's shoulder in the front seat. "So, Lilly, you said you wanted to do some baking. Would this afternoon be good for you?"

His mother paused. "There'll probably be a lot of visitors over to see you soon as they find out you're home. I'll spread the word you're stayin' with me. With that much company, doubt you'll have time for much baking."

"I'll get to work on some cookies when I can today," Bertie said. "That way there'll be something to feed the visitors."

"Let's see how much time we have," Lilly advised.

"I'll deal with everything a whole lot better if I can keep my hands busy," Bertie said. "Farming or baking, I might as well keep on the move, so if you don't need me to help with the bakin', I'll hop on out to the farm and get to work in the garden."

"Ought to stick to baking for the time being, then," Red said, unable to keep his mouth shut about it, though he knew Bertie wouldn't like what he had to say. "Leave the farm to the men."

He wasn't surprised when Bertie's small, strong hands clenched together until her fingertips showed white around the nails. Good. The anger looked better to him right now than her pity.

"I've not been gone from the farm that long," she said. "I still know how to take care of the stock."

"Stock's not what I'm worried about—though I can't see you handling the hay fields all by yourself." He wanted to put his hand over her bunched fists, remind her that this was him she was talkin' to, not some stranger. But he didn't want to push himself on her.

"I can hire help if I need it," she said. "Lots of men coming back home to the area from the war."

He winced at her words. "What do you think *I* am—" he snapped before he could think "—a goat?"

He heard her small gasp, saw his mother's quick, warning look over her shoulder, and cringed when Ivan laughed. He'd as much as told Ma on Monday that he wouldn't be much help on a farm, though he'd discovered since then that there were lots of chores he could still do, they just took him a little longer than they used to.

He realized Bertie was still looking up at him, gaze steady, as if she was searching into his very soul to see what was really going on with him. "I'd say that was a pretty fair description right now," she said quietly.

Ivan laughed again, this time so hard he nearly ran the car off the road.

Chapter Sixteen

Bertie sat beside Red on the very short drive into town and listened to Lilly, Ivan and Edith chatter about Ivan's funny experiences in the Pacific—only the funny ones. Edith asked question after question, drawing Ivan out, complimenting him on his poetry, and wanting to know what had inspired each poem she'd read.

Bertie was glad no one talked about the bad experiences.

Was she a horrible person for wanting to avoid the depressing stories right now? These men had risked their very lives for their country. Didn't she owe them a listening ear if they felt a need to talk about the horrors they'd endured for her safety, her way of life?

Sitting so close to Red, forcing herself not to look at his leg, trying hard not to think about it, she didn't feel she'd be able to bear to hear about what he had suffered. She would want to know later. Right now, with Dad not buried yet, she couldn't face more.

Laughter once again bounced through the car. Was it as obvious to Ivan and Lilly as it was to Bertie that

Edith was keeping Ivan talking to cover the silence between Bertie and Red?

Bless Edith's kind soul.

And bless Ivan, too. He'd never liked dwelling on
depressing things. Like Red, he'd always glossed over
hardships or conflict with a distracting joke.

Bertie wanted to share in the laughter, but it caught
in her throat.

She stole a glance at Red from the corner of her eye,
and saw him staring out the windshield, his eyebrows
drawn together in a grimace. Was he as painfully aware
of her beside him as she was of him? Or was he off in
another world entirely, remembering the experiences
that had wounded him in the war?

From time to time, her insides seemed to spin like the
belt on a lathe, and she couldn't tell if it was her stomach
or her racing heart. It wasn't supposed to be like this.
She should be sitting here with Red's arm around her,
planning what kinds of treatments would best work to
heal him. She felt as muzzled as a mad dog.

Oh, the countless hours she had daydreamed as she
worked at the plant. She'd imagined her father's smiling
face when he welcomed her home, the feel of the humid
Missouri air on her skin, the smell of the wildflowers
that grew along the wooded section of the farm and the
tart taste of one of Lilly's gooseberry pies.

She'd also dreamed about the first time she and Red
would see each other again, how handsome he would
look, and how eager to catch her in his arms and promise never to leave again.

Not only hadn't he caught her in his arms, he'd

shoved her away from him, even before she'd come home.

She closed her eyes. Reality was nothing like those silly dreams. Yes, Red was alive. But this man sitting beside her wasn't the same man who'd written to her, with whom she'd grown up, and teased, and dated.

That man held gentle laughter inside that came out with the slightest encouragement. This man was prickly and bossy.

She grieved the loss just as she grieved her father's death.

From the corner of her eye, she studied Red's grim expression, the firm tilt of his jaw, and she figured he was worrying this situation as she was, like a dog gnawing on a hard bone.

"Well, here it is," Ivan said, glancing at Edith in the rearview mirror as the road curved around the side of a cliff and the sleepy village of Hideaway came into view.

The lush growth of trees, flowers and healthy victory gardens encircling each house reminded Bertie of an easier time, when she, Red, Ivan, John and John's sister, Dixie, would ride their bikes through town.

"You remember when we'd snatch flowers?" Ivan asked, looking in the rearview mirror at Bertie. "You were the worst of the bunch, Bert, making the prettiest bouquets from flowers you snitched from different gardens."

"Nobody missed 'em," she said.

"She didn't keep 'em for herself," Red protested. "She left 'em for the elderly folk to find on their front porches." He looked at her then, almost reluctantly, before quickly dropping his gaze. "Then she'd knock on the doors and ride away before she could get caught."

Bertie felt surprise, then a flush of pleasure at Red's defense of her actions.

"I heard about that," Lilly said, chuckling. "But their worst bit of troublemaking came when Bertie and Red went fishing one Friday afternoon and caught 'em a mess of fish, but did they bring that catch to me for a fish fry? Nosiree."

"I remember that," Ivan said. "I was with them. We left the fish on Mrs. Murphy's front porch, because Mrs. Murphy loved a good mess of fried striper."

Lilly clucked her tongue. "Well, when Bertie rode her bicycle past Mrs. Murphy's house on Monday, the fish were still out there, stinking to high heaven. Mrs. Murphy had been out of town with her daughter that weekend."

Edith's delighted laughter lifted Bertie's mood only slightly. "Bertie's always bragging about how pretty her town is, and I've always wanted to see it. She never told me the half of it."

Ivan drove his Chevrolet around the square, showing off their tiny town to Edith. Bertie suspected he also wanted to show off the car his parents had given to him as a reward for returning home in one piece.

Gerald and Arielle Potts would do about anything for their only child. If there'd been a new car manufactured this year, they would have bought it for him.

Everyone had known for many years that Arielle's plans for her son included an internship in Baltimore, Maryland, at her brother's bank. What most folks didn't know—what only a few of Ivan's closest friends had known for years—was that he had no intention of going to Maryland.

He had worried about the problem since high school, but he had been granted a reprieve by earning a scholarship to the state university in Columbia, Missouri. The war had claimed him immediately after college graduation, but Bertie knew he would soon be expected to take that long-awaited journey to Maryland. If he didn't, it would break his mother's heart.

Ivan loved his mother dearly, but as he'd told Bertie once, he "was a homegrown man," with no interest in venturing into his mother's native world. He identified far more with his father, who liked a good hunting trip, loved to fish, and whose highest ambition was to be mayor of Hideaway as he earned a living with the MFA Exchange feed and farm supply store—a lucrative living by local standards, though not quite what Arielle had in mind when she'd married Gerald.

Three old friends from church waved at them from the sidewalk, and twice Ivan had to stop the car when someone gestured him over to the edge of the red-brick street.

Everyone wanted to talk to the soldiers who'd come home from the war...and everyone wanted to hug Bertie and sympathize with her about her father's death. They also wanted to meet her friend from California. Mrs. Jarvis eyed Edith with suspicion, as if she was some foreigner, but then she warmed to Edith's southern charm in no time.

As Edith explained, no one was actually a native of California. She, herself, had been born and raised in Mobile, Alabama.

The sudden homecoming crowd on the town square was startlingly different from the anonymity Bertie had experienced in California, where everyone she passed on the street was a stranger. She glanced at Edith, and smiled at her friend's expression of growing disbelief.

"You're right, Bertie," Edith said quietly, under cover of another conversation between Lilly and Mrs. Thomas, the owner of Mode O' Day ladies' wear shop. "People are wonderfully friendly here."

Bertie shrugged. "As you've pointed out to me often enough, when folks are isolated from the rest of the world by a long drive and hard times, they learn to depend on one another. They have to socialize."

Bertie risked a look at Red, and for once, he returned that look. Still no twinkle, no light of welcome in those blue eyes, only a brooding watchfulness that tore at her. But there was something else…some barely detectable look of…what? Tenderness?

Her imagination was running rampant.

She wanted to tell Edith that sometimes, no matter how well you knew someone, there was still a stranger inside. No one was ever completely knowable.

They drove past the Methodist church, and Lilly turned to look over her shoulder at Bertie. "We'll have the funeral at noon tomorrow." She pointed toward the cemetery, where the grave had already been dug.

"The Methodist church?" Edith asked, leaning forward to glance at Bertie. "But you attend the Lutheran church in California. I thought you were Lutheran."

"Dad was Lutheran when he came to this country with his family as a teenager," Bertie said. "But there was no Lutheran place of worship in Hideaway when they got here. Dad's parents would never adapt, but my parents started attending the Methodist church after they were married."

"How did that go over?" Edith asked.

"There was a culture clash," Bertie said. "The Germans liked to drink their beer at town gatherings, so there were a lot of eyebrows raised at my parents. But my parents never got used to women not properly covering their arms and legs, even at church."

Bertie remembered some of those conflicts from her childhood. People laughed about it years later, of course, but at the time those differences in customs and attitudes had fueled the German Americans' sense of exclusion in their new country.

At the Meyer Guesthouse, neighbors and friends started bringing food and lingering to talk, reminiscing about old times with Dad. The house gradually filled, and Bertie realized there would be little time to bake anything this afternoon.

That was okay. She had other things she wanted to do, as soon as she could slip out of the house.

Chapter Seventeen

Red wasn't surprised that the first visitors through the front door were Gerald and Arielle Potts, followed by Ivan, who carried a large covered plate. Red knew that the plate would be filled with tiny sandwiches and quiches, bite-sized cakes and meringues, Arielle Potts's specialties.

Red always wondered how the Potts men could be so hale and hearty. Those dainties Arielle made usually wore off in about an hour, and a fella was starving again.

Gerald had met Arielle at college in Baltimore, where she had been born and raised. Both had been smitten at once, and they married as soon as they both graduated. According to Ivan, it'd been quite a shock for his mother when Gerald brought her back to his hometown of Hideaway to settle and have a family.

It had been an even deeper shock, and a huge disappointment to her, when she'd been able to produce only one child.

In spite of these initial disappointments, however,

Arielle Potts had been quick to set about maintaining her pride of heritage, and even in Hideaway, she'd tried to instill a sense of community spirit for the past. She'd attempted to convince Ivan to attend the same college in Baltimore she and Gerald had attended, but she'd been thwarted and disappointed when Ivan didn't abide by her wishes.

Her next great plan for her son was to see him taken under the wing of her brother, a banker, as soon as this war was over, to be established in business.

Ivan was smart, he'd done well in school, in spite of a bit of rebelliousness, and she wanted to see him in politics, maybe even the governorship someday.

She'd always encouraged the friendship between Ivan and Red—she was partial to Red, which baffled him, being a homegrown boy in every way. But Red knew that even after all these years of being a citizen of Hideaway, the wife of the mayor, and running the library, Arielle Potts still didn't have any really close friends. Leastways, not according to Ivan. For the most part, the townsfolk still treated her like an outsider.

Once, when she didn't realize Red and Ivan had come into the house after school, they had overheard her complaining to her husband about the town's "hillbilly mentality." That had been after Gerald had run for mayor and was being criticized for some of his new policies.

Red felt a little sorry for Ivan's mother. She was like a princess who had come to a town of commoners and could never become one of them, hard as she tried. Red suspected a bit of jealousy might be part of the reason she wasn't fully accepted—because of her looks. Arielle Potts was a pretty woman, still slender, with blond hair and dark brown eyes.

Some folks said Gerald had been elected mayor in spite of his uppity wife. Some folks were plain ornery and envious.

"Arielle!" Bertie called to Mrs. Potts, stepping from the kitchen with a platter of corn muffins to set on the table.

The two women hugged each other, and Red thought he saw tears in Arielle's eyes. She murmured something into Bertie's ear.

It seemed, ever since Bertie's mother died in '42, that both Red's and Ivan's mothers competed over who would take Marty Moennig's place in Bertie's affections.

"So," came Ivan's voice from behind Red at the fireplace, "first of all, are you going to tell me why you're covered in dirt? Second, when are you going to change clothes? And third, when are you going to start showing Bertie how much you missed her?"

With a grimace, Red looked down at his dirty old clothes. "Guess I oughta get out of these things."

Ivan put a hand on his arm. "Not until you answer my questions. What are you up to, Charles Frederick?"

Red scowled over his shoulder at his fair-haired friend. "Still checking things out."

"Did you fall out there at the house?"

"Not exactly."

"So what happened? Don't tell me somebody jumped you."

Red gave a long-suffering sigh. "If you must know,

Mr. Noseypants, I thought I heard artillery fire, and I did what any good soldier would've done."

"Hit the ground." Ivan's puzzlement turned to obvious concern. "Somebody shot at you?"

"Nope." Red felt a flush creep up his neck. "Let it drop, okay?"

Ivan seemed about to press.

"And I'll deal with Bertie my own way, if you don't mind." Red crossed the room to Ivan's mother. "Mrs. Potts," he said softly in her ear, "mind if I ask you a couple of questions?"

She smiled up at him. "You're calling me *Mrs. Potts* now? This sounds serious." She gestured toward the sofa in the parlor where Red had sat plotting an investigation with Ivan and John on Monday. "We can close the French doors and talk about anything you like," she said. "Will a little privacy meet your requirements?"

He nodded and led her there, gesturing for her to be seated, then closed the French doors and sat across from her on a straight-backed chair. "I was wondering, since you know so much about history, if you could tell me anything about the Bald Knobbers."

Her perfectly arched eyebrows raised a fraction of an inch. "You want to talk about local history at a time like this?" She turned and peered through the windows into the other room, where Bertie seemed to be in deep conversation with Mr. Potts near the fireplace. "And here I thought you were coming to me for a little advice about romance."

Red said nothing, but glancing toward Bertie, he felt a tug of frustration. "I think the most important part of romance is keeping that loved one safe."

Arielle returned her attention to him. "Well, of course, but safe from what, Red? Do you perceive Bertie to be in some kind of danger?"

"Haven't decided yet, but I aim to do my best to find out." He forced himself to stop casting quick glances toward Bertie like a love-struck schoolboy and focused on Arielle. "I know the Bald Knobbers hung out around Hideaway sometimes. I thought, you knowing so much about local history and such, you'd have a little information about them."

She nodded at Red, her eyes bright with curiosity and concern. "Don't tell me you're thinking of resurrecting that vile group of fiends."

"No, but maybe somebody already did."

She leaned forward and placed a hand on Red's arm. "I remember how much you and Ivan and your friends loved to play Bald Knobbers down in the caves below the Moennig farm. You children found trouble more times than I care to remember for playing where it wasn't safe."

He knew what she was talking about. Those caves had been flooded half the time, and Cecil Martin had almost drowned there ten years ago.

"It was always John Martin's idea to play there," Red said. "He was always hung up on the Bald Knobbers for some reason."

"He might not have been so eager to idolize that gang if he'd known how roughly *they* played."

"Maybe not, but his grandpa told us the caves were an outlaw hangout at one time, so we couldn't resist goin' down there. We'd heard the story about the Bald

Knobbers raiding the place sometime back in the early nineteen hundreds."

"Those wouldn't have been the original Bald Knobbers," Mrs. Potts said.

"Tell me what you know about them."

"The stories are quite embellished, and I think they might be much more legend and myth than fact now."

"So you're saying you think the tall tales about those vigilantes is a load of hooey?"

An affectionate smile lit her face. "Trust you to put it that way, Red Meyer. What kinds of things do you wish to know?"

He shrugged. "Mr. Cooper told me the Bald Knobbers was the meanest, cruelest bunch of men in Taney County."

Mrs. Potts leaned back, resting her elbow on the armrest while managing to keep her posture straight. "Actually," she said, her voice taking on a lecturing tone, as it often did with him, "the Bald Knobbers were a bit of a mixed baggage, or at least the original ones were."

"They sure made a name for themselves," Red said. "Folks still talk about them in these parts, even this far from their hangouts around Forsyth."

She nodded. "They made a lot of people anxious."

"I think I learned in school that one of their methods of warning a victim that they were out to get him was to place a bundle of hickory switches at their door."

She nodded. "If that didn't straighten the poor victim out, then they'd sometimes use those switches on him." She stopped and cleared her throat, obviously uncomfortable with the subject. "These weren't gentle little taps, either. They drew blood. They intended to injure with those switches."

"What would you say if I told you I saw those very same kinds of switches on Joseph's front porch?"

This definitely caught her attention. She leaned forward. "Red, are you certain? Couldn't you have just seen some branches the wind whipped up? Because I have to admit this theory about a resurrection of the Bald Knobbers seems a stretch for me."

"I know, but just listen," Red said. "I heard that sometimes the farmers would have their livestock run off their land when the Bald Knobbers wanted them to leave their property. Joseph was missing livestock, and someone even let Ma's horse out of the stable the day I arrived. There have been several incidents like that, which is why I keep wondering if someone's trying to hide behind a Bald Knobber hood. They was thieves."

"They *were* thieves."

"That's right. And murderers. Masquerading as men providing justice, when they really hurt a lot of innocent people."

She nodded, her dark eyes narrowing at him. "Red, are you trying to compare Joseph Moennig with Bald Knobber victims sixty years ago?"

"I think I remember hearing about copycat groups that sprung up after the first one was disbanded. These folks was more vicious than the originals."

"Were, Red. They *were* more vicious."

"Yup."

She looked pained for a moment, then shook her head. "What we're thinking here is pure conjecture, unsubstantiated by dependable sources."

"I know, but there's still enough old folks around these parts who remember what went on back then."

"Memories can become faulty with the passage of time," she warned him.

"Did you hear about that brick someone put through Ma's window last week? And Earl and Elizabeth Krueger and their five kids seem to have took off. I just heard today that nobody's seen aught of them since. They disappeared in the middle of the night, the same day Joseph died."

She looked down for a moment, then slowly shook her head. "That still doesn't convince me that there has been a revival of the Bald Knobbers. Have you spoken with the sheriff about any of this?"

"The sheriff don't seem interested in my ideas, or anybody else's. So Ivan, John and I plan to check it out for ourselves."

"Well," she said, leaning forward, the affectionate smile back in place, "you're always welcome to visit me at the library. We have some books there you're welcome to check out. I plan to go straight there as soon as we leave here."

He nodded. "I just might do that."

Her expression betrayed her doubt. Red had never stepped foot inside the library except when he helped Ivan and Gerald build the shelves for her.

"I need to change clothes and get a haircut first, then I might check that out." He stood up. "Thanks for answering my questions."

She offered him her hand, and when he took it, she let him help her up. She was always doing little things like that, teaching him how to behave like a gentleman without making a big deal out of it. She'd been the one he'd gone to for advice before his first date.

As if reading his mind, she asked, "I suppose you're thrilled to see Bertie again. It must have been lonely without her." There was no missing the friendly curiosity in her eyes.

He glanced into the living room, where Bertie sat on the sofa, talking to Gerald, who sat across from her in an overstuffed chair. "It was more than lonely."

Arielle patted his arm. "Don't expect to pick up where you left off the day you went away. Bertie's as true as the flow of the James River, but give her time to adjust."

She didn't look at his leg, but he knew what she meant. He decided not to tell Arielle, yet, that he wasn't going to even try to pick up the romance where it had left off. Bertie loved somebody who didn't exist anymore.

Arielle gave his hand a final pat, then stepped out to speak to some neighbors who had just arrived with more food. To avoid the growing crowd, Red slipped out to the back hallway. He would change his clothes so nobody else would ask him if he'd been rolling in the dirt, then he'd hightail it to the barbershop, before surprising Arielle by actually stopping in at the library for those books. He nearly smiled when he imagined her reaction.

Chapter Eighteen

Bertie's arms became tired after hugging so many folks who'd decided to "just drop by" to say hello, welcome her home and offer condolences on her loss. She was grateful for Lilly's warm hospitality, and for Gerald Potts, who stayed nearby, such a comforting presence, strong and supportive as the crowd grew.

"Lilly told me you and your friend are staying here instead of at the farm," Gerald said.

"I don't think the choice was ours. Lilly pretty much insisted."

"Good," he said. "I don't feel comfortable about this whole situation yet."

"You, too?" She sat down on the sofa, and Gerald sat beside her. "Are you saying you don't think Dad's death was an accident?" she asked softly.

He glanced around the room. "I'm not convinced about anything yet."

"Then, as mayor of the town, can't you ask Sheriff Coggins to check further into the case?"

He grimaced and reached down to pat her hand. "Let

me tell you a little about being mayor of Hideaway. If you ever tried to herd a flock of chickens, then you know it can't be done. The position of mayor in our town doesn't pay, and it doesn't earn a person any respect. If anything, it makes a man the object of jokes and a dartboard for any complaints."

"So the sheriff won't listen?"

"He doesn't think there's a case."

"But Red does."

Gerald nodded. "That's right."

"He doesn't even want me to go out to the farm to do the chores, but Red Meyer is discovering he doesn't get everything he wants."

"I'd be honored to take care of the animals for you, but I think Ivan and Red have already taken that task on themselves."

"I would like to go out and get my bicycle, but Red doesn't even seem to want me to do that."

"He's worried about your safety, and I don't blame him. If I'd had a pretty young lady like you waiting for me for three years, you can bet I'd do everything in my power to keep her safe."

Bertie allowed herself to smile at the compliment.

"I know you've had very little time to make plans for the future," Gerald said gently. "But if there's any way I can help, you'll let me know, won't you? After all, you were my best worker at the Exchange before you left, and there'll always be a job for you if you want it."

"Thank you, Gerald. I appreciate that."

"Have you considered further schooling?"

"I'm a certified machinist."

"I'm talking college, Bertie. You're young. You have

a whole future ahead of you, and there's plenty of equity in your farm to help you with that."

She nodded. "I'll be thinking about it in the next few days."

What she intended to do as soon as possible was collect a batch of comfrey leaves from the lower forty acres, which overlooked the James River. She just wouldn't say anything to anyone when she went. If she did, she believed she'd be hogtied and dragged back to town.

Gerald gestured toward the front porch, where Ivan and Edith were holding a lively conversation.

"My son doesn't seem to be able to drag his attention from your friend. She was all he talked about on our way here."

"You noticed that, did you?" Bertie said dryly. "She's been my roommate in California for eight months, and she insisted on coming with me when Red called with the news about Dad."

The screen door opened, and two familiar figures stepped into the entryway of the guesthouse. Bertie suppressed a scowl. Gramercy and Drusilla Short.

"Here comes trouble," Gerald muttered.

Drusilla waddled beside her husband across the living room toward Bertie. There was no smile of greeting on their faces, and no expression of grief over Bertie's loss. Dru was broad at the hips, with heavy legs, which made her waist seem smaller than it actually was. With her gray-blond hair and muddy yellow eyes, her unfortunate coloring made her look as if she was always scowling.

That wasn't the reason Bertie had never found her to be a pleasant person.

Gerald stood. "I think it's time for some crowd control," he said. Then he walked toward the Shorts and greeted them, his voice clear and firm.

From the edge of her vision, Bertie could see Red slip from the sitting room into the back hallway. Escaping the crowd, no doubt. She wondered how many times he'd been forced to explain his leg injury since he'd arrived home Monday. Hideaway folks were a curious bunch.

She figured if she listened for a few moments to any nearby conversation, she was likely to learn more about his injury than she'd heard from him.

Arielle Potts walked across the living room to join Bertie in the sitting area in front of the fireplace. She gave Bertie another warm embrace and sat down beside her on the sofa, offering no explanation about her private discussion with Red.

"Bertie, you can't know how happy I am to see you home again." Her voice, as always, was musical and throaty. She glanced around the large, crowded living room. "Lilly is a gracious hostess, and I know you'll want to be near Red, but you must remember that you'll always be welcome in our home, as well. You may want some peace and quiet after all this."

Gerald reappeared from his welcoming duty and sank down in the chair across from his wife. "That was one of the most pleasant visits I've had with the Shorts."

"Why?" Arielle asked. "Because it was so brief?"

He clucked his tongue and pointed at her. "You've

hit the nail on the head. I've been asking Bertie about her plans for the future."

"And what was her answer?" Arielle looked at Bertie.

"So far she's giving me the runaround."

"Now, Gerald," Bertie teased, "you know that isn't true. I'm not sure what I'm going to do yet."

"I think she should stay in Hideaway," Gerald said to his wife. "If she and Lloyd can sell the farm, Bertie would be able to attend college with her portion of the proceeds, and have a nice nest egg to tide her over until she decides what she wants to do with her life."

"But what if she decides she wants to keep the farm going?" Arielle asked, giving her husband an enigmatic look. "What she needs right now is time to recover."

"It never hurts to plan ahead," he said.

"Her father's funeral is tomorrow, and she shouldn't have to make any big decisions right now. She has a good head on her shoulders, and she'll know when the time is right to make any kinds of changes."

Bertie silently blessed Arielle for her support. Gerald, with his thick, broad shoulders, firm jawline and piercing blue eyes, was the kind of man who made solid, quick decisions, who got things done and did his best for the town, whether or not his efforts were appreciated. His wife provided the tender heart and wisdom, and she wasn't afraid to voice her opinions to her husband. Sometimes firmly.

They were a good balance, even if they did strike sparks off one another from time to time.

"There you are, Bertie Moennig." Louise Morrow, one of her closest—and nosiest—neighbors, rushed to the sofa with a plateful of food. She nodded to Gerald and Arielle, sat beside Bertie, giving her a one-armed hug, and then handing her the plate. "This is for you. Thought you'd be famished. Lilly mentioned you hadn't eaten yet."

Bertie accepted the plate with sincere gratitude.

"How are you holding up, honey?" Louise's graying brown hair was tied back neatly in a bun, her gray-green eyes soft and slightly out of focus—she'd always hated wearing her glasses.

"I'm fine, Louise, thank you." Bertie picked up the fork and cut into the thick slice of meatloaf. With a silent prayer of thanks, she savored the food. Fried potatoes and gravy, cornbread and green beans fresh from the garden, cooked with bacon. The neighbors had gone all out.

She ate without talking for a few minutes while Louise, Gerald and Arielle talked around her, and she caught a few snatches of conversation here and there from others in the room who had already greeted her and offered their condolences.

Bertie had lost friends and loved ones before. She had experience with grief. But missing someone she knew she would see again someday was a far cry from that cold fear that she might be saying goodbye forever. Thankfully, she knew she would see Dad again. He'd had a strong, enduring love for his Lord, as had Mom.

But even though Bertie knew they'd be together again, it wouldn't be here on earth. She already missed him with a deep sense of loss.

She picked up on the conversations around her.

"…was a good man, dependable and honest…"

"…can't understand why Butch isn't checking this out better…"

"…never seen the like…don't know what this world's coming to…"

"…best food in the four-state area!"

"…oughta try the mountain oysters…"

"…what's the filling in the fried pies? Tastes like some kind of berry…"

After only a few bites, Bertie realized her appetite wasn't as keen as she'd first thought.

Arielle gave Bertie another hug, and rose to her feet. "Everyone is going to want to talk to you now that you're home. We'll give you some time to get your bearings, but you must remember that our home is always open to you, Bertie."

Gerald held up his hand. "One more thing, Bertie. I really could use some help down at the MFA Exchange this summer. We're busier than we've ever been, and I need someone in the office with knowledge about farming."

Arielle gave her husband a look of exasperation.

Bertie hesitated. "If I decide to run the farm myself, I won't have time for any outside work, Gerald."

He grimaced. "A young woman like you shouldn't have that kind of burden." His wife tugged on his arm, and he shrugged good-naturedly at Bertie. "We'll see you tomorrow at the funeral."

As Gerald and Arielle walked into the crowd, Louise leaned close to Bertie. "I wouldn't let anybody talk me into selling yet, honey. Wait a while. Talk to your neighbors."

"Don't worry, I won't make any decisions without talking to my brother first."

"That's good. And if you do sell, be sure to come to us first. Honey, I don't know what to say about your father. I feel so awful, after talking your ear off Sunday night when your dad didn't answer your call. I should've known something was wrong, but he's always been such a strong man, so sure of himself, a body doesn't expect something to happen to him." Louise paused for a breath.

"I don't blame you, Louise," Bertie said quickly. "You and Herbert have always been good neighbors." She hesitated. Well, that wasn't exactly true. Dad and Herbert Morrow had argued often about the fence that connected their properties at the back forty.

Dad had never been one to mince words, and he'd thought Herbert was just plain lazy about upkeep. Few people, however, were as diligent about keeping their fences, barns, cattle and homes in as good a condition as Joseph Moennig.

The other farmers who lived and worked on the five-hundred acre section of land closest to Hideaway—the Jarvises, Morrows, Kruegers and Fishers—were hard workers. But they never quite matched Dad's meticulousness when it came to caring for the land. He'd always seen his work as a calling from God—the real oldest profession and the most blessed. He took that calling seriously, which was one reason Bertie had so much trouble accepting his death as a careless accident.

But it was even harder to hold any of their neighbors in suspicion. Sure there had been times in the past when her father's gung ho attitude had rubbed some folks the wrong way, but no one she knew would have resorted to attacking him.

"Louise," she said softly, "did Dad ever mention any problems he might have been having with someone? Another neighbor, maybe? Or someone from town? Have there been any newcomers in Hideaway recently besides tourists?" No one Bertie knew would have paid as much attention to the comings and goings of strangers as Louise Morrow.

Louise leaned back on the sofa, looking as if she intended to settle in for a nice, long conversation. "He hadn't said much recently. You know how he kept so busy. There wasn't always time to sit and chat, besides which, Joseph was never much of one to visit of an evening. I'd heard about the cattle that went missing from his place. He'd asked Herbert about those cows." She paused, leaned closer to Bertie, lowered her voice. "You know I don't mean any disrespect, but I had the feeling Joseph might've thought my own Herbert took the cattle, which of course is ridiculous."

"He never said anything to me about that," Bertie assured her.

"I know the Kruegers *said* they lost some cattle, as well."

Bertie frowned at her. "You didn't believe them?"

Louise spread her hands to her sides. "It isn't for me to say. Herbert went out and checked on our stock when he learned there might be cattle thieves in the area, but we didn't lose any." She leaned close again. "Herbert did tell me about something he overheard at the Exchange the other day. Somebody thought the Kruegers might've—"

She stopped suddenly, as if realizing who she was talking to. "Oh, Bertie, listen to me jabber on. You don't need to be burdened with all this, what with your father's funeral—"

"Louise, what did Herbert hear about the Kruegers?"

"Oh, you know how those men down at the Exchange like to tell their tales."

Bertie nodded, waiting.

"Well, okay, but you need to take this with a grain of salt, and it's probably not even worth that much." Louise glanced around them hesitantly, then scooted closer to Bertie. "I'm not going to mention names, mind you, but some folks have actually come right out and suggested maybe Krueger was the one who took those cattle in the first place. Half the town knew he was struggling to make his farm payments, what with all the money he had to send back home to his parents in Germany."

"What else did they say?" Bertie asked, hearing the quaver in her voice.

Louise patted Bertie's hand. "Now, honey, don't you worry yourself about such gossip. Like I said—"

"They're saying Krueger was the one who killed Dad?"

Louise blanched, eyes startled. "All guesswork. Nobody knows for sure."

"But it would be an easy conclusion to draw," Bertie said, though she couldn't bring herself to believe it. "People are probably wondering why else Krueger would take his family and disappear in the middle of the night."

Louise hesitated, then nodded.

"Can anyone remember seeing any of the Kruegers after Dad was found Monday?" Bertie asked.

"Well, you know, I thought I saw somebody out in their garden that morning, but with that eighty acres between our house and theirs, it's kind of hard to know for sure."

Bertie nodded. She would have felt badly for pressing Louise, but she had the distinct impression that Louise didn't mind at all. In fact, she seemed to want to be pressed for more details.

Bertie got up, taking her plate with her. "Thanks for telling me this, Louise. I know it's just hearsay, but at least I'll know what people might be thinking when they talk to me, and what they're saying when I'm not around."

Louise patted her arm. "You let me know if you ever need to talk about anything. You know where I am."

Bertie carried the half-empty plate into the kitchen, which was unoccupied for the moment.

Louise was a kindhearted soul, but Bertie couldn't see herself confiding in her...unless, of course, she wanted to spread news to everyone in Hideaway and half the folks in Hollister.

At one time, Arielle Potts had decided to start a Hideaway newspaper. With Gerald's help, she'd compiled six pages of up-to-date news and information, using the efforts of several high-school students. She'd used a printing company in Hollister, and had, of course, included some of her own son's poetry, which had embarrassed Ivan half to death.

Most townsfolk bought the first couple of weekly editions for the novelty of it. But it soon became apparent that they couldn't find much in the paper that they didn't already know by word-of-mouth. They did, after all, have radio now, and relatives who kept them informed with phone calls and letters.

Bertie had been sorry to see Arielle's efforts get off to a rough beginning. That paper had been skillfully edited by Arielle, herself, and every word could be trusted as truth.

On the other hand, Louise Morrow never bothered to edit the words that came out of her mouth, and she didn't always bother to check her facts with people who might actually know the truth.

Bertie placed her plate in the sink, ran some warm water and washed the dishes that had already been brought in from the other room. She had managed to speak with everyone who had come to see her. Soon, she would put on sturdier shoes and take a walk.

Chapter Nineteen

Red stepped out of the barbershop, reeking of after-shave and itching around the collar of his shirt. He'd never liked going to the barber, so he always let his hair grow a little too long before getting it cut. In the Army, that hadn't been much of a problem.

As he walked from the barbershop to the MFA Exchange for some grain for Seymour, short hairs continued to poke at his neck. Time to take a bath as soon as he got home—if he could get past all the visitors without being drawn into some conversation or other.

As usual, when he reached the MFA Exchange, he saw a handful of farmers loafing around the large dock where the farmers unloaded their excess crops and loaded up with things they didn't have. Some would've brought grain in to sell, others, like Red, were there to buy it.

The MFA Exchange, the barbershop and the diner down the street were the three favorite places for the men to catch up on local news, find out the going price for grain and let off some steam every once in a while.

A telltale haze of pipe smoke greeted Red before he caught sight of Gramercy Short sitting on a hay bale, jawing at anybody who'd listen.

Not many ever did. Gramercy's word was about as dependable as a cow pie in a hailstorm. But Red did eavesdrop on several conversations as he limped along the aisles of farm supplies, sniffing the sweet grain laced with molasses, the sun-baked hay, the smoke from various cigarettes and pipe tobacco.

"...sure keepin' to himself since he got back..."

"...thought they were sweet on each other before he left. Think they'll get married now that he's home for good?"

"...going to try to run that farm all by herself?"

"...oughtn't to be buryin' a Nazi in a Christian grave-yard..."

He stopped and looked sharply toward the sorry soul who'd made that last remark. Of course. Gramercy Short was still hunched down low on the hay bale, mut-tering to his wife, Drusilla, who stood beside him. Far be it from ol' man Short to let his wife have the only available seat.

True to form, Dru didn't seem to be listening to a word her husband said, but stood thumbing through last year's copy of the *Farmer's Almanac*.

Red's hands clenched at his sides. Gramercy Short, that old hog-nosed bully, had always been a few rows short of a plowed field. What right did he have to call anybody a Nazi? Or complain about who was buried in the church cemetery? He never went to church, or even funerals, unless the dead person was close fam-ily, and no Shorts had died around here in a coon's age.

Not that Red wanted harm to come to any of them, but they sure did cause a heap of trouble for the rest of the town with their constant bickering and their troublemaking ways. Dru was the one that had upset Ma so badly, accusing Red of being AWOL on his last leave from the war.

Red caught Gramercy's eye and held a staring contest with him until the scoundrel looked away. As he walked past the man, he checked Gramercy's shoes. Old work boots, about the right size, cracked at the edges. The shoes looked almost as old as Moses, and probably didn't give much protection to the scoundrel's feet.

Resisting the urge to ask Gramercy to pick up his foot, Red passed by him with a nod.

After buying the grain—Seymour was going to be a happy horse, because Red was the only one who knew what kind he liked—Red greeted most of the other farmers by name, and stood and jawed awhile. Homer Jarvis, another of the Moennigs' neighbors, wasn't as talkative as he used to be. Red having been gone to war for the past three years, could be he'd missed a gradual change in the man. But Jarvis had never been an overly friendly sort.

It was well-known in town that the Jarvises needed more land to grow what they needed to raise their flock of kids. Homer had approached the subject with Joseph a few times, hinting that Joseph might consider selling his land to a neighbor he could trust.

Red couldn't see anyone killing off a trusted and respected farmer for a few measly acres of farmland.

He left the way he came in.

He happened to walk past Gramercy's old Model T

Ford, parked across the street from the Exchange. No
telltale shoe prints around the driver's side, but he did
see one print near the passenger side. A large print, like
that of a work boot. There was a ridge on the dirt that
could've been made from a cracked sole, but it didn't
tell him much.

Red glanced toward the sheriff's car, parked now in
front of the barbershop, and strolled back in that direction. He studied the damp earth around the parking area
across the street from the shop. Right there in mud he
saw another footprint with that telltale crack in the heel,
like the one outside the guesthouse, and the one outside
Joseph's house. But footprints in the dirt wouldn't be
enough to convince the sheriff to open this case again.

Red would have to do more than that. But what?

He limped back to his horse, tied the feed bag on
the back of the saddle, fighting off Seymour's curious,
snuffling nose and thick, seeking lips.

Red wasn't finished yet.

Bertie wanted to check the farm for herself. Sure,
she trusted Red to go over it with a fine-tooth comb and
scare up any evidence of foul play that might be there.
But she would know if something was wrong, perhaps,
simply by walking through the house on her own, seeing if something was out of place, or if Dad might've
been worried about something he hadn't mentioned to
anyone. She'd been in too big a rush to check any of the
rooms while everyone waited for her in the car earlier.

She also wanted to check and make sure the hunting rifle was still in the place where Dad had always
kept it, or if, for some reason, he might've moved it

from the pump house and taken it into the house with him for protection.

Another thing she wanted to do was hike to the spring above the cliffs over the James River and see if the comfrey still grew there as thickly as it once did. Even if Red resisted her attempts to treat him, she wanted to be prepared.

Right now, Red was making her feel useless, treating her like a brainless little woman who didn't know how to think for herself. She didn't need rescuing. She did need to be kept in the loop about what Red might've found out about Dad's death. Was it simply a tragic accident? Or had someone actually attacked him out of vengeance, or had they made an error of some kind? Did someone really think Dad was aligned with the enemies in Germany?

Ordinarily, Louise's inquisitive nature repelled Bertie, but this time she wondered if it wouldn't be a good idea to learn a little more about the goings-on in the neighborhood recently.

But first, it was time to do some investigating for herself—if only she could manage to slip away for a little while.

The coast was clear. The kitchen was empty for the time being. Bertie had slid on her best walking shoes and come back downstairs, and had actually made it to the back of the house without being stopped by any of the guests, who continued to chat in the living room.

She had stepped out the back door and turned to pull it shut when she heard a loud male voice behind her on the porch. "There you are! Bertie Moennig, it's hard to catch you without a whole roomful of people surrounding you." It was John Martin. She recognized the deep sound of his voice before she even turned around and saw him, dark brown hair combed back and held into place with enough VO5 hairdressing to pave the road in front of this house.

"Why, John, I wondered where you'd gotten off to." She hugged him with a little more enthusiasm than she ordinarily would. "I figured you'd be working on the farm, with school being out."

She couldn't tell if his flush was from her exuberant greeting, or from a little too much sun recently.

"I've been working some extra in town when they can spare me from the farm. The school's growing with the rest of the town, and we're building some new classrooms during summer break." He raised his hands. "When I'm not kept busy picking blackberries and gooseberries for my mother."

She saw his hands were scratched, the left sleeve of his denim work shirt ripped and stained black. "Those vines can be hard on skin and clothes." He glanced down at her walking shoes. "Headed out somewhere?"

"Just needed to get some fresh air. If you're hungry, there's plenty of food inside."

He nodded. "Knew everybody'd come to see you." He hung his head. "Bertie, I sure am sorry about your dad. He was always so good to us kids. We'll all miss him."

"Thank you, John. That's a comfort to hear." She gestured toward the back door. "Why don't you go on in and get some of Lilly's German chocolate cake before it's all gone." Her own mother had made that cake for years, using black walnuts in the filling.

John grinned. "No kidding? I guess I'll have to go have a taste before Ivan eats it all. Bertie, you be careful out here." He glanced around the backyard, nodding toward the back fence. "Someone nearly brained me last week with a brick through the back window." He pointed to the largest window at the back of the house, where there was a small sitting room for those who preferred privacy from the rest of the guests.

Bertie gasped. What *else* had they all decided not to tell her about? "Did it hurt you?"

He pointed to a partially healed wound on his forehead. "Got some glass, but at least the brick missed me. We swept on that floor for what seemed like hours to get all the glass up."

"It didn't hurt anyone else?"

He shook his head. "I was up late, and everyone else was in bed. Your father came over the next morning and helped us patch up the window until Lilly could get a new pane. That came in on Wednesday."

"It looks as good as new. Did Red repair it?"

John nodded. "I helped."

Bertie nodded toward the house. "You'd better go ahead and get some of that cake. I'll talk to you a little later."

He nodded to her and walked through the kitchen door.

With relief, Bertie turned away, wondering again how many other things had happened in this town that Red and others were "protecting" her from.

The guesthouse was nearly twice the size it had been before Lilly had started taking in boarders. It had been an ongoing project for the family to build on an extra room any time they could afford the material. The sitting room at the back of the house had been Red's sister's bedroom until she went off to college.

Bertie walked over to examine the large picture window that John told her had been broken. He and Red had done a good installation job.

She walked through the garden and inspected the back fence, which was made of hog wire to keep stray dogs out of the yard. Anyone could have gotten into the backyard either through the horse stable, or by climbing the apple tree, the trunk of which was being used as a fence post.

Bertie had climbed this tree many a time. She'd also helped mend the fence when she or Red or one of their friends had come down on the wire and torn it loose from its moorings.

For old times' sake, she grabbed a low branch and swung herself up and over, then slid easily to the other side. With a quick glance toward the house, she started to turn away when a voice arrested her from inside the horse stable.

"Where are you off to, young lady?"

For an instant, Bertie froze. Then recognizing her roommate's voice, she relaxed. "Spying on me?"

Edith stepped out of the stable. She, too, had changed into her jeans. "That's what I'm here for." She turned and looked again at the building. "How I miss my own horse back in Mobile."

"I thought you grew up in the city."

"I did, but we always kept horses at a stable in the country. I dreamed of living in a place where I could get up in the morning and go for a ride before school."

She climbed over the fence and landed beside Bertie. "You haven't told me where you're going."

"For a stroll."

"Crowd getting to you?"

Bertie cast a wistful glance toward the road. "It's good to see everyone, it really is."

"But sometimes it can be too much." Edith nodded. "I know."

Bertie hesitated.

"Don't let me stop you," Edith said. "I'm well aware that you want to be alone right now, but this is as alone as you'll get today." She looped her arm around Bertie's. "Where to?"

Bertie suppressed a sigh of frustration. She knew better than to argue, because with Edith, she usually lost. "I want to go home."

Edith's arm tightened around hers, and the humor died in her eyes.

"Just for a few minutes. Please."

Edith raised an eyebrow, her eyes narrowing as she held Bertie's gaze. "We should call Red or Ivan to come with—"

"No. Not this time. I don't need either of them breathing down my neck right now. They hover too much, and I can't focus when Red's around. Besides," she said, gesturing toward the stable, "He's obviously gone somewhere on the horse."

"So it seems."

Bertie glanced toward the house again. "I want to do my own investigating, and I want to find my father's hunting rifle, and even gather some comfrey if I can find it. Red's leg obviously needs some help healing."

"Then let's get there and back before the posse can catch us," Edith said gently.

Bertie wanted to hug her. Instead, she led the way around the house to the road.

Chapter Twenty

The birds serenaded Red as he urged Seymour toward the library. Some loud whippoorwill sat in the top of a gnarled old oak tree halfway up the side of the hill Hideaway was built on, not wanting to shut up—probably the same one that had kept him awake half the night. A mourning dove joined in the song, followed by a mockingbird.

What Red wouldn't have given to hear this chorus when he was skulking through a deserted Italian town, expecting any minute to hear the whiz of bullets or feel the burn of metal in his flesh.

And when he finally did get hit, the physical pain had been nothing compared to the damage down deep inside.

The morning he was shelled, he'd closed his eyes and thought of home…of the sounds of the birds in the trees, the smell of the lilac bushes in full bloom, Bertie's smiling face. All he'd had to get him through that day, when the Germans were watching too closely for the medics to get through to him and pull him to medical care, was the bundle of Bertie's letters, which he'd carried right here in his front right pocket.

Could be she'd saved his life that day.

A small voice deep inside asked him why, now that he was out of danger and back home, he couldn't tell Bertie how much those letters had meant to him. How much *she'd* meant to him.

As he rode beneath a tunnel of trees that overhung the road—sycamores and oaks, maples and willows—dappled sun warmed his face and neck, creating gold patches of light against the gray shadows beneath the trees. He allowed Seymour his head once again. The horse knew this road as well as anyone, and Red had more important things to do than tug on the reins.

He pulled a letter from his pocket—the one letter he would never forget, and which had caused him more joy than he'd ever felt in his life. In the past weeks, it had also been the one letter that caused him the most pain.

Sunlight shot through the trees and reflected from the top page with such brightness for a moment that it nearly blinded him.

Dear Red,

I can't believe I've already been in California for over six months! Every day when I go to work, or look at a calendar, I remember how long we've been apart. I know it must seem silly to you, reading about the things that are happening in my life right now, when you're in Italy's trenches, fighting with your life for your country's safety and freedom.

He didn't know how many times he'd read this part, and it always made him feel good. She'd been thinking of him, about how much time they'd been apart. A woman as special as Bertie could've had any number of men callin' on her, but she'd waited on him.

He fingered the sheet and continued reading.

To keep hope alive, I can only think of the future, how good it'll be once we're both back home. Knowing of your sacrifice urges me to keep giving blood, even when I'm still feeling weak from the last time I gave. The hope keeps me knocking on doors, urging folks to buy war bonds. Doing without sugar and meat and nylons is such a small sacrifice, when I think about what we could be doing without...our very lives. You're a hero, Red Meyer, and I've never been prouder to be able to tell people I know you.

He looked up as Seymour reached the town square. Hideaway had a different city plan than any other town Red had ever seen. It was built with the storefronts and offices all facing outward onto a bricked street that surrounded it on all four sides. The town itself was built into the hillside, and overlooked the James River below, which wrapped itself around the hill on three sides in its lazy route to the White River.

He steered the big bay gelding to the right, then relaxed the reins again and continued reading.

He'd discovered a few months ago that Bertie was not only writing to him, but to a few of his buddies. She'd also convinced several of her girlfriends to write, as well. She was like a one-woman campaign to keep the soldiers supplied with letters from home.

At first, he'd been jealous, and had let her know about it. Then he'd been ashamed.

He especially liked the ending to this letter.

Red, you know I miss you something awful, and the months that go by make it harder and harder. Writing

*to other men fighting for our freedom makes me feel
I'm that much closer to you, but don't you worry. You
get the most letters, and you're the one I think about so
often every day. You're the one in my prayers and in
my heart. Always and forever in my heart. You hang in
there and come back home to us. The one thing I want
more than anything else in the world right now is to see
you again, healthy and whole.*

He winced at that, then refolded the pages and
slipped them back into his pocket. She always signed
her letters *Yours with love.* He knew it'd been wrong to
ask her about the other guys she was writing to, but he
couldn't help himself. He'd never been jealous before.

He reached the library and slid from Seymour's back.
Time for some more research.

"I don't know where Lilly's going to put all the food
people are bringing," Edith told Bertie as they strolled
along the deserted road toward the farm.

"Don't worry, it'll be eaten soon enough." Bertie
stepped to the edge of the road, where, if she looked
just right, she could see the curve of the river below.
"Though none of my relatives are coming in for the
funeral, we won't lack for people. They almost always
have a dinner on the church grounds."

"Good, because I'm eager to taste a botten cake."

Bertie cast her a curious glance. "I'm sure you've
had those before."

Edith looked at her blankly. "Not that I can remember. I'm hoping to taste gooseberry pie, and fried may-
apples and mountain oysters, as well—whatever those
are. I thought I'd tasted everything the world had to

offer, but the Ozarks offer foods I'd never even heard of in Hawaii or California."

Bertie grinned to herself.

"So, what is a botten cake?" Edith asked. "Mrs. Jarvis brought one. I've heard of chocolate cake, pound cake, fruit cake and wedding cake, but—"

"You're going to be disappointed." Bertie chuckled, pitying her poor, proper-English friend. "Edith, you have too much school teacher in you. Have you met Arielle Potts, Ivan's mother?"

"Not yet. I helped Lilly in the kitchen for as long as I was needed this afternoon."

Bertie chuckled. "Mrs. Jarvis simply bought her cake at the store instead of baking it at home."

Edith blinked, her dark brown eyes mirroring confusion.

"Boughten."

Edith frowned.

"Store bought."

"You realize, of course, there's no such word as boughten."

Bertie smiled. "You realize, of course, that we're hillbillies who sometimes make up our own language," she said, mimicking Edith's southern accent. "Don't worry, though, you'll still have plenty of new things to taste. I daresay you haven't had black-walnut cake."

"I've had plenty of black walnuts. I'm from Alabama, you know. Have you ever eaten boiled peanuts?"

Bertie made a face. "No, and I don't intend to. As I said, I really think you should meet Arielle Potts. She was a school teacher, she has a college education, she's the town's only librarian, and the two of you speak the same language."

"Well, by all means, I hope to meet this delightful lady. Ivan's mother, you say?"

"That's right," Bertie said. "She's quite a lady. She's also busy, and the library is one of her top priorities. You might stop by there sometime soon."

Edith nodded. "I may do that."

When they reached the farmhouse, Bertie paused for a moment inside the front gate. This had been the only home she'd ever known. Mature elm, maple, broadleaf pine and dogwood trees shaded the house, keeping it cool in the summertime. Or at least as cool as it could get in the humid Ozark climate.

Edith touched her shoulder. "Are you okay, honey?"

Bertie nodded and led the way up the porch steps, frowning at the limbs scattered along the far end, which she hadn't noticed earlier in the day. She didn't know where those had come from. She'd have to ask Red.

She opened the front door and went in, once again accosted by the poignantly familiar smells that threatened to bring tears.

Edith followed more slowly. "You people don't believe in locks, do you?"

"No reason to use them. We've never had a break-in here." Bertie stopped in the middle of the living room, frowning at the closed door in front of her.

"What's wrong?"

"That's odd. I know I left the door open between the kitchen and the living room when I left here this morning. And Red went out before I did."

"Maybe Red came back after he left the guesthouse." Edith stepped up behind her, sniffing. "Did something die in here?"

Bertie sniffed, grimacing. "That doesn't smell like

a dead animal." She pushed open the kitchen door, and the smell attacked her.

She stepped backward. "That's propane gas."

Edith caught her arm. "Must be a leak. We should get out of the house."

"No, wait." Bertie pulled away and went to the stove. She was shocked to find the burner knobs all opened to the widest setting. She turned them off and reached for the back door to air out the room.

Before she could get the door open, however, from the corner of her eye she caught sight of a thick thatch of golden fur wedged between the stove and the back wall.

"Herman!" she dropped to her knees, gagging at the stench of the gas as she reached for her father's barn cat.

"Bertie, what is it?" Edith asked. "We have to get out of—"

"Get the back door open, quickly!" Bertie lifted the cat into her arms. "He's still warm."

She felt the animal's body arch, and then sharp claws buried themselves in her arm as he yowled.

"Ouch!"

"Here, bring him out." Edith shoved the door wide and braced it as Bertie fought the suddenly struggling animal.

She couldn't hold him. When she dropped him into the grass, he scrambled away from her, footsteps as unsteady as a drunk's.

"What was he doing in there?" Edith asked.

Bertie reached for an old washtub at the corner of the house to brace the door open. "I have no idea. He sure wasn't there earlier today, and Red wouldn't've let him in."

"He also didn't open the gas valves on that stove," Edith said, "And he didn't blow out the pilot light."

Bertie turned to her friend as the implications sank in. "Someone's been here."

Eyes wide with alarm, Edith glanced around the yard, looked toward the barn, and looked back at Bertie. "And someone might still be here."

Bertie started back into the house. "We need to call for help."

"Not here." Edith grabbed her by the arm. "What if whoever did this is still in the house? Or what if the gas has spread enough to ignite? Isn't there a water heater in the house, with a pilot light?"

Bertie closed her eyes, focused on her breathing. "I can't believe this is happening."

Edith looked down at Bertie's arm, then released her. "You're bleeding."

"Cat scratched me." Bertie's heart thrummed in her chest. The cat had also ripped the dressing from her sutured finger.

"We'll get you taken care of as soon as we get back to Lilly's," Edith said. "But we need to get there as quickly as possible." She cast another glance around the yard, and then she looked at the kitchen window. Her eyes widened, and much of the natural color drained from her cheeks. "Oh, Bertie," she whispered.

Bertie looked up at the window. Scrawled in thick red lines were the words *Nazi gas chamber*.

Edith grabbed her again. "Let's go. Now! Let's get back to town!"

Chapter Twenty-One

Red opened the library door and stepped inside. The Hideaway library was little more than a large room out back of City Hall. There'd never been a library at all before Arielle married Gerald Potts and came to town.

She had a lot of pet projects—special classes on charm for the young ladies, establishing a town newspaper, hosting a weekly ladies tea, but the library seemed to be her biggest source of joy, other than her son, Ivan.

Here at the library, she prided herself in keeping a wide variety of reading material, with the latest novels and periodicals. The magazine rack was especially well stocked with news about the war, and she always had more than one copy of *Stars and Stripes*, because it was so popular.

She was carrying a stack of books in her right arm and pushing one book into place on a shelf with her left when Red walked in, and he got a lot of satisfaction from the look of surprise on her face when she saw him.

"Fooled you, didn't I?" he said.

The surprise turned to welcome as she smiled at him

and set down the books she'd been shelving. "And here I'd done all my research on the Bald Knobbers because I was sure I'd never see you in here doing it for yourself."

He hid his relief. He didn't have time to go searching through all the books for something that might not even be here. "Are there many books on the subject?"

She pointed to her desk, just inside the entrance. "A total of two. The original vigilante group of men who called themselves the Bald Knobbers formed in the mid-eighties, many years after the end of the Civil War in '65." She picked a book up from the desk and held it out to Red. "What began as a good thing, to enforce law and order, soon turned evil when men allowed their greed for land and power to control their actions. It's much the same today, of course."

Arielle Potts had been a teacher of high-school history for a brief time before Ivan was born—and before she discovered she didn't possess the brute strength it took to corral a schoolhouse full of wild "hillbilly" kids. She'd always taken an interest in history, especially in this area—probably from a need to understand why the Ozarkians were so different from Easterners.

"Just in case you didn't have time to read these books, I've written some notes for you." She opened the cover of the top book and slid out two folded sheets.

Red recognized her neat, very precise handwriting. "Thank you, Mrs. Potts. Do you think my hunch might be right?"

"About a revival of the gang?" She frowned. "There are some similarities, of course. The Bald Knobbers formed after the Civil War because so many men had been killed there weren't enough to contain law breakers. Our war with Germany recently ended, which is a similarity, but we have law and order here. Times aren't the same."

"But we don't even have a police force here in town. We have to rely on the sheriff, and if you don't mind my saying, he ain't the best."

She gave an elegant grimace. "Why don't you let me talk to Gerald about this? He would be the best person to speak with Sheriff Coggins."

"That'd be fine." Red didn't tell her he planned to keep searching for Joseph's killer, no matter what the sheriff decided to do.

Bertie and Edith reached Lilly's guesthouse, winded and perspiring, but safe.

"We can't go inside with this," Bertie said, holding up the rifle she had insisted on grabbing from the pump house.

"I can't believe I let you waste time getting that thing!" Edith said. "What would we have done if we'd been shot?"

"Well, we weren't." Bertie skirted around the outside of the fence toward the corral and stable.

"We've got to tell the police about this."

"Not yet. I've done some thinking about it, and I don't think that's a good idea right now."

"The sooner someone gets out there, the less likely it will be for the intruder to escape," Edith said.

"That intruder's long gone, Edith, you know that. It would've taken some time for the cat to be affected by the gas, and no one's stupid enough to hang around that long. Nobody knew we were going out there."

"Someone at least needs to go inside and check to make sure the whole house doesn't explode with all that gas," Edith said.

"The doors are open."

"You should at least tell Red."

"Not yet." Bertie reached the corral fence and handed Edith the rifle, then climbed into the corral. The stable was still empty, which meant Red wasn't back yet. "First of all, I don't know who's doing this, and so we really don't know who we can trust."

"You can trust Red. You know that."

"And what's he going to do? Ride out to the house just to find that no one's out there? After the funeral tomorrow, I'll tell Red all about it, but I can't risk having him hear about it, and deciding to drag me right back to the train station at Hollister."

"You don't have to let him do it."

"I don't want a big brawl the day before Dad's funeral." Bertie glanced around the stable.

"What are you looking for?" Edith asked.

"Someplace to hide this rifle."

Edith glanced toward the house. "Someone might have already seen us with it."

"I've been trying to keep it out of sight." She reached for it, and Edith handed it to her then climbed the fence after her. "Edith, I didn't want to drag you here in the first place. It's proving to be too dangerous."

"You didn't drag me, I came of my own free will, and I'm not going back without you. My main focus is my best friend, who needs me right now."

"Well, then," Bertie said, carrying the weapon into

the shadows of the stable, "your best friend wants to know if you're any good with a hunting rifle."

"I sure am."

"You are? I thought you were a city girl."

"My husband wasn't. Harper grew up in rural Alabama, and he knew how to shoot practically before he could tie his shoes. He taught me how to handle a rifle before we got married, and I was good." She frowned at Bertie, the strong lines of high cheekbones and firm jaw tense with seriousness. "Whom do you want me to shoot?"

"I told you, I don't know yet. I hope nobody, but if we have to shoot to protect ourselves, can you do it?"

"I guess we'll see, won't we?"

Arielle raised a slender finger and pointed it toward the cane Red had leaned against the table. "Now, suppose you tell me about this injury of yours. I have a cousin in Baltimore who is one of the finest surgeons in Maryland. What can we do to get you healed?"

He shook his head. "Already seen too many docs. The Army surgeon says I should be fine."

"But you obviously are not fine."

"One doc tried to tell me it was all in my head."

"Psychosomatic?"

"He didn't say I was psycho, he said I was imagining pain that wasn't there."

Her lips pressed together with disapproval. "I don't agree. I think the Army may need some new surgeons who can do their jobs correctly without blaming it on your mental acuity."

He nodded. "I appreciate that, Mrs. Potts, but I don't think there's gonna be any more healing."

"I've noticed you and Bertie seem to be avoiding each other this afternoon."

Red tried not to scowl. "Lots of folks want to see her, and I've got things to do."

Arielle shook her head at him. "Don't forget whom you're talking to, Mr. Meyer. I've known you since you were a baby, and there's something wrong. I know the war has changed you, but you haven't been yourself at all today."

"She just got here today, and we haven't seen each other in a year. Give it time."

Arielle leaned forward and rested a soft hand on Red's arm. "Young man, you've fought in the war for three years, with very little leave. If I had been separated from Gerald for three years when we were courting, no one would have been able to keep me away from him—or him from me. Don't tell me there's nothing wrong."

Red shrugged. "War changes things, Mrs. Potts."

"It certainly does. You seem to have forgotten that I prefer to be called by my first name by those whom I perceive to be my friends. Do you suddenly have a problem with that?"

"No, Arielle." How could he have forgotten her habit of opening his life up like a book, reading and discussing whatever page she chose to light on?

She smiled at him. The smile was warm and kind, and he decided he really didn't mind having this lady with a good heart turning a few pages in his life's book.

Chapter Twenty-Two

Streaks of red, blue and white lights raced across the night sky and a deafening firestorm exploded in the blackness in front of Red. He dove for cover, smelling the stink of the explosive, tasting the grit of wet earth as he landed face-first in the bottom of the foxhole. Mud filled his nose and ears, blinding and choking him.

He reached out to feel for the side of the foxhole, and he felt something else. Something soft and cold.

It was human flesh, stiff with death.

He jerked away, dashing the mud from his eyes. Another streak of light flashed past him. He looked down at the body and saw Joseph Moennig imprisoned in the thick, black mud.

Red cried out and scrambled backward, only to fall against another body. Bertie's lifeless eyes stared past him.

Screaming, Red lost his footing and fell...and kept falling.

The mud wasn't soft and deep this time, but hard, flat, painful. He opened his eyes to darkness, and he froze, his breath loud in his ears, sweat dripping down his face. He waited until the square of his bedroom window took shape in the blackness of the wall. His leg hurt, and so did his shoulder and hip where he'd hit the floor. He'd fallen out of bed.

He swallowed to keep from throwing up, and stared out the window at the fading stars in the early morning sky. Why couldn't the dream disappear, like the mist that rose from the river?

The dreams were getting worse instead of better. How much longer would they haunt him like this?

He hoped he hadn't disturbed any guests. If he kept having these nightmares, he'd end up sleeping with the horse in the stable.

In fact, that might not be such a bad idea. At least if he was watching Seymour, no one could turn the horse out of the corral again without getting caught.

Someone knocked at his door, and he groaned. He'd been heard. His mother had moved his bedroom to the first floor of the house, in spite of his protests that he and his cane would be fine upstairs. She'd insisted that she wasn't worried about him and his cane, what she was worried about had something to do with a handsome, single man sleeping too close to his future bride. Folks would talk.

Red had warned his mother time and time again not to get her hopes up about a wedding, but would she listen to him? Nope. She still treated him like he was her rambunctious little boy. Not only did he want to protect her from disappointment, but he wanted to protect himself, as well.

Everything had changed. She'd have to get that through her skull.

The knock came again, and his door handle jiggled. "Red, you okay in there?"

He squeezed his eyes shut. It wasn't Ma outside that door, it was Bertie, and though relief washed through him afresh—proof stood right outside the door that his dream was nothing more than that—he knew he had to keep his defenses up.

"I'm fine," he said. "Just a dream." One of the worst nightmares yet. He needed time to get over it. What he didn't need was Bertie asking questions he didn't know how to answer, when he wasn't thinkin' straight.

"You fall or something in that dream?"

He grunted. A fella couldn't even make a little noise without somebody running to check on him. A person would think he was a cripple or something.

He scrambled to his feet, reached for his robe, then his cane, and was halfway to the door when the handle jiggled again.

"Red?"

He couldn't tie the belt of his robe while handling the cane, so he didn't tie it. His pajamas were decent. Yanking the door open with his free hand, he braced himself for the sight of her. She held a lit candle in her right hand. She held more than that, though. She held the power to convince him to do things he knew he shouldn't.

"Woman, you're not my nurse. Do you think I'm an invalid?"

She caught her breath and took a step backward, the candle fluttering, and he felt all kinds of a heel.

She recovered quickly enough. Her eyes flashed. "Not physically," she snapped. "You might be a little soft in the *brain* sometimes. I heard a thump, and it scared me. For all I knew, somebody'd hurled another brick at the house."

Red grimaced, partly from a sudden pain in his bad leg, partly because Bertie knew about the brick. Too much stuff happening these days. If she'd stayed in California, she wouldn't have all this extra worry heaped on those shoulders.

"You shouldn't have been told about the brick," he said, hearing the instinctive gentleness in his own voice. "You've got enough on your mind. I'm okay."

"No you're not. You're hurtin', I can tell."

He looked away, suddenly thinking his breath must be rank enough to water her eyes, and then wondering where that thought came from.

Still, it was one thing to wake up in the morning with a bunch of battered soldiers who hadn't washed in maybe two months. It was another thing to face Bertie in the bare morning light before he even had a chance to brush his teeth.

He couldn't help noticing she didn't have any trouble with bad breath or an untied sash. In fact, she looked wide awake with her hair all in place, as well as he could tell in the candlelight.

"You already up for the day?" he asked.

She glanced down the hallway, toward the front window that overlooked the road, where the night still held sway, then she shook her head.

He took a step closer, and thought he saw dark circles under her eyes, the skin of her face pale—too pale.

"Mercy, girl, you look like something the cat dragged in." She needed some sleep. She looked like she hadn't had any. Was he the reason for that?

She turned her scowl back on him. This was the old Bertie. The one he'd grown up with, who could fight like a boy when she needed to, and hadn't been afraid to punch him in the jaw once when he was eight and she was six and he locked her in the outhouse at school.

"I'm going to gather some comfrey out on the farm today," she said. "I tried to do it yesterday, but... I got sidetracked."

"You went out to the farm yesterday?"

She hesitated, looking away. "Sure did."

"What for?"

"I wanted to see the house without you breathing over my shoulder and everybody waiting for me in the car."

"I thought I made it clear it wasn't safe—"

"Yes, you made that crystal clear, Red."

He blinked at the sharpness in her voice.

"What you didn't make clear was *why* you didn't think it was safe," she said. "You didn't tell me about the brick, you didn't explain what all those limbs were doing on the front porch, and you never gave me any reason for why you think Dad was killed. What else didn't you tell me?"

He couldn't hold her gaze.

"That's what I thought," she said, voice softening. "Anyway, comfrey'll be the best thing for that leg."

Something inside him relaxed, some burning pain eased that he hadn't even realized was there. She'd been thrown for a loop, seein' him like this yesterday without any warning, but now her nursing instincts were kicking in. She did still care about him.

As soon as the thought came to his mind, he dashed it away. He had no right to her healing touch. He had no rights at all.

"No need to do that," he said.

"I'll boil some of it into a tea, and the rest I'll—"

"I don't like comfrey tea." He hated the stuff. "Your mother made me drink that nasty brew when I broke my arm. I hated it then, too."

"It's not for your enjoyment," Bertie said. "It's for you to start feeling better. I'll sweeten it with honey, and then I'll make a comfrey-leaf poultice for that leg, and—"

"No, you won't." He wanted to grin, but he kept his face straight with effort. She didn't need to go gallivanting over the countryside, what with her father's funeral today. She especially didn't need to go alone.

"Sure I will," she said. "We'll see if we can't pick up where the doctors left off."

He placed a hand on her shoulder, and then realized this was the first time he'd actually touched her in a year. Her shoulder was so slight...so delicate. She didn't need to be takin' care of him, she needed takin' care of.

Now that he'd crossed that great, cold gap between them, he didn't want to let go. He wanted her so much closer.

And yet, he didn't have a right to touch her. He didn't have a right to be giving her hopes about a future together, even if she still wanted that future.

"Don't take to meddlin'," he said, releasing her reluctantly. "And you need to get some sleep." He wanted to take her in his arms and kiss her hard and long and wipe that look of hurt from her face.

He wanted so much more. He wanted things to be different, but they weren't. They were what they were.

Ma was right to move his room.

"I think Ma's gonna need help with the guests this morning," he said. "She's cooking a batch of beans for the funeral dinner, but she wants to bake some cracklin' cornbread and a heap more things. You know what our funeral dinners are usually like."

"I asked her last night if she'd need help, and she said—"

"You know Ma, never one to ask."

Bertie's eyes narrowed. "You're trying to distract me, Red Meyer." But she didn't sound angry. He could hear the slight lilt in her voice.

He suppressed another grin. "Why don't you see about helping her? We'll talk about comfrey and tea and stuff like that later, after this whole thing is over today."

She stood watching him. "You promise?"

"I said we'll talk about it."

"You will let me try to help you?"

"Now, Bertie, you know I don't make promises I might not be able to keep, and I hate comf—"

She pressed her fingers to his lips, and that soft touch sent a warning shock through him. He jerked away.

"Don't press me, woman." He couldn't believe the sharpness of his own voice, but he also couldn't believe how tempted he was, how weak he felt. "Do you know how many doctors told me my leg would be as good as new? I got my hopes up every time, and it never happened." He slapped his leg. "It's not fixed, and a few leaves and a swig or two of nasty-tasting tea won't do any more for me than the doctor's best penicillin, so don't start on me."

"Red, you've seen it work before."

"We'll talk later," he said, then closed the door and leaned hard on his cane, listening for sounds that would tell him she was leaving.

For a few seconds there was no movement, and then she walked slowly back to the staircase and up the stairs—the boards creaking with every step.

He'd have to get the floors fixed around here. Right now, though, he had other things to see about.

Soon as he could get his heartbeat back under control.

Chapter Twenty-Three

Bertie stepped silently through the bedroom she shared with Edith. She couldn't even cry, for fear of waking her friend.

How had it all come to this? Not only didn't Red want her here, he didn't want her to be close to him, to try to help him heal.

He knew she was knowledgeable about the herbs in these parts. Her mother had taught her everything she knew. But he didn't want to try. Not even for her.

She felt the sting of that through and through.

She stepped to the window overlooking the river and stared into the dim gray of the coming dawn. Time to get control of her thoughts. She was tired and over-wrought. Edith was a silent sleeper, but the bedroom had only one double bed, and each was accustomed to her own bed.

Bertie had expected to sleep heavily last night because of her sleeplessness on the train, but her mind had flown from worry to worry, and she'd tried hard not to toss and turn for fear of waking Edith, which had made her more uncomfortable.

Every time she'd begun to drift off, a new problem would occur to her—how was she going to run the farm all by herself? How could she stand on her own two feet and run anything, if she wasn't even allowed to go to the farm alone?

And how could she expect Edith to go with her? Edith didn't know how to cope with cantankerous bulls, or cows with an overly developed protective streak for their calves.

Things would look better once she'd had some rest, surely.

With a quiet sigh, Bertie realized Red was probably more right than she wanted to admit. She *wasn't* ready to make any major decisions right now. The shock of Dad's death was too fresh. She didn't want to make a move that would turn out to be the wrong one.

She leaned against the window sill and gazed into the hollow as it grew dove-gray with morning light. Red had let her know how little he wanted her in his life right now. She'd seen the irritation in his eyes when he opened his door to her, and nobody could've missed the way he'd reacted to her touch. Like she was poison.

Why had she even gone to his room? If anyone else found out, she'd be mortified. A young lady did not go to a man's bedroom. Period.

But this wasn't any man, it was Red, and she'd heard him cry out. She'd do it again in a heartbeat.

"You've been standing there half the night," came Edith's groggy voice from the bed. "Don't you think you should try to get some sleep?"

"I can't."

There was a rustle of covers as Edith pushed back the blankets and stepped into her bedroom slippers. She padded across the floor to Bertie and placed an arm across her shoulders.

"How about some nice, warm milk with honey? That works for me when I can't sleep. Of course, it takes more than milk and honey to get a woman over a man."

Bertie grimaced. "Meaning?"

"Red isn't exactly welcoming to you right now, is he?"

"He's grumpy as a bear in the springtime, if that's what you're gettin' at."

Edith squeezed Bertie's shoulders, chuckling. "When Harper and I were dating, we had an argument about college. I wanted to go, and he didn't want me to. He thought a woman's place was in the home."

Bertie rolled her eyes. "How'd you two ever end up married, then?"

"It took a while. I told him a woman's place was anywhere she wanted to be, and if he didn't like it, he'd better tell me before we got more serious, because I wasn't about to play second fiddle to anyone, much less a man who didn't value me as a human being."

"What happened?"

"We stopped dating for about six months."

Bertie caught her breath. She'd been alone for nearly three years already. If she and Red had that kind of fallin' out now, would they ever get back together again?

Of course, it couldn't get much worse than it was right now.

"Then what happened?" she asked.

"I started dating someone else," Edith said. "Don't get me wrong, I loved Harper, but I knew that if he didn't respect my wishes before we were married, he sure wouldn't respect them afterward. I knew the kind of life I wanted, and it included a college education."

Bertie leaned her head against the window sill. "I don't know if I could date someone else. Red's the only one I've thought about for three years." She hesitated. "In fact, Red's the only man I've ever wanted in my life."

Edith gave Bertie's shoulders another squeeze, then released her and stepped to the window. "Harper was the only man I ever wanted, too. I still dated other men. And I started college."

Bertie knew this. Edith had been in her third year when Harper Frost was killed. Then she'd quit. She'd never returned.

"You must really miss him still," Bertie said softly.

"I do, but I'd go through all of it again, even knowing he would be killed. What we had was worth the heartache."

Bertie looked up at her friend, whose strong-yet-beautiful features were outlined by the bare dawn light that stretched across the eastern horizon, turning the river below the house to a silver stream of mist.

Edith had dark brown hair, dark eyebrows and eyes that sometimes seemed to reflect the night sky.

That pretty face turned to Bertie. "We both have our whole lives ahead of us, Roberta Moennig. If you want to be a wife and mother, then you need to decide now that you will be the best wife and mother you can be. If you want to be a business woman, like Lilly, then you learn all about the business, and don't let anyone tell you what you can and can't do. Not even Red Meyer."

"That'll be kind of hard. What I want to do is find out what happened to my father, and Red's being awfully bossy about it right now. Thinks he's protectin' me."

"Red strikes me as the kind of man who can get the job done if anyone can, and he seems determined to take care of that job, himself. I still think we should tell him about what we found at the farm yesterday."

"I'll tell him later today. There's nothing he can do about it now, anyway."

Edith gave an impatient sigh. "I don't know why I let you talk me into this secrecy. So what else do you want in life?"

"To get Red well, back to his normal self," Bertie said, frowning down at her hands. "Not so broken. That's what'll be hard."

"But that's exactly what you need to do," Edith said. "No matter what it takes."

With a nod, Bertie turned from the window. She threw her arms around Edith and hugged her. "I don't know why God blessed me with such a good friend, but I hope this friendship lasts for a lot of years."

Edith chuckled and patted her back. "I do, too. Now, you need to get to bed for a few hours. Can't go without sleep forever."

Bertie did as she was told, snuggling beneath the covers, feeling calmer than she had in days. It would work out. God had brought her this far, and He would see her through everything.

But as she drifted off to sleep, she once again saw

those words scrawled across the kitchen window. *Nazi gas chamber.*

Who in the world would ever believe the Moennigs were Nazi sympathizers?

Chapter Twenty-Four

The Friday morning sun had barely begun to peer through the trees along the hillside above Hideaway when Red saddled Seymour and headed into the valley. He used to ride the horse bareback, but he couldn't jump nearly so high with this blasted gimp leg, and so he had to use a saddle now to get on the horse. Besides, he needed someplace to tie his cane.

Aside from the cane and the saddle, Red could close his eyes and just about feel like a man again. He could almost pretend he wasn't lame.

The fresh June morning air cooled his skin as mist drifted above the James River, swirling around the trees and hiding the water. The scent of lilacs drifted around him like the finest perfume. The sun crept higher, making a red background against the black-lace pattern of the treetops. Seymour's hoofbeats echoed against the cliffs.

If he could forget everything but this moment, he could convince himself the world was right again.

But the memory of Bertie's touch on his lips kept intruding—and the look of hurt in her eyes that came and went, as if her very heartbeat depended on him. He felt squeezed in a vise, and the nasty situation with Joseph's death turned the crank. He'd done the right thing with Bertie, and yet it had hurt her bad—the very thing he didn't want to do.

Why's it got to be so hard, God?

The prayer of complaint slipped from his mind before he could catch it. What was the use? God sure wasn't listening to him.

He let Seymour have the lead, sighed and sat back, willing the early morning beauty of his hometown—the home he'd longed to return to for so many months—to soothe the ache inside him.

Though Hideaway was a tiny town, far off the beaten path and on a gravel road except for the bricked street that surrounded the town square, it had a goodly share of visitors. The James River was great for fishing and floating, and Hideaway was built high enough above it that even the worst of flooding could never reach the town. There had been some lollapaloozas in past years.

Besides the fishing and floating, there was a lot of good huntin' in the woods around here, and Red knew the best places to find everything from coon to deer to wild turkey. He even knew where to find wild honey, and had supplied his mother with plenty of the sweet stuff over the years.

Before the war, the grocery and dry goods store had been well-stocked for such a small, out-of-the-way place, and the weather was so good the merchants catered to tourists three seasons of the year. Red knew these things well, since his livelihood for so much of his life had depended on those tourists.

He passed the Jarvis home and heard Mrs. Jarvis calling the chickens out back. Her husband, Homer, stepped out on the front stoop, letting the screen door slap shut behind him at the same time Red reached the gate.

Red gave him a polite nod. The Jarvises had never gotten on well with Dad when he was alive, but after he died they'd helped Ma out as much as they could, like the rest of the town.

"What you doin' out so early this morning, young soldier?" Homer asked, settling onto the porch steps with his spittoon can and a plug of tobacco.

Red didn't stop the horse. "Just checkin' a few things out."

"You heard any more talk about that dam the U.S. Army Corps of Engineers is planning for Branson?" Homer asked.

That made Red pull back on Seymour's reins. He stopped in the middle of the road. "I thought they scrapped that idea."

"Only 'cause of the war. Now that it's almost over, I hear they're getting interested in it again. There's talk, anyhow."

"War's not over yet."

"I said *almost*. My sister and her family live down along the White River. A dam like that upriver from them would sure change things. It'd stop all the floodin'. Can't beat that."

Seymour jerked on the reins, eager for a good morning walk. Red pulled back. "You hoping to live on a lake?" he asked Homer.

"Cain't say that I am."

"If they build that dam, the whole holler below us'll be flooded." All that hunting, and the good fishing would be wiped away. There'd be different fish altogether in a lake, with the warmer, sun heated waters.

"Don't see how you figure that." Homer ripped off a little plug of tobacco and slid it between his lip and bottom teeth. "They're damming White, not James." He'd become so good at talking with his mouth full of tobacco, he didn't even slur his words.

"James runs into White, and that dam's gonna be bigger than you and I ever dreamed," Red told him. "It'll reach this far, easy."

Homer shook his head. "You know how many miles we are from Branson?"

"Not far enough to avoid the lake," Red said. "It'll cut us off from Hollister. In fact, it'll cover the whole road. We'll have to drive twice as far to get anywhere."

"Who told you that?"

"I know how to read maps." Red shook his head. "Guess it's okay for some, but it'll sure change things for us around here."

Homer spit into his can. "I can tell Joseph's been talkin' to you. He and Earl Krueger thought the water would flood their fields."

"Joseph was right," Red said. "Can't blame a fella for wantin' to protect his livelihood."

"Well, if they was to have lakefront property, it'd probably be worth a pretty penny."

Red knew Joseph hadn't been interested in having

lakefront property. All he'd ever wanted was his farm. Red had been relieved when the plans for the dam were scrapped. He wasn't one to take to change. Seemed like the whole world had changed too much in the past few years, and he couldn't help wonderin' if it'd be destroyed completely before the war ended. Folks who hadn't been in the front lines of the war—who hadn't seen Italy or Germany or the rest of Europe—didn't know what destruction was.

He waved to Homer and nudged Seymour on, passing by the Moennig farm this time. He'd investigated all he could there. He'd stop and count the livestock on his way back home, but first he wanted to do a little more investigating. He had a hunch that kept sinkin' its teeth into him, and he couldn't shake it.

The Krueger family had lived downhill and across the road from the Moennig place. By the time Red reached their farm—a flat plot of land with good dirt for crops—the sun had begun to warm the air.

This was the farm where Earl and Elizabeth and their five kids had a victory garden so big they'd supplied enough vegetables to keep Hideaway in produce all summer long. Before the war, when the depression was weighing down the rest of the country, the Kruegers had followed Joseph Moennig's example and grown fields of tomatoes for the local canneries.

Red had heard later, though, that they'd still come close to losing their farm a time or two in the past years.

Using his cane so he wouldn't have to climb down from the horse, Red unlatched the front gate to the Krueger place and rode on into the yard. The family had apparently taken their two yappy little dogs with them. Their cattle and chickens, interesting enough, had ended up in the farms of their closest neighbors. If Red hadn't started seein' to Joseph's livestock, he had no doubt they'd've ended up with the neighbors, as well.

Finally, Red reached the porch and slid from Seymour's back. He tied the horse to the front post and limped around the side of the house. Straightaway, he saw something that stopped him.

Someone had scattered limbs at the far end of the enclosed porch. They were small, more switches than thick limbs.

He noted the color, the texture of the wood. Hickory switches. Like the ones Red had seen on the Moennig porch.

He shook his head and glanced around the yard, as if somebody might still be lingering this long after the Kruegers left.

With the aid of the growing sunlight, Red found something else he was looking for—familiar footprints, etched in the thick, congealing mud alongside the house. It had rained last night enough to moisten the earth, but not enough to erase these prints. They were probably made with the style of heavy work boots a farmer might wear, and they were like the ones he'd found in Ma's backyard, and at Joseph's house, and across the street from the barbershop.

The more he thought about it, the surer he was the crack across the left heel had come from an ax head. Someone who chopped wood might've stepped on one. That didn't tell him anything, though. Everybody in the country had an ax.

He shook his head and gazed around the place. This

made three homes of German immigrants that had been attacked in a week. Ma had suspected the Kruegers might've been threatened by someone, but Earl Krueger had always been a close-mouthed guy, a little too proud to let anyone know if he was having trouble. If he hadn't been forced to visit the neighbors asking about his lost livestock, nobody'd have known about it.

Earl and Elizabeth hadn't come to this country until a few years ago, when they could no longer ignore the Nazi threat to their peaceful little rural town in Southern Germany. They spoke with a heavy accent, but until the war began, they'd been treated with as much kindness and dignity as anyone else in town. Lots of folks had accents around these parts.

Other German families who'd recently come from the old country to America had been sent to detention camps. Could that be what had happened to the Kruegers?

But then, why wouldn't anyone know about it? Whole families didn't disappear in the middle of the night for no reason. And there were other German immigrant families in town. He'd not heard they were having any problems.

The switches bothered Red a lot.

Those nasty rascals, the Bald Knobbers used to bully men and teenaged boys into joining their vigilante gang by leaving switches on their front porches to warn them what would happen to them if they refused to join.

It was obvious why the Bald Knobbers did that. The more men who were involved in their terrorizing of the countryside, the fewer there would be to oppose them.

But how would anybody expect Joseph Moennig or

Earl Krueger to even know about something like that? Joseph might have heard about it from elderly neighbors, but Earl wouldn't have any way of knowing about it. Not unless somebody'd told him a little about this area's history.

Red walked back around the house to the front porch. Unlike Joseph's porch, this one wasn't open to the wind, but had a rock wall enclosing it from the elements. Those limbs…

As he studied them again, a shape took form that froze his blood—something he should've seen sooner. Leaning heavily on the cane, he went up the steps and walked across the porch to stand over the switches.

There were eight of them placed together. At first glance, he'd thought they were scattered haphazardly, but these were not. He had a feeling Joseph's hadn't been, either, but the wind would've had more chance to scatter them out of order.

Someone had made a rough Nazi swastika with those switches. It surprised _him_ that he hadn't recognized the shape as soon as he saw it, even though some of the limbs were askew.

The symbol that had stamped his nightmares for three years had been used in an act of terror against these German Americans. He gripped the curve of his cane in anger. He wanted to stomp these switches, to break them into tiny pieces and burn them. He raised his foot…and then he put it back down.

Never destroy evidence.

With shaking hands, he tested the front door of the house, found it unlocked, and went inside. In the kitchen, he found a couple of small, cracked saucers Mrs. Krueger had left behind, and he carried them outside.

Carefully, he scooped the familiar section of footprint into the saucer, and studied it. He figured it to be about a size ten, heavily worn on the outside, but the most helpful mark was that cut in the heel.

No telling how many men had been to the barbershop the past few days. The prints there might not tell him anything, and just because those prints were there didn't mean the man had even gone inside the shop. Red had noticed Ivan had gotten a good haircut in the past couple of days, but then so had his dad, and John Martin, and likely half the town, freshening up out of respect for the dead at the funeral today.

Even tobacco-spittin' Homer Jarvis looked as if he'd had his ears lowered recently.

The one person Red wanted to suspect, Gramercy Short, didn't even go to Bernie's barbershop. Those two'd had a falling out years ago over a fence between their properties, and Gramercy hadn't forgiven Bernie yet. His wife Dru cut his hair, and it showed. On the few times a year he got a shearing, he looked like a shaved billy goat.

Red would have to start paying more attention to shoes for the next few days. One way or another, he was going to find Joseph Moennig's killer and bring him to justice.

Chapter Twenty-Five

Bertie awakened several hours after dawn on Friday morning to the sound of a loud thump that jerked her up from her pillow. Morning sunlight streamed through both bedroom windows, the lace curtains throwing delicate shadows over the polished wooden floor.

The bedroom she shared with Edith was in the second story, front corner of the large guesthouse. It overlooked the road that skirted the front of the property at the edge of the bluff, and Bertie could see the James River from the front window.

She realized the thump had apparently been the slam of a car door. Noticing that Edith had already risen for the day—probably already working in the garden, an activity she loved—Bertie turned over and covered her ears with the pillow. Just a few more minutes of slumber…

But she still heard the footsteps of someone climbing the concrete steps to the wooden front porch below the window. It was too hot in this upstairs room to leave the windows closed at night, and so they opened both to create a cross-breeze. The James River Valley caught that breeze and seemed to direct it upward and into the open windows in the evenings.

Yesterday evening that breeze had been most welcome, because, when not entertaining company, Bertie had spent her time helping Lilly in the kitchen, sorting dried beans for overnight soaking, helping with mincemeat pies and baking black-walnut cookies. And worrying, worrying, worrying about the gas in the farmhouse and the message on the kitchen window.

But she couldn't let herself think about that right now. In a few hours would be Dad's funeral.

Dad used to love Mom's dishpan cookies, made with oatmeal, molasses, chocolate chips and black walnuts. In fact, there wasn't much Dad hadn't loved about Mom, which was why Mom had gone out of her way to please her husband. The love they'd shared had always been an inspiration to Bertie when she was growing up, and it was why she'd been so surprised to discover that other marriages weren't always as happy as Mom and Dad's.

Last night Bertie, Edith and Lilly had baked a huge batch of the dishpan cookies, and Lilly had crowed with delight when she'd taken her first bite. They'd be serving the cookies at the funeral dinner today.

Lilly had fretted about the grieving daughter being forced to cook for her own father's funeral, but Bertie had reassured her she needed the activity to keep from thinking about many things.

The spring on the screen door downstairs groaned as it opened. Someone stepped inside—a man, by the heavy sound of footsteps. A moment later, Lilly called out a welcome from the dining room, her footsteps making the floor creak downstairs.

"Help you, sir?" her generous voice boomed.

In a very short time, Bertie had gotten used to hearing every conversation that took place in the living room, as the staircase directed sound up to this bedroom like a megaphone. It was why she'd heard Red holler and fall out of bed early this morning.

She frowned again at the memory—at the rejection. It was the only thing she could call it. Why should she even bother with Red? He didn't want her. He'd made that clear enough yesterday, when he'd left the house and not made an effort to talk to her the rest of the evening.

The man downstairs asked for a room for himself and his wife.

"Sorry, sir," Lilly said, "but we've got guests filling the house all weekend."

He offered to pay double.

Lilly didn't hesitate. "I'd do it if I could, sir, but we can't turn out our other guests."

Bertie was out of her bed and throwing on her clothes by the time the screen door slapped shut, and the footsteps echoed the visitor's return to his car. She daren't run out into the road half-dressed, though it frustrated her to let him get away. It was because of her that he hadn't been given a room.

She caught Lilly in the kitchen, heaving her bulk from stove to kitchen table with surprising agility as she started preparations for the large country breakfast she always advertised in the Hideaway weekly newspaper. While cooking breakfast, she was also working on the huge pot of beans, and had a cake pan of cracklin' cornbread ready to go into the oven.

Lilly was famous for her breakfasts on Friday and Saturday mornings, which were open to the public. She'd told Bertie last night that she'd begun to make almost as much income from her breakfasts as she did for her rented rooms.

"You can't keep doing that, Lilly." Bertie finished buckling the belt around the waist of her dark blue denim pants as she joined Lilly at the kitchen table. "You can't turn down paying customers like that. It's your livelihood."

Lilly handed Bertie a bowl of flour, a wooden spoon, buttermilk and a crock of freshly churned butter. "Think you can bake me up a batch of biscuits that'll keep our customers comin' back for more?"

Bertie took the items and laid them out on the table. "'Course I can, but you don't need me livin' here with you to do that."

She paused. If they'd had this conversation yesterday morning, she'd have insisted on staying out at the farm and riding her bike in every morning to help with the household chores. But she knew that would be out of the question. At least for today, until after the funeral, she needed to keep her mouth shut about what she and Edith had found.

"Arielle Potts invited Edith and me to stay with them while we're here," she told Lilly. "I hate to see you give up good income for a room."

"I want you here," Lilly told her. "With no college tuition to pay anymore, and no kids to take care of except Red—who's more help to me than anyone could be—I can afford to do what I want with some of my rooms, and I want to let my special guests stay here. That's final." Lilly nodded firmly.

"Then at least let me—"

"And don't even start on me about paying."

Bertie pressed her lips together. "Thank you." She sifted the flour and baking powder, mixed them and added the buttermilk. "Somehow, during any free time I can find today, I need to search through the woods and fields for some comfrey leaves to treat Red's leg."

Lilly gave her a pointed look. "You think that'll help him?"

"Sure it will. Mom used comfrey a lot. It can't hurt anything."

"I heard that it could. Wrap his leg with those leaves and it'll heal the outside fine, but the infection inside the leg would then be trapped, and he could lose his leg."

"Not if we give him comfrey tea along with it. That'll heal him from the inside out, while the leaves work on his wounds from the outside in. Besides, the infection should be gone." Bertie focused on the task Lilly had set before her, taking comfort in the familiar recipe for biscuits. In her mind's eye she followed a trail through the woods back of the farmhouse, where her mother used to gather plants for treatment.

It had been well over a year since she'd been there, but Bertie knew what she'd need. She and Edith both agreed that whoever had been at the house yesterday wasn't likely to linger there. She would probably be safe.

She hoped.

Leastways, she couldn't let a little fear stop her from making sure Red got the treatment he needed to heal.

"Lilly, do you have any idea why Red would refuse to have his leg treated?"

Lilly looked up from her frying. "You talk to him about the comfrey yesterday?"

"Early this morning, actually, after I heard him fall out of bed."

"He fell?"

"Nightmare."

Lilly fixed her with a stern look. "Young ladies don't go to the bedrooms of young men."

"I thought he might be hurt, and I couldn't let him lay there. Anyway, Red's behaving strangely about his leg. Don't you remember that time he broke his arm?"

Lilly continued to level a stern look at Bertie for a few more seconds, to let her know how serious her transgression was. Then she nodded, relenting. "I sure do. Why, he loved all the attention that got him from friends. He made a big joke out of it."

"Of course, he complained about having to drink that comfrey tea Mom gave him," Bertie said, "but he did it, and he knew it helped him heal. Now it almost seems as if he's ashamed of his war wound, which is crazy, and he doesn't seem to even care if it heals."

A war wound like that was something a man would be proud of, wouldn't it? But Red had not mentioned much about the war, had stayed quiet yesterday when Ivan was entertaining the ladies with stories. Where Ivan was proud of his uniform and his medals, and wore them yesterday, Red wore his old work clothes.

Something was eating at Red, and Bertie aimed to find out what it was.

* * *

Red couldn't put his finger on what bothered him as he mounted Seymour again and rode back to the Moennig place. The beef cattle were out in the pasture, with plenty of grass to graze on and a pond full of water to drink. He counted them from the road. All were there.

The milk cows, of course, were already together in Ma's small pasture between the house and the river. Red and his mother had moved them on Monday afternoon so they could be milked more easily and watched more closely.

He guided Seymour across the front yard and up to the porch. Sure enough, the hickory switches looked like they'd been blown around by the wind. There were seven switches on the porch itself, and when he checked, he saw another one on the ground.

Somebody wanted to play Bald Knobbers, and they were smart enough to make sure their victims got the message.

He started to turn back to the road, but then he noticed the front door wasn't completely closed. When Bertie came out yesterday with her recipes, he'd watched her pull the door firmly shut.

Had someone been out here since then?

He nudged Seymour around the side of the house to the back door. It stood wide open. Something red caught his eye from the kitchen window. He froze when he read the words.

Chapter Twenty-Six

Bertie slid a large batch of freshly cut biscuits into the oven and closed the door before the heat could escape. Most folks around Hideaway cooked with a woodstove, but Lilly had the wisdom to know she needed the most modern kitchen setup she could buy, with all the people coming in and out, needing to be fed. She had a gas stove and a nice, large icebox.

There was a smokehouse out back of the house, where Lilly kept hams and bacon and sometimes smoked pork chops and sausage. She rendered her own lard in a huge kettle whenever she butchered a hog. She kept frozen meat at the meat locker on the town square; potatoes and apples, carrots and turnips in the root cellar; and jars of food she canned in the pump house. Lilly was a busy lady.

Bertie knew her way around this kitchen, too. She should. She'd been here enough times over the years.

She washed her hands at the sink and turned to Lilly, who stood carving thick slices of bacon from a slab she had brought out of the smokehouse yesterday.

"I've made my decision, Lilly," Bertie said. "You know Edith and I are beholden to you for letting us stay here, but I'm not planning to leave Hideaway after the funeral. Maybe never. You can't keep giving us free hospitality while you turn away paying customers."

Lilly pulled a cast-iron skillet onto the front burner and turned the switch. Blue flames licked up around the metal. "I think you oughta let me decide how I'm gonna use my own house."

"I've got a perfectly good home, with three bedrooms and indoor plumbing."

"Your pa told me that sometimes the electricity shuts off on him."

"I can work with that. We still have a backup hand pump behind the house, and our old outhouse is still upright."

Lilly paused in her work and placed her hands on her wide hips. "Roberta Moennig, I'm not discussing this with you anymore. Red doesn't want you staying alone out there until he's cleared up this mystery, and that's the way it's going to be. Now, I know you're a modern, independent woman, but you've got to understand that a man's gotta be made to feel like a man, especially when he…when he might have reasons to doubt his abilities."

"But he's a war hero, Lilly," Bertie said softly. "How could he doubt that?"

Lilly turned back to her work, draping strips of bacon into the skillet. They spattered, sending a rich, smoky aroma into the kitchen. It would bring the guests in to breakfast, for sure. Until last year, folks in America had done without a lot of meat so it could be sent to the boys overseas—as it should have. But Lilly had always taken good care of her own right here at home.

Lilly suddenly turned again and looked at Bertie, wiping her hands on the towel. "That shell hit more than Red's leg, Bertie. It seems to've ripped into his heart."

Bertie nodded. "I think more happened than that injury."

"Sure it did. He's decided he's not the man you need, now. He doesn't think he's gonna heal any further, and he doesn't want to burden you with a cripple."

Bertie wouldn't've been more shocked if the stove had suddenly turned purple. "He told you that?"

Lilly gave her a grimace of a smile. "Didn't have to. Don't forget, I'm his ma."

Bertie closed her eyes. *Oh, Red, no.* "He must know me better than that. Does he think I waited for him all this time to walk away when the goin' gets tough?"

"It ain't you that's makin' the decision, Bertie."

"He's not getting away from me that easy."

"Then you oughta have a little talk with him."

"He'll hardly talk to me."

"Keep tryin'. He needs to be showed you're made of sturdy stock, and you can handle anything he was to throw at you."

"I haven't changed."

"Red has. And besides, a feller doesn't want to be a sympathy case."

"I've never seen him as that!"

Lilly put the towel down. "I know you ain't, but he's not thinking straight right now. He's got a lot on his mind, especially while he's tryin' to figure out what happened to your pa. Red'll get to the bottom of things, you know."

"I know," Bertie said.

"Ivan Potts and John Martin think they're helping, but they don't know tracking like Red does," Lilly said.

Bertie felt suddenly chilled in spite of the heat in the kitchen. "Red knows how to take care of himself, but if the wrong person knows what he's doing, he could be putting himself in danger."

"He's still a soldier. He's doing what he has to."

"Lilly," Bertie said, "how long should I let someone frighten me out of living in my own home? I thought that was one reason we went to war in the first place."

She was talking more to herself than to Lilly now. Yes, she was afraid. Terrified. She didn't know if she would be brave enough to go back into that house after what she and Edith had found there yesterday, and yet it made her mad. She didn't want to let anyone do that to her.

"I didn't think I had any enemies in this town," she murmured.

"Your pa didn't have no enemies," Lilly said. "He might've been cantankerous sometimes, but he for sure didn't have no enemies in this town. None we knew of, anyways. That's what makes it dangerous. We don't know who to trust."

"How can it be any more dangerous out on the farm than it is right here?" Bertie asked. "You had that brick thrown through your window."

Lilly's lips parted in surprise, and her blue eyes widened. "Who told you about that? After all you've gone through, you don't need to be worryin' about—"

"John Martin told me yesterday afternoon, and I'm glad he did. I'm not a child, Lilly."

Lilly dabbed at her perspiring forehead with the back of her hand. Her plump cheeks were rosy with the heat. "Never said you was, darlin'. You don't need to get all worked up about other things right now. What you need is time to recover." Lilly gave a firm nod. "I can't stop you from movin' out, but I can sure refuse to rent a room in my own house. It's your room, and it will be 'til I say different. No one else will be stayin' there, whether you and Edith stay or not. I take care of my own."

Bertie raised an eyebrow. "Your own?"

Lilly rested her hands on the table and fixed Bertie with a level look. "The way I see it, one way or another, you're gonna be my daughter."

Bertie sighed, shaking her head. Oh, the stubbornness of mothers. And yet, she hadn't felt this loved and protected in a long time.

Sudden laughter reached them from the garden, and they both glanced out the back window to see Edith and Ivan gathering vegetables.

"You noticed those two together?" Lilly asked.

"How could I not?"

"Ivan is a true gentleman from a good family. Edith's an educated lady. They could do lots worse. Don't hurt to do a little matchmaking, does it?" Lilly asked.

Bertie shook her head. "Not at all." She watched Lilly working, and marveled at the fact that she felt closer to her father right now than she had in a long time.

Lilly had such faith in God's provision. Sure, she'd gotten a brick through the window, had lived without a husband for twelve years, and had a son wounded in the war, but she'd had a thriving business all these years, and she knew how to smile, how to have fun, how to treat her guests with kind hospitality.

The lady also had a bent toward romance. In fact, Bertie had discovered about a year ago that Lilly might even have been interested in Dad. They'd spent a lot of time together, laughing and talking. Lilly had taken several dishes of food up to the house when Dad was alone. Bertie knew this, because Dad had told her about it, and he wasn't unhappy about it, either.

Bertie remembered teasing him about Lilly a couple of times over the telephone, and he hadn't protested. In fact, he seemed to enjoy it.

She glanced up to find Lilly pulling a chair out and sitting down at the table. The smile, so characteristic of her all the time Bertie was growing up, was gone, and lines of sadness creased her face.

Now that she thought about it, Bertie realized Lilly's laughter, though still there, had been forced, her smiles lacking the usual happiness that radiated from her. She had always been such a powerful force in her family's life—because she had to be, and because she was naturally gifted with a joyful spirit. Seeing Lilly so tired and sad jolted Bertie.

"It must've been awful for you and Red to find Dad like that on Monday," Bertie said.

Lilly bowed her head with a somber nod. "He was a fine man."

"I'm so sorry, Lilly. Here I've been grieving my own loss and not given much thought to how Dad's death is hurtin' others. I know Dad thought a lot of you and Red." She hesitated. Should she even mention it? "I even got the feelin' you and he might've gotten to be pretty close…if you—"

Lilly took a breath and straightened her shoulders. "Now, don't you start that. Joseph was a good friend. He helped me here at the house any time I needed it. With Red gone, I couldn't do everything myself, and Joseph knew that. He was always checkin' up on me because he was such a good man, and that's all."

Bertie couldn't suppress a smile. "I heard tell you fed him a few times for his trouble."

Lilly nodded.

"Well, I know…knew Dad pretty well. With Mom gone and Lloyd living far away, Dad and I did a lot of talking. He admired you, spoke of you quite a few times, when he could be sure the neighbors weren't listening to our calls."

Pink crept up Lilly's neck, and she fanned herself with the dish towel. "Roberta Moennig, don't you go teasing me like that. Your pa could've landed himself pert near any woman he'd want in this town. No reason he'd be lookin' at a fat woman like me for a wife. We was good friends, and that's all we was."

Bertie shook her head. Lilly sure didn't see herself the way most other folks in town saw her. Anyone who knew her saw a charming woman with a strong and loving spirit.

Lilly got up and reached to turn the bacon, then sliced more from the slab. "Roberta Moennig, I know you and your tomboy ways, and you'd fight a wild boar if you had a mind to, but there ain't a lot of women around like you."

Bertie watched her, waiting.

"I don't want you to up and decide you're gonna move into the farmhouse in spite of what Red thinks, or what I think."

"Okay. I won't."

Lilly gave her a suspicious look. "You promise?"

Bertie nodded. "Promise."

Lilly nodded. "Folks'll start coming in soon. I've got to finish laying out breakfast on the sideboard. How about whipping me up some of that delicious cream gravy like your ma always used to make?"

Bertie got up, glad for the work to keep her occupied.

Chapter Twenty-Seven

Edith came through the back door carrying a burlap bag of garden produce. She had dirt under her fingernails, mud on the shoes she kicked off outside the door, and a thoughtful smile on her face, the likes of which Bertie had never seen before.

Lilly was in the dining room setting the long table, and Ivan had gone in to help her with the other two tables she used for the breakfast crowd. Their voices could be heard from the dining room, Lilly teasing Ivan about something, and Ivan's laughter filling the house.

Edith glanced over her shoulder at Bertie. "That Ivan Potts is one of the nicest young men I've met in a long while."

"You don't say," Bertie said dryly as she spooned all but a few tablespoons of hot bacon grease from the huge cast iron skillet. "With the heart of a poet, no doubt. Was he quoting his poetry to you out there in the garden a few minutes ago, when you picked green tomatoes instead of ripe ones?"

"Oh, you wipe that smirk off your face," Edith

warned with a chuckle. "All I said was he's nice. He has a good head on his shoulders, he's funny and he's literate. And yes, the man can quote a poem off the top of his head about something as mundane as a carrot."

"I don't know many men who'd care enough to try."

"I don't know many men who could do it even if they wanted to."

"That's our Ivan, all right," Bertie said.

"I told him his talent would be wasted in a stuffy old bank, and that he should be a school teacher."

"Well, maybe he should marry one," Bertie said. "He's going to be a banker. His mother already has the plans made."

Laughter and additional voices reached them through the swinging door between the kitchen and dining room.

"Speaking of Ivan's mother," Edith said, "he told me that Red had been by to see her at the library yesterday afternoon."

"The library? You don't say. I wonder what's up there. Red's hardly ever stepped foot in the library."

"Maybe she's doling out advice for the lovelorn," Edith suggested.

"Then she might oughta think about giving her own son some advice before long, you think?" Bertie sprinkled flour over the grease and stirred until it thickened, then started adding fresh milk to the mixture. She realized, after several seconds, that Edith still hadn't responded.

She glanced around to find Edith staring down at the vegetables she'd picked. Just staring.

"It's not a sin to find a fella attractive, you know," Bertie told her.

Edith picked up a bunch of dirt-covered carrots and set them in the sink to run water over them. "I don't suppose you've given any thought about what you're going to do in the next few days."

"I sure have. Lilly talked me into staying on here for a spell. Changing the subject? You must really be taken with Ivan."

Edith looked up from her work. "You're staying for good, aren't you?"

"I'm leaning in that that direction more all the time." In fact, down deep in her heart, Bertie wasn't sure she'd even considered going back to California. Not seriously. How could she leave again, with Red here in Hideaway?

"That doesn't surprise me," Edith said.

Bertie stirred the gravy, adding salt and pepper. "I'm needed here, and I'm not about to let somebody run me off the land our family worked so hard to cultivate. The question is, what will *you* do now?"

"I told you I wasn't leaving you until I knew you were settled. Nothing's changed since Monday, and I sure don't see you settled yet."

Bertie grinned at her. "I don't suppose Ivan could be giving you a little more reason to stay."

Edith turned to look at the garden. "How far does Lilly's land go?"

"It goes back about an eighth of a mile. The road in front of the house divides her acreage. The rest of her land stretches downhill between the road and the river. She had a lot more before she sold off acreage to the town for the city's expansion. Folks say this town's gonna double in size in the next few decades." Bertie rubbed some dried sage between her fingers over the gravy as she stirred. "Edith, I'm serious, it's not wrong to be attracted to another man."

"It's more complicated than that."

"How?"

"I promised myself at Harper's funeral that I'd never marry another man in the armed forces, or a policeman or anyone who might die on me. I don't ever want to go through that again."

"And Ivan's headed back to the war next week," Bertie said softly.

"That's right."

"So what's the problem? There won't be enough time for you two to fall in love, but you could sure enjoy his company while you're both in town."

Edith placed the carrots carefully on the dish drainer and reached for some snap beans. "You've lost loved ones, Bertie. You know how it rips something apart inside you."

"Yes, and it hurts somethin' awful. And I know I haven't lost a husband like you have, so I've no room to be telling you what to do or who to date."

"Well, I can tell you that losing the person you love most in all the world is like being ripped apart, then being left on your own to grow back."

Bertie knew that. Losing both her parents in the space of three years had been like that.

"And then people think you should be fine in just a few months," Edith said.

"I never thought that," Bertie said.

"For me, it's been three and a half years, and sometimes I think I haven't even begun to heal." Edith picked up a scrub brush and worked at the carrots until part of their skin was worn off, exposing the brighter orange beneath. "Ivan told me Lilly makes the best fried green tomatoes in the state."

"That's right. She has several recipes for green tomatoes. I know folks here in Hideaway who are addicted to Lilly's green-tomato preserves." Bertie looked out the window and saw Red riding Seymour into the corral.

He wore his work boots and jeans with an old plaid shirt that Bertie remembered was his favorite before he joined the Army. It stretched too tightly across his shoulders now.

He stumbled when he got off the horse, but caught himself quickly, reaching for the cane tied to the saddle.

He glanced over his shoulder toward the house, as if ashamed of his weakness and hoping no one had seen.

For some reason, she stepped away from the window. If he hadn't wanted her to know about his injury in the first place, he for sure wouldn't want her to see the weakness. She watched him lean the cane against the stable door and uncinch the saddle, a little unsteady on his feet. At that moment, she felt such a rush of love for him, and pride in him, because she understood. Charles Frederick Meyer was an honorable man. That part of him had never changed. The war had injured him, but it had also taken the good man he'd been before the war and fired him into an even better version of himself. That was what testing did to good men.

Red was doing all he could, with only one good leg, to find her father's killer. Most men who were whole and healthy couldn't do what he was doing. And he was trying to protect her through it all.

Why hadn't she seen?

"Oh, Edith, I've been such a fool."

Her friend joined her at the sink. "How is that?"

"I was angry with him for not telling me about his leg. I did everything wrong yesterday when I saw him, but I was so hurt that no one had told me."

"I heard from Ivan that no one knew. In fact, Ivan didn't even realize it when he first saw Red on the train."

"That's because he didn't want me to know," Bertie said. "If anyone in town had known about it, I'd have heard, and he wanted to wait and tell me himself. And I was so angry with him. It was a horrible way for me to treat a war hero. Especially the man I love."

Bertie slid the skillet from the burner and glanced at Edith. "Do you think you could—"

"I'll find a gravy boat. You go on out and talk to Red. Better hurry, though. I hear people coming in the front door."

Bertie didn't hesitate.

Chapter Twenty-Eight

Red ran a currycomb down Seymour's withers, feeling the tremor of flesh beneath the metal. The horse loved to be groomed.

"What do you think we oughta do now, boy?" He smoothed the glossy hair with his hand. Seymour hadn't even worked up a good sweat this morning, but combing him gave Red a sense of peace that he couldn't seem to find anywhere else right now. "I can't just go around town asking people to show me the soles of their shoes."

He thought about the tracks he'd seen at the back of the house, leading from the kitchen door, and the words scrawled on the window, and he gripped the comb so hard he thought he might hear it crack.

A soft sound of a footfall came from behind him, and he jerked around to see Bertie as she reached the white-washed corral fence. Her hair was tied back with a blue bandana, and she wore a blue plaid shirt and blue jeans.

She climbed the fence instead of walking around to the gate, and he had a good view of her shoes. Sturdy walking shoes.

He ran the comb down Seymour's back. "Sure some good smells comin' from the kitchen," he said. "Guess you helped Ma with breakfast this morning."

"Guess I did. Have you been out looking for more evidence?"

He nodded. "May've found some, too."

"Where?" She reached for the currycomb.

He held it out of her reach. "You don't need to take my work away from me. I can still groom a horse."

"Sorry."

"Why don't you let me do a little more investigating before you start asking questions?" He kept his voice gentle. Her father's funeral was today, and she didn't need to be yelled at.

"I'm not trying to check up on you, I just want to know about my father."

He gave the horse a final swipe with the comb, patted him on the haunch, and hung the comb on a nail in the wall. "I'm checkin' a few things out." He pointed down at her shoes. "For instance, I was out at your house a while ago. Seems you were there before me."

Her eyes widened, and her lips parted in dismay.

"I thought we'd decided you wouldn't go out there by yourself." Still, he kept his voice gentle.

"I didn't."

"Who went with you?"

"Edith."

He took a deep, slow breath. "What happened?"

"I guess you saw the words on the window."

"Yes. Were you the one who left the back door wide open?"

Seymour chose that time to nuzzle Bertie's hair, and

she reached up to rub his nose. "Yes. We wanted to air the house out."

"Air it out?"

She crossed her arms in front of her. "I'm sorry I didn't tell you about it, but I was so sure you'd try to pack me up and haul me back to the train station before I could even attend Dad's funeral, that I decided to wait until after the funeral to tell you about it."

He gritted his teeth. She must think he was some kind of bully. He didn't mean for her to feel that way, but how else could he keep her safe without watching her every minute?

"I wouldn't have hauled you to the train station," he said.

"Good, because I wouldn't have gone, anyway. I just didn't want to fight with you." She took a step toward him, her gaze gentle and…what was the word? Vulnerable? "That's the last thing I want to do, Red."

"Why did you want to air out the house?"

She bit her lower lip and jammed her hands into the back pockets of her jeans. "Someone had turned all the gas jets wide open on the stove, and the pilots were out. All the kitchen doors were closed, and I found Herman lying between the stove and the wall."

He closed his eyes as horror washed through him. She could've been killed! "That's what the words on the window meant. *Nazi gas chamber.*"

She nodded.

"The cat okay?"

"He came to pretty quickly." She held her arms out, and he saw the scratches on them.

He reached for her hands. "The cat did *this?* Are you okay? Did you doctor these—"

"I'm fine, Red." She looked up at him, a tiny smile touching her lips. "Edith and I ran all the way back here."

"Looks like whoever wrote that message used an old tube of lipstick from the house. I found it on the ground."

"But no idea who put it there?"

"I know who I suspect. Good ol' Gramercy. But it can't be that easy."

"Why not?"

"Nothing's ever that easy. Bertie, you've got to promise me one thing." He resisted the powerful urge to take her by the shoulders and shake her. He would shake her gently, of course. But he needed her to see reason.

"I know," she said. "I can't go back out to the house alone."

"Or drag poor Edith out there and risk both your lives."

"Before we ran back here yesterday, I made a side trip to the pump house and got Dad's old hunting rifle and a box of bullets. Edith and I both know how to shoot."

Red grimaced. That didn't make him breathe any easier. Sometimes this woman made his head want to explode. "Did you call the sheriff?"

"I didn't call anybody. Edith wanted me to tell you."

Sure she did. She at least has the sense God gave a goose. He glanced toward the house. "No use in arguing. What's done is done."

"I turned off the gas."

He nodded. "Like I said, no use arguing. And like I also said, breakfast sure smells good. Guess I'd better get washed up and get some of this horse hair off me before I try to sit at the table."

He turned to walk toward the house. Bertie followed him."Red, you've got to stop telling me to go back to California."

His steps slowed, but he didn't turn around. *Now what?* He saw his reflection in the window he'd installed Wednesday. He looked grim, jaw jutting out, red brows drawn into a heavy frown. He tried to relax his expression a little, but it didn't do much good.

"I've decided I'm not going back," she said.

He stopped. In the window reflection, his frown deepened. He saw her standing behind him, and knew she could see how her words were affecting him, same as he could.

"If you'd been here the past year," she said, "I'd've never left in the first place. With you back home, I'm stayin' right here where I've always belonged. And don't go trying to change my mind." She paused, swallowed. "I don't know about you, but nothing's changed for me in three years."

He wanted to groan out loud with frustration, and at the same time he had a hard time keeping a sudden grin from popping out on his face. What *was* it about this woman that could make him act like a five-year-old kid?

He bowed his head, kicking at a stone on the ground with his bad leg. "It won't work, Bertie." It amazed him that he was able to keep his voice quiet, gentle, sane.

He turned around, leaning hard on the cane as he looked at her. "Please don't even try it."

He saw the sudden hurt in her eyes, but she shook her head. "I'm not trying anything, I'm telling you my plans. I'm staying. I know you've got to have time to recover some from the war, but I'm going to be here waiting when you do."

"You didn't ask for a cripple," Red said.

Her eyes flashed with a brief show of her typical spirit. "And *you* didn't ask to *be* crippled."

"You deserve more."

"I deserve better than the treatment I'm getting from you right now. I deserve the man I waited for and wrote to all this time. I deserve a hero."

"That's not me."

"It sure is."

"Not now."

"Lilly told me you've got a whole drawer full of medals you earned over the last three years. You have a Purple Heart. You risked everything for your country, and if your letters were telling the truth, you risked all that for me. I'd like to know who in that army is a hero if you're not."

"Bertie," he said quietly, trying to derail the freight train before she could work up any more steam, "you don't know what all went on over there."

"What makes you think you're the only one who ever went to war?" She glared up at him. Plenty of the ol' fire left in her. "My heart traveled right along with you, into those foxholes and on every dangerous mission. My prayers followed you every step of the way. My body might've been safe here in America, but the rest of me was right there with you."

"You didn't do the things I did. You didn't kill—"

"I devoted myself to you before you ever left for the war, and—"

"Bertie, this kind of thing's exactly why I never made any promises or asked any from—"

"You can't tell my heart what to do, Red!" She stood with hands on hips, face flushed. "And you can't toss it away like so much garbage because you don't know how to deal with it anymore. You're going to have to learn again."

"I can't—"

"Don't try to tell me you can't do something." Bertie bit her lip and looked away. Her chin wobbled very briefly, but she met his gaze again. "You've always been able to do anything you set your mind to, and you can do this. I know your injuries aren't just physical. A fella can't go through a war and come back unchanged. But I'm here to tell you, even if the old Red doesn't ever come back, this Red right here," she said as she reached out and smacked him none-too-gently on the shoulder, "this is the one I want. I'm taking you as you are right now."

She continued to stand there glaring at him for another second or two—or it could've been an hour. Right now, he wouldn't've known the difference. Then she shoved her hands into the pockets of her jeans and turned and stalked into the house.

He felt as if he'd just had another kind of war declared on him. This was one war he suddenly wasn't sure he could win. And he wasn't sure he wanted to.

Chapter Twenty-Nine

Bertie still burned with shame as she sat in Ivan's car once again, this time in the front seat at his insistence, in honor of her loss. Lilly weighted down the back on the passenger side, Red was once more in the middle of the backseat, and Edith sat behind Ivan.

What must Red be thinking now? Of all the cock-eyed things to do. A man was supposed to pursue the woman, not the other way around.

And this wasn't the time to be thinking about such things. *Bertie Moennig, you have the worst timing!*

Edith's dark hair was in perfect order, her dress the latest fashion, formfitting and attractive, military style with broad shoulders and slim waistline. It was one Bertie had helped her make from pieces of an old dress with a McCall's pattern.

Bertie's dark gray dress had been made from the same pattern, with some adjustments by Edith, an expert seamstress, who had sized down the pattern for Bertie's smaller, shorter frame.

Both men wore their military dress uniforms—Red

with great reluctance, and only because Lilly and Edith had both begged him to show some pride in his country and his own service to them. He still didn't wear any medals. It was as if he was ashamed of them.

The drive took barely a couple of minutes. Lilly had protested that they could walk to the church faster than they could all get situated into the car, but Ivan wouldn't hear of it. Any other time, Bertie would've teased him about inventing a reason to see Edith again.

Though the funeral wasn't scheduled until noon, a crowd had already begun to gather at the church by eleven-thirty, with folk huddling in small groups on the grass outside the building. Some strolled around in the church cemetery, visiting at the gravesides of departed loved ones.

"Is there something else happening at the church today?" Edith asked when Ivan pulled in front of the church.

Bertie looked back at her blankly. "No, just the funeral."

"You have this kind of turnout for a funeral?" Edith asked, glancing around at the crowd with interest. "We don't even do this in Mobile. It looks like a party setting up."

"I told you," Bertie said. "Things are a little different here." She didn't know about Mobile, but in California, where everybody was from somewhere else, very little family was present to honor their dead.

Ivan parked at the edge of the church cemetery, where Bertie glanced toward three graves decorated with military headstones. Fresh flowers covered the gravesites, blooming in multiple colors. The families of James Eckrow, Larry Peterson and William Lewis were keeping the memories of their boys alive, though the bodies were destroyed in the Pacific Theater two years ago. The town still mourned the three young men whom Bertie had known in school.

Joseph Moennig was to be buried beside his wife, Martha, near the edge of a bluff that overlooked the James River at the far corner of the cemetery.

Bertie noticed that her mother's grave had been well-tended, with flowers growing around the headstone. Ever the practical man, Dad hadn't been much interested in growing flowers around the house, but when it came to his wife, his practicality had often flown out the window in favor of their strong bond.

Mom had been the one to convince him that they needed electricity and indoor plumbing long before most of the rural residents had anything but outhouses and oil lanterns. Even during the Depression, Dad had worked extra hours to make sure his wife had a few extra things—material for a new dress, even lace handkerchiefs from time to time.

"We've brought in a load of chairs from City Hall," Ivan said, drawing Bertie from her memories. "Dad had them hauled over earlier this morning."

Bertie nodded. It would be a packed church.

Ivan got out, opened the back door for Edith, then rushed around to the other side to help Lilly and Bertie. Lilly, of course, had already helped herself from the car and was halfway to the front door of the church.

"You doing okay?" Ivan asked Bertie softly, under cover of Lilly's greeting to some friends congregating near the door.

"I will be."

"Your father was a fine man," Ivan said. "None better."

"Thank you." Bertie felt the heaviness of grief settle over her again. She'd done very well yesterday, with so many friends around to comfort her and so many things to distract her. But today was different. In spite of the presence of so many, she weakened under the impact of Dad's death. He wasn't coming back. She was on her own.

She glanced over her shoulder toward Red, who had climbed out of the car and limped to the cemetery fence, gazing toward the gravesites of his fellow soldiers. "I can't help thinking of simpler times, when there wasn't a war, when we were just wild kids with living parents and the only thing we had to worry about was whether we'd get into trouble for getting our clothes wet paddling the river."

"Or putting a daddy longlegs in the teacher's desk," Ivan said.

"Or carving initials in the outhouse wall," she said.

Ivan grinned. "You were the one who did that? I thought it was Red. You know he was sweet on you all through high school."

Again, she glanced toward Red, and found him watching her. He looked away quickly, but not before she saw, once again, a deep sadness in his eyes.

Her cheeks burned as she thought about her bold behavior this morning. Not just once, but twice. She'd never pushed herself on any man—never thought she ever would. Sometimes things changed that made a person change with them, and Lilly's words had kept running through her mind.

"He's crazy about you, kid." Ivan put an arm around Bertie's shoulders and hugged her.

She allowed herself to lean against him and accept the comfort of another one of her longtime friends. "He doesn't want me here."

"That's right, but you know why, and it isn't because he's suddenly stopped caring. He wants you safe, same as the rest of us do."

Bertie groaned. "And here I'd hoped I wouldn't hear that tired line for the rest of the—"

"You just listen to your ol' Uncle Ivan." He gave her shoulders another squeeze and released her. "The day we came home, I surprised Red on the train. He was reading a letter from you, concentrating so hard he didn't even see me coming. The thing was worn to a frazzle."

Bertie looked up into Ivan's dark brown eyes. "You sure it was one of my letters?"

He nodded. "You've written me enough, I should know your handwriting by now."

"This isn't a good time to tease me, now, Ivan Potts."

"I may tease about a lot of things, but not this, Bert. You know me better than that. For Red, the sun rises and sets in you. It's always been that way for him."

She sighed. "He's pushing me out of his life as sure as I'm standing here." She'd talked a brave talk to Red in the backyard this morning, but she wasn't nearly as sure of herself as she'd pretended to be.

Ivan glanced toward his friend, and Bertie followed

his gaze, saddened once more by the loneliness she saw in the figure that stood apart from all the rest.

"We're talking about a man who's trying to come to terms with too many awful memories," Ivan said.

"I knew it was hard on him," she said. "He didn't write about it often, but when he did, I could tell it was tearing him up, but it tears everyone up."

"You can't know what it was like unless you've been there," Ivan said. "Red's doing what he can to see to it you don't have that same experience here. He's behaving the way a man would behave if he was in love with a woman and wanted her safe."

She glanced at Red again. "He's acting like a man who's only half alive."

"That's what war does to a man, especially someone like Red." Ivan pressed his hand against her back and urged her to walk toward the church, where Lilly stood chatting with Mrs. Cooper and Edith.

"But he's so different," Bertie said. "It's like he's another person completely."

"I think that's one of the things that's keeping him at arm's length from you," Ivan said. "He knows he's changed, and he doesn't want you to accept him back home as if it were your duty."

"I don't believe Red's changed for good," Bertie said, glancing in Red's direction. "It'll take a while, but the shock of things he's seen will fade over time. Someday he'll even find where he put his sense of humor."

Ivan followed her gaze. "Give him time."

Bertie nodded. Time was exactly what he deserved. Time and patience.

"Mom has the meal planned," Ivan said. "We heard the minister who's doing the service is long-winded."

"Folks'll get hungry, sure enough," Bertie said.

"And they'll want to stick around and visit afterwards, since you've been gone so long."

"And they'll want to visit with you and Red," Bertie said.

Lilly turned back to them, as if just now realizing they weren't right behind her. "Ivan, I've got a big batch of ham and beans cooking on the stove that we'll need to collect after the funeral."

Ivan looked disappointed. "No chicken and dumplings?"

"For the whole town?" Lilly laughed. "I may not be hurtin' too bad, but I can't afford that. Don't you worry, though, you'll get more before you have to leave again." She winked at him. "I did make some cornbread and some gooseberry cobbler."

Ivan grinned and kissed Red's mother on the cheek. "Lilly Meyer, will you marry me?"

As the two continued to tease in their old, familiar way, Bertie caught sight of Ivan's parents, Gerald and Arielle, directing the setup of tables in the shady yard at the side of the church.

Arielle, tall and slender with graceful movements, wore a stylish black suit. Her pale blond hair was drawn back in a chignon, with a black hat and black netting over her face.

In contrast, Lilly wore no hat, and though her navy dress was only a few years old, it stretched tightly across her ample hips and shoulders. Lilly typically dressed more comfortably in roomy house dresses and flats, cooking a feast for her guests. Edith had spent some time beautifying her this morning, and now her golden red hair was neatly gathered in a bun on the back of her head.

Arielle most likely had cooked something far different from Lilly's pot of beans and cornbread. In all these years living in Hideaway, Arielle hadn't grasped the mindset of the typical Hideaway farmer.

Bertie loved Arielle's tartlets and finger sandwiches, but most folks hadn't quite caught on. They wanted something that would fill their stomachs, even if it was ham and beans. Too many still struggled with the aftershock of the Depression.

There had always been a sharp contrast between Arielle Potts and Lilly Meyer, and there'd been times after Mom died that Bertie had felt a little like a rope in a tug-of-war between the two women. Both had been worried about their sons fighting overseas, and their need to mother someone was strong. Bertie had become the object of affection of both women.

Though Bertie had been a grown woman of twenty when Mom died, Lilly and Arielle had paid visits to her at home and at work ever since, until Bertie left for California. Arielle had shared her favorite books with Bertie, while Lilly always seemed to be cooking up a "little too much" for her guests, and needing someone to help her eat the generous leftovers.

Bertie felt more comfortable with Lilly's down-home ways and blunt honesty, but there were times when it was nice to have a little of Arielle's sophistication and social grace.

Edith stepped up beside Bertie and looped an arm through hers. "It looks as if the whole town's coming."

"You wait and see," Lilly said. "That church will be packed in a few minutes, and there'll be folks sitting out in the vestibule and out by the windows. Folks around these parts loved Bertie's pa, and they'll turn out for his farewell."

Bertie glanced at Red, who continued to stand at the edge of the cemetery, as if the rest of the world didn't exist—or maybe he only wished it didn't.

She stared down at his hands, clasped on the hook of the cane. Tightly. It was as if Red Meyer held everything inside as tightly as his hands gripped the wood.

She thought about the words he had written to her from Italy. He'd thought he might die before he saw her again.

How right those words had turned out to be.

Bertie believed in the resurrection of Jesus. What she had to ask herself was if she believed that very same Jesus was strong enough to resurrect Red Meyer, because he seemed so dead to her that she barely recognized him.

Chapter Thirty

Red studied the graves of the men who'd died in the Pacific—friends he'd hunted and fished with and shared farm chores with. He'd visited the parents of all three on Tuesday, not knowing what to say, though it didn't seem to matter. His presence seemed to bring them comfort.

He could've ended up in the cemetery with his friends. What would that've done to Ma? To Bertie? He thought about what Ivan had told him on the train Monday—about bein' better off dead. But what would that have done to Gerald and Arielle?

He heard his mother's strong voice carry across the yard, and glanced around to find her and Bertie looking toward him. He turned away quickly.

What were they talking about? Why had they suddenly gotten quiet? He'd not been able to stop thinking about Bertie, nor keep his gaze from straying her way ever since her declarations this morning.

All through breakfast, while Edith helped Ma serve folks, Bertie had sat at the far end of the table, as far from Red as she could get. Every time he'd looked at her, she'd been watching him, and once she'd nodded at him, as if to assure him she meant what she'd said about staying.

He knew his behavior was hurting her—had hurt her for weeks. She couldn't understand why he was drawing away. If he'd had any doubts about her feelings for him, he sure didn't now. She'd never been one to hide what was in her heart.

"Hello there, soldier," came the familiar voice of Gerald Potts, and Red turned to greet Ivan's father.

Gerald pounded him on the back and shook his hand until it nearly tore off at the wrist—even though they'd seen each other yesterday. Ivan took after his father; both men were built like draft horses and were as friendly as hound pups.

Gerald's thick, graying hair was slicked back, his gray suit jacket too tight across his shoulders.

"Will Bertie and her friend be at the guesthouse for the duration of their stay?"

Red wasn't sure what to say. He didn't feel like announcing to the world that Bertie wasn't going back to California. "I'm not sure."

"Well, I don't think it's safe for them at the farmhouse just now. They'd both be welcome with us for as long as they want to stay."

"They're welcome with us, they know that. But if Bertie takes a notion to move back into her own homeplace, there's not much I can do to stop her."

Gerald chuckled. "You know our Bertie. She can be strong-willed. I may have a talk with her, or have Arielle ask her and Miss Frost to lunch in a day or two."

"That's *Mrs*. Frost," Red said. "Her husband was

killed at Pearl Harbor." He stepped in a hole, and grimaced when pain shot up his bad leg.

Gerald grabbed his arm. "Are you okay?"

"Fine. I'm fine."

"You're still tracking the mystery of Joseph's death?"

"That's right."

"Found anything yet?"

"Maybe a few things, footprints and such. You know about the swastika somebody left on our stable, but did you notice those switches on Joseph's front porch?"

"Yes, I saw them," Gerald said. "I didn't pay much attention. We'd had a decent storm the night before, and you know how things can blow up."

"There were also the same kind of switches on the Krueger porch. All hickory, all about the same length. They'd been placed there, Gerald. They were laid on the porch in the shape of a swastika."

Gerald regarded him with sudden gravity. "Well, that places a question on one theory."

"You thought it was Krueger?"

Gerald nodded. "Still could've been. He might have placed those switches on his own porch in order to misdirect."

"But what reason would he have for doing it? Krueger's whole family disappeared. And yet the threats are still being laid." Red told Gerald about what had happened to Bertie and Edith yesterday.

Gerald shook his head. "I've tried to talk Butch into reopening the case."

"No luck?" Red asked.

"None. You know how stubborn he can be sometimes. I've overheard a few discussions down at the

Exchange. Lots of crazy ideas, all the way from Joseph's neighbors doing the deed, to someone from out of town."

"I think Joseph Moennig and the Kruegers and my mother were all chosen because they're German," Red said.

Gerald's eyes narrowed in thought. "I wondered about that, too. Have you considered the possibility that the culprit is actually a Nazi?"

"You mean someone who's infiltrated the country? Gerald, that's the kind of thinking that's caused so much trouble with folks all around. It's why innocent families were forced into detention camps."

"How do we know all those people are innocent?"

Red didn't have an answer. He didn't agree with Gerald, but then Gerald wasn't German American.

"Red, I trust our government. If intelligence sources have concluded that there are infiltrators sent by that demon, Hitler, they could be anywhere. They could be in any town."

"But the Germans surrendered."

"Publicly, yes. But Hitler started making his evil plans to take over the world long before he started the war. His people and their families could have been indoctrinated for years. There could even be second-generation Nazis under cover, and if they haven't been caught, they might carry Hitler's standard as long as they can, even with Hitler dead."

Talk of such things gave Red a queasy feeling. "But why attack other Germans?" he asked. "And why here in Hideaway? We're so far removed from major defense plants and military headquarters."

"We have no idea how many spies Hitler could have sent to infiltrate," Gerald said. "Now that Germany's lost the war, they could be wanting to do as much damage as they can to their enemy out of revenge, and they see German Americans as turncoats. That's who they want to attack."

Red shook his head. "I don't agree."

"I don't want to think like this, Red. It's frightening to consider that anyone in our neighborhood, any of our friends, could be the enemy, but we have to be realistic. We know what Hitler was capable of."

"But we know all our neighbors. Someone would've had to come here years ago, hide their accent, and have the downright meanness to hurt and kill their neighbors."

Gerald spread his hand, indicating the crowd around the church. "It takes all kinds to make a community, Red. Take your pick. Arielle's parents still have a Swedish accent, but you can tell she sounds purely American." He stood beside Red, studying the newcomers, most of whom walked to the church. "The infiltrators would be trained to blend in."

A large black hearse pulled to the front of the church, and Gerald nodded toward it. "I think we'll be getting started in a few moments. I'm a pallbearer, so I'd better be going." He patted Red on the shoulder once more. "Whatever you do, make sure Bertie doesn't get herself into trouble. I'd like to talk more about this later. Maybe tomorrow. I've already made plans for a fishing expedition later this afternoon down by the caves below the Moennig house. Fish are really biting there right now, and we have an empty drawer in the meat locker."

Red nodded and watched Gerald walk away, wondering at the things he'd said. Could there actually be someone among them who had been spying on their community for years?

He didn't even want to think about it. But he did.

Krueger hadn't been in town long. He'd left the day Joseph was found dead in his corral. Could he, as Gerald said, have placed those switches on his own porch to deflect suspicion from himself?

Though the sun shone brightly today, Red felt as if the whole town was covered by a thick cloud of gray.

Bertie watched from the front of the church as her father's casket was carried through the foyer by the pallbearers. She knew all these men. Ivan Potts and his father, Gerald, John Martin, Fred Cooper, Bernie Wilson and Leon Peterson.

She was grateful to them, and she knew Dad would be proud that such fine men would usher his body to its resting place.

During the funeral, Bertie sat at the front of the church and allowed the organ music to float over her, hearing the words of "How Great Thou Art" in her head.

She stared out the side window at the cemetery. Dad would be buried there in a little while...his body lowered into the earth, to be covered in darkness.

Lilly's arm came around her from the left, and Edith took her hand from her right. *Oh, God, how could You do this to us?* She thought of her brother. Medical science was coming a long way toward curing tuberculosis, but not everyone lived through it, even yet. The sanatorium, in Mt. Vernon, Missouri, was their only hope.

Dad had been the youngest in a family of four brothers. The others were dead, and Bertie's cousins, all boys, were in the Pacific Theater, risking their lives for their country, just as Red and Ivan had done. She had no family here.

She glanced past Lilly to the cane leaning against the pew in front of them.

The whole world was flying apart, and she couldn't keep from wondering if she was flying apart with it.

The service ended and people filed forward to view the body and greet her. She swallowed and forced a smile. So many friends loved her, were here for her. The church was full, and old classmates, former teachers, her church friends, all came by to tell her how sorry they were, and remind her about what a wonderful man her father had been.

As if she needed reminding.

The final person filed past. The funeral director—who had driven over from Hollister—bent toward her, gesturing for her to approach the casket.

But as she started to rise, she realized she couldn't do it.

Lilly gently urged her to stand.

Bertie wanted to shove her away, but she didn't. She just didn't stand. Edith, bless her, just sat holding her hand.

After a few moments, Edith said quietly, "You can't go with him, no matter how much you probably wish you could right now."

Bertie looked at her, saw tears in Edith's eyes, and realized she was reliving a loss of her own.

"Your time hasn't come yet. You have to keep going," Edith said.

Bertie nodded, then slowly stood. The people waited outside for the casket to be carried past and into the cemetery. She would go with it.

But the life she had known was over. What would happen next?

Chapter Thirty-One

Red stood apart from the crowd that circled Joseph Moennig's grave. He wished he could be strong for Bertie, holding her up and encouraging her the way Edith and his own Ma were doing, but try as he might, his mind was on the battle. He couldn't let it go, not even when he saw Bertie turn around and study the crowd, and her gaze lit on him.

She was probably seeing the old Red, with his threadbare suit and red hair slicked down for church. She was seeing the boy she'd grown up with, played baseball with, fished with, worked with.

She wasn't seeing what was inside him now. She used to be able to look at his face and know what he was thinking, long before they'd started seeing each other in a...romantic way.

Back when they were both in that ol' one-room schoolhouse out past this church, she only had to look at him to know if he was gonna go fishin' after school, or if he had to get home to the farm to help with chores.

But she didn't know him anymore. He was a soldier

home from war, with one more battle to fight, and he didn't have the weapons he needed for this battle—wasn't even sure he could win this one.

It ate at him that he didn't have the strength to fight it alone, without this blasted cane.

A soldier had to be on guard all the time, and Red was.

John Martin stepped up beside him, looking even more awkward in his old suit than Red did. John had kept growing after high-school graduation, and the sleeves and legs of his jacket and slacks exposed a little too much of his long limbs. Fashions these days were skimpy on material, saving all the excess for the war effort. Even Gerald Potts, who could afford a new suit, wore one he'd had for at least ten years.

"I think you're hopeless, Charles Frederick," John said. "Bertie Moennig's a fine woman, and she needs you over there with her, helping her through her loss, not over here brooding by yourself."

"I'm not brooding, I'm thinking. Besides, Bertie needs something I can't give her."

"That's silly. It doesn't take much to stand beside her, let her know she's not alone."

"And how'm I gonna do that?" Red demanded, gesturing toward his ma, Edith, Ivan and Ivan's dad, who all seemed to be competing for Bertie's attention. "They've got her well in hand. I can't even get close to her right now. Besides, I've got other fish to fry."

"I don't see you frying any fish," John grumbled. "I see you avoiding Bertie because of that limp of yours. You're all hung up about—"

"You can't tell me how to behave with this leg if you ain't gone through it yourself," Red growled back.

John glared at him. "At least you got to come home as a wounded war hero, and you're still alive. Others came home in caskets. And still others are living in shame because they weren't counted worthy to fight for their country."

Red flinched. He knew John had tried to enlist more than once.

"I'm not a coward, Red Meyer," John said.

"I know that," Red said gently. John simply didn't know, and there was no way to explain it to him.

"I'd have done my part if they'd have let me. I'm doing my part here every time I can. I give blood so often I must—"

"Didn't say you was a coward," Red grumbled.

"Yeah, well, sounded different to my ears, but then maybe that's because of the chip on your shoulder. The words must bounce off that big old chip and sound like other words by the time they reach me."

Red sighed. He was tired of apologizing for being so tetchy, but he didn't know how he could manage to act differently. Right now, everything seemed to simmer below the surface, ready to boil over with one word, one wrong look. He knew it, he hated it. He wanted to do something about it, but what?

"You notice anybody who oughta be here but isn't?" he asked, shooting a look around at the crowd. Even the Shorts were here, unwelcome as they were with their foul thoughts and mouths.

"Kruegers aren't here," John said.

"Anyone else?"

"Other than that family, nobody's missing that I'd have expected to be here."

Red turned and studied the individual faces in the crowd. Could there be someone here who wasn't surprised by Joseph's death? Could someone here even have been the one who caused it?

Bertie stared at the casket as others wandered away, chatter growing louder as they prepared for the meal on the church grounds.

It was time to cry now. It was time to say goodbye. Even Lilly and Edith were sniffling beside her, and Arielle was holding a handkerchief to her eyes.

Somehow, though, Bertie's eyes remained dry. She felt as if the tears she had held inside since Monday had petrified in her heart like that forest had done in Arizona.

She stood over the place where her mother's body had been buried for more than three years.

Edith placed a hand lightly on Bertie's shoulder. "You never told me how your mother died. Do you realize she and my Harper died only a few months apart?"

Bertie nodded. She and Edith had never discussed death much. Thoughts of it were too close to both of them. "Mom died of polio. Hard as the doctors and nurses worked over her, nothing they did could save her. Dad and I had already tried every potion Mom ever used on the townsfolk and neighbors around Hideaway—hot onion poultices, hot mustard plaster, mullein, coneflower that grew along the roadsides. Nothing worked, even though these things had done the job many times before."

"You said your mother used to treat sick neighbors?"

"That's right. Mom was the closest we had to a doctor hereabouts, and folks came to her from all over. Hill folk, mostly, who didn't trust modern medicine."

Edith stood beside her in silence.

"In the end," Bertie said, "the doctor accused Dad and me of keeping Mom home too long. He said we were 'experimenting' on her with our 'crazy witchcraft.' I don't think that doctor could've done any more for her if she'd gone to him at the first sign of illness, because there'd been an epidemic in Hideaway, and three of the townsfolk died in spite of all the doctor tried to do."

"Your mother treated them?"

Bertie nodded. "That's the sad thing. Mom caught the polio from a neighbor who had it and refused to travel the long distance to see a doctor. Mom treated this neighbor with those same plants. The neighbor lived."

"Which neighbor was that?"

"Elizabeth Krueger."

After Mom's death, Bertie had cried for days, until she'd begun to wonder if she'd ever stop. Even last week she'd dreamed of Mom and had woken up teary-eyed.

Now she was afraid of those tears. She was going to have to be strong, stand alone.

"It sounds to me as if the herbs worked better than medical science," Edith said.

"But try to tell anybody that," Bertie said, glancing toward Red, who had wandered down toward the riverbank, leaning heavily on his cane.

Lilly placed her heavy arm around Bertie. "You said something to me this morning about treating Red with comfrey. It grows in the woods on your place, doesn't it?"

"Yes, above the cliffs over the James River, where the caves are."

The arm tightened. "Honey, it's about to break my heart, watchin' him brood the way he is. You really think it'll help that leg of his?"

Bertie nodded. "If he'd let me try it, I think it could help."

"I know most folks would scoff. They'd say no leaf could help where a doctor's best medicine won't bring healing, but I'm desperate. It could be just your loving touch that'd help more than anything."

That was all Bertie needed. "I think I'll have another talk with Red."

"That's my girl." Lilly gave her shoulders a final squeeze, then looked down at Joseph's casket. "Your father was always so proud of you, Roberta Moennig. He had every right to be. You're the sweetest possible combination of your mother and your father, with a whole lot of just plain ol' Bertie thrown into the mix."

With those words, Bertie said her final goodbye to her father, then walked away from the burial site, past the churchyard, where most of the women, and at least half the men, were involved in setting up for the meal, while children played on the grass.

The ladies of the church knew how to set a table with all the best produce from their victory gardens. Lilly had already sent Ivan to the house to collect her beans, ham, cornbread and cobbler. John's mother, Cora Lee Martin, carried another cobbler, proud of the berries her son had picked.

You've got people who love you, Bertie. They'd told her that, and she believed it, but *someone* in this town didn't love her. It was hard to feel welcome with all that was going on.

She walked steadfastly toward Red's receding figure, not knowing what kind of reception she'd get from him. He was so moody lately, one minute making her think he still cared about her, and the next minute shoving her away from him, almost like she was poison.

No matter what happened between them, she'd do the best she could to help him heal—as much as he'd let her do—and she would stay in Hideaway. In spite of all the wondering about who might be behind Dad's death, in spite of the ugly messages someone had been leaving, this place was home. She loved California, sure enough. It was beautiful. The mountains and the ocean, which she'd never seen before this past year, made her think of God's majesty. His bigness. His power.

But these Ozark hills had been made by God, too. He had created the medicinal, nourishing plants that grew here. It was here, if anywhere, that Red would finally find healing.

The tears came then, as she realized how afraid she'd been this week. And she was still afraid of the future. Mom had always told her not to trust feelings, but to trust in the Word, because the Word would last through feelings. Mom had always quoted Job, "Though He slay me, yet will I trust Him."

But what was trust? Sure, Bertie knew she'd be in heaven when she died, but was that all there was to trusting Him? What about here and now, on earth, when loved ones died or went to war and came back changed?

Besides a happy afterlife, what did she have to look forward to?

As old, familiar voices of longtime friends drifted across the cemetery, Bertie fought the loneliness and fear with silent prayer.

Neighbors and friends had all spoken to her today, hugged her, told her, "If there's anything we can do, just holler."

She'd nodded and thanked them, knowing she probably would never holler. But also knowing that at least some of those friends would be there when she needed them.

Chapter Thirty-Two

Red was halfway down the bank to the river's edge when he heard soft footsteps behind him. He turned his head just enough to recognize Bertie's blond hair.

She didn't give up.

He turned around, leaning on his cane. "Been a bad week for you," he said.

She climbed down an incline and stopped in front of him, but didn't say anything. He knew that look in her eyes. She had something on her mind. Still, she needed to hear what he had to say.

"Awful bad week," he repeated. "I know you don't believe it now, but it doesn't always hurt this way."

She nodded and turned to step down closer to the water's edge. "I know you wouldn't say that if you didn't know it was true. But you still have your mother and brother and sister. Sometimes it seems I'm about to lose everything and everybody I've ever cared about."

He winced. "I know it does."

She kept walking.

"Bertie?"

She stopped and turned, looking up at him.

"I've done a lot of things wrong," he said at last, scrambling over some rocks to her side. "I shouldn't've been so hard on you this week. Seems like everything I say turns to—"

"You did fine," she said gently. "I know you've had a lot on your mind, too. I know you thought a lot of Dad. You're just trying to keep me safe and find out what happened at the same time. That's a hard job. I know all that."

He waited for a but. It didn't come, and he just stood there for several seconds looking down at her stupidly. "That's right. I'm glad you understand."

She held a hand up. "I understand that just fine."

Oh, no, here came the but.

"What I don't understand is why you didn't tell me about your leg."

He sighed. "What is it you want to know about it?"

She looked down at the cane, which he leaned on heavily. "Why didn't you tell me before I had to see it for myself?"

"I didn't want you to worry."

She frowned up at him, eyes narrowing. She could see through him better than anyone he'd ever known.

"I kept thinking it'd get better," he said, not able to meet her eyes. "Didn't want to worry anybody."

"You didn't want to *worry* anybody? Why did you stop answering my letters, then? You don't think I was plenty worried about that?"

He grimaced and looked out across the rippling water. "At first, I just thought I'd heal and it'd be fine, so I didn't say anything about it in my letters. Didn't want to sound like a whiner."

"And so when you didn't heal? Why didn't you tell me then?"

He still didn't look back at her. "You know me too well, Bertie. You'd've known something was wrong if I'd tried to write to you then. Besides, a lot of the time I was hurting too bad to do much but lay there and wish I was dead."

"You gonna tell me about it now?"

"Not much to tell."

"You got shot?"

"Got shelled."

"From what I hear, a shelling could blow a man's leg clear off. Or his head. Or make mincemeat of his whole body."

"It didn't. Just sliced through muscle and bone."

"When did it happen?"

He sighed. "Last of March. Medic couldn't get to me for a few hours, because of the battle, and it was daylight. Then they couldn't get me to a hospital because we were still under attack."

"It's a special blessing that your leg was saved."

He gritted his teeth. He didn't want to hear about blessings right now. "Guessed you'd say something like that."

"You're alive, Red. After everything I've read about the war, your very life's a special blessing. At least it is for me."

He looked at her then. When she was like this she could talk a stubborn mule into plowing the moon. "I don't see it that way," he said. "You don't have any idea where I've been or what I've done, so don't go talking to me like you know all about it."

She frowned at him. "Now you do sound like a whiner, and I know better. Red Meyer's never been one to complain about the hard things that had happened in his life, the things he'd had to do without after his father died."

"Red Meyer's always been healthy before."

"You're walking," she said. "Even if it is with a cane."

He shrugged. "They say penicillin's a miracle drug."

"I'm sure they're right, but just because they've treated you with their miracle doesn't mean God's other miracles are worthless now."

He nodded.

"So you'll let me use comfrey on that leg?" she asked. "I overheard Gerald say he's going fishing this afternoon. I know his favorite fishing hole is down on the river, just below the comfrey I need to collect."

"No."

"I'd be perfectly safe if he's there, too."

Red groaned and turned away. "Bertie, don't start this."

He heard her step up beside him, and he moved away. "I didn't come down here for company. I came down to do some thinking. Alone. You need to go back to the church." Without looking at her, he limped along the river's edge, leaving her behind.

Bertie watched Red's retreating back, feeling grief threaten to overwhelm her again. But she wasn't going in that direction this time. Instead, she allowed her loss to fuel a quick spurt of anger.

"Don't you dare treat me like this!" she called after him. When his steps slowed at the sound of her words, she caught up with him. "I'm only wanting to help you, and you're treating me like a pesky puppy."

"You don't know anything about this, Bertie, so just simmer down."

"Well, I *should* know about it." She risked his anger by stepping in front of him. "You don't think I've earned just a little more respect from you? I've been true to you for three years. With all those pages of letters I wrote to you, I could've written a dozen books."

He blinked at her, swallowed, nodded. "Maybe more." He didn't look mad.

"But I wanted to write to you. You're the one I've put all my hopes in, the one I've waited for."

"I didn't ask you to." It amazed her that such a harsh statement could be spoken with such gentleness.

"You said that to me this morning, too. I'm tired of hearing it." She heard a quiver in her voice, and that tiny sign of weakness made her mad all over again. "Something's bothering you that you haven't told anybody, because I know you better than this. You don't mope, and you're not the cranky type. Not the way you've been since I got back."

He grunted and closed his eyes. "You don't know me now."

"So you keep reminding me, and that's just ridiculous. A fella doesn't change the core of who he has been all his life. Maybe your outlook on life is changed, but who you are inside won't change. Not your character. Not the person God made you to be."

He shook his head. "You can't even guess, Bertie."

"Yes, I can. Up until a few weeks ago, I got letters from you all the time. You weren't afraid to tell me what was going through your mind. So something happened just before the end of things over in Italy." She gestured to his leg. "Something more than that. Don't shut me out like this, Red. It isn't fair to me."

He looked down at the cane in his hand, then turned and gazed toward the edge of the forest across the river.

For the longest moment, all was silent except for the birdsong echoing from the trees, and the sigh of the wind through the leaves.

"You're right," he said at last. "It isn't fair to you." He looked down at her and laid a hand on her shoulder, and all the love she'd ever seen in his eyes or read from his letters was suddenly, amazingly, plain on his face. "You need to understand why everything's changed, and then you need to let it go."

Chapter Thirty-Three

Before Bertie could respond to the touch of Red's hand, he pulled away, as if he'd done something wrong.

"A week before I got hit," he said, "our scouting team was captured by the German Army." The soft, matter-of-fact voice contradicted the shock of the message.

Bertie felt the jolt of his words all the way to her toes. She swallowed and didn't say anything, not wanting to break his momentum now that she had him talking.

He gave her a brief glance, then looked away again. "I haven't told anybody about this."

"You can tell me."

"I'd appreciate it if you..." he paused, then shook his head. "No, that ain't right. I can't dump bad news on you and then expect you to keep it bottled up. I did that to Ma."

"Red, I won't say anything to anyone unless you want me to." She reached out and touched his arm, and felt the hard muscles underneath the sleeve of his suit coat. Her Red. "Just tell me. I want so much to understand."

He hesitated. "I will, but you've gotta promise me one thing."

"You name it."

"Don't go giving me a sermon about how I should get over this and move on with my life. I don't want a pep talk."

"I promise."

"And don't go trying to remind me about the great blessing of life."

She flinched at that. "Okay. I guess it was pretty stupid of me to try to tell you about blessings when you're suffering so with your leg. I know how I felt yesterday when Mrs. Fisher sidled up to me and whispered about how happy I must be that Dad's now with the Lord."

His brows lowered. "She said that?"

"Yep, she did. I'm sorry, Red. I for sure won't do that to you again."

A bare nod as he looked toward the sky, jaw muscles working. She could see from the strain in his expression that he was suddenly reliving something awful.

She almost told him to forget it, that it wasn't any of her business, and it wasn't worth making him go through it all over again, but she needed to know. She felt, after everything, that it most certainly was her business. Maybe her very most important business right now.

"One of our captors was this young kid," he said at last, turning to stare back up the bank in the direction of the church, though the church wasn't visible from where they stood. "Looked to be fifteen, sixteen, mouthy and mean, always beating up on us, pulling ugly tricks on us, then laughing." Red took a deep breath. "Always stirring up trouble."

Bertie swallowed hard. She wanted to ask how long they'd been captured, just exactly how mean this soldier was, how they were rescued, she wanted all the details quickly. She pressed her lips together and squeezed his arm, wanting so badly to wrap her arms around him that it became a physical need.

But she knew he needed her not to. He was a grown man who didn't want mothering. He'd already made that clear enough this morning.

He looked down at her, as if memorizing the features of her face, then he looked away again. "Kid's name was Fritz. Blond hair, dark, snapping eyes, never took guff off anybody, even though he had to've been the youngest in his squad."

He closed his eyes. "He could've been a Moennig, Bertie. Could've been a bratty little brother of yours. He looked so much like you and Lloyd when we were growing up."

The thought stung her. She still had relatives in Germany, of course. But just because he'd looked like her didn't mean they had a blood bond.

"I decided to see if I could talk to him," Red said. "I know a little German I picked up from Pa's side of the family, and I tried a word or two on him."

"What did he do?"

"Laughed at me, mostly. Made fun of me to his buddies. I kept trying, anyway, for those few days they held us." Red looked down at his leg, then turned and walked along the rough track beside the river.

Bertie held on to his arm and walked beside him.

"He released us all one night."

She stumbled on a rock, and felt Red's arm tense beneath her hand, steadying her. "The bully released you?"

Red nodded, not breaking his stride. "Came to us while we were sleeping, untied our bonds, and kicked us awake. Just like that."

"But why?"

His steps slowed. He sighed, shook his head. "I never knew."

"He didn't say anything?"

"He didn't know our language, as far as I could tell." Again, that shake of the head. "At first, we were afraid it was a trap. We were sure he was just releasing us so they'd have a good reason to shoot us while we were on the run, though the Germans never needed an excuse to kill their prisoners. They just killed them."

"But he let you go."

Red disengaged from Bertie's grasp, fumbled with the cane, and bent over and picked up a flat rock. He drew back with his right hand and skipped the rock across the smooth surface of the moving water. It skipped six times, if Bertie was counting right. His rock-skipping skills were getting awkward.

"I'm pretty sure that runty soldier saved all of us," Red said, bending over to pick up another flat rock. "I'd understood a few words that passed between the men the day before, though I'm so rusty with my German I only knew a little. From what words I caught, it sounded like they were planning to kill us soon."

"That's why you thought the release was a trick," Bertie said. "But why did he—"

"I don't know. Our team talked about it later, as we

made our way back to camp. We couldn't come up with any reasons, 'ceptin' it was a miracle from God." He looked down at her. "Yes, there you go, I said it. I believe it was a miracle. Some answers to all those prayers you were prayin'. We were so glad to get out of there with our lives, we didn't hang around and ask questions." He paused and closed his eyes. "Didn't even take the time to thank him."

"Word never reached us back home that you were a prisoner of war," Bertie said.

"We weren't missing long enough. We went right back to work when the next battle broke out." He tossed the rock into the water, not even trying to skip it this time—as if the act of sinking that rock into the river was satisfying enough.

She waited for him to continue. Yes, it would've been a horrible experience to go through, wondering if he was going to be killed by his captors at any moment, but he'd lived through three years of that kind of threat.

"Four days after we reached our company, fresh battle broke out," he said. "I think the Germans knew time was gettin' short, so they decided to kill all they could while they had a chance."

"That's when your leg was hit?"

He stopped, leaning heavily on the cane. Splashes from ripples along the river's edge filled the silence. "I got caught in a foxhole, separated from the rest of my team. Two men had been there before me, and didn't make it out. They were dead at the far end of the hole. I heard footsteps coming toward me, and I saw a German helmet peering over the edge of the hole." His eyes closed. He swallowed, as if words had suddenly caught in his throat. "I shot him. Got him straight-on in the chest, killed him just like that." Red snapped his fingers.

Bertie waited, holding her breath.

"He fell into the mud beside me without a single cry. Face-first into that thick mud." Red looked at her, his blue eyes filmed with moisture, his face filled with horror. "It was the kid who'd saved our lives."

She felt the shock of his words through her whole body, felt a shadow of the pain he must be feeling. Instinctively, she reached for him, but he backed away, as if he was afraid of her touch, her comfort.

But at the moment, she felt as if she was the one who needed comforting. Just seeing what Red had gone through cut her deeply.

"When no one else followed him into the foxhole, I went to him and turned him over. There were those blue eyes, staring without life into the sky, looking like he could've been a brother of yours. I couldn't stay there, Bertie. Not facing what I'd done."

"Red, it was war. You did what you had to do, what you were taught to do."

He cast her a sharp glance.

"Sorry," she said, glimpsing the raw memory of that moment in his eyes. She knew she would always see it there. Nothing she could say or do would help him heal that wound. Only God could do that, and she'd promised not to preach.

"Anyway, you're right. That's when I got hit. There've been times I wished the shrapnel had found a more deadly place to lodge."

"But it didn't, and you can't go wishing your life

away. Did you ever think, even though Fritz let you go, he would've shot you then?"

He gave her another sharp glance.

She couldn't hold his gaze, nor her tongue. "I said I wouldn't preach, and I won't, but I didn't promise to keep my mouth shut completely."

He continued to watch her. She grimaced.

"Don't know how I'm going to live with this," he said, looking away at last. "I for sure don't expect anybody else to put up with me while I try to find a way through it. I've heard stories of men in the first war who were shellshocked and never came out of it. I couldn't put anybody through what they put their families through. Especially not my Bertie."

Those words—my Bertie—felt to her like a physical caress.

"We've already had this fight," she said gently. "I'm not changing my mind."

"You don't have a choice." He turned from her then, and walked along the riverside, shoulders squared, back stiff.

"You're right," she called after him. "I don't have a choice. My heart already belongs to you." She didn't follow him, but watched him go. She wasn't finished with him, and whether he liked it or not, she'd developed a little more perseverance about waiting since he went off to war. She could be patient.

Chapter Thirty-Four

The last thing Red wanted to do was mingle with a bunch of people after reliving that harsh memory to Bertie, but after a long, silent talk with himself, he returned to the church grounds. He could talk to people while he ate his ma's ham and beans and Bertie's dishpan cookies, discussed the crops and the price of cattle and hogs with Herbert Morrow and Homer Jarvis.

Homer Jarvis, he discovered, thought Earl Krueger had been the culprit in the recent livestock rustling, because he'd needed the money the stock brought at the sale barn to make his yearly mortgage payment, which had been overdue for a month.

Furthermore, Herbert Morrow believed Joseph Moennig had tracked down Krueger and confronted him as the thief. Then, after killing Joseph, Krueger took off with his family. When Red asked Morrow who might have been behind the vandalism at Joseph's house on Thursday, Morrow thought maybe Krueger had slipped back into town when no one was looking.

It seemed quite a few folks thought Krueger was a Nazi sympathizer, and they were glad to be rid of him.

John Martin's mother, Cora Lee, interrupted their discussion. "Red Meyer, you need to try a helping of my raspberry cobbler." She handed him a dish with red berries oozing from beneath a crispy crust, topped by ice cream. "John cranked the ice-cream freezer himself."

Already full as a tick, Red accepted the dessert and thanked her, excused himself from the group to walk around the churchyard.

He tried hard not to look at Bertie, but sight of her drew him like being pulled around by a mule on a thick lead rope. There was no missing the sadness in her eyes that he'd put there with his own confession.

He saw Arielle Potts working beside his mother at the serving line, and recalled what she'd told him about the Bald Knobbers. The real reason those rascals ran so many people off their farms in Taney County was because they knew the railroad was coming in.

It was only hearsay, of course, that the property of those farmers who were frightened into leaving their homes just happened to be on that line. He'd probably been gazing down at some of those very plots of land when he rode the train in on Monday.

There was no railroad going in now, but there were plans for a dam. Which would mean a lake. The Moennig and Krueger property might all be lakeshore in a few years. A fella might buy it cheap, and make a killin' on it in a few years when the dam went in at Branson, if he was willing to wait that long.

From what Red had heard, it seemed the Kruegers were about to lose their place. If the bank foreclosed on the loan, it could do pretty much anything it wanted to get that money back. Red wondered who might have profited from that.

He'd spent some time with Wyatt Brown in Italy last year, before Wyatt got shot up and sent home. He'd heard Wyatt got a job over in Galena, the county seat, after he recovered. It was a wild guess, but could be someone had already made a move on the Krueger place. Maybe Wyatt could look up that information for him.

Definitely a crazy theory, but worth checking into.

Hideaway was already a resort town, with many wealthy folks from all over the country vacationing here. How much more popular would it become with a lake? The Moennig place would for sure be on that shore.

Could Joseph have lost his life because someone wanted his land?

Red took his dish back to the serving table and handed it to Cora Lee Martin. "Have you seen Bertie around anywhere?" he asked her.

"Sure did, Red. She took off walking down the road a while back. Poor thing. I know she's plumb worn out from all this."

"Did anyone go with her?"

"Not that I noticed." Cora Lee glanced at him skeptically. "She's a grown woman, Red, she can walk herself home, I expect."

He thanked her and went to find Ivan, who, predictably, was sitting on a blanket under a shady tree, talking to Edith, who was taking a brief rest from serving.

Red asked Edith if she knew where Bertie had gone.

"I'm sure she just got tired and went to your house," Edith said. "She probably needed a nap, since she barely slept last night."

"She didn't say anything about going to gather comfrey leaves, did she?" Red asked.

"I don't think she would go by herself," Edith said. "Not after our experience yesterday."

Red figured he knew Bertie a little better than her roommate of eight months knew her.

"Not to worry," Ivan said. "Even if she did go, Dad's gone to his favorite fishing hole, and that's just below the Moennig place. She'll be safe." He stretched his long legs and leaned back against the sycamore tree, looking relaxed and happy to be home.

Red turned away. He would check the house, and if Bertie wasn't there, he'd saddle Seymour and go—

He turned back, and looked down at Ivan's shoe… where there was a deep gash in the left heel.

"Ivan, are those your shoes?"

Ivan frowned at him, then looked down at his shoes. "They are now. Why?"

"Where'd you get 'em?"

"Dad gave them to me to wear today. He's breaking in some new ones."

"They're your *father's?*"

"Well, did you expect me to wear my combat boots to the funeral? All my others were too tight on me. These are Dad's old shoes. Not dressy, but for everyday."

Red realized the mistake he'd made, thinking the print he'd been tracking was from a work boot because the shoe was so wide and long. Extra width for a sturdy work boot. But the extra width on these shoes was because they were a larger size shoe, made to fit a man with a larger foot. Like Gerald Potts.

The very thought led Red to other thoughts that made him suddenly sick.

"I've got to get to Bertie."

"Why, Red?" Ivan asked. "I told you, Dad's going out that way."

"How do you know he's there yet? I don't feel safe leaving her alone. You know how much trouble Bertie can get herself into without thinkin' twice."

Ivan looked at Edith, and together they got to their feet.

"We'll take my car," Ivan said.

Once upon a time, Bertie had been able to ride her bicycle anywhere she wanted, even out into the field to take water to Dad and Lloyd when they were planting or gathering—when she wasn't working alongside them. With a hundred and twenty acres of land—ninety of which were good for crops—it had taken the whole family and sometimes several of the boys from town to help gather the hay into their big barn.

This morning she walked, carrying a scratchy burlap bag from Seymour's stable over her arm. She would collect the comfrey she needed, then carry it back to the house and scrub herself down to remove any summer critters that might have hitched a ride on her clothing—Lilly said it had been a bad summer for ticks.

Then she would boil the comfrey for tea; the large leaves she would use as dressing. The leaves were a perfect size for that kind of a poultice.

The old cow trail was still a well-used path to the riverbank, with gooseberry bushes and blackberry brambles only a few steps from the trail. She would come back another day to pick berries. Today, she was gathering something much more important.

Red would most likely put up a fight, but now that Lilly was as determined as Bertie to help him heal, she thought between the two of them they'd convince him to at least try it.

Oh, Lord, touch his heart and heal him, she prayed as she stepped over an old tree root that used to trip her when she was a kid. *He's been through so much.*

She couldn't imagine how she would have reacted to the horror Red had endured these past three years. She was surprised more men didn't come back from the war shellshocked, unable to function. She hated war with a passion.

And yet she knew the alternative could have been a whole world under the evil reign of Nazi Germany— with Hitler the supreme commander. Red and Ivan and the men who had fought this war were heroes. Why couldn't Red realize how much his sacrifice meant to her? To everyone?

She found the comfrey plants exactly where they had always been, watered by a tiny spring on the hillside, just above the cliffs that dropped down to the largest of the caves at the foot of the hill. She was bending down to collect the first few huge leaves—which would work so well to wrap around Red's knee and thigh—when she heard voices below her.

She couldn't quite make out the words, but she did recognize Gerald's deep voice. That was nothing new. The riverbank below was a popular fishing spot for the locals, who knew where to catch the best striper on the river. She'd known he would be down there today.

But as she continued to collect the leaves, the tone of Gerald's voice changed. He sounded angry.

Frowning, she broke the final comfrey leaf from its stem, eased it gently into the bag on the ground, then, curious, she stepped over to the edge of the cliff and looked down. All she could see were the tops of two heads, two men in separate flat-bottomed boats, directly below her.

Gerald wore the old fishing hat he always wore. Gramercy Short was the other man, his balding head already turning pink in the sun.

"Look, we had an agreement," Gramercy snapped, his voice echoing along the water. "My silence for a price. You owe me."

As the words registered, Bertie took a step backward. This didn't feel like a place she wanted to be right now.

"We agreed this would be a long-term investment of our mutual time and silence," Gerald said.

"Don't give me your highfalutin words. I don't want no long-term nothing! I'm not waiting 'til the lake comes in. I could be dead by then. I want my share now."

"You should know I don't have that kind of money. Where would I get it?"

"Don't try to pull that one on me, Potts. Everybody knows your wife's family is loaded to the gills."

There was a silence, then came Gerald's voice, low and cold—so soft, Bertie wouldn't've heard him, except their voices carried from the water up the side of the cliff like a natural amplifier.

"You leave my wife out of this."

There was a wicked chuckle. "But isn't that what this is all about? Me leaving everyone else out of our little discovery?"

"It was an accident!"

"Hideaway needs to have another accident. Or did you talk little Miss Moennig into selling?"

"I never said anything about the Moennig farm."

"You said you'd see to it that—"

The ground shifted beneath Bertie's feet. She gasped, scrambling backward. The voices hushed below as rocks and pebbles splashed and echoed.

She needed to grab her bag of leaves and get out of here before—

The ground beneath her gave way completely. There was a shout from below, and she screamed. Suddenly she was tumbling down amidst mud and gravel. Rocks dug into her legs and gouged her shoulders.

She hit the river with a splash of shocking cold. Water stung her nose and she gagged. Her feet touched the rocky bottom as more pebbles rained down on her from above.

When she broke surface the stones had stopped falling, but as she blinked her eyes and her vision cleared, she saw something more dangerous.

Gramercy Short was on his knees in the boat, and he had his paddle raised over his head, directly above her.

"Short!" Gerald called from behind him. "What are you doing? Are you crazy?"

The paddle started down. Bertie didn't wait. She dove beneath the surface again, clawing her way beneath Short's boat to avoid his weapon. She came out on the other side, gasping for breath, only to find Gramercy in the water with her, reaching for her, his face twisted with some kind of vicious determination.

He snagged her by the hem of her skirt as she tried to swim away. She went under, choked, fought her way back to the surface, coughing.

"No!" Gerald shouted behind her.

"Looks like trouble has decided to pay us a call," Short said. "Probably another one of those Nazis you're so eager to kill."

"Let her go, Short!" Gerald said. "Bertie isn't a part of this."

"Sure she is," Gramercy said, treading water, gripping his boat with one hand and more of Bertie's skirt with the other. "This little gal's up to her neck in it, 'specially if you're collecting lakeshore land. Her father's gone, and I've heard her brother has tuberculosis. With her out of the way, we'd have that much more stock in our company."

"There's no stock! No company!" Gerald snapped. "Let her go, Short. Now!"

Gramercy dragged Bertie under. She kicked and struggled against him, but here she couldn't touch bottom, couldn't reach the surface.

She was going to die.

Fingers dug cruelly into her arm. She kicked and shoved and tried to dive away.

She heard a shout that was loud enough to penetrate the water and her terror. "Short!"

She fought those hands, kicking, thrusting her body toward the surface, fighting with desperation for her life. He shoved her again, and as her body went down, he kicked her hard in the ribs. His fingers dug into her throat, squeezing. Darkness surrounded her. Blackness smothered her.

Then suddenly, it ended. He released her. She floated for a bare second or two, unable to find her bearings. Before she could force her arms and legs to move, her hair was caught in a painful grip, and she felt herself being jerked upward.

Air kissed her face, and she sucked it into her lungs in greedy gasps. Strong hands pulled her to the shore. She blinked, then looked up to see Gerald hovering over her, his face pale, wide, terrified eyes suddenly filling with relief.

"Bertie? I'm so sorry."

She looked back where she had been. Gramercy Short's thick body floated face down in the water, bumping against Gerald's boat as it tried to float downstream with the current. His arms were splayed out beside him, bald head shining in the sun, with a gash in the back of it that had stopped bleeding.

Gerald reached down and pulled the man over, pressed his fingers to his neck, then closed his eyes and shook his head.

Gramercy Short was dead.

Chapter Thirty-Five

In spite of the cane, the pain in his leg, the weakness, Red had no trouble leading Ivan, Edith and John through the brush and up the incline to the top of the cliffs, where he heard splashing, where he'd heard shouting just seconds before. Now, he heard someone gasping for breath.

"Bertie!" he shouted.

Red crested the cliff and nearly fell down the other side, where the earth had obviously given way, providing a long slide of rocks and dirt from the cliff top into the river twenty feet below.

What he saw froze him, and he held a hand up for the others to use caution as they joined him. He dropped to his knees. Bertie was lying on the riverbank, drenched, coughing.

Gerald stood half in half out of the water, staring down at Bertie, his face white. Gramercy Short lay in the water, and his lifeless body was bumping against Gerald's flat-bottomed boat.

Bertie turned to Gerald, still catching her breath.

"I killed him," he told her, his voice carrying upward. "I didn't know what else to do. He just about had you."

Gerald looked down at the oar, and at his own hands, and then back at Bertie. "He was killing you."

"Dad!" Ivan cried, and started down the cliff.

Red grabbed him. "Wait, Ivan. Something else is up."

Ivan tried to pull away, but Red held him firm. "We need to have a talk with your father."

Ivan turned to him. "Why? Isn't it obvious what happened? Short's been up to his old tricks. Looks like he tried to get to Bertie this time."

Red looked back down at his best friend's father, the man he and Bertie had known all their lives. "What was it, Gerald?"

Gerald didn't answer. He dropped to his knees beside Bertie.

"Dad?" Ivan pulled from Red's grip. "What's he talking about? What's going on here?"

Still on his knees, Red turned to his side and released his cane. Using his hands, ignoring the pain, he slid down the steep cliff side, using the dirt from the recent collapse to break his fall. He reached Bertie where she lay drenched and shivering, and pulled her into his arms.

"Dad?" Ivan said. "Tell me what's happening."

"I didn't mean to do it—"

"Gerald," Bertie said softly, "Gramercy said something about a deal you two had made. Why did he try to kill me? What's going on?"

"The sheriff's coming," Red told Gerald. "You'd better practice your story on us."

"I don't have a story, Red." Gerald sounded utterly beaten. "It was all a horrible mistake."

"You can tell that to the sheriff, too," Red said. "I don't suppose you'd believe that your own wife and son are the ones that helped give you away."

Gerald looked up at Ivan, and tears filled his eyes. "Oh, son, what have I done?"

"I don't know, Dad," Ivan called down. "Tell me. Please. Help me understand what's going on here."

"The shoes you were wearing when you laid all those limbs," Red said, "and turned our horse out and put your vile mark on our stable were the same shoes you let Ivan wear to the funeral today."

He felt Bertie's shoulders shake with sobs, and drew her to his chest.

"I didn't do those things, Red," Gerald's voice, already too soft, sounded as if it was losing strength. "I made some bad moves, did some wicked things, but I would never have hurt Joseph if I'd known it was him."

Red felt Bertie tense. She pulled away, dashing the tears from her face with the back of her hand. "You killed my father?"

Gerald covered his face with his hands. A moan came from his throat. "I never meant to kill him," he said, then looked over at Gramercy's body. "I never meant to kill anybody. With Short, I didn't know what else to do to save you, Bertie. I couldn't get to him in time to wrestle him away from you. There was no other way."

Bertie shivered again. "I can't be hearing this. Not you, Gerald."

"Dad." Ivan's voice thickened with pain. "You killed Joseph?"

Gerald closed his eyes and covered his face with his hands. "I didn't… I didn't know it was him, I swear it."

"Who did you think it was?" Red demanded.

Gerald reached a hand out as if to touch Bertie. She shrunk away from him.

He shook his head. "I thought it was Krueger, and I thought Krueger was a Nazi infiltrator. I still think that. I *knew* he was the cattle thief, because I caught him at it. I didn't even mean to kill him, just run him out of Hideaway."

"And get his land?" Bertie asked, remembering something else she'd overheard between the men when they were arguing.

Gerald winced. "I'm sorry. I didn't see that it would hurt anyone, with the cattle thief gone."

"And you hit my father instead of Krueger?" Bertie asked. "Why? What were you doing on our land?"

"It didn't happen on your land," Gerald said. "It was on Krueger's land. I'd just followed him from your place, where he'd tried to rustle another calf from your herd. I'd gotten tired of waiting for the sheriff to help us with our rustling problem and the vandalism, and I decided to take it on myself to find who was doing it."

"So it really was Krueger doing the rustling?" Red asked.

Gerald nodded. "I didn't realize Joseph had also been watching him. By the time I followed Krueger back to his place after his failed attempt to catch the calf, it was getting dark. I turned and saw a shadow of someone behind me, thought it was Krueger, and that he was coming after me. I grabbed the first thing I could find to hit him. It was a board. I didn't realize until afterward that it had nails in it. When I saw that it wasn't Krueger, but Joseph, I think I... I know I went a little crazy."

"But why did you try to hide it?" Bertie asked.

"I'm sorry, Bertie. I didn't mean to hurt you. I never meant to hurt your father, I was trying to help. But when I discovered what I'd done, and Krueger witnessed it, I threatened to tell the sheriff that Krueger was the one who killed Joseph. It would have been easy to convince Butch, especially since Krueger was the rustler. I was also thinking of my wife and son. How could I let Ivan come home from that war to find his father had killed the father of one of his best friends?"

"But Dad, you lied to save yourself," Ivan said. "You let Bertie and Red and the rest of us wonder all this time who could have done this. You even encouraged Red to try to find the killer. Why?"

Gerald shook his head. "I thought Red would surely come to the same conclusion everyone else has. I told Krueger if he would pack up and leave immediately, I wouldn't tell the sheriff anything, but I wanted that land."

"For Ivan's future," Red said.

Gerald nodded. "Forgive me, I was thinking of my wife and son. The Exchange is doing okay financially, but we don't have land, nothing to leave for our son. Nothing from me. Only from Arielle's family. I'm a proud enough man I need to know I've passed a legacy on to my son and grandchildren."

"With the dam coming in a few years," Red said, "Krueger's property will be lakefront property."

Gerald nodded. "Like I said, I'd do anything for my son."

"What about the swastikas, the gassed cat in Bertie's house?" Red asked.

Gerald shook his head, gesturing to Gramercy's body. "I'm thinking he did it. There's no other reason he'd have been at Krueger's house the night of Joseph's death, because he never made a secret of the fact that he hated Krueger. He came to me later and told me he saw what I did, and he wanted a cut."

"He was blackmailing you?" Ivan asked.

Gerald nodded, then looked at Bertie, sorrow etched deeply into every line of a face that seemed to have aged far too much in the past few minutes. "That wasn't why I killed him, Bertie. You have to believe that. I couldn't let him hurt you. I'd rather go to prison for the rest of my life than be responsible for your death."

Red's arms automatically tightened around her as Ivan scrambled down the cliff side to his father.

This was just one more wound that would haunt the history of Hideaway.

Red and Bertie made it to the top of the cliff before Edith returned with a blanket and wrapped it around Bertie. Its warmth felt good, in spite of the heat of the day. Bertie wasn't sure she would ever recover from the chill that had settled deep inside her.

And yet, the healing touch of Red's concern, his obvious caring, his dedication to her safety was beginning to work its way through the icy feel of her skin.

Edith hugged her tightly. "Are you going to be okay, honey?" she whispered in Bertie's ear.

Bertie lied. "I'll be fine."

"Then I'll leave you in Red's capable care. The sheriff's loading Gerald in his car. John's with Ivan, and they're going to go tell Arielle what's happened."

Bertie nodded. "You go on. I'll be...okay."

Edith kissed her on the cheek, squeezed Red's arm, and turned to follow the trail back to the farmhouse.

Bertie felt battered as she walked beside Red up the cow trail behind Edith. She couldn't bear to think about Gerald. How could she ever face Ivan or Arielle again? How would *Gerald* ever be able to face his family?

"I kind of know how Gerald feels," Red said, his voice quiet, filled with the sadness that Bertie felt.

"You didn't kill a neighbor, then try to hide the truth for your own benefit."

Red looked down at her. "Who is my neighbor? Someone who lives down the road from me? Or is it someone who saved my life once?"

"Red, you were fighting a war. You did what you had to do."

"Gerald was trying to find the cattle rustler. Yes, he lost his way, and didn't own up to what he did. You may never forgive him for what he did to your father. I figure there'll always be someone in Germany who'll never forgive me for killing their son, their brother."

"But it's not the same thing."

He stopped and turned to her. Still leaning on his cane, with his free hand he reached up and cupped the side of her face. "I've been doing some thinking, and I've decided you're not gonna get any easier to handle."

"You make me sound like a plow mule."

A shadow of the old Red peeked from his eyes. "As

long as you keep stepping into trouble, you're gonna need somebody to follow along behind and get you out."

"You have anybody in mind for that chore?" she asked.

He shrugged. "I figure there's nobody around who knows you better than I do, so I'll have to take the job to make sure it gets done right."

She gazed up into those beautiful blue eyes that reflected the color of the James River on a sunny day. "What are you saying?"

"I'm saying I'll have to do all I can to get this leg better if I'm gonna keep up with you. I think you came out here to gather comfrey."

She nodded.

"Then maybe we should get started on those treatments as soon as possible."

"You mean now? Today?"

He nodded.

She threw her arms around him. Finally, he realized it was possible to heal. Her Red was coming home at last.

"There was another death two thousand years ago that covers everything we've seen in this war," Red said, still holding her, his touch gentle, loving.

"He paid it all then," she said. "The Savior willingly laid down His life for me, for you, for Fritz."

"For Gerald."

She nodded.

"It helps me to think about that when I think about Fritz," Red said. "I don't know if Fritz or his family will ever forgive what I did to him, but I know now that I had no choice. It was war. I had to fight, or I could've died, and then you and Ma and a lot of other people would have been going through what his family must be going through now."

"You'll probably always have that ache in your chest when you think about Fritz, but living with the constant guilt isn't the best way to honor Fritz's death."

Red reached up and touched her cheek. "I think you're right."

"I'm sorry. I'm preaching," she said. "You told me not to do that."

He pulled her closer. "Do you know how much I've missed you? I didn't realize a feller could miss a gal so much, especially when she's right up on the next floor in the same house."

She let him draw her to his chest, so grateful to see signs of her old Red back in place, she wanted to sing in spite of the day's pain. Instead, she kissed him. And then she kissed him again, and very nearly swooned right over when he kissed her back with all the fervor of the old Red.

She let him wrap her in his strong arms, and she rested her head on his chest, and thanked God in her heart for the touch of the man she loved more than anyone else in the world.

"I don't suppose you'd ever given any thought to my question last year," he said, his voice rumbling deep in his chest.

"Which question?"

"The one where I asked if you'd be interested in never leaving Hideaway again, once we returned."

She leaned back to look up at him. "Why, Red Meyer,

if that isn't a proposal, then I've not learned to read you as well as I thought I had."

He drew her close again, tangling his fingers in her hair. "Will you marry me, Roberta Moennig?"

"You'd better believe I will, Charles Frederick Meyer. I've been waiting to hear those words for far too long."

"How about these words," he said, brushing his fingers against her cheek and looking into her eyes, his gaze serious. "I'll love you 'til the day I die. That's a promise you can count on."

Epilogue

On August 15, 1945, the day after World War Two ended, Bertie grinned at Second Lieutenant Charles Frederick Meyer as she watched him walk to the front of the church, cane-free, with barely a limp.

He turned to wait for her, his attention completely on her, his blue eyes shining with the love he had shown her throughout the war in so many ways—through his letters, his constant thoughts of her, his determination to protect her at any cost, even if it meant denying his love for her.

There was no denial of that love in his expression now, a fact that no one in the packed church could miss.

Red wore his full dress uniform, his Bronze Star and his Purple Heart amidst several other medals across his chest. He wore them with pride.

Ivan joined him, to stand beside him as best man. In spite of all, their friendship had remained strong, and Bertie had grown to admire her good friend even more in the painful weeks since Gerald's arrest. His mother, Arielle, had stepped into the breach at the MFA Exchange, and was now running the place during her husband's absence. Ironically, what would ordinarily have been the family's disgrace had served to unite Arielle to the town of Hideaway as nothing else had done.

Bertie fumbled with her bouquet as she struggled to battle tears. How she loved this town. This church.

This was the church where, two months ago, her father's funeral had been conducted. The contrast between that day—the result of pain upon pain—and this day of joy and triumph could not be more dramatic.

Edith Frost, Bertie's dearest friend, walked ahead of her down the aisle, holding a small bouquet of yellow roses from Lilly's garden.

The past two months had been a battle, for sure, right here in Hideaway, as Bertie learned to forgive those who had hurt her and her family, and as Red learned to trust her to help him heal physically.

Yes, this day was a triumph, indeed.

Bertie took Lloyd's arm and followed slowly behind Edith. Bertie proudly wore the pale green dress of chiffon and lace her mother had worn at her wedding.

The church was full of people she loved. She winked at Louise Morrow, who stood smiling at her from the aisle, eyes filmed with tears. She squeezed Lloyd's arm as they passed by his wife, Mary, and his children, Steven and Joann. God had answered their prayers. Lloyd didn't have tuberculosis. He'd been able to return home to his family.

Recently, he and Mary had decided to move back to Hideaway. They had enough money saved for a down payment on the Kruegers' old place, and the Moennig property was now double the size it had been.

One of Bertie's most difficult decisions had been to forgive the man who had killed her father. She hadn't thought it would be so hard. After all, it had been an accident. At the time, Gerald had been trying to protect the town. It had turned out to be more painful than she'd expected, but the day she went to Gerald at the jail and told him to his face she forgave him, had been the day his whole family began to heal.

He would be home soon, and she knew she would have yet another battle to fight with herself as Gerald struggled to regain the trust he had broken with friends and family.

Bertie was distracted from thoughts of Gerald by the sight of young Pearl Cooper standing between her parents, eyes as wide and hopeful as any young girl's as she watched Bertie come down the aisle. Pearl was a beauty, and she had taken every chance to sit by Bertie at church on Sunday—when her parents allowed her to attend church at all. Bertie prayed as she walked that Pearl would be able to overcome tribulations in her own family history, and build a new legacy.

As Edith reached the front, she turned to stand beside Ivan. Those two lovebirds had a strong start. Edith had stood beside Ivan throughout his father's trial and jail sentencing, and had become good friends with Arielle, assisting her at the Exchange. If Edith ever left Hideaway, Bertie would be amazed.

Cecil Martin, proud Marine, stood watching the procession from near the front of the church. He, too, was home to stay, and was already preparing his high-school classroom for upcoming science projects.

Bertie reached the altar and released her brother's

arm as she held her hands out to Red. Together they turned to face the minister.

Today was their triumph, a triumph for the town, a triumph of the heart. Red and Bertie Meyer would soon have a whole future to explore together.

When their union was sealed with a kiss, the whole congregation applauded their approval. The old Red was back. Red and Bertie Meyer would be a force for good in their beloved town of Hideaway.

* * * * *

*Evicted from her home, Joanna Nelson and her two
children seek refuge on the harsh Montana plains—
which leads her to rancher Aidan McKaslin's property.
When outside forces threaten their blossoming
friendship, Aidan decides to take action. Can he
convince Joanna to bind herself to him permanently or
will it drive her away forever?*

Read on for a sneak preview of
High Country Bride *by Jillian Hart!*

"Where are you going to go?"

His tone was flat, his jaw tensed, as if he was still
fighting his temper. His blue eyes glanced past her to
where the children were going about their chore.

"I don't know." Her throat went dry. Her tongue felt
thick as she answered. She trembled, not from fear of
him—she truly didn't believe he would strike her—but
from the unknown.

Of being forced to take the frightening step off the
only safe spot she'd found since she'd lost Pa's house.

When you were homeless, everything seemed so
fragile, so easily off balance. It was a big, unkind world
for a woman alone with her children. She had no one to
protect her. No one to care. The truth was, Joanna had
never had those things in her husband. How could she

expect them from any stranger? Especially this man she hardly knew, who seemed harsh, cold and hard-hearted?

And, worse, what if he brought in the law?

"Let me guess. If you leave here, you don't know where you're going and you have no money to get there with?"

She nodded. "Yes, sir."

"Then get you and your kids into the wagon. I'll hitch up your horses for you." His eyes were cold and yet not unfeeling as he fastened his gaze on hers. "I have a shanty out back of my house that no one's living in. You can stay there for the night."

"What?" She stumbled back, and the solid wood of the tailgate bit into the small of her back. "But—"

"There will be no argument," he snapped, interrupting her. "None at all. I buried a wife and son years ago, what was most precious to me, and to see you and them neglected like this—with no one to care…" His jaw clenched again, and his eyes were no longer cold.

Joanna didn't think she'd ever seen anything sadder than Aiden McKaslin standing there in the slanting rays of the setting sun.

Without another word, he turned on his heel and walked away, melting into the thick shadows of the summer evening.

Don't miss
High Country Bride *by Jillian Hart,*
available October 2018.

www.LoveInspired.com

Love Inspired®

Save $1.00

on the purchase of ANY
Love Inspired® book.

Available wherever books are sold,
including most bookstores, supermarkets,
drugstores and discount stores.

✂

Save $1.00

on the purchase of ANY Love Inspired® book.

Coupon valid until October 31, 2018.
Redeemable at participating retail outlets in the U.S. and Canada only.
Limit one coupon per customer.

52615896

Canadian Retailers: Harlequin Enterprises Limited will pay the face value of this coupon plus 10.25¢ if submitted by customer for this product only. Any other use constitutes fraud. Coupon is nonassignable. Void if taxed, prohibited or restricted by law. Consumer must pay any government taxes. Void if copied. Inmar Promotional Services ("IPS") customers submit coupons and proof of sales to Harlequin Enterprises Limited, P.O. Box 31000, Scarborough, ON M1R 0E7, Canada. Non-IPS retailer—for reimbursement submit coupons and proof of sales directly to Harlequin Enterprises Limited, Retail Marketing Department, Bay Adelaide Centre, East Tower, 22 Adelaide Street West, 40th Floor, Toronto, Ontario M5H 4E3, Canada.

5 65373 00076 2   (8100)0 12379

U.S. Retailers: Harlequin Enterprises Limited will pay the face value of this coupon plus 8¢ if submitted by customer for this product only. Any other use constitutes fraud. Coupon is nonassignable. Void if taxed, prohibited or restricted by law. Consumer must pay any government taxes. Void if copied. For reimbursement submit coupons and proof of sales directly to Harlequin Enterprises, Ltd 482, NCH Marketing Services, P.O. Box 880001, El Paso, TX 88588-0001, U.S.A. Cash value 1/100 cents.

® and ™ are trademarks owned and used by the trademark owner and/or its licensee.

© 2018 Harlequin Enterprises Limited

LICOUP89584

Looking for inspiration in tales
of hope, faith and heartfelt romance?

Check out **Love Inspired**® and
Love Inspired® **Suspense** books!

New books available every month!

CONNECT WITH US AT:

Facebook.com/groups/HarlequinConnection

Facebook.com/HarlequinBooks

Twitter.com/HarlequinBooks

Instagram.com/HarlequinBooks

Pinterest.com/HarlequinBooks

ReaderService.com

Love Inspired®

LIGENRE2018R2

Inspirational Romance to Warm Your Heart and Soul

Join our social communities to connect with other readers who share your love!

Sign up for the Love Inspired newsletter at **www.LoveInspired.com** to be the first to find out about upcoming titles, special promotions and exclusive content.

CONNECT WITH US AT:

Harlequin.com/Community

 Facebook.com/LoveInspiredBooks

 Twitter.com/LoveInspiredBks

LISOCIAL2017